R0200756310

12/2019

D0929961

BRAND OF LIGHT

Books by Ronie Kendig

BRAND OF LIGHT

THE DROSERAN SAGA
BOOK 1

RONIE KENDIG

Ours is a journey stamped indelibly on my heart: In 2006 I entered *Brand & Bound* (the original title) in the ACFW Genesis Contest. It did not win or even final because it received a score of 62. After the contest, I was told that 62 was the highest score a particular judge had awarded. Later the coordinator informed me the judge had so liked the story that he wanted to talk with me. Little did I know that low score would become the most prized of my scores because it connected me with a creative genius who went to the ends of the earth for other writers. Your humble heart would not even let me name you *mentor,* but instead insisted you were my *advocate,* who championed my writing. Challenged me. Taught me. Brainstormed the Discarded Heroes series with me. It is for you I have named Rico Ohlson, Marco's *advocate.*

Thank you, John.
For your guidance, friendship, and generous soul.
For being my advocate.
I hope this story makes you proud.

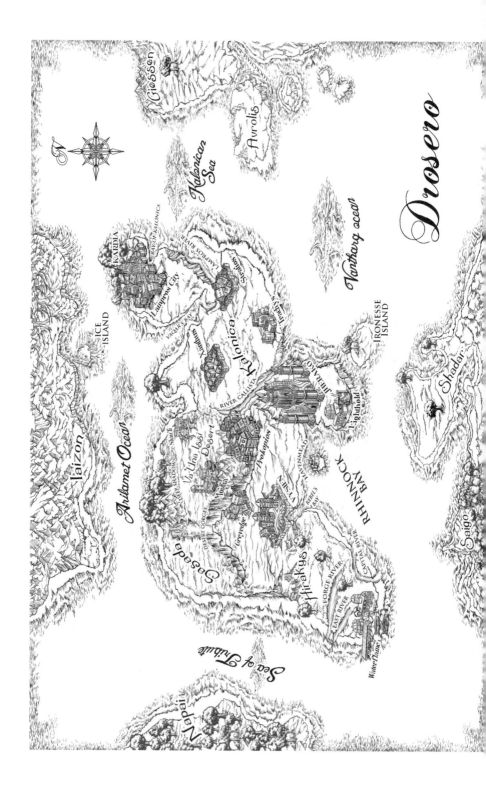

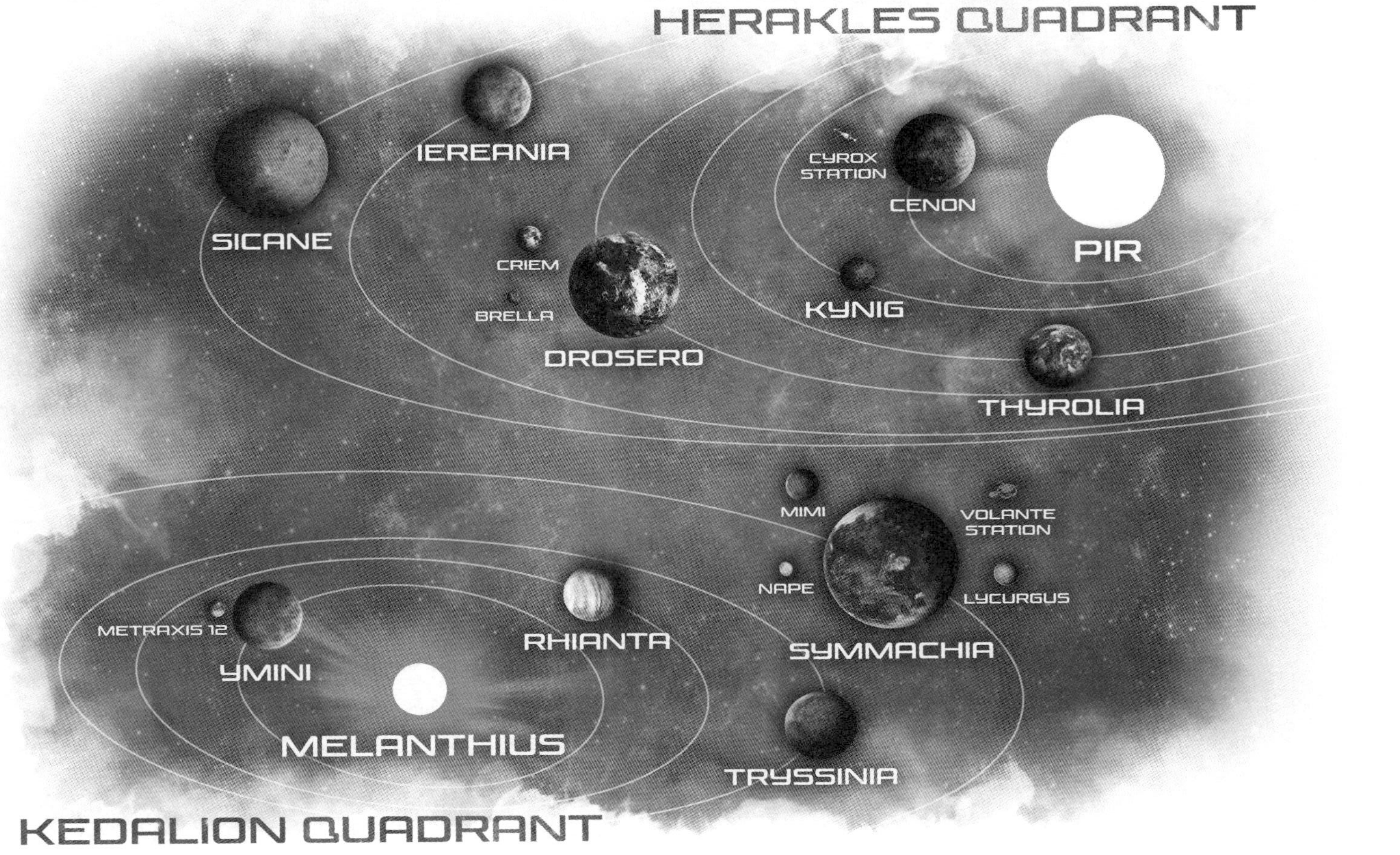

HERAKLES QUADRANT

PIR

CENON

CYROX STATION

KYNIG

THYROLIA

VOLANTE STATION

LYCURGUS

MIMI

NAPE

SYMMACHIA

TRYSSINIA

DROSERO

CRIEM

BRELLA

IEREANIA

SICANE

RHIANTA

MELANTHIUS

YMINI

METRAXIS 12

KEDALION QUADRANT

PROLOGUE
KALONICA, DROSERO

The *tap, tap, tap* of rain drilled into Achilus's brain, holding him captive against sleep. He flopped over yet again, kicking the confining coverlet, and stared into the darkness. Would this reek-cursed night never end?

A strange light fell from the sky and glided over the rain-pebbled window. Blinking, suddenly aware of a deep thrum that had run under the rain for the last several minutes, Achilus threw off the coverlet and scrambled across the mattress. He landed with a thump on the thick rug and scurried to the large window that towered over him. Rain sprinted down the beveled glass, blurring his view. He squinted after the ominous blue light that now fled the palace, as if on orders from his father. But it was not the light itself—unnatural and clearly not born of any torch—that held him rapt, but the way it moved.

Flying.

Like an aetos from Mount Kalonica, which stood guard over Lampros City. Chills wormed through his bare feet as he watched the fading illumination. Fear played havoc on his stomach. What had it been? Why was it here in Lampros City? Was it dangerous? And it stunk! He held an arm over his nose, hating himself for being afraid and it for irritating his senses.

Blood and boil! Must the reek be so rotten?

"Riders!" came a shout from the watchtower. "Riders from the cliffs!"

Achilus stilled, breath trapped in his throat. The cliffs—that was the direction of the light! But people out in the rage of the Kalonican storm? The matter must be urgent. Pulling his unwilling gaze from the now-black night sky, he craned his neck to see the portcullis. Pushed onto his tiptoes. If he were just a little taller, a little older, he could see who disturbed his father's sleep at such a late hour.

"Open the gate!"

Cursing his age and height, Achilus wished himself older. Father promised when he was ten Achilus would be present during receptions. Which meant he could stand by the great fire pit in the solar as the intruders presented themselves. Surely their news must be terrible for them to tempt the peril of the hour and storm.

At the clanging of chains raising the gate, he pressed his nose to the window. His breath bloomed on the leaded glass, fogging his view. With a grunt, he swiped it with his sleeve, looking past the raindrops sparkling like crystals. Torchlight scampered across the bailey. Shadows shifted but he could discern nothing save the drenching rain.

Noises in the hall yanked him around. Achilus threw himself at the door, catching the knob. With a light press against the brass, he eased it open. In the hall, Father's broad shoulders faded as he descended the stairs. The sadness and anger trailing him drew Achilus into the open. Straining to discern what prickled the hairs on his neck, he stared into the recesses of his brothers' rooms, darkened by the night. What had he—

A shadow moved toward him.

Cold dread chilled Achilus. Braced, he pulled in a breath and watched the shape glide across the black floors.

"Achilus?"

Air whooshed from his lungs as his younger brother shuffled closer. "You should be in bed, Silvanus."

Rubbing an eye, his brother grunted. "The banging woke me."

"Go back to the nursery. Check on Darius."

He swatted at the air. "Aw, all that baby does is sleep. I don't know why we needed another."

"Go back. Now!" Jaw jutted, Achilus waited until his brother started for the nursery. Voices from the grand foyer turned him. He tiptoed to the balustrade and glanced over the rail. Two golden aetos twisted in battle glared up at him, their tangled shapes set into the marble floor.

He descended, the smooth rail guiding him down the twenty-four steps. In the great hall, that chatter rose to a dull roar. Heart racing, Achilus stopped on the last step. Many voices. Many ... *smells.*

Fear choked him. "I am in my own home—the castle, for boil's sake! There is nothing to fear." Jaw tight, he left the safety of the stairs and inched toward the great hall, breath harnessed.

Swirls of cool air slammed him, freezing Achilus just across the threshold, while his gaze swept the room. A whirl of black erupted—a man. Large. Eyes black and fierce. Shoulders larger than the great pit! Achilus gaped. By the Ancient, he looked as big as a Zeev! Long black cloak matched his pants, belted tunic, and hair slicked into a queue down his back. A faint blue glow came from his hip—no, his wrist. Something he wore gave off dim light.

The man leaned toward him.

Though everything in him screamed to run, Achilus stood rooted. Balled his fists. Lifted his chin. Fury or friend, he'd fight.

The stranger chuckled. "Good, boy. Good." With a twist, he snapped off a small piece of the glowing thing on his arm.

Achilus tried not to flinch when the stranger pressed the thing to his throat, but it was cold and ached with an odd vibration. Then it trilled and white flashed.

"So high?" The man's voice and smell betrayed surprise.

"You and your technology, Roman!" Ma'ma rushed to Achilus, and her purple overcoat wrapped around him, as if to protect him. "I did not want this for my son."

"*Want* is irrelevant, Athina. Despite Droseran hatred of technology, the device is never wrong. He *is* gifted. It cannot be argued. Life here for him will only be strained. Give him over to what he is called."

"Athina," Father said quietly. "You're frightening him."

"I'm not afraid, Father."

Shuddering through a breath, Ma'ma held him at arm's length, her face screwed tight and crying. Watching her, smelling her sadness—he might as well walk the rope bridge over Kardia Falls during a windstorm.

"No more." Gold cords swung across the stranger's chest.

Achilus stepped back with a choked breath. Widened his eyes. He knew—*knew* what that meant. *A master hunter!* A Kynigos. But what was *he* doing in Kardia? May and true, they had authority everywhere, but here? In the castle?

Clicking the device back onto the wrist strap, the stranger stalked to Achilus. Clamped a hand on Achilus's shoulder and bent, staring through a terse brow. "You are brave, yes?" Dark eyes seemed to stab at the fear within Achilus.

Mutely, he nodded.

"Then you will ride strong and fearless."

"Ride? In this storm?" Achilus looked to Father. "Where are we going?" He recalled Father and Uncle speaking of sending him away for protection should war come. "Is there war?"

Ma'ma pushed away, stifling a sob with the back of her hand. "Mercy ..."

A bitter burst of sadness erupted from behind. Achilus glanced over his shoulder. The stairs. Silvanus came flying into their mother's arms. The two embraced as if their lives would end. It was not comforting or helpful.

Father moved between him and the master hunter, then led Achilus to the foyer. "Remember the night you were able to ferret out the servant boy who had stolen your bow?" His grip tightened, the pressure almost painful. "No one could find him, but you did—said you could smell his fear."

"I'm not sure I could really *smell*..." An unfamiliar rush pelted his courage like iced-rain in winter. Suddenly, he understood why the master hunter had come. It seemed appropriate that he would arrive on a night like this. Tales spun over feasts and large fires colored them as haunting. But ... how? How could this be? He shifted his gaze back to him. "You've come for me."

"I have."

The doors swung open with a bang, jerking him around. Black night poured in, rain splattering the floors. Destriers stamped in the inner bailey as the storm raged. Guards worked to steady the war horses, who seemed impatient to be on their way rather than stand still. Achilus could relate to their restlessness.

"Achilus." His father knelt before him. "The Ancient has blessed you with gifts that will help bring justice to the lands. Ride with Roman."

Going with the Kynigos meant one thing: those who went never returned. Achilus bit his trembling lip and tightened his fists. He would be strong. Yet never again seeing Ma'ma ...? His gaze wandered to her and Silvanus. "Is the journey long, Father?"

Hands squeezed his shoulders. "A lifetime, my son."

Swallowing hard, refusing to be weak, Achilus lifted his chin and followed Father and the master hunter into the bailey. The hunter mounted and Father lifted Achilus easily onto the horse. "Be strong, Achilus."

A tear defied his will and dashed to his cheek. "*Vanko Kalonica*, Father."

The beard twitched, rain dancing on it. "*Vanko*, Achilus." Forever.

They rode out of Kardia, his family disappearing in the inky, rainy night. The hunter's arm held him tight as they raced through Lampros City and out toward the raging sea. There, beneath the cliffs, hummed a large metal ship. It was bigger than the royal carriage and horses. Waves crashed behind it and swelled over the sleek hull as if to swallow it.

The master hunter reined in the horses. "Have you ever been in a ship before?"

He tried to shake his head but a shudder ran through him instead.

"You will find there is much to fear in our system." The hunter dismounted and reached to Achilus. "But not technology as your parents believe."

Eyes locked on the ship, where another hunter opened a panel, shooting more light across the stormy night, Achilus felt a sting of excitement. Tried to remember what he'd promised his father. Tried to believe the hunter's words, but he had sharp awareness that many terrors awaited him.

"You are sure of this, my lady? It's Myles." Weighted eyes drove home the point. "Our fiercest."

"It was a fair draw."

"Aye, but—"

"Let it not be said that I, the lone female in the training yard, whinged." Not when she had pleaded so hard for training. As it was, she was thankful Uncle Rufio had left express word before he left for the middle lands that she should be allowed to continue her levels.

Jamming her fingers into thick hide gloves, Kersei Dragoumis stalked toward her destrier. She smoothed a hand over Bastien's broad skull, then pressed her forehead to his and closed her eyes, stroking his powerful neck. "May I serve you well, friend." She swung up into the saddle, ignoring the heat and dust that clung to her. Thank the Ancient women in Kalonica wore split pants to accommodate arduous tasks. At least in this she conformed to tradition.

Squinting against the strength of the full rise, she stared down the training yard at her opponent. Courage curdled inside her.

Seek strength where it may be found.

Approaching on her left, Minos lifted a javrod. "Myles will not take into consideration that you're a female, nor that you're a second-year. He is ruthless."

"Then I must be at my best, aye?"

Minos thrust the javrod into her grip. "You have the iron of the machitis in your blood, Lady Kersei." His sun-leathered face grimaced. "Ancient help us all."

She laughed, more because of her nerves than out of amusement. "Now you sound like Darius."

Had he been here, he would have forbidden her to spar against Myles, one of Father's favorites. Myles had gained the rank of aerios faster than most—faster, even, than Darius—though only by a month. Yet her father would threaten his position on the elite guard of the realm if anything were to happen to her today. She'd never taken on a warrior of his caliber. Still, she knew Minos was right: Myles would give no quarter, while everyone else *had* taken into account that she was a female and that her father was Xylander, Elder of Stratios, one of the Five, and Chief Counsel to Medora Zarek.

Minos secured the strap around her arm. "Prince Darius will have my hide and your father my shield if harm comes to you."

She cut him a glare. "Then I am glad neither is here."

With a sigh, Minos backstepped.

Kersei again studied her opponent. "He thrusts at the last second," she muttered.

"And at an angle. Give it room to bend." His eyes held the worry of a warrior facing his last battle. "Pull off if—"

"Blood and boil!" someone shouted. "Kersei has drawn Myles!"

"She can't be going through with it. She wouldn't be that—"

"Aye, she would." Another laughed.

Kersei blew out a breath as her periphery filled with the grubby green tunics of machitis lining the edge of the hay-strewn training field. She ignored their mocking murmurs and focused on Aerios Myles, who sat in quiet confidence on his mount, bored. Even though he wore a training jerkin and armor, it was *how* he wore it. Stretched taut against his chest and arms. Comfortable as a second skin. The destrier stamped impatiently. Myles had long been intent on proving she should not be here. Her mother liked him for that reason alone.

With gloved hands, Kersei slid down the face shield. Mentally patted armor that should protect her ribs and stomach. Wouldn't Ma'ma love her to come home the night of Adara's Delta Presentation with a black eye or broken limb?

Then best not get injured.

"Riders, ready!" Minos called over the chatter of the other machitis.

Both she and Myles hefted javrods to readiness and nudged their mounts into position on either side of the long dividing fence.

"Ho! Look to the ridge," a spectator called. "The Kalonican lion!"

Sucking a breath, Kersei flicked her attention to the rise overlooking the training field. Royal banners snapped in the breeze. A cluster of horses cantered ahead of the detachment coming down the hill. One rider broke ahead in a full gallop. And though she could not see faces at this distance, she knew that golden-brown hair.

"It's Prince Darius!"

Now he returns? No no no. He had always said she should not spar or joust. If he saw—

Her gaze darted to Minos. He held a fist to his chest in recognition of his prince. "*Vanko Kalonica*" rang out from the warriors. *Blood and boil!* Darius would end this match.

"Ready," she shouted, hunching into Bastien.

"Ready!" The shout from the other end of the field pulled her up straight.

So, Myles is as anxious as I. But which of them would stand proudly before their prince when this was over?

Kersei swallowed. Tucked the javrod into her shoulder, its length standing straight. Lighter than a lance, it was a formidable weapon even if she were dismounted.

Aerios Minos lifted an arm, then violently swung it down.

"Huah!" With a jab of her knees, Kersei committed.

Bastien reared, his raw power surging beneath her. He vaulted forward like the mighty war horse he was. She leaned into the charge. Breathing in through her nose and out through her mouth, she urged Bastien to eat up the distance.

As Myles stormed her, he grew. In size. Formidability. Ferocity.

Heart thundering with Bastien's hooves, Kersei focused her advance. *Bend with it.* Darius's instruction from their days of sparring nudged attention to her rigidity. Expecting failure, she loosened taut muscles. Lay upon the buffeting wind streaming between her and Bastien.

As she aimed her javrod, Myles did the same.

Shouts pushed past the wind to reach her ears.

Her javrod wobbled in her grip. It vibrated up her arm. Shook her. She stiffened, fearing she'd lose the rod before even engaging her opponent.

Bastien responded, tensing beneath her stress.

Kersei shed the fear. The expectation of failure. Guided Bastien to the rail and firmed her grip. Felt it nock perfectly into her gloved hand. Targeted down its length to Myles's chest.

Just forward more. Almost there …

As she thrust, she held her breath. She must do this. She was Kersei, daughter of Xylander, the fiercest machitis in Kalonica!

The thick, dulled tip of Myles's javrod beamed right at her. Firm. Solid. No uncertainty. Pure experience. Ferocious determination. His scowl bled into focus behind the rod. Dark eyes. Forbidding. His rod swung down.

Ah! Just as expected. He'd miss. She would stand before Darius. She would—

Thud!

Horror struck Darius as the thick rod punched Kersei from her mount. She flew through the air like a limp doll. Black curls loosed. The terrible grate of armor rang out as she landed in the dirt with a heavy thud.

He drew up his mount on the training field. Vaulted off his horse. Sprinted across the sandy yard to her unmoving form. "Kersei!" He snapped a glower to Minos. He would hang the man over the cliffs for this. "Get the pharmakeia! Iason!"

Darius visually traced her limbs for obvious breaks. Cradled her head in place as Iason probed her abdomen with practiced fingers. "Kersei," he said, staring down into the face he'd known since they were children. The face of a lady and warrior. Dark lashes dusted the freckles from all her days in the sun sparring. "Kersei, can you hear me? *Kersei?*"

Iason pressed on her right side.

Kersei arched her back and groaned. Yelped. Then collapsed in silence again. He met his man's eyes. "Break?"

"Likely," Iason said with a grim nod. "Possibly just a deep bruise. Either way, she'll breathe fire for a few days." He gestured to her face. "That she's unconscious is of concern—it could be a serious head injury."

"Kersei," Darius called again to her. He knew what it was to be knocked out, to lay thick in that vat of darkness heavier than a sodden blanket. "Kersei!"

She groaned. Squinted and winced. Whimpered. Then her eyes opened. Blinked. Fixed on him as she stilled. "Oh no."

Long had they argued over her training. "Aye." Though he would love to string her up for this foolishness, his anger with her never lasted.

She started to sit and tensed.

"Easy," he said, shifting to slide an arm under her shoulders. "Slowly, now."

Swallowing, gaze skirting the aerios and machitis, she tucked her chin and allowed his assistance. She guarded her side and squeezed her eyes, breath tight.

"Iason says you'll breathe fire for a few days. I've sent for the pharmakeia. You're injured and should wait for him."

"I'm fine," she said through gritted teeth and stiffly came upright with his help.

"You're a bad liar, Kersei," Darius said with more frustration than he had intended. "You are injured."

"No," she insisted, pushing up from the ground. "Merely winded." As usual, she would not yield to him. She straightened, met his withering glare, then nodded to the yard. "In case you missed it, I was"—she seemed to work hard to find the correct words—"*removed* from my mount."

"Thrown. With great *force*."

"As you see." By all the Ladies, if she did not have a grin prying those lips apart.

Chuckles flickered through the afternoon, fueling her mischievousness. Darius flashed a glare at the machitis. "Who authorized this?" he demanded.

Kersei started, shifting to him—then shriveled beneath the pain of her injury. "Leave them," she bit out. "You have been gone these two years, and in that time I have leveled up in my training under my uncle."

"My lord prince." Minos inclined his head, his expression of deference yellow with fear. "Master Rufio said the lady could train with the others. Authorized javrod lessons."

"*Lessons*, yes," he roared, his face reddening. "Not trials. And most ardently not with *Myles*!" He jabbed a finger at the aerios who now lumbered toward them, wiping blood from his upper lip. "What sense in pitting a lamb against a lion?"

"Lamb? How dare you!" Kersei flared.

Darius spun on her. He rarely exerted his title over her, but he would now, for her own good. "Forget you to whom you speak, Lady Kersei?"

Only after an intense internal battle that she had many times—in private—made quite external, Kersei withdrew her objection.

Blood. Myles. Darius looked at the warrior who'd unseated her. "Did you not see whom you fought, Aerios Myles? What manner of warrior drives a javrod into the chest of a lady? What does that speak of your character? Of the family whose jerkin you wear?"

By the Ancient, why was his nose bleeding?

"You are right, my lord prince." Myles frowned, shoulders stooped and gaze down. "While I did hold back, ensuring she would not have been badly injured, I was out of line."

"*Hold back*?" Kersei's objection mirrored Darius's own, but for entirely different reasons.

Kersei rounded on the aerios. "You … you *coward*!"

She moved quickly for someone with an injured rib—so, not fractured. But Darius caught her arm. Assaulting an aerios was a punishable offense.

Myles seemed to grow by spans as he turned a thick-knotted brow at her. "You know I—"

"Enough!" Darius ran a hand over his mouth. Restraint. *You are a Kalonican prince.* "Myles, return to your training."

"Sire." With a curt bow, the aerios retreated and left the training field.

Darius shifted back to Kersei. He must reason with her, but there had always been little *reason* with Kersei. Aye, he had been gone for two years, training in the middle lands, scouting the southern border, and receiving training from the Plisiázon, which both he and Father agreed would be of benefit to him in his role as commander of the armies. In all that time, none of Kersei's fire had dimmed. She had a passion for training, for being a warrior. He had a passion for his family, for the crown, for … her. And she very nearly ended any hope of joining their houses. "What were you thinking?" A hot breeze spilled from the west and tussled his hair into his face. "And on the night of your sister's presentation?"

Indignation crawled through her expression. "What was I thinking?" she hissed. "I was *thinking* I would train, that I am willing to take a bruise to better myself and learn to defend our lands like any machitis."

"You are *not* machitis!" Why did she persist? Why must she feel the need to don leathers and take up sword? "You are Kersei, *daughter* of Xylander, Elder of the Stratios, one of the Five."

Her cheeks glowed with fury that ignited those dark eyes. "If you want a weak-kneed woman then find one. I will not be her. I *am* Kersei, daughter of Xylander—the greatest warrior in all of Kalonica." She wrested from his grasp.

At her resistance, a tremor raced through his guard, who tightened their protective perimeter on him. Darius stilled them with a lifted hand.

She finally registered her breach of conduct and hesitated, eyeing him. But much had changed while he was earning his title and sword, his right to sit on the throne should his brother Silvanus, the crown prince, die or abdicate. Gone was the young girl who'd clacked wooden swords with him along the boundary river between Lampros City and Stratios lands. She was a lady—complete with fire, beauty, and curves. Even in the dingy britches and dirty tunic. He was heir to the land on which they stood. But they had a connection, a friendship built on years and understanding. Was he wrong to think that could become more? That she would understand what would happen tonight?

Darius erased the gap between them. "Is this the example you want for your sister, the legacy you choose to leave?"

Guarded, she lifted her gaze. "You have been gone. What know you of Adara?"

Darius nodded toward the golden fields where swalti grain waved for leagues. Standing on the lower rung of the training yard fence, arms hooked over the top rail, Kersei's sister held a mock sword. Her light brown eyes and posture as defiant as Kersei's.

"Blood and boil," Kersei muttered.

Darius arched an eyebrow at her epithet. "Lady Stratios has always said you were not to encourage her. For you to let Adara to choose her own path."

"I don't need—" She bit back a yelp, holding her side again.

He touched her elbow, wanting to be near. Wanting to ease her pains. "Are you well?"

Her scowl darkened. "Better you had stayed wherever you were than treat me like this."

"'Tis for your wellbeing and reputation that I intercede, Lady Kersei." He did not recall her being so petite—or himself so much taller.

"What is this?" she whispered, not pushing him away. "We never allowed titles between us, Darius."

He gave an acknowledging nod. "We are no longer children with fancies to pursue."

She raised her chin. Turned to her sister and waved. "Be right there." Then flung her anger at him once more. "Aye, not children indeed. Seems your training injected you with foulness as much as looks." Her gaze scraped down him like the old Kersei. The one he'd sparred with—and not just with swords but with words. Yet there seemed something else in her gaze just then.

So she had noticed the changes in his physique. He grinned, angling in. "Then you find me much changed?"

Without another word, she stalked away.

"Lady Kersei." Iason stepped forward, an edge to his words.

It was hard to stand there and allow his man to do what he must.

"'Tis unacceptable to show your back to the prince regent."

Her old defiance flared, and he was sure she thought to offer more than just her back to him. Her gaze traveled the men around him, then finally came back to Darius. Kersei tucked her right foot back and curtseyed with a tight-lipped smile, before slipping away.

Who was he to come and destroy a perfectly good sparring match? Angry with the pain in her side—she should've seen the thrust—and the way Darius ruined everything, Kersei trudged into the armory, tugging at the buckles of her greaves. She had worked hard since he had left to complete his training as prince regent. He had no right. She secured her practice armor in the tack room and stalked out of building.

"Mayhap he would have a better chance with his courting were he not throwing around his title and ego," she hissed, rounding the corner. She drew up sharply—grabbing her side as pain lanced her.

Myles blocked her path. His deep frown, interrupted by a scar that ran down his chin into his neck, shook what little confidence remained.

"Aerios." Kersei lowered her gaze, recalling what her refusal to back down had caused him. "I beg your mercy for my hand in the dressing down given you by Prince Darius." Silence stretched between them, forcing her gaze to his angry countenance.

"You did well," came his gravelly response.

Surprise held her fast, but she knew he must only jest. "Aye, I flew well from my mount and pounded the earth." She started walking, unwilling to face his mockery.

"Not many manage to unseat me."

Kersei stopped short. *She* had unseated *him*?

"Sir?" Symmachian Commander Tigo Deken of Eidolon Detachment 215 couldn't have heard right. The Coalition had a strict pact with the Droserans. He stared at the comms screen. "Please confirm—Drosero?"

"Your coordinates are confirmed, Commander."

"Sir." He gritted his teeth. "Entering Droseran space—"

Rear Admiral Jair Krissos silenced Tigo with a hand. The band of admiralty around the thick neck glinted even in the low lighting as he leaned toward the viewer, the cerulean blue planets of his rank visible. "We know the uneasy relationship—"

"Uneasy? It's downright hateful." Tigo tried to laugh. "On a good day. In fact, there is no relationship. To send Two-one-five there ... if we're detected—"

"Careful, Commander," Krissos said, his voice terse, his facial features tight beneath that regs-approved goatee. "The admiralty has done its homework. Believe it or not, we are aware of the tensions there."

Aware, yet ignoring. Sensing the reprimand hanging beneath the sarcasm, Tigo withdrew his objections. "Of course, sir."

"The target is there and extremely dangerous. It's vital we remove him from Droseran soil before he can do harm there and unleash a war nobody wants. Am I clear?"

"Crystal, sir."

"I'll wave you the details and this goes no further than our communication. Give Baric the coordinates, then make it happen."

"Yessir."

His brown eyes squinted beneath a nod. "Don't fail me, Commander."

"Death first."

"Well, let's not go there. I'd have to face your father if anything happened to you, and he'd likely rip the planets off my neck—from behind."

Tigo almost smiled. "I believe he would, sir." After the Miritol Descent, a mission on an uncharted planet, grew dangerous, the strike group had been abandoned by a panicked officer. All died. Admiral Domitas Deken had brought the full measure of his anger against the captain in charge, leaving him stripped of rank and working the mines on Tryssinia. His reputation remained notorious—and that went tenfold when it came to his son.

"Orders are incoming. Of note, pay attention to the drop-suit settings. They're provided by a source on the ground to work in tandem with the environment."

Tigo glanced at the gauntlet display strapped over his tac sleeve. Low body temps. Stealth protocol. And— Tigo jerked. "Sir? Oxygen levels—"

"Your team has handled worse. The Ymini-Rhianta mining incursion, you went low-intake—"

"Yessir, due to lethal gas levels. Rhinn spent a week in a depri chamber."

"Are you saying I need to send Two-two-five?"

Tigo tightened his jaw. "No, sir."

"Then get those coordinates to Baric and get underway."

"Aye, sir!"

The screen winked out and Tigo hung his head. Closed his eyes. Forbidden planet. Hostile relations. Violent target. Low oxygen.

What in the black were they extracting?

KALONICA, DROSERO

So foolish. So strong. So fiery ... so *very* fiery.

Darius stood outside the solar, hands behind his back, enjoying the cool breeze drifting up to Kardia, the royal residence that had been his home. He had missed it. His gaze traced the fields, the Hill of Andrios, to the great turrets of Stratios Hall—a formidable sight in the near south—and the blot of black stone fortress in the far west belonging to the Xanthus. More than a day's ride, that. The sea to the east and the falls above that bathed the air in moisture. His focus returned to Stratios Hall, where Kersei had grown up. Where she now most likely walked, experiencing a blistering remonstration from Lady Nicea.

By the aetos, she deserved one.

"You are a Tyrannous, Darius."

"Yes, my lord Father." He did not pull his eyes from the hall, nor his thoughts from the dark-haired beauty. Long had he intended to claim her as his bound.

"You must choose carefully," his father-medora continued. "Though Silvanus is crown prince, you are second in line. Should anything happen to your brother, Ancient forbid, you will be medora. That means whomever you take as bound will be kyria. Even as prince regent, you will have duties heavily invested in the people, as will your bound." His father's presence loomed behind him. "You are certain this is the path you want? You're sure ... about her?"

Turning, Darius faced his father. Inclined his head. "I am."

"Does it not bother you, Brother," Silvanus said as he stood from the gilt chair with a chalice in hand, "that you cast this girl off more than two cycles past? That she chooses to wear britches and tunics, and engage in battles with hardened warriors?"

"Kersei need not wear omnir and a bliaut to be feminine or beautiful. And full well do I understand my duties as a prince of Kalonica." He jutted his jaw and rested his hand on the hilt of his sword, but it did nothing to dislodge her accusation on the field. "Long have she and I been friends. She understands me better than any other, and I her." He shifted to their father. "She *is* a daughter of the Five—there is a fire in her veins that will make her an asset to this kingdom. It will do Kalonica well to blend our lines and houses—you have said so yourself."

"Aye, with the intent of Silvanus binding with the eldest daughter, Lexina."

"And he has been slow of wit and guile in securing that alliance." It never hurt to get another jibe in at his brother's expense. "I am ready, my father-medora."

"But what of her?" His father sighed and raked a hand through his silver-black hair. Zarek IV was said to bear a striking resemblance to the Ancient, of whose line the medora of Kalonica had descended. And yet, Darius did not have those looks, favoring—he was told—their mother's fairer features. "You yourself said she has no intention of binding."

Darius could not help but laugh. "She was but fifteen when she said that. Four cycles past."

Pale eyes, the same blue as Darius's, sparked with amusement. "Then she no longer wishes to train, to fight?"

Knowing he had never been a good liar, Darius chose a safer path. "Kersei will accept the petition."

His father moved to the soaring arched windows, a great weight settling on his shoulders. "It is not she who must accept. The laws only require her father's consent, but I would not bring a woman unwillingly into our house.

We are fortunate in that Drosero's other ruling houses are comfortable enough
not to threaten war or demand bindings for the sake of peace." Hands behind
his back, he faced the realm. Wind toyed with his black, shoulder-length hair,
a few rogue strands of silver betraying his age. "You must know there are
concerns over how she might fill the role of princessa."

"Fear not, my lord Father." Pride dented, Darius bristled. "May and true,
Kersei has a heart that takes flight for the protection of our realm, but she
also possesses the grace and beauty of a lady. Truly, her courage, her *adunatos*
would match that of any Lady of Lampros, or even a Lady of Basilikas."

"Guard your tongue." His father glowered.

"Aye, he speaks like she's a Faa'Cris." Silvanus sniffed.

"Had Kersei unimaginable gifts and wings, mayhap." Darius would not
be dissuaded, nor would he allow his brother the upper hand. "Would you
have me bind with a weak woman so you feel better about yourself, Brother?"

"Darius." Disapproval knotted his father's brow. "I do not question her
strength. What gives me pause is her impetuousness. Her heart is as untamed
as her beauty."

"Mayhap." He thought of watching her flying off that mount. The heavy
thud when she hit the ground. How she lay, unmoving. But … she had
unseated Myles.

Rubbing his full, silver-strung beard, Father let out a sigh as he returned
to the center of the deliberation room. "Pray, when did you last converse with
the Dragoumis heir?"

Darius shifted. Glanced at his brother. "Prior to today, two cycles past."

"Two cycles," his father repeated, eyeing the clouds in the distance. "And
to what end?"

"Sir?"

"How did that conversation end?"

Darius shot his brother a glare. So, his father had been informed of his last
moments with Kersei before he departed for his final training and education.
"Strained."

"Why?"

Gaze on the pearl floor, Darius stifled his frustration. "She was angry
because I …" He was tempted to leave out the parts that would put ill favor
on Kersei, but he knew better. Silvanus had betrayed his trust. "She was angry
because with my departure, she lost her only sparring partner, the only one
who gave little measure for her being a woman."

"The only one," his father repeated quietly. "No other machitis would fight the girl in full combat—as no man should!"

"She and I had an alliance," Darius argued, his defense of his honor weak. "We battled well. I knew her tactics, she mine." He heard his voicing rising and forced himself to calm. "We are friends and respect each other. It is a natural connection."

"Yes." Silvanus cut him off. "When you were frolicking in the fields and woods. But here?" He raised a hand to the stone walls that ensconced them safely in Kardia, the heart of the kingdom. "As a princessa, a representative of the Kalonican kingdom?"

Heat infused Darius's chest. "Of what concern is that to you?"

"Every concern." Silvanus frowned. "One day I will hold the throne. I must have reassurance that whichever bound you choose will honor our family's name, the realm, and the people."

"At least there is a girl I am willing to take as my bound. What of you? Last I heard, you ran scared at the thought of binding."

Silvanus straightened, indignation as thick as his quilted and embroidered jerkin. "I take my role as heir apparent seriously. My bound will be kyria. I will not blaze a path to this sacred vow as you are doing."

"Our father-medora has ordered us to bind. Be the fault mine that I have a perfect candidate?"

"Enough."

Darius felt his hope slipping that his petition would be granted. "My lord Father, did you not once tell me that our mother had a wild heart and spirit as well?"

His father shook a finger. "Do not betray her memory to buy favor." He stalked to the deliberation chair and sat.

"Fath—"

He lifted a hand, silencing him. Breathed out a long sigh as he considered him. "I will allow your petition, Darius. However, be warned: You've chosen a wild daughter of Stratios. Binding hands is much easier than binding hearts."

TSC *MACEDON*

Tigo made his way to the Command deck, where the door took a biometric scan before snapping aside to grant him entrance. Somehow the muted grays and blues softened the din of activity as the crew focused on their tasks at four curved stations around the central work area.

The *Macedon*'s executive officer, Wellsey Dimar, stood in the center, a vidscreen in hand as he talked with the engineering officer. Blue lights from the screen dancing off his flexing jaw muscle, he looked up. "Commander Deken," he said with a drawl that easily betrayed his Capital Colony heritage. "Welcome to the bridge."

"Thank you, XO."

Dimar glanced at the channeler Tigo held and arched an eyebrow. "Orders?"

Tigo gave a small nod.

"Might want to leave your weapon out here. You know—"

"Regulation 17.925 requires Eidolon to be armed at all times."

"Letter of the reg, not the spirit."

"No, I'm the spirit." Tigo grinned.

With a huff, Dimar angled his head toward the captain's office. "Tread softly—he's in a black mood." He returned his attention to the petty officer.

When isn't he? "Understood." Tigo crossed the bridge and palmed the reader embedded in the bulkhead. As he waited for the captain's approval to enter, he slid a glance at Dimar. "Shouldn't have hung up your wings."

"Better lost wings than lost legs." Dimar's hair was still cut in the tight crop of the Eidolon. "I didn't want to make that *Nephesh* moniker literal. Too much risk."

Nephesh—ghosts—from the Eidolon's ability to get in and out without being seen. Tigo wore it like a medal. "Without risk, what fun is there in life?"

"A wife, a family—"

Tigo snorted. "I said 'fun.'" The door sprung back, admitting him into the glaring white of the captain's office.

"What is it, Deken?" Baric barked, his gaze glued to a half-dozen screens. While the man might be mean and easily agitated, he was a competent captain, and Tigo had heard word floating around that TSC was looking to promote him. It'd be smart to stay on his good side. If he had one.

"Orders from Command." Tigo clicked the disc into the nodule on the captain's desk and stood at ease.

Ignoring the disc, the captain used short, irritated gestures to sort through the scans and streaming data on his oversized displays.

Tigo watched with unabashed curiosity as Baric swiped away a topo map and a system chart he didn't recognize, then pulled up new files. Spotting a brain scan, Tigo frowned. Splaying his fingers against the display, the captain opened an overlay Tigo recognized. The Engram.

Something hot and white shot through Tigo. He hated that machine. Couldn't believe Symmachian Command hadn't destroyed every scrap the day its use was declared inhumane. Squinting, he eyeballed the dates and names.

The dates were recent. *Slag me.* They were *using* it? Where? "I thought TSC overruled use of the Engram."

Baric jerked around, his eyes black with indignation. Snapped his fingers and the screens went blank. "You may have authority to commandeer my ship for your excursions, *Commander*, but you have no authority to peruse the files of the ship's captain. Might I remind you that regulation 13.491 of the—"

"Easy, Captain," Tigo said with a lazy smile that took more effort than he'd admit. "I know regs. And I'm not commandeering your ship, though you do have to answer to TSC if you defy orders and don't deliver my Eidolon team as instructed. As for perusing intel? No effort was made to conceal it, so I had no reason to suspect it was classified."

Glowering, Baric lifted his channeler and glanced at the file. "Going to"—he flung a scowl at him—"Drosero? You know what will happen if this gets out, right?"

"To you?" Tigo grunted. "Not a thing in the 'verse. To my team—"

"This could cause an all-out war! Drosero has refused every attempt we've made to establish a way station there. They won't allow colonization."

"Which is why my team and I aren't colonizing." Tigo hauled his annoyance into line. "Do I need to wave Command that Two-one-five has no transport?"

Lips tight, Baric stared him down, anger flickering in his gaze. "No."

"You have the coordinates. Per SOP, Dimar should probably monitor for hostiles or unusual activity."

"They don't have technology—what hostile acts are you expecting? Swords? Spears?" He plucked the disc and tossed it back at Tigo. "Remember, this is my ship. You don't give commands."

Tigo's irritation skidded into his hands, balling his fingers into fists. "We need to be over Droseran airspace in two days. From our current coordinates, that's plenty of time." He left the Command deck and took the lift down to Hangar Deck 14. As he walked, he tapped into his channeler, which was rigged with faster and higher tech than most, ordering his unit to report to the corvette that would take them planetside. Though they had some time before the *Macedon* arrived at Drosero, they might as well get started on the prep work.

That his boots were squeaking jerked his attention to his location. He wasn't on a hangar deck. Rubberized floor … This was M Deck. What in the black?

But then life didn't disappoint, did it? Because heading toward him was the *Macedon*'s chief medical officer, Dr. Teeli Knowles. She'd been cold as space to him, but he'd win her over. He always did. She was no different from most women he aimed his attention at. And she seemed to need some positivity in her life.

Deep in conversation with an orderly, she glided past Tigo without a glance. Huh. Maybe a little different.

"Well?"

Tigo flinched at the Eidolon who appeared beside him. "Blood and boil, Esq. Always sneakin'."

"So's it true? We dropping?"

Tigo nodded. "Two days."

"Hoyzah!" She pumped a fist. "I am so *sick* of this ship and its whiny, petulant popsicles. I'm ready for warm air and warm blood. Catchya down there later."

She banked right, and Tigo went left, where the passage opened to the medical bay. Again, he spotted the long, lean figure of Dr. Knowles. Black hair, rich mahogany skin. She was from Tryssinia, a planet replete with ore and mining colonies … and one plague after another. Most Tryssinians didn't survive much past young adulthood. But here was the beauty of them all.

"Dr. Knowles."

Turning with a data pad in hand, blue lettering scrolling over the screen, she didn't look up. "Yes?" she asked, shaking her head. Then she swung back to the orderly. "Wait—no. Tell him I can't do that. I won't." Slipping the pad into its sheath, she pivoted back to Tigo. "How can—" Delicious caramel eyes widened. "You." With a huff, she started down the hall.

So maybe a lot different. "Hold up," Tigo said, trotting after her. "I just wanted to see if you had an answer yet."

"I supplied my answer when you first asked. I won't repeat it."

"Then I'll ask a different question. Will you have morning rations with me?"

"Wow, can you make that sound more romantic, Captain Deken?" She lifted a patient's chart, read the vitals, then moved on.

"Um, I'll bring a candle—a cell-powered one, since fires are banned—"

"The only thing that changed in your question, Captain Deken—"

"Tigo."

"—was the meal. Last time, dinner. Before that, lunch."

"So Tryssinians don't eat?" He grinned, determined to be unflappable.

She gave a longsuffering sigh. "No. We don't. Not with egotistical, adrenaline-seeking, womanizing *Nephesh*."

"Hey!" He paused. "I'm no womanizer." He harnessed the charm that had done him many favors. "But I do know how to recognize a woman who is as intelligent as she is beautiful."

"Unless you're in a med-bed, I don't have any intelligence to waste on your kind."

"My kind?"

"You PICC-necks."

Tigo stiffened at the nickname derived from the ports implanted in the Eidolons' necks that fed vital boosters from their mech-suits straight into their spinal columns. Without them, an Eidolon could become incapacitated by injury during battle or an imbalance after a hard-g drop, but the ugly truth was they were also a quick and easy way to inject other things. And despite regs, some Eidolon did. Still he'd never expected that kind of vitriolic labeling from Knowles.

"You're all alike," she snarled. "And anyone who would authorize that machine and on my medbay—"

"Wait." Tigo's pulse jammed, recalling Baric's intel wall. "What machine?" *Tell me he isn't doing this.*

Lips compressed as if to hold in further words, she pointed to a door where a dozen engineers worked with drills and other tools. He looked more closely. Doors had been thickened. Walls padded with some film.

His channeler on his arm buzzed. He glanced down and saw a curt *WE NEED TO BRIEF FOR THE DROP. WHERE ARE YOU?* from Diggs. "I have to—" When he looked up, Tigo froze. He stood alone.

Dr. Knowles was at the far end of the bay, talking with a patient. Her black braid coiled at her nape. The gray medical coat way too blasé for her fierce personality and stunning looks. And Knowles had more than beauty. In that head was a mind that had gotten her not just a medical degree from the Tertian Science Academy, but honors qualification that planted her on a battle cruiser. That took persistence. They had that in common. She might have rejected him a few times, but he wouldn't give up. He glanced back at the door. But what was she upset about?

Two days later in Hangar 14, his team was prepping gear and readying for their mission. He checked his weapons and ammo, then performed a safety inspection on his mech-suit. After preflight checks on their corvette, the *Renette*, he donned the nearly skin-tight flight suit that would monitor his vitals and oxygen mix. Next, he stepped into the lightweight body armor and tested his comms, night-vision, thermals, heads-up visor displays, and ballistic protection. With an ear out for the telltale click, he stuffed his feet into the grav boots of the mech-suit exoskeleton, then threaded his arms through the upper appendages and felt the suit auto-adjust and mold around his body. He locked the dome into place and angled his neck back, engaging the PICC-line, which infused him with a lightning-fast shot of icy fluid that carried the digital neura, connecting his suit and brain.

He trunked over to the deck, where they inspected each other's gear.

Lance Corporal Theodore "Diggs" Diggins, the team's pilot and senior communications officer, secured the shoulders strap of his rifle as their eyes met. "Where to, Commander?"

"We're heading to Planet Nine—"

"Drosero?" Lieutenant Jez Sidra jerked around, her grav boots thunking heavily on the deck that radiated with objections to their destination. Though she had more curves and "pretty" than any woman should, Jez also had a spine and attitude of steel. Sharp like a blade. Nobody got close without getting hurt. And she liked it that way.

"Complaints noted and understood," Tigo said, holding up his hand. "We have a priority-one fugitive hiding out in the mountains of northeast Kalonica." Tigo splashed the specs of the location to their displays. "He's dangerous, so be on alert when we hit ground."

"Ice," Esq grunted, then whined, "I wanted *heat*, Commander."

"Hey, I'm hot, Esq," Corporal Sevart "Rhinnock" Crafter taunted.

"Not even close, Rhinn."

Two pats on his shoulder by Rhinn said he found Tigo's mech-suit in order. "Sending O$_2$ and ambient suit settings now."

Beeps registered the receipt. "What the slag?" Diggs turned near-black eyes to him in question.

"I know," Tigo conceded. "O$_2$ is *low*. Thermals are scuzzed."

"That should be good for AO, right?" Rhinn said. "He has already ice in his veins."

Corporal Jaigh "AO" Eggleston said nothing. Annoyed or amused, his expression never changed. But he was the fiercest and most controlled of the team. And the oldest—yet newest to join Symmachian Marines. Which is where he'd gotten the nickname, Ancient One. A blasphemous one if you, like a lot of downworlders in the quads, believed in an ancient being who orchestrated lives and wills.

"What're they sending us after?" Diggs asked.

Tigo splashed the image of their target.

"What has he done to earn the wrath of Tascan?" Jez asked, using the nickname for Tertian Space Coalition.

Tigo shrugged, a gesture only roughly translated by the mech-suit. "We all know Drosero is an uncoop, so we need to get in and out before anyone is the wiser. No weapons unless absolutely necessary. The less proof of our presence we leave, the better."

"We scuz this," Diggs said, "and we're torched. Nobody will know either way."

Tigo grinned as he started toward the light corvette, which was thrumming after Diggs's preflight check. "Then we've got nothing to lose!"

"Hoyzah!"

Rigged in, they were cleared for launch by the *Macedon* and were soon making their descent. As they broke Droseran space, staying high to avoid being spotted, Tigo reviewed with 215 the schematics of the cave system they'd search.

"This image is sanitized," AO's growl from the jump seat raked the comms. Tigo's gut clenched. *Exactly what I thought.*

"Why?" Esq asked. "How can we catch him if this doesn't look like him?"

"Memorize the structure, the eyes," Diggs replied. "They don't change."

"Unless he's got enhancements," Esq countered.

"This is Nine, remember? No tech." Rhinn leaned forward and met Tigo's gaze. "This already feels off."

"Jitters?" Tigo teased. "Thought you were Nephesh." The team getting buggy before they hit atmo was a bad sign.

Onboard lighting went red. Tigo braced as the light attack craft tore through the atmosphere. To avoid being spotted, they approached from straight north of their targeted landing spot, keeping clear of the populated areas south of the mountains in question. Still, they could only hope nobody was looking up at this moment, or they'd see a shooting star. The hull groaned like a wounded beast. Might unnerve a downworlder, but Tigo found the sensation thrilling—it meant he was about to deploy.

He couldn't imagine life on a planet with no technology. Lights. Comms. Toilets—did they have toilets? Weapons. It was like one of those digitals Esq loved reading when she thought nobody was looking, men with no tunics riding horses bareback. Women stuffed in the hut pushing out buns—from the ovens and from their wombs.

Archaic. His mother would've never put up with that.

Entry complete, Tigo and 215 clomped to the bay door as Diggs maintained high altitude and aimed toward the jagged peaks. He gave the all-quiet signal. Engines silent, they rode an air current to forbidding, snow-packed cliffs.

The landing countdown blipped on their heads-up display.

The *Renette* settled with a thump, and the bay door started opening.

Wind buffeted his suit, gusting up into the corvette. Advancing, he monitored the formidable cliff for unfriendlies through the heads-up. But who was he kidding? Nobody would be here. Brutal cold. External readings were in excess of negative forty temps.

Ahead, Diggs and Jez hustled to the yawning maw of a cave, indiscernible from the air. But it'd been right where intel stated it would be.

AO, Esq, and Rhinn fell in behind Tigo as they breached the mountain. Dark emptiness constricted in a tight tunnel. He slowed his breathing as the passage narrowed, nerves grating when his mech-suit scraped rock. Nothing anyone could hear, but in the vacuum of the suit, it was like metal on metal.

"Ambient adjustment," intoned the digital voice of his suit as it detected and compensated for the darkness, affording a thermal cave readout.

His muscles contracted beneath the chill. On any normal mission, his suit would keep his core static. But the numbers demanded a low core temp.

"This is wrong," AO subvocalized, his teeth chattering.

"Quiet," Tigo hissed back, then mentally kicked himself. This place must be getting to him—the suits were soundproof. Anything they subvocalized wouldn't be heard outside their comms.

Shake it off. Tigo pressed forward, nearly cursing the passage as it squeezed tighter. And tighter. Until it forced him to turn sideways to pass. He shoved himself through and stumbled into what felt like gaping emptiness. Slack jawed, he stared around the gaping chasm. His visor glimmered, switching from a gridded scan to a navigable map of the cavern. But what it relayed froze him. They stood in a large area with four square openings around its perimeter. Doors. Doors hewn from granite. A drop that had to be easily a hundred meters separated them from a small circular cleft in the center.

As he processed the information, the surreal and impossible setting, Tigo realized the chill he'd felt had nothing to do with atmospherics. That AO had it right. Something was off. The chill was a death knell.

03

KALONICA, DROSERO

"You are not to speak of it," Kersei said, gritting against the pain that had grown as she and her sister returned to Stratios Hall. She cradled her waist, protecting ribs that seared with each breath. "Do you hear, Adara?"

Snapping her wooden sword against grain sacks along the inner bailey wall, her sister groaned. "I heard you the first thousand times."

"And I will insist another thousand times until I am decided you understand. It is your presentation night. There are oras of preparation remaining, and no doubt Ma'ma has been looking for you. She will be most displeased to learn you've been to the fields." As they made their way through the side entrance to the house, she nodded. "Now, be gone with you. And say naught."

"Thank the Ancient," Adara breathed and darted up the stairs.

Kersei slowed, eying the steps, and moaned. Why were there so many stairs? She huffed and took the first one, the move clenching her breath in a fist of pain. Wincing and twitching, she climbed. There were sure to be bruises, but those could be hidden. An awkward gait could not. And oh Mercies! If she were made to wear bindings—*Ancient, be kind, please!*

She climbed ... and climbed. Made the landing of the main level and turned, deflating at the next hundred—or so it seemed—up to the residence wing. Teeth gritted, she caught the rail. Thoughts pushed her on: blood on Myles's lip. His amused smirk. Her victory at unseating him had truly been sweet, even with the ruin of Darius's chiding and her injury.

As she gained the residence level, Kersei dragged herself toward the apartments—and froze.

Tall and gracious, auburn hair secured in a meticulous plait atop her head, Ma'ma stood with hands clasped. Had she watched Kersei's entire ascent? By the disapproval on her imperious face, she had. She glided forward with a smile. "Daughter."

That was a warm welcome. Mayhap she did not know.

"Ma'ma," Kersei managed, stiffening for the embrace sure to come.

Her mother's cool fingers tipped her chin. "Stand erect, Kersei. You're a lady."

Every fraction she straightened made tiny daggers pepper her abdomen. Cry out and she'd reveal herself, so she bit down that which begged for freedom.

With a nod, her mother shifted aside, sliding a hand to Kersei's back. Another to her stomach. "Straight." She pressed.

Kersei cried out, tears blurring her vision.

Ma'ma held her gaze, void of remonstration or anger, which made it all the worse.

She knew. Blood and boil, she knew. Tears slipping down her cheeks, Kersei closed her eyes. Breathed through the agony. Gritted her teeth as she tasted the full measure of her mother's displeasure.

"You were with the machitis again." The Lady of Stratios held court right there in the main hall, for all to hear and see. Sergii shuffled along the shadows, intent on their duties and pretending not to hear. "On this day, the very day I expressly forbade—"

"I unseated him, Ma'ma," she blurted.

Fire slashed through her mother's schooled features, her chest rising and falling unevenly as she let silence hang between them. "And you are injured. On the night warriors gather to honor your father's house, you disgrace him."

The words stabbed hard. Pierced Kersei's stubborn veil. Father. She had wanted to make him proud. Could Ma'ma not understand that she ached for adventure, for freedom from the cold stone walls of Stratios?

"When Xylander's daughter cannot stand erect as he presents his final heir to the crown and the Ancient One, what will be said of him?" Her mother huffed through the next several breaths. "Very badly done, Kersei. Even he who might ignore your foolishness would not approve. Can you not think beyond yourself for one tick of the clock?"

Hurt cloyed with shame, beating at her victory, which seemed silly now. "I beg your mercy."

"It is not mine you need beg." Her mother tossed her head in the direction of the private wing. "Go. Soak and have your injuries tended. Rest. Whatever it takes, be ready to stand tall as a daughter of Stratios. And though you would wretch from pain, do not disgrace your father before his entoli and medora."

Kersei trudged to her chambers. Reaching the bed, she eased—ever—so—slowly—against the mattress. Why had the draw determined she ride against Myles *this* rise? The one day she need be Xylander's daughter before all? Her effort to gain his approval, to show him that though he had no sons, he did not have weak heirs, had failed her. And him.

Palms pressed to her eyes, she fought the sob that tightened her abdomen—and cast flames through her muscles. Her hands were burned from losing her grip on Bastien's reins. Raw proof of her irresponsibility.

The door opened and Conti strode in. "Let us get you out of those clothes, mistress. If the lady sees you—"

"She has already." Kersei pried herself upright, grimacing. Lifting her hand hurt. Lifting her arm much more.

As she removed Kersei's tunic, Conti groaned then clucked her tongue. "That be right angry, mistress."

Kersei peered at her side. Red and purple vied for supremacy—yet it was no more ugly than the black marks that coiled in sinuous lines the length of her right forearm. Mother refused to speak of the brand—which was an odd term, since the lines were not burned into her, Ma'ma promised.

"Keep it concealed, Kersei. They will not understand." Beyond that, she would say no more, no matter how Kersei cajoled.

She rotated her arm, eyeing the lone line bisecting the half-arcs that ran randomly. She'd tried to research it, sought texts from the Readers. But there was very little about brands or the unique marks.

"Just embarrassment," she murmured, pressing the arm to her side and stepping into the tub.

Hazy and vague, a memory rose—the brand had burned after the fall. Probably just more of her imagination, as everything had hurt afterward. At least the discoloration on her torso would fade with time. Years had already proven the marks on her forearm indelible.

"Don't give it no thought," Conti said as she bathed her. "The pharmakeia can make up a right good salve for this."

"Can he do something for this?" Kersei said, splashing her arm into the water.

"I know it ails your heart something fierce, mistress, but it's a holy mark."

She snorted. There had been no iereas in Stratios Hall in her memory. Lexina said Father had forbidden the priests further entry when Kersei was just a babe. "A mark none will or can explain."

"Not all in life can be explained."

Kersei rolled her eyes. She carried her mother's beauty, her father's passionate nature, and this mark of the Iereans, the Holy Order of Iereania. At least, that's what she'd read in her academics—all brands were tied to them.

Well into the darkening day, Conti ministered to the injuries with a bitter-herb tea, a pack of chilled fruit for her ribs, and salves the pharmakeia had sent up for the swelling and scrapes.

"You should have seen him, Conti," came Adara's squeaky, lighthearted voice as she flew into the room, bathed and hair in coils, but no dress yet. "Myles flew through the air, unseated by *my* sister!" Pride puffed the small chest. "I thought for sure there would be a hole in the ground where he hit." Her giggles riffled the cool evening as she clambered over the bed to where Kersei lay resting, as ordered.

"Give care, sister! It hu—"

Adara plopped down, sending shards of pain through Kersei. "I can't believe you beat him!"

With a smile, Kersei looked at the hand-embroidered coverlet beneath her. But she did not see the corals and sage greens. She saw the fierce machitis bearing down on her. Myles! "I did not. He unseated me as well—as is plain."

"I wish I could tell Ma'ma!" Adara was on her knees, bouncing the bed, jarring Kersei with those daggers of pain again.

"Cease!" she hissed, then relented, moving to the chair for relief and so Conti could work her hair into something manageable and less voluminous. "No word of that will be spoken beyond this chamber."

Her sister dropped against the gold-threaded coverlet, her enthusiasm sinking with her. "But why?"

"*You* weren't supposed to be there," Kersei reminded. "Ma'ma has forbidden it."

Arms crossed, Adara pouted. "It's not fair that you can train, and I am not even to watch."

Kersei tensed beneath the twisting and tugging turning her scalp to embers. "You must find your own path, Adara. She wants you to make your own choices, not follow mine."

"But I like your path. I don't want to learn how to carry a book on my head when I can carry a sword!" Her sister hefted an imaginary weapon and swung it in wild arcs. "When he came out, I thought for sure you were going to meet the Ancient."

In the reflecting glass perched before her, Kersei lifted her shift and eyed the darkening bruise once more—then the cut on her cheekbone—and set the pack of chilled fruit aside. "Hush before Ma'ma overhears."

Adara's smile slipped, her wide eyes darting to the side. "Too late."

Releasing her shift, Kersei turned toward the side door, a passage between apartments that afforded the family unfettered access to one another. Kersei stood, hands pressed to her thighs, mustering every bit of etiquette, and instinctively covered her right forearm. A chill traced her shoulders, making her acutely aware of her bare arms.

Wreathed in grace and beauty, Ma'ma remained poised and somehow above every menial element in this realm, including Kersei. She could never rise to the level of elegance that defined Nicea Dragoumis.

Eyebrow arced, Ma'ma glided toward her. "You allowed your sister to watch, to be swayed by your insanity and disregard for the welfare of Stratios?"

Adara hopped off the bed and dashed to their ma'ma. "I wasn't in danger. I watched from the fence as Kersei unseated the aerios."

Curse her naïveté!

Rich brown eyes fastened onto Kersei. "Leave us," Ma'ma ordered.

Oh no. Kersei braced as Conti gathered Adara and left.

Ma'ma trailed a slow path around the chamber, then stood on the balcony, where the doors were spread wide to invite a breeze.

Kersei dreaded this part—the silence. The long pause designed to let the guilt fester. She moved closer, hoping to convince her mother to speak and end the painful void.

Yet, no conversation came. The silence exceeded the point of being unnerving. Ma'ma had never held onto her anger this long before. And in truth, Kersei did regret—well, not her actions, but her timing. But should they not be readying for the ceremony? Anything to get this over with. "I—"

"You have always been so … strong."

The gentle words pulled Kersei's gaze to her mother, who stood facing the fields below. What was this? No remonstration? No chastisement?

"Sometimes," Ma'ma said as she lowered her head, "the price we pay for what we want with all our hearts is … very high." With a heavy exhale, she turned. Came to Kersei and slid her hand to the brand on Kersei's forearm. She squeezed. "Other than the bruises, you are … well?"

There was something beneath the soft question. Something worried, concerned.

Though curious, Kersei did not dare invite more lectures. "Yes, Ma'ma. I thank you."

Relief seemed to flood her mother. Then her eyes clouded. Glossed … tears? *Tears?* From Nicea Dragoumis?

After another squeeze, Ma'ma glided away, then hesitated. "You should change. We ride within the ora for the Plains of Adunatos." Sadness clung to her like the first-rise dew on the fields. "Never doubt, Kersei, that …" She straightened. "No matter what comes, know that I love you and your father very much. Had there been another way ..."

Kersei stared. Frowned. "Another way to what?"

Shaking her head, Ma'ma seemed to throw off some great weight. "The blue dress tonight, Kersei."

She blinked at the change of topic. "I'd planned the green—"

"*Blue.*"

Kersei watched her ma'ma leave the chamber, wondering at the near command to wear blue. It was a Delta Presentation. The wearing of green signified unification with the medora, with the heart of Kardia.

Why would Ma'ma insist she wear blue?

KALONICA, DROSERO

"Eyes out." Tigo firmed his grip on his weapon, wishing that his orders had not required stun only. He traced the layout, recalling the low oxygen. The strange settings. All so that their suits would not register. But against what? There was no technology here.

"This is wrong," AO muttered again.

The team filtered around, arcing into the space, their mech-suits seeming strangely appropriate in this harsh environment.

"Do you know, Commander ..." boomed an unfamiliar voice.

"Registers as an external," Diggs reported.

Their target.

"... what is more noticeable," the voice continued, "than the stench of space swine?"

"Where's that coming from?" AO growled.

"I don't see anything!" Jez said.

"Is he calling us pigs?" Rhinn complained.

"Quiet!" Mind buzzing, Tigo swiped the pad on his forearm. "Recalibrate metrics," he ordered his mech-suit. Weapon up, he circled, scanning, letting his mech-suit search out the enemy.

"Negative on visual," AO said.

Tigo signaled the team to spread out along the circumference of the ledge that overlooked the drop. He punched the external mic on his suit. "Enlighten us."

"The absence of smell and heat." A shape dropped straight down from the fathomless heights above. The landing proved soft, the slightest of thumps against the hewn stone. Three meters ahead, the man unfolded his frame, draped in a long black overcloak.

His insertion stunned the team, leaving them immobile for a fraction. Then light danced and splayed across the gaping void. Blasts sparking from the muzzles.

But just as fast, the shadowed form launched away. Legs. Arms. Flurry of movement. Blending back into the shadows from which he'd come. Not spiderlike, but not far from it either. Soft thumps and thwaps carried along the walls.

AO cursed. Someone went down.

Confusion coursed through Tigo as he whipped around, trying to sight the target and realizing at the same time a terrible truth: this man had been waiting for them.

So. Ambush or trap?

"Target lock," Tigo ordered his suit as the reticle slid in and around, trying to home in on the lightning-fast man, who seemed to ricochet off walls. Hit one, bounced off it to another. Hit and bound.

"What the slag?" muttered AO.

"Is he even human?" Jez whispered.

Tigo tucked their distraction and awe away to focus on the blurring shape. The shadow that flittered here and there. Flipped in the air. Leapt from one ledge to another as if he were some creature. Body bent to the side, he kicked Jez backward and simultaneously punched Diggs so hard his visor cracked.

"What is he?" Rhinn growled. "Stun has no effect."

"Switch to low yield?"

"Negative," Tigo barked, losing sight of the target for a second. A blur from the side. He ducked but felt the *thunk* against his helm. Rattled, he pushed upward, trusting his sighting technology. Let it guide. "Anticipate," he said to himself.

"Esq is down!" Jez said.

"My visor isn't working," Diggs noted.

"Tech won't work on this guy," AO said. "Go manual."

"Manual?" Rhinn objected. "I can't see him without the visor."

That was the point. They were relying on the suit too much. "He's right. Go manual." Tigo pressed the button at the base of his neck ring. The visor hissed up and the suit's quiet hum vanished.

"Why aren't the stun blasts working?" Diggs asked.

"No idea," AO said, shouldering forward. He backed up against Tigo, who closed his mind to the chaos. Listened to what he couldn't see.

A gentle thump to his right.

Tigo came around. Threw a fist. Connected with something hard—a jaw. The man grunted. But still came.

After a heavy thunk against his suit, Tigo flew backward. The armor ensconcing him crunched as he landed, the man atop him. Hands on Tigo's neck, but the suit's steel ring prevented him from tightening that grasp. With a thrust of his leg, Tigo kicked him in the back of the head.

The attacker pitched forward.

Using the suit's amplified strength, Tigo flipped, landing atop the man and throwing a fist—that hit solid rock. Even though the gauntlet cushioned his hand, pain exploded through his knuckles. Distracted him long enough for the target to upend him again. Though Tigo fought it, he could not prevent the thick shock of his mech-suit's spine colliding with the stone. His head rattled in the helmet. The man punched him, and stars sprinkled across his vision.

"Webbing!"

Tigo heard AO's shout, and despite his instincts, he flattened himself.

He heard the *thwump* of the webbing ropes wrapping around the man. A whistling preceded the man being hauled backward, and the acrid scent of small electrical charges burning flesh filled Tigo's helmet.

Tigo scrambled around. Hurried to the man writhing in the webbing ropes. Held the anchors to prevent escape. "Sedative!"

Jez slid in and aimed the injector, but their fugitive had a life to lose and seemed intent on fighting. He bucked and Jez shifted back, waiting. Came in again with the sedative.

The man focused his energies and threw his weight at her, knocking Jez and the needle backward. She scrambled for it, snatching it before it lunged into the gaping chasm. She spun around, glaring. "Kill the webbing charge and hold him!"

Diggs dialed back the charge, then he and AO dropped on the target. Tigo fell across his legs as Jez shoved the injector against his thigh. A click, then a hiss.

They hopped away, the man still jerking and fighting until he slowed … slowed … went limp.

"Scuz me," Diggs muttered, lifting a hand. "What is he?"

"Not what we were told." Tigo glowered. This man wasn't a fugitive. In fact, Tigo was pretty sure by the marks on the man's face that this man hadn't committed a crime. Ever. Which made exactly no sense at all.

"What do you mean?" Jez squatted beside Esq, who was sitting up, looking dazed but otherwise unhurt.

But he wasn't going against orders—not from High Command—and leaving their quarry behind. "AO, help me," he said, bending toward the target. "We've been here ten too long." They hoisted the burly man up and ferried him out of the passages. Moonslight washed over them as they exited the cave, revealing AO's expression. The seasoned veteran had realized the same thing Tigo had. No need to talk about it. "Not here."

AO quietly said, "You know what will happen—"

"Too well."

"Two treaties were broken—"

"Not. Here."

"They—"

The sound of Jez swearing broke into their muted discussion. She had forged ahead out of the cave and now spun slowly in a circle with her arms splayed in mystification. "Where's the *Renette*?"

Tigo glanced to the side. He stilled, his mind refusing to take in what his eyes told him. The corvette was nowhere in sight. Had something happened—avalanche, maybe?—or had the *Renette* been stolen? Or worse?

They lowered the prisoner's body and Tigo keyed his mic. "TSC *Macedon*, this is Eidolon Two-one-five. We need an emergency evac."

Crackling silence met his distress call.

"Repeat, TSC *Macedon*, this is Eidolon Two-one-five Actual—come in. We are stranded and—"

"Two-one-five Actual, this is *Macedon*," came Captain Baric's very flat voice. "You are breaking radio silence—"

"Request immediate evac. Our exfil is compromised and we are heavy one package. Over."

"Negative, Two-one-five. We are forbidden in Droseran airsp—"

"*Macedon*," Tigo bit out. "Repeat—we are heavy one package and six Eidolon stranded." Silence filled the connection, agitating him. He shifted and groaned. If they left them down here ... "*Macedon*? Mace—"

"Easy, Two-one-five Actual," came the calm, distanced voice of Commander Dimar in warning to Tigo. "Research One is en route. Glad you're alive. Thought you'd gone Nephesh for real when *Renette*'s signal blinked out."

"Thanks, Commander. I owe you."

"Oh, I know," Wellsey said. "I'm already working out how to make you pay."

Tigo almost smiled. "Roger that. Two-one-five Actual out."

"So," Diggs asked, "lost or stolen?" He'd moved to the top of a nearby boulder and stood surveying the snow-laden landscape. "No smoke. No sign of any ship. I thought this planet was filled with backbirthers, so how would any of them even know how to pilot a corvette? Who could have stolen it?"

Tigo had no answers but to look at their fugitive. "The same one who fed Krissos intel on this man."

"Who is he?" Jez asked, her brown eyes filled with concern.

"Look at the sigil on his face." He nodded to the arcs and swoops winging out from the man's nose to his eyes. "He's a hunter."

The team shifted, some stepping back. However, Jez moved closer. "A *Kynigos*?" She visually traced his face. "I've never seen one up close."

Diggs growled. "Did you know who we were coming after before—"

"No." Tigo wasn't foolish enough to go up against the one form of authority in their universe that transcended planets and territorial boundaries.

"Word gets out about this," Diggs hissed, "it's war."

"Then word doesn't get out."

SAHNSI, LYRIST

The scent of fear reeked in the hot twilit air, rifling highly attuned receptors. Marco inhaled deeply. There were many types of fear, each one carrying its own unique scent. Reverent fear was not painful to receptors, but it often offended his sensibilities. Too many bowed to empty idols and statues. Threat-based fear given off by someone being attacked was stringent. But fear flooding from a quarry who had committed a crime and knew justice had come …

How sweet the stench.

Crouched at the base of the sanctuary spire, a lofty height that provided a hazy view of the river churning off to the south, Marco Dusan had the perfect vantage for a hunt. He rotated, each foot resting on a different ledge—one facing the lower sector, the other the square. The church sat in the armpit of the alley, as if deliberately diverting traffic from the town square to the lower village overrun with miscreants, vagrants, and gypsies. The emanating smells proved putrid. Thankfully, a north wind sifted the scents.

Voices, barking dogs, dinner cooking … The onslaught of sensory information could paralyze him—were he a hound, a first-year at the Citadel. Experience and time had taught him to wade through the scents plaguing a heavily populated area and ignore the irrelevant. Home in on the one he sought—fear. Separate it from ancillary smells and signatures—the hormonal and chemical combination unique to each person.

Marco fisted his hand and closed his eyes, angling to the side as he mentally navigated the odors of the passage and its trespassers.

A crisp, clean signature struck him. Mixed with a touch of frustration. Roman deBurco.

Aye, this quarry had proven most elusive. Yet it should not surprise the master hunter since the Decree requested three Kynigos. The revered hunters had jurisdiction to hunt on all planets of the Herakles Quadrant, save Drosero, unless a quarry had gone to ground there.

A warm, bitter efflux puffed down the alley and into Marco's receptors.

Eyes still closed, he searched, splaying his hands, fanning the scent to himself. Scent could not hide in the shadows. It required no light to betray.

The smell of fear grew stronger. The quarry was closer.

Opening his eyes, Marco scanned the dark passage. *Come. Show yourself,* he willed the fugitive. Eventually he would. They all did. He unhitched the monocle from the rhinnock vambrace on his right arm and peered down into the depths. No good. Too dark. He reattached it and verified there were no waves from his brethren.

At last the crisp scent swelled. Both Roman and Rico Ohlson, his advocate, had drawn in as well. Strong bergamot drifted through the alley—by that particular scent he knew the man had been with a chatelaine. Fear roiled— then collided with balsam, stinging Marco's nostrils. Panic. The Brethren had been spotted. The quarry knew he was hunted.

Marco slowly rose, keeping his movement organic so as not to draw attention. Fear tumbled, leaving a heady lure. Coming nearer. The reek watered his eyes and urged him from the ledge. Warm night air buffeted him as he silently dropped the six feet to the cobbled path. Touched down, reacquiring as he came to his full height.

A woman started and shouted as she shoved away, realizing who he was. What he was.

He rolled his shoulders, unfurling his long black Kynigos cloak with its stiff collar, hyperfocusing his gift. Receptors filled with the scents, he shifted naught but his eyes as he scanned crates, alcoves.

Here. He is right *here.*

Yet ... where?

A shadow darted out of the alley and up the building.

His pulse ricocheted. The shadow had gone *up*, not down. "He runs!" Marco called to his brethren. A laugh stole into his shout as he vaulted across the passage. Grabbed the downpipe of a dwelling and scaled it. Thrust himself to the right, toeing a ledge, before swinging up onto the roof. Spied a shadow spiriting away and threw himself in that direction, hopping over a ledge and the gap between row houses.

Behind came the telltale thumps of his brethren closing in. It was Roman's Decree, so Roman must finish it. The Creed cared not what aid came in completing the Decree, only that it must be completed or all honor would remain suspended until then.

"Marco, this way!"

He skidded to a stop at a corner, confused. Rico called him toward the clock tower, but he clearly scented the quarry north. *Trust those before you.* In a sprint to reach his advocate, Marco felt the taunting edges of frustration.

Exquisite odors of yeast and sugars rose thickly from the baker on whose roof they came to a slow, maddening stop.

"Where?" He trotted to his advocate.

"I …" Roughing a hand over his face, Rico shook his head. "I had him— just past the chimneys. Then he was gone."

"Marco, backtrack south," Roman growled as he joined them, moonslight grabbing his well-worn duster. "I *will* fulfill the Decree. My honor will not be impugned by this miscreant."

Inclining his head, Marco eased away, annoyed that he had been pulled from the scent. He flung himself around. Back to where he'd last had the scent. With a running start, he leapt across a narrow alley, landed in a roll, and came up jogging, scanning. He veered right, grateful the same wind that had carried away the stench of the lower sector now guided him in the hunt.

Yet as he reached the river, the scent wafted out. Marco slowed, eyes closed. Chin tucked. He drew in a long, slow draught of air and licked his lips, using every receptor in his nose, throat, and mouth to find the signature. But … nothing. How was this possible?

Scowling, he traced the shadows, the rooftops.

Need to get higher.

Marco launched at the wall. Bounded to the right, where another building jutted up, and then caught the ledge to his left. He flipped up and over it, then shot upright. Basilica light caressed him as he turned a slow circle, smelling. Tasting. He stilled. Cocked his head to the left. Craned … a … little … mor—

There!

Marco bolted toward the basilica, noting the bustle and lights of the square grew as he two-handed a ledge and sailed over it. Used the next as a launch point. Eyeing the edge of the commons building that rimmed the southern portion of the square, he grabbed it and sailed over, immediately sighting the façade for a toehold. Found one. Dropped to it. Shimmied to the window. Shoved off. Twisted around and landed, facing the fountain.

He groaned inwardly, hating how water and moisture dampened scents. Thickened and blurred them. Smart of the quarry to come here. "Cut off the fountain!" Marco shouted to a sentry, who gaped, then scrambled to comply.

"Kynigos!" The pronouncement swelled the crowd into a frenzy. Villagers fled to the passages. Interfering with a hunt warranted branding. And yet, their very flight could provide the quarry a throng in which to escape.

Rico burst from the side, wide eyes hitting Marco. Asking if he had him. Knew his location.

With a shake of his head, Marco hopped up on the ledge of the fountain and turned his back to the now-still water.

Fear smells like honor. Because that scent was strong and foul, making it easier to track. Making it easier to fulfill a Decree and gain honor.

Ahh. There.

He tilted his head to the left and grinned. "They cannot hide for long."

Formidable Roman stormed forward, his Kynigos cords swaying against his black vest. His long cloak swung back over his shoulders as he angled forward, his thick dark eyebrows tightening and nostrils flaring.

Deathly silence blanketed the previous buzzing. Readying themselves to capture the fugitive, Marco and Rico started in opposite directions to make a slow circuit around the fountain of the goddess Eleftheria, who held a tipped jug.

"To the Decree," Rico said.

"And the hunt," Marco added.

"For honor." Roman breathed a long sigh, as if centered by the mantra.

A heavy lemon smell wafted on the hot winds, drenching Marco's receptors and piquing his thirst. Grimacing, he glanced down at a large barrel. Filled nearly to the top with dried flaxinella petals, the bin sat like a sentry at the magevo's shop. He swiped a hand through the petals and grunted.

Fear and anger scents slammed him from behind. He spun in time to catch a woman throwing herself at him.

With her neck in his vise-grip, she widened her blue eyes. Cried out. Dropped a knife, the metal clattering against the cobbles.

Processing her smell in a tick, Marco grunted. Rage. Vengeance. Innocence could stay his hand from marking her, but she had none. "Consider yourself marked." The small iron was in his hand in a flash, searing her crime into her throat.

Screaming, she sagged. The Kynigos sigil blazed against her skin. "You beasts!"

He glared as he released her. "It would serve you well to leave."

After a glance at the magevo's shop, she shuffled away. Her efflux reeked of worry.

What had she been looking at? Finding nothing, he slowly backstepped. Something here gave her concern.

Marco wiped his forehead as he surveyed the shop. Then the lingering scent on his hand stilled him. He stared at his palm for a tick, then slowly raised it to his face. The faint odor of lemon mixed with a distinct … *signature*. He considered the barrel again. The scattered dried petals around the base.

He grinned. Over his shoulder, he caught Rico's gaze. With a gentle nod toward the magevo's shop, Marco inched closer to the waist-high crate. "Have you heard, Brethren, how flammable certain plants are?" He scooped a handful of the dried white flowers. He held them above the barrel and let the petals fall through his fingers. "Flaxinella is particularly potent in hot climates—highly flammable, if I remember correctly."

Roman smiled, palming his webbing gun and activating its charge, should the quarry again run. "It was a double rise day."

"Indeed." Marco nearly laughed at the acrid balsam erupting now—panic. "I'm sure this entire barrel would be enough to launch a Symmachian warship."

"At least," Rico said with a wink.

"Shall we test it?" Marco took a step away, as did Rico. This hunt belonged to Roman. Only he could attain the honor it would imbue.

"I have a sparking stone here." Roman lowered his head and relaxed his arms at his sides, fingers rolling. "What say you—two sparks enough?"

Petals flew upward as a body launched from the barrel. "No!" the dusty man gasped, a rebreather in hand. "Mercy, no!"

Roman grabbed the scruff of the man's neck, fury coursing through his dark eyes. "Firkin, you have cost me my honor long enough."

"I beg your mercy, Master Hunter. I've changed my ways."

"What? Bedmate with Symmachia now?" Rico taunted.

It was an old jest among the Kynigos. Those who claimed they changed their ways had either taken up with Symmachian warlords or claimed to sing Eleftheria's praises in the high temple.

The man's face fell. "How do you know about that?"

Marco tensed, frowning at his brethren.

Firkin shook his head. "I didn't know they were going to use my work to kill people. I swear!"

KALONICA, DROSERO

Pain, she decided, was merely another name for retribution.

A column of machitis escorted her family. On most days, she would ride Bastien out this far, but this ceremony was sacred and beasts were not allowed past the river. Kersei rode behind her father and mother, who led the machitis and councilmembers toward the Plain of Adunatos. The forty-minute journey on horseback was nothing compared to the ensuing twenty on foot, where she stumbled on every uneven patch and hole in the road.

Kersei felt Ma'ma's glower and refused to meet it. Instead, she lifted her chin as the proud daughter of Xylander Dragoumis that she was and kept walking. Teeth gritted.

Relief swept her at the distant sight of the basalt arcs of the Delta platform. Already a sea of Stratios swelled around it to attest to Xylander's final heir presentation. Kersei marveled at the structure. A triangular stone platform sent three arches up from its corners, the fingers joining in the center to uphold a large crystal orb, as if offering it to the stars. It was, in reality, an offering to the first Lady of Basilikas, who emerged when Vaqar returned after a cycle-long journey to bless the lands of Drosero and present him with his heir. Just as the Lady presented her heir, each elder and those of his entoli presented their heirs to Vaqar, the Ancient.

There, the story diverged. Some said the heir the Lady presented was a son, Kynig, strong and equal to none, save his immortal father. Others said the heir was Eleftheria, the Lady who watched over all daughters born to the medoras of Kalonica since.

Once her father took his place on the dais with Adara, Kersei joined her mother and eldest sister at the base. Behind them, rows of machitis and the entirety of the Stratios entoli and other clans who ventured into the night for this celebration. Those who did would be rewarded with festivities. Cakes, music, and dancing.

A horn blast was quickly followed by the slap of overcloaks as the machitis snapped to attention in anticipation of the royal family.

Kersei stole a glance at her elder sister, reading there the expectant glow as she watched for the crown prince. Willowy, yet fuller through the hips and breasts—and ego—Lexina skated a look down the long path formed by striking green uniforms of the machitis.

The medora strode into the column, tall and proud. The Light of Kardia sat atop his head. In full regalia, he was an imposing, handsome figure. More than either of his sons, may and true. Father had spoken of the medora taking a new bound, yet he had not. He had remained true to Kyria Athina after her death. His crown somehow caught and dazzled torchlight across its twisted vines that held five different colored gems, representing the five provinces of the Kalonican kingdom. To his right and back two steps strode Crown Prince Silvanus, but the only thing remarkable about the bland-faced prince was his military regalia that squared his shoulders. The Great Star of Kalonica pinned to the gold sash marked him a member of the royal family, but the blue garter sash was that of the heir apparent. His straight black hair hung in a plait or queue, she guessed.

Kersei twitched her nose. Too skinny. Too pale. Too stuffed full of himself. Though some might call Silvanus beautiful, as Lexina had over and over, he had no allure for Kersei.

On Medora Zarek's left and back four steps, Darius cut an impressive figure. Closer to his father's height and good looks. Though his near-blond hair made rumors fly that the kyria had shared someone else's bed. But the square jaw and piercing blue eyes affirmed who'd sired him. He wore the gold sash and white cord of a Tyrannous heir, but unlike his brother, Darius was adorned with the gold belt and cords of the commander of the aerios. It was not merely a hereditary title but one of experience and expertise. It said much of his fighting skills. Below his heart also rested the Great Star of Kalonica, mark of the royal family.

He was more handsome than his brother in the green-and-gold jerkin and black pants, but still too … pretty. Though she'd never call him that on the sparring field. The thought plied a smile from her lips—which drew Darius's gaze. There was something strange and intense in his eyes tonight. His brow rippled as he took in her gown—blue, as Ma'ma insisted. Not green. Was he offended that she had not worn Kalonican colors?

As the medora took the dais with his sons, thirty aerios, the medora's personal guard, arced out behind their sovereign. It was an impressive sight. And she smiled at the way Adara beamed up at their father, who squeezed her hand as they stood at the front for the presentation.

"Hear ye, hear ye!" a caller proclaimed. "Give ear and witness to the events this sacred night of the Delta Presentation, following in the manner of the first Lady and Vaqar and this eve presided over by Medora Zarek, Fourth of his name and ruler of Kalonica."

After a speech from the medora about the importance of this night, he asked, "Xylander Dragoumis, Praeceptor of the Realm, Elder of Stratios and one of the Five, have you a presentation to make?"

"I do, Your Grace."

"Bring forth your heir."

Taking Adara by the shoulders, Father moved onto the platform. The aerios shifted, encircling her father, Adara, the medora, and the princes.

"Who is this child?" Zarek asked.

"Adara Nicea, daughter of Xylander," her father replied, lifting his bearded jaw, "born of Nicea Dragoumis. Sister to Lexina and Kersei."

"Has she ten cycles, Xylander?"

"She does, my liege."

Medora Zarek lifted a Lampros ampule and held it overhead. "On this night, beneath the light of the Ancient and the Deltas, I, Zarek, Medora of Kalonica and ruler of the Five, acknowledge Adara, third heir of Xylander."

He set the wreath on her head, then lifted his scepter to the entwined orb overhead. They waited until moonslight struck the orb then danced into his scepter, which he touched to the small ampule dangling above Adara's eyes.

Ahhs filtered through the crowds, followed quickly by applause.

It seemed that light also somehow found its way into Kersei's arm, the brand exploding with shards of fire.

"Fare you well?"

Entering the hall resonating with music and dancing, Kersei smiled up at her father. "Aye." She watched her sister turning a circle as she stared, near cross-eyed, at the still-glowing ampule on her forehead.

"You were in pain, Kersei." Concern touched his eyes. "After Adara's presentation—I saw it in your face."

The memory of that startling moment singed her, but this night was for her sister and her father. "What you saw was my jealousy. Did you see how brightly her ampule glowed?" She laughed, keeping her arm close to her side, convinced the fire that had burned at the presentation would betray her. "Go, dote on Adara. She has earned her celebration."

"If you need rest—"

"And miss all the dancing?"

"I was told you were thrown by Myles."

She started to react but tempered it. "Actually, by his javrod."

Consternation creased his dark brows. "You'll be the death of me, Kersei."

"Not till your head is silver and your heart roiling with grandchildren—borne by Lexina."

His expression grew serious. "And by you, I would hope."

"After training. You promised."

"Foolishly mayhap." He laughed, pressed a kiss to her forehead, then strode off.

As the crowds thickened, there again came a great shout from the caller, announcing the arrival of Medora Zarek and the princes. Here? Why would they come to Stratios when other entolis had also brought heirs to be presented? Mayhap because Stratios was closer to Kardia.

Regardless, there were too many bodies pressed into the space. Kersei pushed herself to the far side of the great hall, where the many doors had been removed to allow the party to flow onto the veranda. She hung near the sheer curtains, not quite brave enough to dance and risk pain from the injury.

And the nagging, nervous curiosity zipped through her again, drawing her gaze to her forearm, sheathed though it was in blue fabric. What had caused the marks to hurt so much? It had never happened before.

"Blue, an interesting choice."

Kersei lowered her arm. "The gilded prince," she teased Darius, who joined her by the doors, hands behind his back as he watched the dancing. "Can you breathe, Darius? Your collar looks a bit snug."

"There is air enough around you, my lady," Darius said, his tone light. He pivoted and extended a hand. "A dance?"

Her gaze connected with Aerios Myles passing nearby. "I beg your mercy, Prince Darius, but I would dance with Myles."

"I fear you will not," Darius said in a low warning. "I must have a word—"

It was this behavior that forbade her from ever thinking of Darius as anything more than a straw-stuffed target. "I beg your mercy, but I must. I promised Myles the first—"

"Kersei!"

She pivoted and winced at the flare of pain from her side as she sought the one who had called her and spotted the scruffier version of her father.

Wider through the belly, but just as quick and wise, Uncle Rufio had been the machitis who started her training. Her heart vaulted. "Uncle!"

His hairy arms welcomed her into a thick-chested hug—yet he did not crush her. "Little Warrior." His voice rumbled in her ear, then he cupped her face. "How fare ye?"

"I am well," she said, tucking aside mention of her injuries and hooking her hand in the crook of his arm, grateful when he led her from Darius. Guilt forced her to glance back, not surprised to find that stern expression he was so very famous for—that temper.

"You unseated Myles," Uncle Rufio said with a rueful expression.

She breathed a laugh. "Poor aerios—his ego must be severely wounded, much like my side."

"Bet your prince didn't like that."

"He is not *my* prince." But then she nodded with a smile. "But yes, Darius went into a rage."

His laughter echoed as they returned to the great hall, where a fire roared in the corner and warmed cordi had been prepared by the barrelful. "I am sure he means well. It is no secret he intends—"

"I hear you have been to the south," Kersei blurted, anxious to not spend more time speaking of the prince. May and true, she wanted to know how the meetings fared. Few ventured past Prokopios lands.

"How came you by that news?" He scowled, then waved. "I forget you have those brown eyes to work your wiles."

Heat bled through her cheeks as they navigated the crowd, making their way toward the tables at the front of the hall. "No wiles. I merely asked."

Again, he laughed. "I have no doubt, niece. There is yet to live a machitis who can resist Nicea's daughter."

"You make me sound the seductress, Uncle. We both know it is not my appearance but my position—they seek the favor of Xylander, mightiest of the Five."

His expression sobered as they reached the inner columns. Now he seemed forlorn. "Kersei." He took her hands. "I—"

A blast of the horn of Kardia dropped silence on the crowded hall.

Turning, Kersei frowned and tried to see the head table. Had her father already gained his seat beside the medora? That was fast. Why the rush?

"Stratios!" Her father shouted to be heard in the far reaches of the hall. "A petition has been set!"

Hoyzah! shouts went up.

Kersei grabbed her uncle's arm. "Lexina!" Excitement rang through her. "He has finally done it. Silvanus has set petition for Lexina." She let out a caustic laugh. "I will at long last be rid a sister who whines more than she flutters. Come. Let us move closer." She started through the crowd, fighting her way to the family table, but when she glanced back to catch his hand, he was gone. She frowned and searched for him amid the throng.

On the dais, her father bowed aside for the medora, then returned to the family table. "A petition has been set this eve," Zarek announced, drawing her attention once more. All petitions for binding were brought to the medora for permission or denial. Normally, an entoli elder would preside over the austere occasion, but with the medora present, the task was his.

Kersei gained her parents' side at the head table, grinning at her sister.

Crown Prince Silvanus and Prince Darius joined their father on the dais as he presided. Unorthodox, yet a nice gesture about the match to be made between the crown and the Stratios.

Medora Zarek held a scroll. "The petition has been set"—eagerness thrummed through the crowds—"for Kersei Dragoumis."

She shouted, glancing at her sister, excited for—

What? Her heart staggered to a stop amid crackling silence, then the roar of exultation that rang through the hall. The machitis and aerios grew raucous.

"No," Kersei breathed.

Pulse thundering, Kersei could not move. Could not breathe. No. This was … wrong. She swung her gaze to her parents—father was proud, Ma'ma lowered her gaze. Lexina threw daggers from her eyes.

It should be her. It needed to be her. "You mean Lexina," Kersei said, her voice quiet, uncertain. Shaken. She nodded to her sister with a doleful smile. Zarek was medora. He could not be expected to know the names of all in the realm and keep them clear. "My sister," she said more firmly. He had merely mixed up their names. "*Lexina* Dragoumis, you mean."

Her father shifted, clearing his throat.

She shook her head. Then saw something in his expression that struck her dumb. Terrified her.

No.

"Kersei Dragoumis," the medora called, his deep voice rattling the beams overhead, "stand present."

"No," she whispered, digging her nails into her palms.

"Kersei," her father said, an edge creeping into his voice. "Our medora summons you."

She caught his arm. Like a lifeline. "Father, 'tis a mistake. This is not …"

He nudged her forward.

"Nay," she hissed, planting her feet and nearly crying out at the pain that flared under his pressure.

"Be not a fool, Daughter." His grave eyes sparked. Firmed. "Do not humiliate me and the entire entoli. This is a great honor. I would not have otherwise accepted the petition."

Panic squirmed through her restraint as Kersei licked her lips, then surrendered, allowing her father to guide her before the medora.

Medora Zarek nodded, his expression … grave.

This gives him as little pleasure as it does me. Then why?

Zarek towered over the whole of Stratios on the dais, but his great height and broad shoulders that bore the weight of all Kalonica demanded respect. As did those sharp blue eyes that had overlooked her many a time and did even now, as he scanned the great sea of warriors to find the machitis fool enough to take her to bound. To claim the wild daughter of Xylander. She was not ignorant of what others thought of her, nor did she give care in that respect.

He lifted his chin. "Who has set petition for Kersei, daughter of Xylander? Speak now and set petition before her father, entoli, and medora."

"It's a mistake, Father," she whispered aside, but he squeezed her shoulders to make her face forward again. This was wrong. Who would saddle her with obligations she did not want? Her periphery was ablaze with green capes. Who? Could it be Myles? Her heart skipped a beat—would he do this to punish her for unseating him? Put her in her place by getting a child on her? Mayhap. He *had* seemed intent in the bailey.

She skidded a glance in his direction but found only bored irritation.

Movement behind the medora distracted her for a moment and her gaze hit Darius's. He seemed amused, his eyebrows raised. Annoyed that he found sport in her humiliation, she huffed and glanced away. To each side to rout the traitor.

"The petition is mine, my lord Father."

Amid a raucous cheer from the aerios, exulting in their commander's petition, Darius broke rank from his father and brother.

Kersei hauled in a breath as he hopped from the dais as if dismounting a horse. At her side, he swung around and looked up at his father. His neck was lovely and long. Easily snapped in two, had she a javrod. Mayhap more easily strangled. Or severed.

Curse his black-hearted *adunatos*. He *knew* she did not want to bind. Not yet. Not until she'd finished training.

"What are you doing?" she hissed at him.

"The petition is claimed by Prince Darius, second in line to the throne of Kardia," Medora Zarek announced. "Prince Darius, make your request known to her entoli leader and father."

Taller than her by a couple of hands, Darius smiled at her, faced her father—a move that put his shoulder directly in front of her—and extended his palm in a gesture of submission. "Elder Xylander Dragoumis, I, Darius, son of Medora Zarek of Kalonica and the Great Seas, set petition and cause to be bound to your daughter, Kersei Lysandra. To claim her as my own, to protect and honor her, to assume the role you have served since the Ancient gave her breath. Will you grant my petition, sir?"

Wonder and rage warred within her. In her fists she crushed the sheer overlay and taffeta of her gown, heart thundering like a summer-tide storm. "No—"

Her father clamped her shoulder. Drew her back.

Darius's light brown, shoulder-length hair hung in waves like the shores of Kalonica. His boyish charm that had always drawn dithering females like maggots on rotting flesh had vanished amid the stubble etching his jaw.

Handsome, yes. Arrogant, definitely. Fool, absolutely!

We were friends. Why ...?

The clap as her father's palm met Darius's crackled through the hall and severed her thoughts. Marveling at their stacked hands, she watched her father receive the petition and with it, the bound price of yet another measure of land. Sealing her fate. Bartering her off like a prized bovina.

Breathing hurt. Living more so.

Her father offered a broad smile. "'Tis an honor, Prince Darius, to welcome you to Stratios, where you will sit in council among our leaders and be second only to myself among the Stratios."

Was that it? Was Medora Zarek after more control in the kingdom? Is that why Darius would so wholly defy her will?

"Long have you and Kersei been friends," her father continued. "It is an honor now to call you son." Father jutted his jaw. "In the ways of the Ancient, by the strength of Vaqar, and the blessings of the Lady of Basilikas, I grant you the hand of my daughter."

Darius's chin and chest lifted. "Thank you, Elder Xylander." He shifted back to the medora and caught Kersei's hand.

She resisted. Clenched her fist and yanked it back but felt his grip tighten. The surprise in his blue eyes. The warning, subtle yet clear. Her arm trembled as they stood in a silent duel. But there, too, lay her defeat. If she refused, her father would be shamed. The Stratios would be shamed. Perhaps even lose their voice among the Five. Grave repercussions, especially with the lingering threat of the Symmachians trying to insinuate themselves on Drosero.

Strong and warm, her father caught her other hand. Fingers coiled tight. Easily, he could hurt her. But he did not. And that forced Kersei to tear her gaze from the medora's knees, where it had locked, and travel the distance to her father's chest. Up his shoulders. To his face. Those dark eyes. And there she pleaded with all she had been gifted.

Please do not allow this. True and blood, I do not want to bind. I don't want to be restrained, forced to bear children rather than armor and sword.

Kindness. There had always been kindness in his gaze. Though he whipped and sharpened his warriors, he was a loving father and husband. Always had he given her latitude. Yet not this time. This time he stood resolute.

Tears stung before she could stop them. This was it. He was giving her away. Sending her away. *Forcing* her away.

He lifted her hand, kissed her knuckles, and nodded. Only then did she realize they were not the only ones privy to her resistance. She felt the glower of Zarek and Silvanus. The concern of the aerios. She had stood on their training yard and demanded respect. Would she now act the child when she had not gotten her way? Stiff-backed, she would be better than this. She would fulfill her role. It could be worse—she could …

Blood and boil! There was no worse. This was the end of all she knew and loved.

Darius raised their hands to eye level and spoke to his father. "Medora Zarek, in the presence of the aerios and machitis of Stratios, Elder Xylander Dragoumis has accepted my petition. Therefore, I present myself and the Lady Kersei to Your Grace for approval and anointing of her to join the royal family and represent your kingdom as princessa."

Kersei pulled in a startled breath. Princessa. She had never thought to bear such a title. The room swayed.

"Speak now, my lord Father," Darius continued, "and make known your will before all."

The medora motioned them onto the dais, and it startled Kersei to realize how very tall and broad he truly was. Cupping their hands with his own, he looked to the people. "With honor and with pleasure, I authorize this petition." He smiled at Darius, then to Kersei—and she saw there was no truth in his words—there was no pleasure in his acceptance of her, but a flash of warning and disapproval. "From this night that Kersei Dragoumis shall be known as Princessa Kersei of Kardia and Kalonica." He elevated their hands until she was forced to go to tiptoes. "Tonight, the royal House of Tyrannous and the House of Stratios are joined!"

Shouts thundered through the great hall, drowning her will and raging heart. It felt like a childhood game of pretend they'd played, vowing to save each other from mere mortals. To cut down the worst of diabolus. Escape to the high mountain where they'd live forever and train longer.

"Prepare the hall," her father shouted over the din, which escalated at the proclamation.

"What?" Kersei gaped. "*Now?*" But her father didn't hear or respond as he launched into motion, barking orders. She balked, shifting to Darius. "Why now?" she demanded. "I would have preferred time to prepare …"

"Prepare a pack and horse to run?" he taunted, then lost his smile. "When set by a royal, petitions are always carried out immediately. Leaves no time for harm to befall the intended."

"Or for them to flee, apparently," she murmured, eyeing the excitement as sergii worked to dress the hall for a binding ceremony. "Why, Darius?"

But he was pulled into a strong-armed back-pat by Myles, who offered his congratulations. More aerios lined up to congratulate their grinning commander.

Kersei's anger rose to boiling. How dare he!

He turned to her. Leaned in.

Her stomach protested, realizing he meant to kiss her. She angled aside, his kiss hitting her coils. "How could you do this?" she hissed in his ear.

A frown flickered through his smile as he laced their fingers. "Smile, Princessa." His tone was cold. "You will see this is good for both our families." He was drawn into conversation with another aerios.

Oh that she could speak her piece, ride his thick hide to the sea and back. *You beast!* Tingling heat trickled into her cheeks and neck, no doubt coloring them with a wretched shade of crimson.

When he faced her again, Darius wavered. He touched her arm.

She yanked from him, then schooled her reaction when her father and Medora Zarek glanced their way.

"You are truly angry," Darius said as he guided her aside.

She took refuge behind a column, finally breaking Medora Zarek's piercing gaze. "*Now* you discern my thoughts?"

"Kersei, we are a good match," Darius said, his tone calm and maddening. "You know me better than any woman, and I you."

She glowered. "You think you know me, yet you do *this!*"

He drew back. "Do you feel so ill toward me?" The softness in his tone was gone. In its place, an almost impatient, hurtful tinge. "Think about it. These long years we have been friends and sparring partners. Is being my bound so wretched?"

"Friends *play*. Sparring is training. Those who are bound …" Heat infused her cheeks at the thought of what would come later. She glanced away—just in time to see her mother and sergii gliding toward her. Kersei groaned.

Her mother inclined her head. "Prince Darius, we must take your bound to dress her for the ceremony."

He hesitated, no doubt thinking she might flee. That she might humiliate them all. Curse the man because she had more honor than that. She would not hurt her father. And she would have a lifetime to make Darius regret this.

Marco stood at the balcony overlooking the great city of Vaqar, capital of Kynig and home to the training grounds for all hunters, the Hall of Judgment, and barracks. A weight had settled into his thoughts after Roman gained his honor finishing the Firkin Decree. Something ominous thrummed in the air. Unlike others, he could not discount it as lack of sleep or—he looked at the near-full tankard of warmed cordi juice he held—inebriation.

As a hunter, he sensed things others could not. But it took no great imagination to realize something had changed. He unlaced the forearm plating and tugged it off, wondering at the heat that'd been there earlier when they returned to the gathering hall to celebrate. He'd given no real thought to the marks—they had no purpose he could discern and wearing the armor and vambrace hid them. All children brought to the Citadel were taught to shut out the past and their lineage, to claim the honor and training of a hunter. Now the mark was demanding attention. Distracting him.

A hand slid along his shoulder then down his chest as a woman curled in front of him. "Come inside, Marco," she murmured, kissing his jaw and pushing up to catch his mouth.

He angled way, lacing up his plating. "Not tonight, Ezretia."

She pouted. "But—"

"Not tonight."

"You say that every time," she whined, pushing herself against him once more. "You deserve pleasure. Everyone knows *you* saved Roman's honor."

Anger doused the distraction. "Enough." He straightened. "Do not speak against the master."

"I speak against no one." She huffed, planting her hands on ample hips. "Come, let me work that tension out of you—"

"Will he still not yield, Ezretia?" Rico taunted from the hall.

Marco glanced at his advocate, who was being led away by a chatelaine, the two laughing and kissing as they stumbled toward a bedroom. Irritation flashed. It was common, acceptable—nay, a supposed *honor* for a woman to bed a Kynigos. An allowance supposedly approved by the original hunter, Vaqar the Tahscan, who had said no greater honor was to be had than the love of a woman.

But had Vaqar intended *this*? How could this be honor? It was weakness.

Ezretia was plying him again with her wiles. Her scent reeked of rotten onions and soiled clothes.

Another arrow that severed the Kynigos from other enforcers across this quadrant—no heirs. They were committed to one thing only: the hunt. For that reason, they did not bind. They did not divide their loyalties. Which was why, most likely, they allowed the strained interpretation of law and allowed hunters the pleasures of women.

"Come, Marco. Warm me."

Annoyance struck hard and fast. "Release me, woman," he growled.

She huffed. Hands dropped to her side. "Fine." She shuffled to the hall. "Julian wanted me anyway."

Did she think to make him jealous? He snorted. More he should pity Julian.

Glad to be rid of her and that scent, he gripped the rail and stared out into the star-littered night. Something was happening, changing. He felt it. Smelled it. Lived it. Dreamed it. Not just his mark. Whatever surged through the air stirred in his veins, too. Made his blood itch for relief, much as he had as a boy when he'd first come into the scents.

"For one who handed me a victory, you are much chagrined," came grave words and the scratching of boots on the stone floor.

At that voice, Marco straightened. "Master. Think I would make it easy for you, handing a victory of such importance—if even I could do such a thing?"

"So humble." Roman chuckled as he joined him in the cool of the evening.

Marco grinned, then leaned against the balustrade as a shuttle departed Keighra dock and climbed to break atmo. Another hunter off to fulfill a Decree.

"You are not taking your pleasure."

"I beg your mercy, but I am." Marco nodded to the sky, to the stars. "Great pleasure."

"It is allowed—"

"Just because it is allowed does not make it right," Marco countered.

"Still holding fast to that?"

"It guides me."

"The Brethren talk."

"It's what they do best when not hunting."

They stood in silence watching the stars for a several long minutes and, in the far distance, the busy Onoria port with drop ships and passenger shuttles. It was not long before he wondered why the master lingered.

Hair streaked with the light of the moons, Roman stared at the starry sky, his expression blank. Similar in build to Marco, he wore his hair in the tradition of the Kynigos, queued back loose. "We've been summoned."

With a sidelong glance, Marco considered the words. Hunters received Decrees, but they chose which to accept, which to deny. To be summoned was unusual and typically indicated a monarch or ruler of some note held the Decree. That Roman had not yet mentioned the holder ... "Who?"

"Iereania."

Marco jerked. "The Holy Order?"

With a slow nod, Roman sighed. "Much to my chagrin."

A religious order did not mix well with mercenaries, which is how they often referred to the Kynigos. The hunters had gained respect for their decisiveness, their ability to rightly pick a Decree, but mostly for their effectiveness in delivering fugitives for justice. Worlds depended on their swift action. Symmachia, the Tertian Space Coalition, and most worlds in their nine-planet quadrant authorized Kynigos to operate autonomously.

"What have we to do with the religious?"

Roman shrugged. "Nothing, unless a purse is dropped."

It was part of the process—money deposited after the subject of the Decree was established, along with details of the guilt. The Kynigos then decided whether to accept or refuse, a decision never made lightly. And at the point of the purses, rarely refused. "But ... *priests*." Marco's lip curled.

"Aye."

"No good comes from the White City."

"Agreed."

"Yet you consider giving them audience?"

"Honor is the hallmark of who we are. Personal feelings have no place in a Decree. We hear the accusation, consider the subject, weigh the laws, then— if convinced justice has been truly maligned—we accept." He took another sip of his drink. "Our honor is not tied to preferences, Marco. You know this. It is tied to what is true, what laws govern and keep this mad, twisted 'verse from collapsing."

"Of course, Master. It's just ... they pervert truth to bend wills."

"Give care. You know not what Decree may be your next." Roman eyed him, smirking. "Prejudices can negatively affect your ability to hunt."

"That would not happen." Marco straightened. "To the Decree."

Roman inclined his head. "And the hunt. For honor. Rest you well, Marco." He slapped his shoulder, then disappeared back into the gathering hall.

Marco's gaze shifted to where the sun slumbered in the north. Lyrist was bad, but to be thrust into the rigid, archaic dictates of the Iereans …

Curse the reek!

KALONICA, DROSERO

Green. They dressed her in Kardia green. The bliaut danced beautifully with gold threads over the green brocade. Gold ribbon embroidered with the Lampros torch trimmed the bodice, waist, skirt, and gathered section of the sleeves. White gossamer flounced dramatically from green puffs at the shoulders and dangled to where the white petticoat flared at her calves. There were no omnir pants now. No comfort and practicality. Just … Green. White.

Holding something, Ma'ma dismissed the sergii who had assisted Kersei into her gown. Only four in Stratios Hall knew of the black marks scrawled over her arm. Some of the black arcs reminded her of a scythe, others of the fingernail of the farthest moon. "I will have to tell him."

"He will know soon enough." Ma'ma fastened a brooch over Kersei's left breast, then tucked a train of gold lamé through the fitted part and over her shoulder, the material dangling past her feet.

Kersei cringed. The brooch was the crest of the royal house. But it could not shield her from the marks. "He will cast me off, break the vows."

"He cannot. Will not," her mother declared, securing the buttons at the back of the gown.

"His father is medora."

"Exactly the reason he will not break them. It would shame the Tyrannous name, bring dishonor to a house that holds honor above all—"

"Is that why you said nothing?" Kersei asked, an edge to her words she had not intended.

Her mother straightened. "You think I would do this—allow this if I were offered a choice? It is not decided at a woman's table, but an elder's chair."

"I beg your mercy," Kersei said miserably. "I … I have never felt so powerless."

"You know not what it is to feel powerless," her ma'ma said. "Not yet."

"I cannot do this." She dropped her head, tears stinging.

"You *will*. And you must." Ma'ma lifted her arm and tugged down the brocade sleeves, overlaid with lace that hung in fluttering waves from her wrists, and secured the hooks, then slipped the ties around Kersei's middle fingers. It kept the material drawn tight and also ensured the sleeve did not slide up and reveal the mark. "Gather that iron courage, Kersei. There are days and times ahead that will test your mettle and make you wish for the whip, but remember—you *can* control much from this point forward."

Curiosity caught her by the throat and forced her to eye Ma'ma. There was something hidden in her words, a meaning Kersei could not grasp. Though nearly fifty cycles, her mother had not been touched by wrinkles. "You give me a fright, Ma'ma."

"It will be in your power, Kersei," her ma'ma said, "to sway the heart of the prince, who holds the ear of the medora. That is a great honor, a great power. Few have it."

She let her eyes flutter closed for just a moment. "I wanted what you and Father had—love."

Grief pursed her mother's lips. "Our situation was unique. You know that." She held Kersei's hand, gaze downcast. "I paid a very high price for that love."

A high price? What was this? Kersei studied her ma'ma, the weight in her expression. A thought crept into her mind she'd never considered before. "You regret it?"

Serenity wreathed Ma'ma's face as she shook her head. "Nay. I would give a lifetime of grief for the love of Xylander. I have known no better man." She touched Kersei's cheek. "And he gave me three beautiful daughters."

A light rap came at the same time the door opened. Lexina slipped in, seething but aiming her gaze at Ma'ma. "They are ready."

Her ma'ma smiled at Kersei, then embraced her again. "Know happiness for as long as you can, Ker—" Her mother swallowed, convulsed, looking aside and down as she rushed to the door. "Father and I will wait at the foot of the stairs. Come when you are ready—but do not dally."

Why was she ...? Kersei stared after her, confused. "She was crying," she murmured.

"Have you considered," Lexina snarled, "that Ma'ma is sad you're only binding to the second in line?"

"If you believe that, you know our mother not."

"What do *you* know? Always off with smelly men, riding horses, pretending to be a son! When I marry Silvanus, you'll know your place then."

"Why would Medora Zarek bind his last son to another Stratios?" She regretted the sharp dagger she'd just thrown in her sister's heart.

Lexina's expression darkened. Then grew panicked. "Why did you do this? I'll hate you forever!" Her sister whirled out of the room, slamming the door behind her.

Defeat strangled her. Realizing this would be her last night here, Kersei turned, taking in her room. Her bed. Simple compared to what she would have in Kardia, she imagined, yet lavish compared to the Stratios, who lived in uncomplicated homes within the keep. Should she take something? A memento?

Strange, but there was nothing here she would miss.

The door creaked, and she spun, half expecting to find Father insisting she come. Instead, a pair of smaller eyes peered at her. Wide with awe. "You're going to bind with Darius?" Adara asked.

Arms open to her little sister, Kersei had been wrong. There was something she would miss: her family. When Adara collided with her, she tensed against the pain that slashed her ribs, yet savored the hug. "I will miss you, beloved sister."

"Will you wear this?" Adara produced a small amulet. "So you won't forget me."

Kersei eased back. "Oh, Little Aetos, I could never forget you."

Small hands worked the crystal pendant around her neck. "There. Now you can't forget."

"Thank you." She straightened. "We should go before Father sends machitis in search of us."

As she allowed Adara to lead her from the room, Kersei refused to look back. Refused the grief that stood sentry this night. As she passed the guest wing, a shadow shifted at the far end. She squinted, catching sight of a man slipping into a room. Was that Uncle Rufio? What would he be doing in the guest wing?

"Father is waving," Adara warned.

Shifting her focus, Kersei found Father at the bottom of the stairs, waiting—impatiently—before nearly a hundred Stratios. Two columns lined the path into the great hall.

Had she any idea the beauty she possessed? She could make a prince a pauper with a mere turn of those dark, fathomless eyes. Hair bound atop her head with a riot of dark curls kissed by flowers and pearls, Kersei wore a thick ribbon woven through her near-black strands. Some loose curls covered the Tyrannous star, a brooch that gathered the train now identifying her as a royal. As his.

"On this eve," his father began, "before the eyes of the Stratios and under the authority and blessing of House Tyrannous, by the power granted me by Vaqar the Ancient, I urge all gathered to join in the uniting of these two great houses and two young lives—that of Tyrannous Darius and Kersei Dragoumis." His father peered down at them. "Stretch forth your hands."

Darius lifted their hands, glancing at Kersei. He had not missed her consternation or her rigid posture—was it the pain of her injury? But he had also not missed her determination to see this through. To honor their ways, her father. He had known sense would prevail. That she would understand the necessity. The rightness.

The ceremony began to blur, his focus drifting to the fact that he would have the honor of loosing her hair, a symbol to all that she was bound. And those curls would forevermore bear a tiara.

"Darius."

He stiffened, realizing he'd not been paying attention. Kersei faced him now, her cheeks flushed as she held her other hand to him. Right. The double blessing. He placed his palm over hers. Standing on either side, their fathers wove a leather cord around their hands, reciting the Prayer of Eleftheria in unison.

Darius watched the strap tighten, a symbolic gesture of the binding lives. He smiled at Kersei, but stilled at her blanched complexion. Uncertainty hit him again.

"For the—"

Thud!

Was that his heart?

Thud!

Startled, Kersei glanced over her shoulder from the dais and Darius followed her gaze. Across the field of white-and-green-clad aerios, beyond the green-tunicked machitis, stormed a blur of red.

"Halt!" a deep voice, angry and authoritative, rent the air. "The daughter of Nicea cannot be bound to the Kalonican prince!"

07

VAQAR, KYNIG

In the training yard, Marco ran along the foot-wide wall to where brick ended and sky began. He pitched off it and spread his arms, savoring the weightlessness, the freedom, and the gentle stroke of air against his face. He dove at the ground and tucked into a roll, then came up running toward bars. He vaulted at them. Grabbed steel and used the momentum of his body to carry him up and over. Hopped onto the one-inch bar. Toeing it, he eyed the rope dangling midair. Then threw himself at it.

Hand over hand, he pulled himself up to the wood platform at the top, twisted and let himself fall backward. Sailed out and caught the rope one more time, feeling its burn as he slowed his descent, then dropped onto the sand. He broke into a jog around the rest of the yard.

Nothing invigorated his receptors more than a full-body workout. Despite technology that assisted the Kynigos during hunts, Marco had determined to never allow himself dependency on machines. He'd been mocked for it, but he'd rather be in tune with his body than in tune with a grave.

He snatched his towel from the bench and wiped the sweat and matted hair from his face. Breathing hard, he lifted a corked bottle of water. Took a mouthful, swished, and spit it out. Time for a shower and—

A shout went up near the gate to the yard. Several Brethren hurried out, their scents weighted with surprise. Anger. Concern. Even panic.

What is this?

The strangeness of those scents here at the Citadel forced Marco after them, allowing the paved path circling the Fountain of Tears to guide him toward the commotion. Alarm and anger roiled through the Citadel.

Marco broke into a jog again, following the scent, which added voices and shouts as he stepped into the main building. Dozens of hunters huddled around the door to the intelligence wing, where they researched and studied the worlds under their jurisdiction.

"—downworlders took him."

"—didn't have a chance."

"The master will have their heads."

"Let's drown them and seize honor!"

"Mayhap you need more lectures on the meaning of honor," Marco said as he edged through the crowd, noticing how hounds, first-years, gave him berth. Though Marco was not a master hunter or even an advocate, it was not for lack of eligibility. He waded to the front, where a glass separated them from a conference room. Inside, Roman, Rico, and Apelles the Curator argued heatedly with Urbain, Kynig's premier, who shared first rank with Roman and Valerik, the head of Academics.

Not good.

Rico's gaze struck Marco with fury and outrage.

Seeing Viator, the training yard master, Marco edged closer. "What is it?"

The blond man huffed. "Nobody knows for sure, but there's word that Dolon is missing."

Marco started. "Thought he was on a hunt."

"Never reported in," Viator said.

A thunking noise snapped their attention to the glassed-in room. Roman rapped against the glass, motioning Marco inside. He sidled past those gathered and entered the din, surprised at the scents in the air.

"Master," Marco acknowledged as he closed the door. "What has happened?"

Roman huffed, glancing at the curator. "It seems one of our own has gone missing."

So it was true. "Unusual." Most people knew to steer clear of hunters.

"Very."

"Who?"

After exchanging a long look with Apelles, the master said, "Dolon."

Marco twitched. One of the six master hunters. Gone missing. "How does a master go missing?"

"Exactly," Roman said, folding his arms over his chest.

The door swung open and in rushed Palinurus, another of the Six and the master hunter in charge of flight instruction.

Apelles stood, looking at his brother. "What did you find?"

"It is a good thing we have our own technology," Palinurus said. "The primary Symmachian transponder on the shuttle was deactivated or damaged, but our locator is giving off a faint signal." They'd acquired their entire fleet of small fighters from the Tertian Space Coalition, but had, of course, made modifications.

"And where is his ship?"

Palinurus sighed. "Where suspected—Drosero."

Eyes sparking, Apelles turned to Urbain and Roman. "We must all agree on this action."

What action? What had he missed? Marco skidded a look to his master, not surprised at his firmly fixed scowl.

"I as well do not like it," Valerik said, "but we must recover the ship. Perhaps that will tell us what happened to Dolon."

"We all know what happened to him," Palinurus hissed. "Droserans are not savvy enough to interfere with a shuttle. It must be the Symmachians."

"That is a leap, Brother," Roman countered. "We have long been allies with the Coalition. Though not cozy, we have cooperated. Why would they violate a pact? Why create a breach, knowing what our response will be?"

"Symmachians have been aggressive on every other front in Herakles. And though subordinate to the TSC, they have never been quiet about their demand for greater autonomy and power—or a station in Droseran orbit or a colony there," Apelles said, stabbing the table in front of him. "We *must* confront this."

"Agreed," Valerik said.

"Swiftly," Palinurus added.

"Doing this," Roman spoke quietly, his thoughts weighted and plain in his hard expression, "takes us down a path for which we may not be prepared."

"*They* dragged us down this path by taking Dolon."

"We do not know that for sure." Roman seemed angry, frustrated, but held his emotions in check. "We must first confirm what happened. Rico will find the jumper and bring it back for analysis. Then we decide which course to pursue."

KALONICA, DROSERO

"You have no say here," Kersei's father growled to the red-robed iereas.

"We beg your mercy," the iereas said, "but we have every say." His gaze slid to Kersei on the dais with Darius and lingered, making her uncomfortable. He turned back to her father. No! To *Ma'ma.* "Nicea, would you have us speak plainly here?"

Her mother started, then went white. "No." She met Xylander's stare, then both started for a side door, leading the wake of blood-colored robes out of the great hall.

What in the plagues was that? Since when did her parents yield to a holy order? Shifting uncomfortably at the chitter spiraling through the room and the warmth tingling her forearm, Kersei started forward.

"Stay here," Darius barked as he strode off the dais with his father and brother, who were in step with her parents, as well as several aerios.

Kersei balled her fists. *I am no dog to be commanded!* Though a couple of aerios moved to protect—and restrain—her, she waited, then slipped in the opposite direction. It was her home and she knew the passages. Reaching the main foyer, she slid around the long, oval table arrayed with food and flowers. Grabbing fistfuls of brocade skirts in both hands, she started running, gritting through the throbbing pain of her bruised ribs.

Though she heard voices and her sister's call, Kersei continued.

"Hurry, lad!" a voice—her uncle—ordered.

Not slowing, Kersei diverted toward where she'd heard her uncle's command. Saw him slip past a hidden door. What …? She slid to a stop and caught the door before it closed. What was Uncle Rufio doing in the secret passages?

"If you want to live, hurry!" his voice carried.

The words, so unreasonable and so unlike him, pulled her into the dank, narrow space. Enveloped in darkness and curiosity, Kersei plowed ahead, having had the black halls memorized since childhood. She rounded the last corner and came up short when only pitch-black swallowed her. Silence clapped her ears.

Hair teasing her chin, she looked over her shoulder. Where had he gone?

A warm breath touched her face. Twitching, she vaguely recalled that this passage led out of the fortress. Why would he go this way? Tentatively, she felt along the cool stone walls. Letting it guide her, she was surprised as the stone grew warmer with each step. Or was that her excitement warring with her fear? Why was it warm?

She paused. Peered back. Mayhap she should return. Father and Ma'ma— the iereas! Why had she let herself get distracted? She had to know what reasons they gave for interrupting—

"Niece, what are you doing here?"

Kersei snapped to the front and found her uncle a few paces away, his face haggard and awash in a red glow. Alarm made her hesitate. "I …" She lifted her chin. "I could ask the same of you."

He huffed. Grabbed her arm. "Blood and boil!"

Kersei yelped at the stabbing through her side when he wrenched her. "You're hurting me!" But he continued on, unheeding, uncaring, hauling her down the passage that grew redder and hotter. "What is this? What is that light—heat?"

They broke into a wide cave, and she stumbled at the step she'd missed. Righting herself, she looked up. Sucked in a hard breath. There, at the mouth of the cave, sat a … a metal contraption. "What is that? Where—"

"Quiet! You can't have your answers and your life, too." He thrust her toward a ramp up into the glowing metal maw. "Get in!"

"What?" Kersei spun to him. "No! These things—we can't. We aren't allowed—we don't. It isn't right. I'm binding with Prince Darius tonight. They'll—"

Uncle Rufio shoved her hard, right at another man, whose face she couldn't see but who wrapped her in beefy arms and lifted her up. Something in her ignited. She kicked and screamed, but the injuries blinded her. Still she fought, using every bit of training and fire as he carried her into the ship.

Writhing, she only hurt herself—hand smacking the hull and foot scraping a sharp corner. He threw her against a strange chair, then all but sat on her as he wrestled straps over her body. Assaulted by the places he touched that no man should, Kersei punched him. He staggered back, even as the ship lifted and the ramp slowly raised.

The ship's scream bled into her own.

A distant call gave her hope. She tried to peer over the lifting door, but it was no good. Had she heard someone? "Help!"

The ship canted and she felt herself sliding off the chair, toward the door. She grabbed whatever she could and held on, terror clawing through her breast. Battled to secure the buckles.

Uncle Rufio's voice came from the front, talking to the other man. How did her uncle even know how to fly one of these things? They weren't allowed on Drosero. He had rejected the technology like the rest of Kalonica.

As they lifted, the front where her uncle sat rose so high, Kersei's panic thrummed. Her limbs trembled and she struggled to hold on as the ship reared like Bastien when she jabbed his flanks.

A small laugh trickled—he found so much pleasure in this. Why?

"Uncle, why are you doing this? Why did you take—"

The ship shot forward, pinning her. Pressing her back so forcefully that she felt as if her spine would pass through the fabric and steel. The fire of her bruised ribs proved excruciating. Her ears went strange, like she was underwater. Her vision danced and the edges blurred gray.

"Watch—"

The ship bucked. Flung sideways. Spun and tumbled. So fast. So very fast. Shuddering. Shaking. Her vision ghosted as the ship flew into a frenetic spin. Vision failing, Kersei felt the tears streaking down her cheeks.

Boom! Boom! BooOOOOoom!

Light exploded through the darkness and sucked her into its void.

TSC MACEDON

Unavailable.

Tigo slapped the desk in frustration. His third attempt to reach Krissos. He roughed a hand over his face and stared at the flex screen. It wasn't unusual for the rear admiral to be busy, but it was remarkable that he hadn't been available on three separate occasions. Since Tigo reported to Krissos, he was supposed to have unfettered access to the officer. He'd toyed with going over Krissos to Acrisius, but the justification wasn't there. Yet.

Tigo tossed the screen on the desk. He paced, plagued by an ominous feeling he couldn't shake. Whoever they'd extracted from Drosero was a hunter. And Kynigos had autonomy. Which, according to the treaties between the Coalition and the hunters, could mean Tigo would lose his commission. His command. His team. Unless there was a very, very good reason he'd been ordered to retrieve the hunter.

He tapped a message to Diggs into the channeler. HEARD FROM KRISSOS?

While he waited, he threaded his arms through the sleeves of his tactical shirt and slid it over his head.

A beep signaled a reply from Diggs: NEGATIVE.

If Krissos wouldn't talk to him, Tigo could go over him to Acrisius, but the vice admiral got twitchy about chain of command violations, and he also wasn't exactly fond of Tigo.

So. No Acrisius.

Which left exactly one option. He raked his short-cropped hair as he left quarters and headed down to the brig. Within a yard of the door, he was scanned by the security hub, which flashed his identity on the panel and then whooshed aside the door.

An ensign turned from where she worked at a data wall. She set aside a flex screen and strode to a chest-high wall, the glow of the recessed lights stroking her blonde hair as she smiled. "Commander Deken. How can I help you?"

Not knowing her name, he was at a distinct disadvantage. That's what happened as commander of a strike group on a battle cruiser with a complement of over two hundred. "I need to see the prisoner my team delivered last night."

A frown creased her brows. "Prisoner?" Fingers hovering over an intake port, she cocked her head to one side, then to the other. And back. Until she was shaking her head. "I'm sorry, but there were no prisoners brought on—"

"*I* brought him here." He rapped the counter. "Last night. We picked him up from Planet Nine."

"Nine?" She scowled. "We're not allowed—"

"I *know* what we're allowed, Ensign." He huffed, looking for the chief petty officer in charge of the brig. "Where's Fenske?"

"Off duty—"

"Great." Tigo nodded to the opaque glass that separated them from the holding rooms. "Let me check."

"Sir, I can't. Not without prior approval."

"The only approval you need is me. That was a high-value target. My orders came from Rear Admiral Krissos, so unless you want to answer to him—or unless you are ready to shoulder the responsibility for any harm a missing prisoner can do ..."

She swallowed.

"I just need to visually verify—"

"I can't."

Annoyed, he palmed his weapon, but thought better of it. "Feeds." He looked at the bank of monitors behind her. "Put the cells up there."

"I—"

"Do it." He fingered the activate strip on his weapon, the somber tweetle making her eyes enlarge. "Or I will."

Hands shaking, she keyed in a few codes.

Why did they have her working the brig if she was easily frightened? What was the point? The wall behind her washed in crisp images of each cell. All empty, save one. A woman lay on a cot, curled on her side.

He punched the wall with a curse. Spun around. Where was the hunter? He thought to order her to sound the alarm, but according to her records, there hadn't even been a prisoner. What in the black was going on? What if he'd gotten loose on the ship? He stormed away, lifting his arm to hail Diggs again when the channeler vibrated.

Instead there was a message from Jez: MIGHT HAVE A PROBLEM.

Tigo let out a frustrated breath and responded: WHAT NOW?

GET TO MEDBAY.

Medbay? He skipped into a jog, his gut clenching at the thought of the prisoner filling beds in the medical bay. EN ROUTE, he typed back. Krissos would roast him over the Eternal Pyre if he lost this hunter. If the Kynigos got free and told his brothers, there would be hide to pay. It took ten minutes to reach Level M. When the doors whispered back, he stalked down the passage and found Jez hurrying toward him.

"You're not going to like this," she warned.

"There's a lot I'm not liking today," he growled, hesitating by the lift. "Our prisoner is missing from the brig."

Jez's expression went strange, swimming in wariness.

"What?"

"He's not missing." Her gaze skipped over his shoulder.

"Commander Deken."

The sultry voice pulled him from Jez and cranked his adrenaline a few notches as Dr. Knowles approached. But any idea of flirting fled at the shadows rimming her eyes. The fury roiling off her stiff walk.

"Dr. Knowles."

She skated a look to Jez as she closed the gap. "Thank you."

Tigo glanced between the two officers. "Did I miss something?"

"I was desperate," Knowles admitted as she indicated the main bay, "and nobody was listening, which sometimes happens because officers tend to be a bit cavalier about—"

"Doctor," he said, wrangling his irritation. "I have an emergency situation I need to deal with. If you could—"

"I asked Lieutenant Sidra to wave you because, of all the officers on this ship, you seem to be the only one who shares my views on … certain measures."

"You lost me."

She sighed and shared another look with Jez, then back to him. "Do you have a minute to talk? In my office?"

Tigo hesitated.

Jez whispered, "Eyes out as you go. I'll keep watch." She quietly headed to the lift juncture that flung two corridors apart.

Fine. He'd go along. He turned to the doc.

"You'll follow?" Hope rose in her brown irises.

"Like a lost puppy." As they started away, he glanced back at Jez— what was this all about?—and found her watching, concerned. Or was it something else?

Dr. Knowles waited and he caught up, a bit unused to her actually paying attention to him with anything other than rejection and superiority. They made their way around the nurse's station and he noticed several eyeing them. Past the next corridor, a half-dozen uniforms lingered near the door that had been under construction a few days ago.

No. Not lingering. Posted.

"So, I'm sure you'll understand why I need to run this twice," Dr. Knowles said, her words a diversion.

"Of course."

Two sentries tensed, shoulders squaring, but instead of approaching them, Tigo and the doctor banked toward her office. As he passed, he met the steel gaze of one ensign.

"Here." Dr. Knowles accessed the door and slipped inside the room.

Tigo trailed her, squinting as lights sprang to a dull glow, as if they were unsure whether or not to illuminate the space. "You normally keep the brightness this low?" He took in the space—a small sofa with a blanket and a workstation.

She bent over her desk and started typing into the terminal. "Did you see them?"

"Ship's security—Fenske's men. Why are they there?"

A faint glow warmed her features as she nodded to the terminal. "Come see."

Tigo swung around the desk and leaned in beside her. A room swimming in lights and images glared back. A dark mass in the middle focused his attention. "What …?"

Knowles nodded. "It's the Engram."

He twitched. "Here? In the medbay?" His voice pitched.

Another nod. "They put your prisoner in there last night. Erased all evidence of his presence."

He struggled to accept what he was seeing and hearing, then that she had access to the feeds at all. Why would Baric do this? He'd been livid when Tigo got the order to set course for Nine. He objected to the mission. Yet he took custody of him? In secret? Subjected him to this? It didn't make sense. Baric was just the mode of transportation. He was outside this mission.

Of course, this explained Baric looking brain scans at in his office. But it didn't explain why the Engram was here when the Council voted it inhumane. So, who authorized this? And why? How had they gotten the Council to reverse their vote?

Or they don't know.

"How are we seeing this?"

Knowles wet her lips.

Palms on the table, he met her eyes as they stood in frozen silence, shoulder to shoulder. Mere inches apart. She made him feel like they were in zero-g.

"I think that's your prisoner in there."

He knew it was. Yet ... "How do you know I brought someone back?"

"I was ordered to assess your prisoner at about two-two-five hours."

He straightened and let out a long exhale. "By whom?"

She arched her eyebrow and cocked her head as if to ask who else would give that order. "Let me show you something else." Knowles palmed the roller on the control pad. The screen to her left blurred in motion, apparently running the feed backward. She hit a button twice. "At four times speed."

Tigo watched as guards pitched the hunter into the room and locked the door. For a while, he tried kicking down the door—and that mark on the bridge of his nose was so distinctly Kynigos. Apparently searching for an exit, he sprang along the walls crawling with strange images and symbols, blurring so fast, Tigo felt sick. Eventually the Kynigos sagged against the wall. More time lapsed and he lay on the floor. Then curled. In the end, huddled.

Dread clawed Tigo. "What time was he put in there?"

"Three-forty-three hours."

He glanced at his channeler. "Ten hours."

Knowles nodded. "Ten hours and he's fetal." She turned to him. Touched his arm. "Commander, you have to do something. The Engram is cruel and its effects irreversible, but I've never—*never* seen a subject collapse that fast."

"Any idea why?"

"None, but I am not versed in Kynigos physiology."

Anger coiled through his gut. He nodded. "I need to contact Admiral Krissos." Another long look at the screen. "You have my direct channel?"

She met his gaze. "I—uh, no." A blush filled her cheeks.

Hold up—was that a reaction? From the non-reacting doctor? "Two-one-five-six."

A hint of a smile touched her lips. Then sincerity. "Thank you."

He'd been handed something beautiful but fragile with this exchange— her friendship. "Don't thank me yet. I've tried three times to reach the admiral and failed."

Her eyes widened. "You think he knows about the use of the Engram on the hunter?"

"No." But it would make sense, since Krissos gave the order to drop on

Nine in the first place. It also appeared Baric knew more than he'd let on. His channeler flashed orange, indicating a message from Wellsey.

REPORT TO THE BRIDGE.

"Duty calls." He started for the door.

"Commander."

As he reached for the touchpad, Tigo glanced back.

She came and laid a hand on his arm again. She really had no idea what that did to him, did she? "Please—if they find out I contacted you …" She'd risked a lot asking him to help.

He winked. "Afraid they might think we're an item?"

She sniffed, but didn't get annoyed like normal.

"Your secret's safe with me."

She breathed a smile.

"But I might bribe a meal out of you."

Folding her arms, she arched an eyebrow.

"I know—"

"Get your prisoner out of there, and I might be inclined to say yes."

Tigo stilled, startled at the possibility of her offer. "On it." Though he felt light as he left her office, the reality of the situation kept him focused.

Once he rounded the corner, Jez came toward him. "So?"

"I've been summoned to the bridge."

"No, I meant—"

"I was *summoned* to the bridge."

Jez slowed, hesitated, then her gaze lifted to one of the security nubs mounted in the ceiling. After the barest of nods, she headed in the opposite direction. He wasn't sure if they'd been spying on him, if that's why they'd summoned him, but it was a safe bet. Especially with his prisoner in the Engram. They'd want to contain that. Still, his adrenaline spiked in the hollow silence as the lift delivered him to the bridge. Thermals scanned and matched his ID and granted access.

Executive Officer Dimar stood to the side, arms folded—he'd been waiting. Relief shoved through his expression. "I need you to ready your team."

Tigo hesitated, peripherally scanning the deck. No Baric. So this wasn't about the Kynigos? Somehow that made him angry. "Why?"

Dimar motioned him over to the waist-high table that threw holographic maps onto the glass above it. He nodded to an officer. "A'Zenia, Nine please."

Tigo's heart skipped a few beats. Maybe this *was* about the hunter. Even as the thought zapped his brain, the planet appeared. The petty officer rolled the angle, the planet tilting in accordance, and focused a northern section—far from where he'd extracted the hunter—into sharp display. Though lush and green, the area of interest was scorched black.

He scowled. He'd studied Nine many times, trying to understand why a planet would not accept or want technology and assistance. "What is that?"

"A terrific explosion," Dimar said grimly. "By the radius and devastation, I'd say matter-antimatter, but—"

"But it's Nine."

Dimar nodded.

"What'd Baric say?"

"Said it's Nine, so he can't do anything. Suggested you look into it, since you were just there."

Tigo's neck burned with the subtle accusation. "He thinks I did this?"

The XO lifted a shoulder in a shrug.

Anger spiked through Tigo. "Where is he?"

"Off-ship for the next two days."

That grabbed Tigo's attention. "*Off-ship?* Doing what? He's captain!"

"And therefore not answerable to you."

Frustration constricted Tigo's gut. He gritted his teeth, but then something from the drone image registered. "Wait." Hand out to the petty officer controlling the view, he squinted. "Pull back to orbit. Left quadrant."

"What?" Dimar asked, unfolding his arms as he eyed the screen.

The planet swirled and shrunk.

"There." Tigo craned his neck, then tapped the glass, his touch sending information to the petty officer. "Tighten here."

She swung the link and homed in on the anomaly.

A ship. Not just any— "My corvette!" How had the *Renette* ended up adrift in Droseran space? Who piloted her out of atmo? And what were those black marks on the hull? The right rear thruster was missing.

But even as he noted the ship, as he thought through how it might've ended up there, how he'd been called to the bridge, how Dimar said to ready his team, how he'd just happened to see the ship because of the angle ... "You wanted me to see this."

Dimar dipped his head, eyeing the glass. "It's just inside Droseran orbit."

"Bleeding plagues of the apocalypse," Tigo growled. Inside their orbit meant Symmachians couldn't do anything. Meant their hands were tied.

"Your earlier mission put the *Macedon* at risk of discovery," Dimar said.

Is that why Baric suddenly left? To avoid shouldering the blame? And yet—Baric's order put the Kynigos in the Engram.

"You and your captain have no honor," Tigo muttered as he walked around the projected image. "Life signs on my corvette?"

"Readings indicate there is at least one person alive, but vitals are … compromised."

Tigo shifted, glancing to the XO. "Sounds like they might need a medical assist."

Dimar slanted him a look. "Maybe," he agreed hesitantly. "Still in Droseran orbit. We touch this …" He shook his head.

"Sir," the ensign said, her voice piquing, "vitals are falling."

Tigo wasn't going to stand by while someone died—and on his corvette! *Macedon* couldn't touch this. But 215 could. "Get as close as you can. Draw it in with the beam."

"We do that and we violate the treaty. I won't be respon—"

"And how will you explain to the Droserans that you had a chance to save one of their own and didn't?"

Jagged pain tore Kersei from a black sleep and made her scream. Blinking, she groped for bearings. Agony renewed its vicious bite and wracked her body, strangling thought and understanding. She threw her head back, cracking hard against cold metal.

Sobbing, she shoved through the fog of pain. Her leg hurt. Now her head as well. And … The tide of pain swelled and surged, rushing over her. A choke-growl wormed up her throat. Fire pulsing through sinew and bone, she reached toward the most grievous of hurts—her leg. A new pain seared as she touched something sharp protruding from her thigh and it sliced open her palm. Blood slid across her wrist and arm. She glanced down but only saw black.

A distant, pervasive throb snaked through her overwhelmed senses. Somewhere in the torrent of information flooding in, awareness grew of the deep black that enveloped her. 'Twas not unconsciousness, but *darkness*. Cold, forbidding darkness.

Where am I? What happened?

She wrestled her thoughts into submission to find the last thing she could recall. Rufio. In the passage. Following him. The—

Kersei twitched, shock riddling her system. She dropped back, feeling the cold thud of steel against her shoulder. How had she landed on the floor of the ship, when she'd been strapped in?

A light blinked somewhere at the front. Its tiny glow revealed windows covered by a steel panel. That lone red light seemed a beacon, washing bloody over a slumped body.

Breath ragged, she lifted herself. Squinted and tried to shift—but an explosion of fire and wet warmth pulsed down her leg. She cried out, slumping against the steel floor. Eyes clenched, she bit through the pain. Flattened her slick palm against the floor. Cold. Very cold. Why was it so cold?

Her gaze traveled up the gray steel to the front where she once more eyed the body. One there. And herself. Where was her uncle? She squinted and angled, aiming for a better view without angering her pinned leg. Barely could the co-pilot's head be seen.

"Uncle?" she called. "Uncle Rufio?"

A groan from her left startled Kersei. She flinched and sought the noise—behind her, to the left. She turned there, but the steel shaft stabbed her rebellion, sending shards of fiery darts up and down her leg, bleeding her of clear thought and willpower. Slumping, defeated, she breathed out a choked cry, hot breath blooming across the steel.

Crack!

The ship canted. Kersei felt herself sliding, but her leg, the one with the shard through it, resisted. "No," she gasped. Terror seized her, knowing if her weight shifted too much, the shaft could rend her leg in two. She scrambled to grab hold of something. To brace herself. "No no no." But every twinge of muscle punished her.

Crack! Crack!

"Augh!" Kersei caught the half wall, stopping herself from sliding as the ship yet again bucked. She vomited at the vicious pain. Her hearing hollowed, her vision ghosting, her body surrendered to the chaos.

Shrieking and hissing streaked through the heaviness that cocooned Kersei, dragging her from unconsciousness. It took every semblance of strength and Dragoumis willpower to push open her eyes. Steel and orange-red chunks nearby welcomed her back to the horrific reality. She shifted her leg—and the shaft punched its presence back into her awareness. She cried out and stilled, gritting her teeth.

Thunk! Thunk!

What … what was going on? Strangely still without power yet immersed in an ominous thrum, the craft lifted. Sucking in a breath, Kersei steadied herself, vainly trying to dig her fingers into the floor. She was scared. Injured. Her gaze rose and scanned the interior. What was happening? Looking to the front, she gave a start. Her heart climbed into her throat at the empty cabin. Where were they?

Trembling, she whimpered. "Uncle?" Her voice cracked. "Uncle Rufio!" Was he in a different part? *Were* there more compartments? Terrified of being alone, floating in space … "*Uncle!*"

A series of clanks and thuds pervaded the small ship. She glanced around the metal contraption, searching for the source of the noise. Noticing the strange vibrations beneath her palms and body. "Hello?" she called. "Is someone out there?"

They were in space. The darkness … the cold … They had to be. How could anyone be out there? How would she get home?

Then a white-hot line framed the door she'd been dragged through a lifetime ago, when Uncle Rufio had forced her into this nightmare. Bright light pierced the dull gray.

Thud! Thud!

Kersei jerked her head away as air gusted her hair from her face and renewed the stench of her vomit. Dimly, her mind registered people silhouetted against the brilliant glare of the opening. "Help me! I'm inj—"

"Hands! Show us your hands!" Large, odd shapes poured through the opening. They wore big metal armor, unlike any she had seen.

"Slag me. Bet that stinks."

"Tossed her cookies, poor downworlder."

Navy, deep red. Helmeted faces. Masks, blacked out and angular like a rhinnock's, swung toward her. As did their weapons. She'd heard of the sky walkers, but she hadn't seen one before.

Were they … Symmachians?

Oh Ancient, let it not be those savages.

"On your feet!" The strange voice came from the one nearest, his words tinny and stiff. He snaked into the small, cramped space, moving around and behind her.

"I cannot," she said, her back and side aching from the position. "My leg is pinned."

"Get a medic and engineering," the first one ordered. "She the only one onboard?"

"Yessir," another said in that grating voice—was it produced by their armor?

Wait. The only one? She jerked toward the front, breath caught in her throat. "No." She couldn't be the only one. "I heard him groan—just before I passed out. Before you … got in here." She looked back to the red-armored soldiers. "My uncle was driving it."

"Medical's here," someone announced.

A woman in a pale gray suit climbed in and knelt by Kersei. Her features were dark as those from south, but her nose and eyes were wrong for Hirakys. "You'll be okay," she said around a wan smile, then pressed a thin metal cylinder to Kersei's arm. It pricked, but the pain was of no consequence compared to her leg.

"Commander Deken, you asked for Engineering?"

"Remove it," the suit-voice answered.

My leg? "No!" Panic thrummed as heaviness tugged at Kersei, pushing her back to the floor. To her vomit and blood. "Please ..." Alarm chased her into the pitch-black again as two soldiers knelt by her leg with a glowing white rod.

TSC *MACEDON*

"Why aren't you stopping this?"

Outside the officer's mess a few hours later, Tigo rounded in surprise at the vitriolic tone from Knowles. "Excuse me?" He thought they'd passed that hatred.

"Two people pulled off Drosero end up in my medbay. One in that blasted chamber!" She glowered outside the surgical bay. "How can you so callously defy treaties when it suits you?"

"Suits me?" *Calm down, calm down.* He had to remember who she was, where she'd come from. What Tryssinians went through before Symmachia bargained a peace treaty with her planet. How her people still mined ore, leaving them with a debilitating disease that killed many before they reached adulthood.

"They are protected under the Droseran-Tertian Pact of 0723.99, and your conduct dictated by the Ymini-Rhianta Alliance Codes. Eidolon cannot simply remove them—"

"Back your jets up there, Doc." His temper simmered. "First, we didn't remove her. She was adrift in space in a corvette that is assigned to me. Stolen from me during a mission. What was I supposed to do, leave her to die of hypoxia, a death twice as painful as cryo?"

Knowles deflated. Rubbed her forehead. "No." She sighed. Shook her head. Offered him an apologetic look. "I just ... I'm scared he'll use the *device* on her, too."

"He won't. I'll make sure." Tigo hated the words as soon as he spoke them. What had he been able to do about the Kynigos? This girl didn't stand half the chance of a trained hunter. So maybe they should make sure she got off the ship fast. "We'll want to return her as soon as possible. How is she?"

"Fortunate," Teeli said with a nod. "The shard missed her femoral artery but gave her a hairline fracture. She's weak from blood loss."

"That's fortunate?"

"She could have lost the leg."

"Ah."

"She's also young."

Which begged the question for Tigo. "All I want to know is how she got my 'vette—did she steal it?"

"I doubt that." She arced an eyebrow. "Recall that she said her uncle *drove* the corvette." She smiled at the words. "Also, remember, you were on a world you should never had been on."

"*She* was in space. I didn't drop to Nine this time. And last—"

"Commander Deken!"

Tigo tensed. Not because his name was barked. But because of *who* barked it. "By all the rings ..." He saw his own annoyance mirrored in Knowles. Why did it give him so much pleasure that she didn't like the captain either?

"Captain Baric." He held back the longsuffering sigh as he shifted toward the officer stomping into the bay. "I was told you were off-ship for the next two days."

Shoulders squared and silver hair cropped into a perfect V at the front, Baric loomed closer. "So you thought to take advantage of my absence and commandeer my ship—"

Again? "I commandeered nothing."

"Then how in the black void did the *Macedon* intercept a corvette in Dro- seran orbit?"

"It was adrift and in distress, sir. Tascan protocols dictate we—"

"Doctor," Baric growled, "where is the prisoner?"

Anger churned. "*Commandeering* more prisoners, Captain?" Tigo asked, winging an eyebrow and knowing the tricky line he toed. "What? Is a girl barely out of her teens a threat? Or maybe her religious beliefs scare you."

"That girl," Baric spat, "is wanted for the murder of her entire tribe."

Tigo stilled. Murder? "That's ludicrous!" His gaze mentally skipped back to the bay, to the riot of dark curls spilled over a too-skimpy-for-space gown, which hung in sharp contrast to the gray-and-red thermal uniforms of the Symmachian fleet.

"Show me," Baric said, ignoring Tigo's objection.

"Of course," Knowles replied too sweetly. "Commander Deken and I were just headed that way."

I was? But he took her cue and followed as she brought the captain to the observation corridor of the medbay. Passage lights dimmed and a tremor raced through the black wall, revealing the girl sedated in a nanotube, her leg elevated in a sleeve. She seemed peaceful and demure, harmless.

"Outside your staff, nobody goes in there," Baric said, "unless they have my direct authorization."

Lips tight, Knowles nodded.

"Captain, you can't believe she's responsible," Tigo argued.

"Over two hundred dead." Baric pushed from the glass. "Including a king and his sons. She survived by being on that corvette. For a tech-free world, why would she be on that?"

"She's a child!" Tigo objected, wrestling with the intel.

"That girl is a *murderer*—"

"She said her uncle was on the corvette, *driving* it. That doesn't sound like someone familiar with piloting a craft."

Baric gave him an apathetic glower. "And when you opened it up, did you find anyone else?"

Tigo stilled. The captain hadn't been there, but somehow he knew they hadn't found anyone else. "No."

"Exactly. So don't get caught up in pretty eyes, Commander. Remember your duty and rank. That murderer is my prisoner." Baric shifted to his men. "Crichton, Crowley, nobody in or out unless they're medical."

"Yes, sir!" Benjt Crichton said.

Baric pivoted to Knowles. "I want to know when she's awake."

There was no way that girl was responsible for murder. Tigo had always been able to call a situation. And when he'd boarded the corvette in the *Macedon*'s shuttle bay, he'd seen a terrified, injured girl. In shock, just as Knowles said. Chalky complexion, no doubt sick from the wound and being in space, obviously overwhelmed by her surroundings. She did not have the makings of a violent criminal.

He watched Baric storm out of medical. Something was going on.

"Why is he so determined—"

"I don't know." Tigo plucked free his channeler and sent a comm to Dimar. REQUEST FOOTAGE FROM DROSERAN RECOVERY OF TSC CORVETTE. He nodded to the girl in the pod. "You think she's capable of murder?"

"I do not know." Knowles sighed as she glanced into the room. "Her left hand had lacerations—probably from the shard in her thigh, but her palms were calloused." She brought soulful eyes back to him. "Those are not the hands of an innocent maiden who embroiders, tends children, or launders clothes."

"Many Droserans work the land," Tigo argued. "It's hard, vigorous work."

"I'm aware of what hard labor is like." Had Knowles worked the mines of Tryssinia before going through the Tertian Universal Academy? "You know why he wants to be informed when she's awake, right?"

Tigo's gaze slid to the other guarded door. The Engram. He gritted his teeth, thinking back to his visor scans of her vitals. All out of whack. But if she wasn't guilty, who killed her clan? How'd she end up on the corvette? In space? It sure looked like an escape.

"Give me a lead on when that happens, okay?"

She drew back, surprised. Wary.

"Just a few minutes. Let me talk to her first."

"Agreed," she said, then extended her hand to him.

He frowned, then realized she was giving him something. When she dropped it in his palm, he was surprised to find a necklace with some wire-entwined crystal.

"To remind you she's not just someone in your stolen corvette. She's a young girl in a heap of trouble."

He closed it in his hand and nodded. "Noted." He started away, then spun around, walking backward. "I still plan to get that hunter out, so you'll owe me a meal."

"Duck."

"You want du—" His head cracked against a box mounted on the bulkhead. He cringed, then grinned at her, realizing she'd been telling him to duck, not that she wanted to eat one. "Duck it is."

She rolled her eyes—but she was smiling.

As he made his way to his quarters, Tigo tapped out to 215 an all-hands in the hangar. They had to talk about what was happening on the *Macedon*. Kynigos were revered through the quads. He admired the way they operated with little tech, though it seemed a lot of work when you could use a suit for half of it. Still, he respected their connection to the physical. The same conviction drove him to return this Kynigos to his natural habitat.

But if he did that, it could lead to open hostility or war. And an entire loss of all Tigo had worked for in his career.

Why hadn't Krissos linked back after ordering 215 to Nine?

"How's the girl?" burly AO asked.

"You're too old," Esq said, flaring with hurt and indignation. She'd long had a thing for the older newb.

"Surgery and nanites are now repairing her leg, so she's sedated," Tigo said. "She'll probably be up in no time."

"That is," Jez added, coming through the side door, "unless the captain puts her in the reminding chamber like he did that hunter."

"Beastly," Esq said, shaking her head. "Just when I think the 'verse can't get any more twisted …"

"I want to find a way to shut the Engram down or get that hunter out," Tigo said.

Silence clapped through the bay. The team considered each other, then him, realizing the cost of pursuing that course.

"You realize," Diggs's deep voice rumbled through the chilled, treated air, "doing that could put us on the wrong side of Tertian law."

"The Council voted it down," Tigo reminded them.

"Yes, but it would not be here if someone high up the chain didn't authorize it."

"Pretty sure dropping on Nine put us on the wrong side before all this," Esq muttered. "We're pretty much scuzzed."

"No way," Rhinn countered. "We had orders."

"Yeah, but I'm noticing the captain ain't talking. And Krissos never followed up, did he?" AO asked. "Which makes me wonder if something's wrong. Or if he lied to us."

"Or used us," Jez supplied.

They were echoing Tigo's own thoughts. "We had orders. We followed orders."

"But?" AO asked.

Why did AO always have to call it? "But I can't link Krissos, nor is he linking back. The hunter is fetal and nonresponsive. Now they have the girl, and proof or no proof, Baric is 100 percent sure she's a murdering traitor."

Jez pulled straight. "So you think Baric will put her in it?"

Something in Tigo coiled, ready to snap. "I've given up expecting him to act with honor or compassion." So what was driving the captain's actions? "There was *no* reason to put the hunter in there."

"Unless he tried to escape." Rhinn hopped onto a crate and sat, using a dagger to peel an apple. He waved the knife. "I mean—that would make sense. If a Kynigos tried to escape, then Symmachia would have to respond. Take it as a threat."

"A threat?" Tigo snorted. "We *pulled* him from where he was *hiding* on Drosero! And what's he escaping? They are autonomous, given authority via a treaty signed by TSC and pretty much every world in the Herakles."

Rhinn pointed the knife at Tigo, who lifted an eyebrow at the offensive gesture. He withdrew the blade. "Nine is not his planet. Those hunters are from the Citadel of Vaqar on west Kynig."

"They're *autonomous*," Jez repeated, widening her eyes for emphasis. "Did your ears get snuffed on that last drop?"

Tigo planted his feet. "Don't care where he's from. Only care about why he was on that planet and why we were sent to retrieve him."

"And why Krissos didn't tell us we were going after a Kynigos from the start," AO said. "That would've been helpful intel."

"So again—they set us up?" Jez always had a way of reading his thoughts, even ones that hid from him.

"Careful," he warned. Entertaining that thought went against the one thing he wholly believed in: Symmachian Command. Say that anywhere else and they would all be branded traitors. He'd lose his commission. Get sent home in a brig. Shower disgrace and humiliation on himself, but worse—his father, the fleet admiral.

"Well?" AO gruffed.

"I don't know." Tigo scratched his head, hating to admit the truth. "This is slagged. None of it makes sense. How did that girl get the corvette?"

"How'd she survive is what I want to know," Esq said. "Heard there was damage to the *Renette*."

"Yeah, saw that on the feed before we pulled it in."

"Think maybe the explosion that killed her family took it out?" AO asked.

Tigo nodded. "Makes sense. Trying to break atmo with a damaged 'vette could explain why they were adrift. Surprised it didn't break up."

"She mentioned her uncle was in it," Jez noted.

Tigo frowned. "Yet she was alone …"

"So you don't believe her?" Jez asked.

"No, I do. That's the thing—can't be possible. But it didn't seem like a lie."

"'Less she's an expert," Rhinn muttered. "Faking us all."

"Diggs," Tigo said with a thrust of his jaw. "Can you get into the Engram programming? Find a way to shut it down?"

Hesitation guarded Diggins as he skated a glance to the others. "Without them knowing it was us?"

Tigo nodded. "Yeah, the whole court-martial thing wouldn't look good on our résumés."

Diggs squinted at Tigo. "We sure that's a good idea? I mean, would Baric really have an operational Engram if someone on the Council hadn't authorized it?" The guy was always exploring options and possibilities. "If we shut this thing down, they could come after us …"

"Have you seen what those things do?" Jez balked. "It's horrific! They make a person relive a crime over and over."

"Good," AO said. "Some of the brain-bleeders need that after what they've done."

"But it's not her crime—or that Kynigos's!" Jez argued, impassioned. "How is that right? And even if someone committed a crime, this form of punishment is inhumane. Not to mention the complete lack of a trial!"

"From what Dr. Knowles says," Tigo said, "this hunter is collapsing faster than any she's seen before."

"Is he cracked?" Diggs widened his eyes. "Is that why he was hiding in the caves? What pile of slag have we stepped in here?"

"I have no idea." Tigo nodded. "Find a way to shut that thing down. Quietly. I'll keep trying Krissos or Acrisius to see if they know about the Engram."

"Look," AO said, his broad chest seeming to grow. "This is some pretty serious slag. We went to Nine against our better judgment because we had orders—but we ended up with a hunter. Now this girl is here. A Niner. The blasted downworlders are invading my calm. I'm game to fight, you know that. But I am not going to lose my clusters for some backbirthers."

"We're Eidolon," Jez snapped. "We protect, no matter race or creed."

"Enough!" Tigo barked, then sagged. "I hear you. All of you. I do. But this is my call." His channeler buzzed. He glanced at it, then huffed. "Doc's waving me—the Droseran is conscious. I'll check in with them, then talk to the XO and wave Krissos again. Eyes out, people. We need to figure out what's happening before it bites us in the rump." He gave a sharp nod, then started from the bay. Probably should verify with Knowles that crashing the Engram wouldn't have some negative effect on the patient.

At the medbay, a nurse looked up and smiled. "She's in her office."

He banked left down the passage that fed into the break room and locked scripts supply closet, then left to her office, eyeing the guards still protecting that machine.

At her desk, Knowles studied a flex screen in low illumination. The soft glow gave her an ethereal look. It helped that she had shed her medical jacket and sat in her form-fitting uniform. Black hair hung in a coil around her elegant neck as she kneaded her shoulder. He hadn't noticed her hair was that long that before.

Tigo rapped on the door and crossed the threshold. "Headache again?"

She looked up with a smile. "Always."

There were different kinds of smiles—tolerant ones, smirks, happy ones, elated—and nervous ones. This was the latter. Why nervous? Did "nervous" mean attracted? Was it possible?

"She's in the pod, which enables me to keep her paralyzed from the neck down. Thought it'd be smarter to talk to her that way until we know ..." She reached for her medical jacket draped across the thin gray sofa that would serve torture better than comfort.

Tigo snagged the jacket, intent on lightening the mood, relieving some stress with laughter.

With an annoyed look, she held out her hand.

He caught it and tugged her closer. "You have to ask." These lines had worked on other women, made them smile. But with Knowles, somehow things were ... different.

She dropped a demure look, not meeting his gaze. "My jacket." She tried to wrest her hand free.

He stepped in, erasing a few more inches. "*Please.*"

She glowered, but color fanned her cheeks. Her gaze never quite met his but danced around his face. "Commander," she said, her voice holding a warning—and yet also a smile. "*Please* may I have my jacket?"

"One condition."

Her gaze skipped to his eyes and away, then she nudged him back. "I'm not kissing you, if that's what you think."

He grinned, liking that her thoughts went to a kiss. "Use my name."

"What?"

"Ask me for your jacket using my first name."

She hesitated. "That's inappropriate."

"The only inappropriate thing would be that kiss you mentioned." He gave her a mischievous grin. "But I'm known to be a rebel, so if you'd prefer that—"

Breath drawn in, she tried to step back, and that's when the bruises, the marks along her collarbone gaped.

He stilled. Frowned. Something protective rose in him. "What happened to your neck?"

In a flood, the softer Knowles stiffened and the rejecting Knowles returned. "Do you want to talk to the girl or not, Commander?"

He released the jacket. "I do."

She glowered at him, threading her arms through the sleeves as she strode into the corridor. "She told me when she came to earlier. Her leg is repaired, but I'm nervous about her reaction when she comes to."

They entered the medical bay where the nanotube thrummed. She went to the pod and used her security protocols to access it.

The dome over the face shifted from opaque to clear, revealing the young, pretty face of the Droseran.

He whistled. "She has a lot of hair."

Dr. Knowles rolled her eyes. "Translator is on," she noted. "Kersei, are you awake? Can you hear me?" She scanned the display. "Her levels indicate she's not in a coma."

"Eyes," Tigo muttered, meeting the rich dark eyes of the girl. She seemed groggy, heavy-lidded. But definitely awake.

"Kersei, I am Dr. Knowles. You're in a medical pod that is healing your body. You can't move right now, but that's because of the medicine we've given you. Don't be alarmed. This is Commander Tigo Deken. He retrieved the shuttle you were on and saved you."

That had a nice ring to it. "Hello, Kersei."

Her gaze bounced between him and Knowles.

"Can you tell me how you got on that shuttle?"

She swallowed. Nervous.

"I just need to know how you got it. Do you know how to fly it?"

A ridge formed between her eyebrows. Her heart bleeped faster on the machines.

"How did you get on it?" Tigo insisted.

"My uncle," she said quietly. "He made me."

Tigo nodded. "Good." But she had been alone. "So, you know how to fly it?"

"No." She frowned again. "My uncle drove it."

Tigo hesitated, glancing at Knowles. "You were alone on the shuttle."

He saw the panic fill her face, saw her control it.

"Kersei," Dr. Knowles said quietly. "I need you to calm—"

"I wasn't alone. Uncle Rufio—where is he? Why are you asking me these things? Why am I—"

Knowles tapped a sequence into the control panel. Air gusted against the girl's face and hair. Her eyes slid closed. Knowles turned to him. "Sorry. Her vitals were elevating too fast. She wasn't ready."

"So were mine," Tigo muttered. "Why does she think her uncle was on that corvette?"

Bathed in the orange glow of the setting sun, Temple Iereania glared at those who dared tread her sacred ground. And Marco dared, with a decent amount of irritation and annoyance. Sun gleamed off alabaster walls, throwing its light in his eyes. He squinted up at Mount Basileus surging, reaching effortlessly toward the sky as if in worship. There atop the southernmost peak, a stark white temple embraced the thin air and defied those on pilgrimage up its steps.

Reek! Three hundred accursed steps. With another glower at the hewn rock and altitude easier reached by shuttles, Marco huffed.

"You should welcome the challenge of the climb to strengthen your body, refresh your mind," Rico said.

"Shed his foul mood," Roman added.

Chastised, Marco continued the ascent, watching as the ground fell away on both sides. He had never feared heights, but when faced with a thousand-foot drop, a man grew a healthy respect for terra firma.

"Stay close," Roman warned, several steps above. "Be aware—you will not detect their scents. It has long been a mystery as to why, but those who embrace the Ancient's ways here in the Temple are such."

"That rumor is true? No scent? It's … unnatural." Marco fisted his hands. "It would be a great undoing if—"

"Most say it is the Ancient's protection."

"And the others? What do they say?"

"Many different things. There is a mineral in the plants here … there is something in the water that neutralizes scent …"

"Impossible," Marco balked. "Pheromones can't be smothered by water."

"Then you accept that it's the Ancient?" Roman gave him a sidelong glance.

"I accept it is unnatural."

"Mm," Roman murmured. "Very."

Marco pitched himself up, easily closing the gap as they gained a broad landing and the first sign of iereas. Priests in their crimson robes—much like the blood of innocents spilling over the alabaster steps—fluttered around with tipped-up chins and the stench of arrogance.

Unease slithered across Marco's shoulders. His forearm prickled. He flicked his wrist to adjust the plating strapped there. Sometimes the rhinnock armor irritated his skin.

"I am with Marco—would it be so sacrilegious," panted Rico as they reached the large terrace that fed up and around to more stairs, "to allow scouts to land on that knoll?"

"Indeed it would." Roman's voice rumbled with laughter and seemed to scale the slick walls. "It is bad enough that we disgrace their halls. We need not undo their robes with shuttles and technology."

"Then we're not to mention the vambrace?" Rico said, mischief pinching his eyes.

The master hunter quirked an eyebrow. They reached the final rise. There waited a series of arched colonnades with three domes, gilt and as gleaming as the marble columns.

"Why would anyone seek this way?" Marco asked. They had many quirks that left him wondering. For example, iereas were not necessarily natives of Iereania, though most resided there. And "iereas" could be one or many. Quantity mattered not to Marco, since they were all corrupt or sought to corrupt.

A small structure sat in the shadow of the Great Hall and delivered a handful of iereas into the main courtyard, which was divided into four parts around a fountain tossing water from one winged goddess-like creature to another.

"Are they supposed to be Faa'Cris?" Rico asked, eyeing the powerful build of the figures. "I did not think they had wings."

The suggestion made Marco pause to consider the supernatural creatures of myth—female warriors given protectorship over people. But then he noticed the closely shorn heads turning almost in unison as the iereas became aware of their arrival. Red robes swirled, the crushed fabric dusting the ground—mayhap that was how the alabaster had become so polished—as the priests fell quiet and still, openly staring.

Marco's boots thudded against the marble as they approached the great hall. The best of Kynig now stirred holy air with ruffian breath. He nearly smiled.

Then … *I smell nothing.* As the master had warned. Yet he still tensed, homing his receptors in futility. He slowed, scanning. Sensing. Shared a long look with his brethren as the doors swung open.

They advanced, unhindered, into the great hall. More stairs surged off on either side of the main foyer, like wings arcing up to a landing. Movement atop drew his gaze. Four iereas wearing white shimmering half-cloaks over the crimson albs condescended to consider the Kynigos. Clasped hands seemed especially pale against burgundy chasubles, made of thinner material and stitched with gold. Cords around their waists pointed tasseled fingers down at the hunters. The half-cloaks served the high lord.

A growl crawled up Marco's throat, but he subdued it.

A fifth iereas with a blue sash across his chest and a gold mantle glided forward. "Hail, Brethren of the Kynigos," his voice rang out, melodic. "I am High Lord Kyros. Thank you for accepting our invitation and dispensation to enter the Blessed Sanctuary. My senior, High Lord Theon, would typically receive such esteemed guests, but he is not here at the moment."

Marco rolled his shoulders, irritated. *Get on with it, so we can leave.*

Glancing around, Roman expelled in a breath, a subtle way of expressing his displeasure at being talked down to, literally. "Is it he who offers the Decree?"

"Nay," Kyros said slowly.

Roman shrugged. "Then let us dispense with formalities. Your parchment sparked interest among the Brethren, High Lord." He inclined his head, sounding magnanimous. "Let us hear your Decree."

Entourage of red and white close behind, Kyros descended. "Please," he said as he reached the bottom, his robe billowing like blood on snow. He pointed to glass doors to the right, which swiftly swung open. "Join me in the Reflecting Chapel."

Instinct told Marco to leave. Honor demanded he stay. Stomach churning, he allowed his receptors to open wider and swept the inner courtyard, hoping to put a finger on the storm brewing in his gut. But here scents were well-guarded.

Not good. He had long heard the iereas were without scent, but he'd never experienced it. Whatever the reason for the lack, the Brethren were glad it wasn't something that could be produced and marketed, making their gift ineffective.

Teeth gritted, he followed his brethren and Kyros into the antechamber.

Kyros moved into the room, catching both doors and closing himself in with the them. The expressions of the other iereas said they were as annoyed as Marco at the barrier. Once curtains were drawn to afford privacy, Kyros motioned to the sofas by the narrow pool. "Please."

Roman squared his shoulders. "We are prepared to listen."

The high lord eyed them, then sniffed. "Not very trusting." He eased onto a large blue settee that yielded to his thin frame. He as much looked like a sovereign on a throne as any king would. "Since you warriors are so attuned to your surroundings," he began, his voice carrying smoothly across the tranquil blue water, "I am sure you are aware war is inevitable—and close—in Herakles. No doubt you have heard that on Drosero there are roughly two-hundred dead after an explosion."

Attention receptors perked up. The Brethren had discussed the unusual death of the Droseran clan. "You speak of the Stratios, Xylander Dragoumis's clan."

"On Drosero they call it an *entoli*, but yes"—Kyros waved off a servant pouring drinks—"I speak of them."

"What has that to do with you? What worry does an iereas have over such a trivial matter as a local skirmish?" Roman widened his stance, ever ready.

"Does the number of dead make them less worth being concerned over to you, Master Hunter?" Kyros asked.

"No such words were spoken."

Kyros nodded. "It was not a skirmish between rival entolis, as you have suggested."

"Regardless," Roman growled with a shrug, "Kynigos will not involve ourselves in any such dispute or war. Our business is delivering justice."

"Justice, yes." Sipping his drink bought the iereas time. "Xylander's middle daughter was in the hall just before the collapse, but her remains were not recovered. It is believed she survived, but is … missing."

"Missing." Marco looked to his brethren.

"You know this how?" Roman asked, narrowing his gaze.

"A high lord and two of his attendants arrived shortly before the explosion."

"To what end?" Roman demanded.

"That is a matter for the Temple and has no bearing on this Decree."

Three iereas dead? Was that a bad thing?

Long fingers trilled the air and a servant came forward, handed Marco a rolled flex screen. He eyed the high lord. "I thought you eschewed technology."

"It is forbidden among the acolytes, but as those higher in the Order serve across this system, it is beneficial to have a means of communication." Kyros pointed to the flex screen. "That image was taken shortly after the explosion leveled Stratios Hall."

Iereas and their strange ways … Marco unfurled the flex screen and stilled. Frowned. "This is Drosero." A satellite image taken on a planet with no tech?

"And in the upper right corner?"

Marco tapped the area and zoomed in. Squinted. "This makes no sense."

"What is it?" Roman asked as he crossed the room.

"A Symmachian corvette in Droseran orbit."

"Verify the time stamp, if you please," Kyros said. "The timing cannot be coincidental. What else do you notice, Master Kynigos?"

Marco shared a glance with Roman. He hated being played and baited. Still, his curiosity had been piqued. After careful study of the outlying regions and finding nothing, he came back to the shuttle. Something … He amplified it again. Grunted. "The shuttle is without power—no lights. No apparent distortion from the thrusters."

With a strange elegance, Kyros came off the settee. Handed off his goblet to the attendant and rolled his fingers again toward Marco. "And the next image."

Without taking his eyes off the high lord, Marco flicked to the next image.

"What care do we have that a Symmachian corvette is adrift so near a battle cruiser?" Rico indicated the new image. "Clearly they recovered their craft and their people."

"Did they?" Kyros said, amused.

Rico huffed. "We have no time for games, iereas."

Though Kyros arched his eyebrow at the slight, he nodded. "In that you are right—there is little time. I cannot and will not explain how I have come by my knowledge, but it is our belief the Dragoumis child was on that corvette and has been taken into custody by the Symmachians."

"Droserans refuse technology, and their treaty with the Tertian Space Coalition forbids Symmachian incursions on their planet," Roman balked. "They would not have had any such craft, and a girl would certainly not have knowledge to pilot it."

Marco studied the new image, which showed the drifting corvette dwarfed by a Symmachian battle cruiser.

"That assumes all on Drosero have abided the accord to eschew technology. A planet full of people and nobody rebels?"

"It's a stretch," Marco argued. "Even if what you claim is true, why would they take her, knowing as all in the quads do that Droserans are simple in their ways?"

"We made overtures to the Coalition on behalf of Nicea Dragoumis, who was once a part of our Order, but our requests were met with silence." Kyros strolled closer, his green eyes amused yet … "However, we are not without our resources. We have learned the Tertian Space Coalition will declare the girl a traitor and a murderer."

"Again," Marco said, frustration coiling, "to what end?"

"Come, Master Kynigos." Kyros sighed, apparently annoyed.

At last, something in common.

"It has been no secret that the Symmachians are intent on gaining Drosero for an orbital way station. By capturing the"—he waved his hands as if making a great commotion—"murdering fugitive daughter of a man renown as the mightiest of the Kalonican warriors and who served as the right hand of the medora, they show themselves as allies to the Droserans. Peacekeepers."

Rico uttered an oath.

"Mm, yes," Kyros said, amused. "Were we given to epithets, I might have spoken that very one."

"This is a lot of conjecture." Roman stepped forward. "High Lord, know you the statues required to present a Decree to the Kynigos? Know you the penalty for summoning the Brethren with an ill-supported—"

"What I have and what I know is supported. You need not fear this to be frivolous or impetuous."

"Then state your Decree," Roman demanded.

"You hunters would do well to learn civility," Kyros said. "I have already stated the Decree—we want the Dragoumis heir found and brought here. Alive."

The iereas stood before Marco with eyes that probed deep. As if searching for something. But no … there was more. As if digging with a sharp iron tool into Marco's being, in his *adunatos*—his soul, his essence. A deep, personal place.

Heat spiraled through Marco. He shifted.

Kyros lowered his chin, those beady eyes unwavering and fierce.

Fire bit its way up Marco's shoulders. Through his neck. He again rolled his shoulders, trying to shake it off. Not draw attention—he did not need meddling iereas learning of his mark. But it stabbed—right into his skull. Though he braced, he faltered.

Reek!

Marco blinked as that heat crawled back down his arm and beneath the flexible plating of his vambrace. Fingers curled into his palms, he traced the forearm muscle coming alive with fire and gritted through it.

He knows … He knows of the mark. But how?

Kyros tilted his head to the side. "Would you remove your arm shield?"

Sweat dribbled down Marco's face from the intensifying heat. He glared at the high lord. "What majuk is this?"

Shoulders straight, Roman moved between them.

Another fiery wave hit. Hissing, Marco gripped his arm. Shook it vainly. He stumbled, grunting.

Roman's hand clamped around the priest's throat, thumb pressing into the soft spot. "Release him, iereas." Few dared oppose the powerfully built master hunter, but there was no cessation of the agony writhing through Marco's veins.

"Augh!" Desperate for relief, Marco gasped and ripped off the armor. Stared in disbelief at his arm. The once-black tattoo now glowed pale blue. "It feels as if my flesh is sliding from my bones!"

"*Release* him or I will kill you to break the spell," Roman growled.

The priest's head twitched as if he tried to shake it. His eyes betrayed fear, though his scent still told nothing. "It is not me!"

Rico dragged Marco to the pool. "Thrust your arm in!"

In agony, Marco complied. Water hissed beneath the fury of the mark. Steam rose in a cloud, yet the fire persisted. "It does no good."

In a flurry, Roman swept a boot behind the high lord's legs and knocked him back, pinning him to the marble floor. "*Now*, or I will end you."

"It's not me. It's not me!" Kyros choked out against Roman's grip. "It's the brand."

Without warning, the fire vanished. Blue faded again to black. Marco sagged against a column, sweat dripping from his brow as he stared uncomprehending at his arm.

Roman shoved off the high lord, knelt beside Marco. "Brother, are you well?"

"Are you restored?" Rico kept guard and glanced over his shoulder.

Shaken, but determined to defy whatever majuk the priest had worked, Marco nodded. "I'm … well." Struggling to stand on shaky legs, he tried to re-fasten the vambrace, but the buckle slipped against his sweaty palms. His strength renewed with each breath. He stormed toward the cowering priest. "What have you done to me?"

"As I said," Kyros said, holding up his palms, "I did not bring you harm or pain. Though I am at times able to draw out the flames of a brand, this time it was not me. Your brand is awakening. That is all I know. Instruction came—"

"Instruction?" Roman scowled. "From who? A Decree cannot be delivered by an intermediary! You are violating—"

"The Decree is mine," Kyros said quickly. "I deemed it the best way after receiving … direction." He lowered his gaze. "That is all I can say. I dare not speak more."

Roman held his arms wide. "You've made a mockery of my hunters, and now you utter foolspeak. Mayhap we should leave. I can convince the Citadel to declare this null."

"If you must. But please." Kyros hurried toward Marco and looked at his arm. "What brand?"

Marco frowned. "I do not understand."

"Brands are tied to prophecies. Do you know which yours is?" A hint of a smile reached his eyes. He reached out, hesitant. "May I see it? Please."

Irritated with the questions, Marco tried to draw in the iereas's scent to no avail. And it made him want to defy the priest more.

"I intend you no harm, Kynigos. I've studied brands. Mayhap I can read it."

"Read a brand?" Rico demanded.

"Yes, all are tied to some prophecy, and I am familiar with the more common ones." Kyros offered a faint shrug. "What could it hurt?"

"Besides all the Fires of Pir coursing through my arm again?" Marco shook his head. "No, thanks."

"Let him read it," Roman spoke, his voice authoritative but also tinged with something indecipherable.

Teeth gritted and vambrace in his left hand, Marco extended his fisted right, looking to the pool as the iereas took hold of his forearm and turned it one way, then another. He shifted around, touching shoulders with Marco as he squinted. Grunts and *hmm*s.

"Enough," Marco growled, yanking his arm away and setting the vambrace on it.

"Well?" Roman asked.

"Usually," Kyros said, inclining his head, "when one is branded, there is a sept of the Order whose mark is borne, indelibly worked into the pattern. I hoped to identify the brand, and thus its purpose." He glanced at Marco's arm again. "I confess I've never seen this one in any of our texts. It has familiar aspects, but the entwining, the arcs are very unusual. Distinct, but connected to what prophecy or sept, I cannot say."

It was not smell alone that warned the hunters of dishonor. Eyes were just as loud, and Kyros's spoke of lies. But why would he? And why did Marco feel … exposed?

"As the Decree demands, find the girl," Kyros said, fingers threaded before himself, "and bring her to this temple before the Winter Solstice."

"Impossible." Marco stretched his neck, regaining some of his equilibrium. A thought struck him, offering him the chance to cast off this insanity. "If she was in that corvette and Symmachia has her, we can do nothing. Our Codes forbid us to hunt on their vessels and the Codes allow for the Decree to be refused based on hunting grounds—"

"Yes, I am aware," Kyros conceded. Then he gave a solemn nod. "However, the girl will be free in less than forty rises of the first moon."

"Which moon?" The iereas likely referred to the larger of Iereania's moons, but hassling him gave Marco a perverse pleasure.

"Marco," Roman chided.

Marco's smile faded and he chose a more serious question. "If they refuse to admit they have her on board, how can you know she will yet be free? And *how* will she get free?"

Arrogance returned, Kyros adjusted his outer robe and donned his apathetic expression. "When she is free, word will come to you." He motioned to a tall gold table nearby. "The purses are there."

Irritated, Marco glanced to the table, startled to note the velvet pouches. Had they been there before?

Roman grunted.

When Marco turned, the Brethren were alone in the room, the reflecting water undisturbed. "By the reek." Ghosted darts of fire coursed through his veins. That iereas had known about the brand. How?

Mattered not. *Just leave. Get out of here.* Forget the gold. Forget the Decree. Forget his honor. It was not worth being their pawn. He started for the door.

"Marco," Roman called. "The gold."

"I care not." He'd reached the door, when a vise gripped his arm. Flung him around. He slammed against the marble column, air punched from his lungs, and he found himself staring into the darkening eyes of the master hunter.

Roman pressed in. "You heard the Decree," he hissed. "The Code forbids you abandon the hunt."

Damp hair in his eyes, Marco glared back. "The man disappears like the wind after nearly setting me aflame, *knowing* I had a brand, and you say I must accept?"

The master's face lost a measure of its intensity. "To the Decree."

Nostrils flared, Marco did not want to finish the oath. While he would readily deliver that iereas's head from his body, he would not disrespect his master. "And the hunt."

Roman slapped his chest, as if to say "good boy," and eased off. "For honor." With a nod that held as much sympathy as agreement, he looked at the purses.

Rolling his anger and indignation beneath his cloak, Marco moved to the table. Naught could be done save fulfill this Decree. Hunt down this girl. He eyed those reeking purple pouches. A tremor raced up his hand; it itched to upend the table. Send it careening though the window. Instead, he snatched the coins and stormed from the temple, feeling as if he'd sold his honor—no, his very *adunatos*.

Light bloomed where there was no sun. A breeze blew where there were no trees. Kersei blinked against the white that blinded as snow during the wintering. She squinted around her from the hard bed. Machines worped and hissed as she lifted her shoulders from the cold, forbidding surface. Tensed, she anticipated pain where the shard had pierced her leg, then realized that only a dull ache crawled through her thigh.

How was that possible? Kersei raised the gray blanket and glanced at her leg. Pale lavender tunic and pants blocked her view. The clothes were not her own, and despite being thin, they felt heavy. And somehow warm. The edges of her mind latched onto the missing piece—the necklace Adara had given her. Patting her throat, she verified its absence. Whimpered.

Rubbing the nagging throb in her temple, she sat up, perched on the edge, and glanced around. Opaque glass walls defined the length and breadth of the room. They glowed brighter than touchstones, yet less than the ceiling panels. How?

Curiosity urged her from the bed. Tentatively, she toed the floor, not surprised to find it cold and hard as well. She stepped carefully, testing her weight on the injured leg, and yet again, no pain. It made no sense. How long could she have been unconscious? Palming the walls told her what she already knew—like everything else, they were hard, cold. It seemed the way of things here. Even the wintering at Stratios did not drill cold into her bones as this place did.

And the quiet. It was eerily quiet. Why was there no noise? No birds. No chatter of leaves. Hum of insects. No laughter. No bleating. Nothing. Save those machines. Never had she felt so locked away from the world.

It's wrong. It's all wrong. I shouldn't be here.

"Hello?" She slapped the glass. "Hello! Is anyone out there?" Fingers tracing the slick surface, noticing the way her fingertips left a strange trail on the glass, she searched for a groove. A way to open it. There was none. It was smooth and solid all the way around.

"Can anyone hear me?" She slumped against the wall. "I just want to go home," she called. "Let me out, please. Let me out!" There was no door to kick in, so she kicked the wall. Drove her heel at the glass.

Hissing clanked through the room and light fractured in a perfect rectangle.

Kersei stumbled back, startled as the wall darkened before her eyes. She drew up and away, feeling an impending threat. Opaque glass turned dark gray and snapped into the wall.

Two warriors stormed at her.

Kersei yelped and spun to flee—but they were upon her. Gripped her arms. Shoved her face first against the metal bed she'd lain upon. "Stop!" Pinned her shoulders down, arms out, face smashed to the cold surface. "Leave me be!" she cried.

In the blur of chaos, another man entered. Hands behind his back and hair threaded with silver and tipped up, he bore a gold crescent moon on his shoulder. By his bearing and the way two more trailed him inside, he was in charge. He ordered the guards in a language she did not understand, but one twisted her right arm. Slid up her sleeve.

Kersei gasped, struggling. She never showed that arm.

Then the hands freed her. She flew away from them, backing up until hard walls dug into her shoulders. She hugged herself, feeling naked. Feeling … violated.

The leader pinned her with an icy gaze. Just like the rest of this place— cold and hard. He lifted a device, set it on the table, and spoke words that made no sense to her. Yet a moment later, a strange, hollow voice overlapped his and familiar words reached her ears. "You are Kersei Dragoumis, second daughter of Xylander Dragoumis."

Hearing her name straightened her spine, as Ma'ma had taught her. "H-how do you know my name?" She twitched, fisting her hands to her side as her own words somehow changed in the air between them. "Where are my clothes—a necklace. I want it back!"

He smirked. "All your things were incinerated. What you wear is appropriate for your duration here." He rubbed his jaw. "I'm amused—you murdered your family and thought to hide in the stars after your horrific crime? And you ask after a trinket?"

Kersei lurched forward, her mind ringing with the terrible word: *murdered.* "Wha—no!" Murdered her family? What words were these?

The guards pivoted and snapped their weapons at her.

Hand to her stomach, she staggered back. "My parents—sisters—" Tears pricked. "No! They are not dead. I was just with them."

"That was two days ago. And I assure you, they are all dead. At your hand."

"I would *never* hurt my family. Return me to them. At once!"

"Captain Baric!" A woman rushed into the room, her eyes dark with anger. "What is the meaning of this?" Her face—a memory stirred. She was the one who'd tended Kersei on the shuttle. "You should not be in here! She is convalescing. The nanites have not completed their work. Please—"

"She walks. That is enough," the captain barked. "Bring—"

"No." The woman lunged, inserting herself between Kersei and the officers. "I will not allow you to remove my patient from the medical bay. I have every right by the Codices to overrule—"

"Under the articles of war, *Doctor*"—he leaned in to her—"you have no authority to supersede action a ship's captain deems necessary to protect his ship, crew, and the Coalition."

"War?" The woman gaped. "What war? She—"

"She is guilty of murdering her entire clan. Step aside, Dr. Knowles."

"Captain." A soldier hurried into the room, his voice only slightly more delayed than theirs. "There's a Kynigos scout on course for us, sir. They've requested an audience."

The captain muttered something, then shook his head. "Ready a team in the hangar to greet them." He nodded to the soldiers. "Two-two-five, you have your orders!"

The heavy clang of boots startled Kersei. They closed in. Caught her arms.

"No! Release me! Let me go!"

Two held her to the floor, knees in her back, the pharmakeia shouting for them to stop hurting her. Two slipped a heavy colorless blanket over her head. As they dragged her upright and tugged it down onto her shoulders, she realized it wasn't a blanket but a tunic of some kind. Snaps clapped together along her sides, startling her. It had a disturbing weight. As if the entire world had crashed on her. Her knees buckled. The guard to her left tightened his hold, gloved fingers digging hard into the soft spot under her arm.

Kersei cried out—not over the pain. But at the awful thought of her family … dead. "No," she whispered, shaking her head. Was it real? How? Her gaze somehow found the woman's again, but she was blurry. "I …" The room whirled. Her legs went weak. "Stop! No, this is wrong. Please!"

The guards lifted Kersei off her feet.

"Captain! I must insist—"

With a sweep of his hand, the captain motioned the guards into the passage. The pharmakeia lunged again, but a third guard appeared from outside, his weapon trained on the woman, who pulled up, her eyes bright with disapproval. "This is wrong! Don't do this. She's a *child*!"

Kersei fought confusion. "Please!" She looked over her shoulder to the pharmakeia. "What happened to my family? Please, tell me!"

"Do this and I will report you, Captain," the pharmakeia threatened.

Hauled down the cold corridors, her feet slapping hard to keep pace with the armored guards, Kersei caught sympathetic looks from the other Symmachians. They were supposed to be cruel and heartless. But what she saw on their faces, how they watched …

Kersei thought she had known panic before, but their expressions, the way one covered her mouth and another shook his head. They were all so … stricken.

"Unhand me!" Yanking her arm to wrest free only pinched her shoulder muscle and earned a crushing grip. "You cannot do this. I am not Symmachian. You have no authority over me." But they weren't listening. Only moving. Dragging her onward. "I didn't kill my family!"

The captain pressed buttons on a panel and a hole opened in the wall. He stepped aside and the guards thrust Kersei forward.

The warrior's daughter in her awakened. Years of training roared to the front. Screamed at her not to be their victim. To stop this at all costs. As Darius and Minos had trained her. Head high, she righted herself. Stopped fighting and started assessing.

"*Weapons need not be swords or daggers. Weapons can be the simplest of objects,*" Darius said.

Again, the walls were barren. Floors slick. Nothing to pry free or break off.

"*And if there be none, the Ancient gave you four weapons,*" Minos had shot back with a barked laugh.

So be it.

Kersei glanced at the nearest guards—*immobilize them and block the path so others can't enter.* Sliding between them, Kersei threw her right elbow out and swung around, simultaneously snapping a knifehand to the throat of the guard on the left.

Gasps and gargles clogged the air. Shouts went up.

Locking onto the third, Kersei slammed her heel into the guard as he lunged. He stumbled into the other. She spun and sprinted back in the direction they'd come.

An explosion of pain punched the air from her lungs. Pitched her onto the hard, slick floor. Her head bounced. Darkness rushed in greedy and angry.

"I show you this medical bay out of the sincerest desire of Symmachia and the Tertian Space Coalition to prove we hide nothing, nor have we done anything illegal," Zoltan Baric said to the hunters. It was a gamble, lying to them, since these hunters could smell fear. But he had nothing to fear because the Engram fully contained sound. That applied to smells as well, right?

The youngest hunter—easily the same age as Deken or Wellsey—glanced around the passage, scowling beneath black hair. His perceptive, pale gaze knocked against Zoltan's confidence.

"Is there a problem?"

Concern flickered through the hunter's brooding brows. "There is … something strange here."

Zoltan laughed. "How often are you on a battle cruiser, Master Kynigos? It is very strange. We grow used to the vacuum of space and the toll it takes on our bodies. It can get quite rank sometimes."

The hunters shared a look.

It was working. Beautifully.

Dr. Psalter pointed them into another bay. "This is the last one."

The hunters stepped in and looked around. The brooding one moved to the tube where the Droseran had received nanotherapy. He tucked his chin and rolled his shoulders.

There was no way they could smell her presence from days past. Or that she lay compartments away in an airtight chamber … Could they?

"Tell me," the master hunter said, stalking the medical bay, "if a ship was adrift and you retrieved someone deemed hostile, where would they be kept?"

Zoltan's pulse thumped against his chest. "In the brig, which you saw already."

"And if they are injured, here?" The third hunter, shorter and more wiry than the other two, placed both hands on the tube. "What is this?"

Nerves jounced beneath Zoltan's sleeves as he watched him.

"This is used for nanotherapy," Dr. Psalter said, easing forward. "If a patient needs extensive repair of muscle tissue or bone, this puts them into stasis and controls the environment of the nanos."

"Airtight?"

Dr. Psalter slid Zoltan a look but nodded.

The hunters were toying with the crew. It irritated Zoltan, the arrogance of these three. Their kind.

"Does our presence bother you, Captain?" the master hunter asked in an unaffected tone as he faced him.

"It does," Zoltan conceded. "I've spent ample time with you, verifying there is no fugitive on my ship. Yet you ask questions about things of which you have clear knowledge." He moved deliberately back into the passage, and turned an impatient glare on them.

"You accuse us of deceit." The master hunter feigned offense. By the way he regarded Zoltan, he was clearly used to dealing with those in authority.

"Indeed," Zoltan said. "It is no secret that Kynigos scouts built by Sherigger Corp were subsequently modified and outfitted by a particular contractor with personal stasis and alembicus repair pods. So you know well the answers before you posed questions to my medical officer." He cocked his head. "Tell me, Master Hunter, why do you lie?"

"In what have we lied, Captain?" the master demanded. "We are Kynigos and hunt with honor. Is a simple verification that what you have on your ship has not been modified or otherwise altered a lie. Are you so threatened by casual questions that you challenge us?" He winged up an eyebrow and looked to the other hunters. "One would wonder if he has something to hide."

"His scent sure speaks of it," the wiry hunter suggested.

Zoltan stiffened. "I have wasted enough time. Lifts are down there." He pointed to the end of the passage. "My officers will escort you to your scout. Good day, hunters."

Kersei jolted awake and jerked upright, only to find darkness glaring back once more. She groaned at the eruption of drums in her ears, her pulse whooshing her panic. Alone. Darkness. Like the shuttle. But then … wait. Those black walls were glass. Whispers of shapes moved beyond them. She pushed to her feet and moved closer.

On the other side a group of people stood at a juncture, talking. The gray-and-red Symmachian uniforms were joined by three men in black armor and cloaks. One with ebony hair and one with brown wore it oiled back in a queue. The third wore his hair loose and wavy, the ends curling against the collar of his cloak, which only seemed to emphasize his intensity. He was large and powerfully built. His curly black hair framed eyes that were pale and scowling. They had curious marks on their faces, lines and arcs across their noses. Through the strange box she'd heard the soldier call them by some foreign name she couldn't remember. Their ferocity startled her, made her stomach squeeze. Why did they look so angry?

The captain seemed furious with these men. The encounter was much as she had witnessed with her father when he confronted a machitis he knew to be guilty of a crime but had yet to prove such guilt.

The intense one's gaze shifted from those he had gathered with to the floor. Then across the juncture. Traced the wall. It was peculiar—as if he were looking for something. His gaze suddenly and terrifyingly pinned Kersei to her spot. Her heart thundered, unsure what she should fear. Were they here to harm? Why did his eyes register no reaction at seeing her? It was like he looked right through her. Searching.

The walls. She eyed the grayish-black surface. *They cannot see me.* Kersei threw herself at the glass. Smacked it. "Help me! I do not belong here!"

The intense one lifted his head. His thick brow rippled as his gaze skipped around.

She stilled, thinking he had heard. Seen her somehow. "Help! Get me out of here!" She kicked and slapped.

The men straightened then indicated to soldiers, who stepped aside and motioned the marked men to the left. They were leaving!

No! Kersei slapped the wall again. "No, please! Help!"

The intense one did not easily surrender, giving her a breath of hope that he would discover her. With one last glance over his shoulder—looking almost perfectly through the glass into her eyes—he allowed himself to be led away.

"No! No, don't leave. Help me! Get me out of here!" She kicked and screamed. Pounded. Searched for some weapon. Something to drive at the glass. Break it. But when she turned back, the corridor was empty. The marked men were gone.

Hope was gone.

Slumped against the wall, she slid down it. Hugged herself. Banged the floor, fighting the sob that clawed its way up her throat. Shifting, she lay on her back. A stream of dust particles danced across the beam reflecting on the shiny ceiling. Why would a ceiling be shiny?

"... *guilty of murdering her entire clan.*" The captain's words thudded against her conscience.

My family! How could they be dead? Stomach seizing, she rolled onto her side. *Please tell me it's not true. Please.* It couldn't be. Ma'ma. Father. Adara. Tears streamed down her face, hot against the chill perforating her heart.

In his scout, Marco powered thrusters just enough to lift them from the belly of the *Macedon*. Once clear of the battle cruiser, he accelerated and banked back toward Drosero, annoyed to no end by what he had sensed.

"Something bothers you," Rico said.

"Aye."

His advocate tilted his head. "Did you detect a scent?"

Marco guided the scout around. "No—beyond those we interviewed, but there was something …"

"Mm," Rico murmured. "I felt it, too. Something was off."

"She's there," Marco said, conviction defying everything they'd seen. "I don't know where, but she's there."

"And we can do nothing for it," Roman sighed.

Futility rose. "Then to what end did we board?"

"To get a sense. To understand our adversary."

Marco eyed his mentor in surprise. "Symmachians are our enemy now?"

"I said adversary, not enemy," Roman corrected gravely. "There's a difference. I believe you are right—Baric has her, but we do not know where and Codes forbid us from interfering with Symmachian ships."

"So what do we do?" Marco fisted his hands.

"We wait."

The door slid open, brilliance erupting around her.

Just like the explosion.

When she lifted her hand to shield her eyes, Kersei grunted against the weight that seemed to press her arms down. Large shadows filled the square of light, pulling her from the memory. This time, the Symmachians entered in full-body armor—and masks—weapons humming with threat. She had been foolish to fight them. If any doubt of her guilt existed, she had erased it with her actions. Reaching to wipe a tendril from her face, she grunted at the heaviness. Why did she feel so weak that she could not lift her arms?

"The conformity apron contains sensors." The captain strolled into the room as if taking an afternoon walk. "It wouldn't bode well for me with the Coalition if I reported your termination due to another escape attempt."

Termination. The word yanked her gaze to his.

Lifeless eyes watched. "The sensors in your suit serve as a conduit to reprimand and subdue. Using a magnetic field, they anchor you to the floor."

Slowly, she looked to the heavy tunic. Every handspan there was a black-and-gold circle.

Pacing before her like a predator, he continued. "The suit affords varying levels of control. The primary, which currently weights and slows you is the lowest. It allows normal movement, yet prevents you from leaving the suspended location. Secondary—" He tapped into the wall panel.

A force she could not see yanked Kersei down. She narrowly avoided a collision with the hard floor. It snatched the air from her lungs. Humiliated her. She gritted her teeth, fury rising as her breath plumed on the shadowed glass.

"—well," he said around a laugh, "secondary stretches you prostrate. Not pleasant. Agreed?"

Kersei tried to look up at him, but vibrations jounced her muscles, forbidding her from moving.

"Now, my favorite," Captain Baric said, "is tertiary."

Steeling herself, she expelled a breath as she had been taught in training when anticipating a blow.

"But since it has crushed beings larger than you, I believe we will forgo the demonstration."

Kersei knew her eyes betrayed her.

He snickered. "Merciful, eh?"

Her gaze never made it past his shin-high boots. But her anger? That made it to the ceiling.

"I would be careful with that pounding heart of yours," he said with a chuckle. "It betrays how stubborn you Niners can be."

Niners? What did that mean?

The thrumming lessened, a notable difference that bounced along her body yet released the crushing restraint. Breathing was a chore, but she forced herself up. Slowly. To all fours. She slumped, exhausted. "I am no threat that you must do this."

Baric's eyebrows arched. "You knocked out one of my men, bruised the throat of another." He pursed his lips. "I call that a threat." With a lazy shrug, he wiped his thumb along his lower lip. "Tell me, did your family believe the same thing the night you burned them alive?"

"Burned?" Gasping at those words and the images they conjured, Kersei balled her fists. Is that how they died? "I did not kill them." The thought strangled her.

"Your sister screamed a lot—"

Kersei shoved upward.

Searing vibrations rattled her teeth. Paralyzed her. Yanked her hard and fast to the floor. Crying out, she tried to break her fall. But her arms defied her and swung aside. Cheekbone collided with steel. Pain shot down her temples, spearing into her neck and back.

Laughter crackled, joined soon by slow clapping. "That was brilliant," Baric taunted. "I guess I forgot to mention that the sensors are *sensitive* to an action's rate of speed. They respond. If you move too fast, they register a threat. And zap—you're on your face again."

He crouched before her, the buzz of the magnets sounding like a plague of insects. His laughter carried over the noise. "Now we understand each other. Right, Princess?" He grunted and straightened to tower over her. "To be found adrift in a stolen jumper after killing the entirety of your clan …" He motioned the men out of the room. "It will be well worth the time to peel back the layers of such a pretty, fiery woman to see what, exactly, motivates a downworlder. And how long you can endure the reminders."

Reminders?

With a hiss, the weights pinning her to the floor released. Hesitantly, she wiggled her fingers, then slowly drew them close and pushed from the floor. Moved to the side, away from him.

The captain's gaze darkened. "Kersei Lysander Dragoumis, you have been found guilty of the murder of your mother, Nicea Dragoumis, Lady of Basilikas." His voice, resonating with supreme authority and condemnation, ripped through her like a javrod.

Basilikas? It must be a mistake.

The walls around her sprang to life with floor-to-ceiling renderings of her mother. Mesmerized, Kersei gaped at the larger-than-life images. Ma'ma's voice and laughter filtered from nowhere, yet everywhere.

How did they bring her ma'ma to life here? "Where are these from? How do you have her likeness?" Her mother appeared younger, more innocent than she remembered.

"And of your father, Xylander Dragoumis, leader of the Stratios, warring tribe of the Kalonicans, and hand of the king."

Her mother's face shrunk, making room for her father. At the sound of his rich, deep voice, Kersei's heart twisted. Squeezed.

"Of Adara—"

"No!"

"—your younger sister, and your elder sister, Lexina, bound of Prince Silvanus, eldest heir of King Zarek."

"They were not bound nor pledged—not yet." It was a moot point. Kersei steeled herself as the semblances of Adara, Lexina, Silvanus, and Medora Zarek joined her parents. Her legs grew leaden.

"Then the great tragedy of the ruling king, Zarek, and the crown prince, Silvanus. I will not name the nearly two hundred warriors who also lost their lives as I am short on time." He checked a device strapped to his wrist. "Lastly, of your bound, Tyrannous Darius, second eldest of Medora Zarek."

Bound … They had not completed the ceremony. His image burst on the walls, and with it, Kersei thought for sure she could hear his stern remonstrations. Always trying to make her more subdued, more like Lexina. Less … herself.

Baric moved to the door. "For your crimes, you are sentenced to daily reminders of those whose lives you have ended. Upon these four walls, the floor, and ceiling, their images will play out until twenty-two hundred hours each day and resume at zero eight hundred." He was far too pleased with himself. "Should you close your eyes for more than two seconds, the sequence will rekey and your suit will give you a … reminder." His lips twisted into a grin. "See, we have technology, Kersei, that can take impressions from the part of your brain that stores memory. These we can lift and the computer interprets them into images. Quite accurately. So, while the tube repaired you, we also retrieved your memories from that fateful night."

"If you did that, then you know and can see that I did not kill anyone!"

"What we saw was you fleeing to safety on a shuttle just moments before the hall was destroyed." He clicked his tongue. "Gruesome, Kersei. We've also gone to great lengths to recover the footage of Stratios Hall in flames and crumbling. This chamber is designed to reform those who have turned to violence to gain their means."

"Like you?"

He glowered. "Give care, Princess. Remember who is in control of that suit's settings."

Nausea roiled. "Have I no trial?" Kersei gaped as he strode from the room. "Where is my guilt defined? I have not given testimony, nor defended myself against these charges!"

The door hissed shut, silencing her objection. Leaving her alone with the dead crawling the walls. Circling, she trembled at the horror of the punishment assigned—there was no escape. Under foot, over head, behind her, in front of her ... everywhere, the taunting reminders blasted her. Breaths came in stuttered measures as bold and handsome Darius filled her field of vision.

Hands shaking, Kersei reached toward him. "Darius," she whispered, tears stinging.

Bright light exploded, momentarily blinding her. Kersei flinched and yanked her hand back. Yellow and orange flames coated the walls. Gory, burning figures ran in wild terror to escape the fire consuming them. Their screams raked her soul.

Kersei's hands flew to her mouth—she covered her eyes.

"Sequence reset," a strange voice announced as a jolt shot down her spine. She cried out.

Gasping, she watched as one of the enormous timbers lining the roof of the antechamber whooshed down like a giant hammer, pinning her ma'ma beneath its massive weight. As if the horror wasn't enough, the picture zoomed in on her crushed form. Something ... underneath...

Kersei stepped closer, tilting her head to discern the crystal-clear images amid the dancing flames. "No," she breathed as she met her little sister's lifeless eyes. Instinctively, she reached out to touch the dark strands ... Lively, precocious Adara—her bright, mischievous eyes ... blank.

Kersei stumbled back. Tears, though hot, felt cold against her flaming cheeks. She wished they could wash away this nightmare. Wished they could cleanse her mind of the horrid ... atrocities.

Below her, the images swam up, taunting. "Stop. Please—I didn't kill them. They can't be dead. It's not real. Stop this!"

Dropping to her knees, she hid her face from the images. Bolts of electricity erupted, singeing and searing her flesh. Hot pain echoed the terror on every surface.

"Stop!" she cried, opening her eyes so the electroshock punishment would halt.

True to Baric's promise, the sequence restarted.

"No," she sobbed. "I didn't kill my family! It's a mistake. Please, make it stop."

Overwhelmed by the images, Kersei's eyes once again slid shut. She heard the sequence re-queue and the humming suit zapped her. She writhed. To whatever extent she'd failed her family, Kersei prayed that one rise, she would find a way to make those responsible pay.

I'm dead either way ...

Whether she challenged him or stayed quiet, Teeli knew her life would end. The mine plague would slowly eat away at her. If she did this, she was gone today.

And is this how you make decisions, based off months left to live? Had she really grown so calloused that she considered only her own life? What about the girl?

Hands cupping her mouth, she stared at the vidscreen of the chamber. When she'd accepted the assignment as the *Macedon's* chief medical officer, she had expected challenges. Moments when she wouldn't agree with some decision, code, or method. When she'd have to pull rank. She just hadn't imagined such an egregious breach of morality. She was mortified when the truth revealed itself. Baric, of course, not only ignored her, but ordered her to stay out of the chamber.

If she reported this situation with the hunter and girl, if she challenged Baric again, she would lose more than her assignment aboard the *Macedon* because the technology must have come from Symmachia, the central planet of the TSC. He'd promised her as much, along with an epithet about her mental abilities and her race.

As a Tryssinian, she was considered a third-class citizen by those in command, though many would never outright voice it. A means to an end. Her ancestors had bartered their way into the Tertian Space Coalition, buying a slice of paradise with the labor of Tryssinians. Nobody could have known then what years in the mines, producing the primary ore that fueled ships and kept the industrial capital of Helio running, would do to its people.

The insidious, unavoidable disease grew more virulent and prevalent because of a genetic predisposition passed down through their lines. Early onset included fatigue, trouble breathing. Next came easy bruising and trouble concentrating. Then brittle bones and thinning blood that wouldn't clot. A nosebleed could kill. Health went downhill fast from there. It was why

Tryssinians who survived to adulthood symptom-free fled the planet—in the hopes of breeding out the gene.

Teeli rubbed her right clavicle, where little feeling remained. Around it a gray shadow, visible to the eye but hidden—*thank the Fires*—by her uniform, evinced the choked nerve endings. The bruising. Symptom-free well into her adolescence, she had left Tryssinia with high hopes of survival. No longer. Slow, stealthy, and undeniable, the disease would take her sooner or later.

Balling her fist, she reached to switch vidscreens to the small secure medbay where the catatonic hunter had been relocated. The chamber was hyperbaric, used against decompression sickness, so why he insisted the hunter remain there … she could only guess it was to hide his presence.

"Dr. Knowles?"

She twitched as her assistant rushed into her office. "What is it?"

Zilla clutched something to her chest, face wrought. She handed over a flex screen. "I was following orders. Monitoring them every hour. Vitals were weak and growing unstable."

Teeli didn't have to look at the screen to know she meant the hunter. "He's failing …" She strode from her office.

"No," Zilla breathed as she followed her. "He's *gone*."

Wheeling around, Teeli collided with the energetic girl. "Dead? How?"

"No! He's *gone*, as in"—she lifted her hands and shrugged—"not there. *Gone*."

The words would not compute. Teeli blinked. "What … how—you think he escaped?"

"Hardly." Zilla snorted as they started toward the chamber. "*Everything* is gone. The sheets. Vac lines. Fluid bags. Everything."

Storming down the halls, Teeli felt a terrible thrum of panic. If he was gone—had he died? Was Baric trying to hide what he'd done to the poor man? Quickening her steps didn't help. Neither did accessing the security panel and opening the door. Reality glared back from the empty chamber. Just as Zilla said.

"When?" Absently, she lifted a warming blanket, staring around the bay. "When did you last check on him?"

"Quarter after—f-forty minutes ago."

Moving a patient in that hunter's condition would take time, navigating only via freight elevators. Teeli turned, breath trapped in her throat. "They could still be on board." She hurried out, one goal in mind. But where—? How? There was one person … She glanced at her personal channeler. She tried to wave him, but her system wouldn't work. "For the love of—"

"Ithoughtyoumightaskhim.He'sontheathleticdeck." Zilla's words spilled out in a rush. "Don't be mad. All medical channelers are down for some reason."

"To prevent us from interfering, likely." Touching the woman's shoulder, Teeli managed a quick smile. "Thanks." She jogged down the hall and grabbed the first access tube. Rode it to the athletic deck, where crew members could keep their bodies from atrophy while in space.

She hurried to the clear walls separating the rest of the quiet deck from the workout bay. But she didn't see him. Inside, being assaulted by the heavy, musky air, Teeli walked the outer wall, searching around the equipment. Mostly women.

Laughter spiraled from a running track. Three women in teksuits huddled around a very sweaty yet still quite handsome Tigo Deken.

His gaze swung toward her and he grinned. When he broke from the group to join her, Teeli drew up, self-conscious. "Evening, Doc."

"We have to talk," she said, noticing those around them gawking. "Privately."

Tigo lifted his head and glanced around. "Okay, give me five to breeze off and change."

"Might be too late." She tried not to notice the way the sweat seemed to dance over his still-elevated pulse. The way his trapezius muscles were quite defined.

He frowned. "For what?"

"They took that … patient."

"The girl?"

She shook her head.

Eyes widening in understanding, he bobbed his head toward the showers. "C'mon. Brief me." He tossed the towel in the receptacle and headed to the blasters. Reaching over and between his shoulder blades, he gripped his shirt. Tugged it up, his spine glistening, then stripped it off. He angled to a locker and pulled out his channeler. In silence, he manipulated the device. His gaze was fierce. Eyes dark with intent and jaw set. As a doctor, she had to admit he was one of the finer specimens of the human race. As a woman … she understood the effect he had on her sex.

At the maze of shower booths, Teeli stood on the other side, grateful they concealed what he had no trouble baring. Air and chemicals hissed their cleansing spray over him. Opaque tubes recycled resources for the sake of conservation on the ship.

"Zilla said he went missing within the last forty minutes," she called to him.

Turning for the spray, he tapped the screen. Pressed his comms implant. "Jez. You there?" His fingers blurred on his channeler, then he hesitated, listening. "You in the system?" His features were strong—olive complexion, not quite as dark as her own. Straight nose. "Good. Check the transport bays."

They could get in a lot of trouble for piggybacking security vids. Who was she kidding? "I probably shouldn't be here while you do this."

Tigo smirked again. "Grab my kit?" He pointed to the locker from which he'd retrieved the channeler. "First one."

She seized the chance for distraction and snagged his duffel. Handed it over the half wall as the jets fell silent.

Stubble lined his jaw, a muscle twitching as his gaze struck hers again. Since when were his eyes the color of honey? Warm, inviting. "Don't worry, D—" He touched his implant, gaze and attention snatched away. "Yeah, go ahead."

He slid on briefs, then stilled. Lifted his head. Brows tightened into a knot. "Mm-hm. Copy." He stepped into black tactical pants. Then hesitated again. Scowled over her shoulder, then tugged her into a private room. Grabbing his ruck, he caught Teeli's arm and guided her to a corner.

"Wh—" Heat climbed through her cheeks as he pressed his still-bare and freshly cleansed chest almost to her face.

He shut the door.

"Now wha—"

Tigo touched a finger to his lips, indicated to the two-by-six-inch window that afforded a view of the corridor. She glanced out and spotted two security officers stalking toward them … then past. Right. Of course—no witnesses to their collusion. She backed away from the glass, bumping into Tigo.

"Didn't think you'd want them to see you with me half-dressed," he said, his breath hot against her ear.

She shuddered and hated herself for the involuntary reaction. For feeding his overblown ego.

Still framing her shoulders with his chest, Tigo bent to eye the screen, his close-cropped hair tickling her face. "Yeah. Yeah," he said, angling the channeler to Teeli.

She glanced at it, but in her periphery, his bulging bicep taunted her. Would he put his shirt on already?

"Seeing it," he said, his voice rumbling along her spine. "Can you mal the doors?"

Teeli frowned.

"Just try, Jez." He nodded as Teeli extricated herself from his cocoon, grateful he was distracted with the work he and his first officer were doing. "Yeah. Make the malfunction look normal." He huffed. "I know it's not as easy as that, but *you* are as good as that." His frown smoothed into a smile.

Finally, he lifted his shirt from the bag. Then stilled. "Slag." He grunted. "No, no ... Yeah. Thanks for trying." His hand hesitated by the comms behind his ear. "I'll be there." He tapped the implant, ending the wave.

"What's wrong?"

"She had a location but it erased as she read it."

"Does that mean the man is dead? Baric's hiding his trail?" She'd been too late. Teeli groaned. Scrubbed her hands over her face.

"Unknown. Was he alive when he left the bay?" Chest. Bare chest. He was too close.

Teeli jerked away from him. Closed her eyes. "Put your shirt on, Commander." She swallowed. "Please."

He snorted a laugh, snagging her attention. Something spilling into his brown eyes that had too much meaning. Too much draw. She felt it. Felt the fire between them. Always had. He was a charismatic officer with the looks and arrogance to draw dithering females.

Which she was not.

His breath teased her cheek. "Teeli."

The warmth of her name slid across her shoulders. Made her gaze dart to his. But he wasn't looking at *her*. He was looking at her lips.

And though she'd shoved him away countless times, though she'd rebuffed his many flirtations, though she'd laughed at his invitation and mocked his date requests, she wondered ...

A breath from kissing her, he hesitated.

Her mind buzzed, nerve endings strangely tingling.

"Pretend," he whispered.

"Wha—"

His lips were warm against hers.

Teeli's breath caught. Mind dazzled by the connection that told her not to argue. Not to reject. To ... enjoy. She did not know how long she'd be here. And ... it was *him*.

His mouth was inviting. Gentle. Caressing. Testing. Tasting. Directing, guiding. His touch firm at the small of her back as he pulled her tight.

Teeli rested a palm on his chest, surprised at the thunder of his heart she felt beneath her fingers. The ragged rise and fall.

"Hey, who—"

Teeli jerked, startled by the intrusion. A uniform stood in the door.

Tigo swung in front of her. Shielding her. "Ah. Hey."

"Sorry, Commander. But …" Curious eyes peered over his shoulder at her. Teeli ducked. Turned away, suddenly ashamed of herself. Of her weakness. "You know these rooms aren't for—well, you know."

"I do. Yeah. Sorry," Tigo said with a chuckle, threading his arms through his shirt as he continued to block her. "We'll clear out. It's all good."

"Okay." The security officer backed out.

Humiliation swarmed Teeli with realization: this hadn't been a moment between her and the commander.

Pretend.

He'd kissed her to distract security. Tigo had told her to pretend. She hadn't understood. She'd lost her ability to think when he'd kissed her. And she'd—like a stupid, dithering female—swooned. He'd used her.

Tigo's stormy eyes came back to her. He smiled, then it fell. "Tee—"

"*Doctor* Knowles," she growled, drawing the line in the sand. Putting him in his place—far, far below her. Dragging the back of her hand over her mouth, she fled the room, just as her brains had done with his kiss.

"Wait," he called. "Te—Dr. Knowles." His grunt chased her. "Wait. Was that patient dead?"

He didn't deserve an answer.

"Listen," he said, his steps heavy as he fell in behind her. "Hey." His voice grew soft, different. He caught her arm and drew her around. "I'm sorry. About—"

She wrested free. Plastered a smile on her lips. "We were *pretending.* That's what you said, right?" Why did the truth sting so much? She told herself to relax her mouth and stance, stop being petulant.

Something flicked through his gaze. Almost like … hurt. But it wasn't. He was wondering if she was okay. If she understood that he gave out kisses the way drill sergeants handed out reprimands. Tigo Deken was notorious for his way with the ladies. All of them. Even her apparently.

"I have no idea about the patient's status," she reported, struggling to get back into character. "He was removed from the medical bay without my knowledge or permission."

The commander—she'd never again call him Tigo—ran a hand through his hair. "And the … uh, the girl?"

She entered the lift. "What? Do you think you're King of the Quadrants come along to—"

"So you still have her?" Ferocity had stamped into his expression and words.

Great Fires, Teeli, get hold of yourself. She tugged her tunic straight. "As of fifteen minutes ago, still there. But she is a child. We can't let her continue to be subjected to this any longer. Do you think … can you do something?"

Tigo scowled. "I don't have authority—"

"Easy answer." She cocked her head in a snap. "Sorry to have bothered you. I had hoped to find someone with strong enough morals and character to protect the innocent, but I see I must look further."

"That's not fair. This is complicated slag, Teeli."

"Good day, Commander."

Tigo pivoted from the turbo lift and threw a punch into the wall. Pain pulsed up his arm, but it had nothing on the barb Teeli had just driven into his chest. Is that what she really thought of him?

Scuz, he shouldn't have kissed her. He'd thought it'd be a kiss. One simple kiss. But … they'd opened a black hole. Void's Embrace, he'd never had such a good kiss. The way she responded lit something powerful in him.

"You okay?" Diggs drew up alongside, eyeing Tigo's bloody knuckles. "Bet that hurts."

Tigo started down the passage toward the lift to the transport bays. "Doc thinks the hunter is dead and they're taking him off-ship."

"That'll be some messed-up slag if they killed him—"

"It'll be messed up period if Kynig learns about any of this."

Diggs cursed. "Heard word they were here days past."

"Who?"

"Three hunters. Rumor has it they were asking about the girl."

Tigo paused. Glanced back as if he could see up a dozen decks and into the medbay. "The girl?" How did that make sense? "You're sure?"

Shrugging, Diggs pursed his lips. "That's what they say."

"What'd they want with her?"

"No guess." As they boarded the lift, Diggs thrust his chin toward the corridor. "This gonna be a problem?"

"If they find out—"

"No," Diggs asserted. "You and the doc."

It took everything in Tigo not to react, saved by the thump of his comms. "She's like every other officer on this ship." The lie was bitter as he tapped his comms. "Go."

"I found him!" Jez hissed.

He shifted. "Where?" Tigo hit the all-stop on the lift.

"In the recycle bay," she said and he pressed the new destination on the panel. "There's a dozen guards down here with this stasis pod."

"So, not dead."

"Why guard a body?"

"En route."

13

KYNIG

The juncture where the two wings met provided too much temptation for Marco to resist, especially when his nerves were jouncing. Eyeing the corner, he sprinted the last twenty yards down the training field and threw himself at it. He toed the right wall, shoving up and to the left. Toed that one. Back to the other side. Caught the stone with his fingers. Dug in and thrust himself up. Up … up.

He vaulted sideways. Gripped the edge of the roof and swung his legs up. In a crouch, he sat on the lip, watching the yard, the heat of Pir baking him and kneading his taut muscles. In the yard, the recruits sparred. Up here, he could breathe. Get away from the clamor of noise and voices. Distraction. Stressors.

Well, not completely. This Decree … he rotated his right arm and stared at the mark. Tattoo. Brand. Whatever it was. He ran his fingers over it. Smooth to the touch. Fisting his hand, he wished he could recall where he'd gotten it. He hated that the iereas knew of it, said it was an Ierean mark. Tied to a prophecy. But like his childhood, the origination of this wretched thing lay shrouded in the past and intense training by which he had set aside his family and life before Kynig. He had no regrets. But it irritated him that this thing he'd long covered up and ignored now demanded attention and significance. No. He was a hunter. He would yield only to that.

An annoyed efflux flung at him, bringing his gaze back to the yard. To the flight wing. Just outside the door Roman stood with Rico. He'd returned—had he found Dolon's shuttle? The two glaring up at him. It was against Citadel practice to scent-search the Brethren within the walls of the Academy, but sometimes it couldn't be helped.

Marco sailed into the air, aiming for the second ledge from the right. Caught it. Pitched himself back in a zigzag as he had in climbing up. With a subtle thump, he dropped to the ground. Jogged across the yard. His advocate and the master were now waiting inside.

He stepped into the cool embrace of the air-conditioned structure. Voices pulled him right, toward the hangar wing. His heart skipped a beat. Had they found Dolon's shuttle? He hustled down the stone passage and shoved open the door with a sign that read, EAR PROTECTION REQUIRED.

The far bay door was open, allowing the sun to glare off the seemingly undamaged shuttle in its early morning light.

"What'd you find? Where was it?" Marco trotted over to the half-dozen gathered.

"Drosero."

"Dro—" Marco jolted. "It's a protected planet."

"Aye." Rico huffed. "The ship is wiped, so we got nothing."

"Wiped?" He studied the fuselage. "It looks in good condition."

"It is." Rico motioned him to the other side, where the scout's bay door stood open. He peered inside, where four of the six masters stood conversing at the top of the stairs from the engine compartment.

"Dolon wiped it so nobody could get our intel," Marco suggested.

"Or someone else wiped it to hide who took him."

Doing that would reveal a fatal flaw in the kidnapper's plan. "That'd mean they didn't know about our secondary security protocols." A mischievous grin hit his face.

"Palinurus is pulling the data now," Rico said with a nod.

If they hadn't found anything yet, why had his advocate and master summoned him?

Roman emerged from the shuttle talking with Urbain, their heads together, expressions stern and disapproving. He shifted and his gaze fell on Marco. With mutual nods, the masters broke apart.

Roman eyed them and continued walking. "With me."

Marco and Rico hurried after their master into the main courtyard. Past the training yard far to Marco's left and on into the headquarters. Taking them back to his office—if one could call it that.

The building consisted of a main hub that split off into six wings, each a residence for a master. Far better accommodations than those of the recruits, who bunked in one of twelve halls, or hunters like Marco, who had private rooms no bigger than a closet. They needed nothing more. Some dorms were doubled, forcing newer hunters to share with another. Advocates were housed in apartments, with a reflecting room, a sleeping room, and a bathroom.

But this … Marco had entered this space only a couple of times. Large and open, the sitting area served that function, yet it doubled for personal training, the climbing wall subtly built into stone that rose from floor to the ceiling of an upper level, which contained a sleeping quarters, bathroom, and another room Marco had never entered. To his right was a kitchen and dining area. All done in near luxury, though after seeing the extravagance of the Iereans, it paled.

Roman strode to the refrigeration box and drew out a jug of water. He poured a glass, motioned for them to help themselves, but Marco didn't dare accept the offer. Neither did Rico. It was considered rude. Besides, it was maddening that their master drank water rather than divulge what he had learned.

"You did not come all this way for water," Rico teased quietly, palming the cold gray stone counter that separated them.

Roman fisted his hand, then set down the glass. Grave and heavy, his expression came to Marco. He flicked something on the counter.

Marco glanced at it. A gold arc—a pin. "A crescent." He lifted it and thumbed it around his palm, recalling the one on the captain's shoulder on the *Macedon*.

"So he was taken from his shuttle?" Rico asked slowly.

The master drew in a long breath, then slowly released it.

"Symmachians took Dolon?" Marco couldn't wrap his mind around it. "They wouldn't dare. That would violate the pact with Drosero as well as the Kynig-Tertian Accord. Absolutely no interference, not with our hunts nor with our hunters."

"Why?" Rico growled. "It makes no sense! Why would Dolon even be on Drosero?"

"Protection," Roman suggested. "He had no Decree, and that is the only plausible—"

"You do not think he was meeting with them, do you?"

Roman glowered. "Speak not against the Brethren without proof."

"But this ..." Rico's gaze skipped around the kitchen. "To drop to Drosero and pull a hunter. Acrisius knows our influence with downworlders—"

"Do not refer to them as such." Roman's tone was dark. "The Symmachians use the term to elevate themselves over those not from their tertiary alliance. We are Kynigos. The Brethren make no distinction between those in space or on land."

Rico inclined his head, but his temper still flared. "You side with—"

"I side with the Code." Roman's gaze blazed. "It has kept the Brethren from erring in judgment and action for centuries."

Chastised, Rico lowered his head.

The master went to the fire pit in the middle of the room. Hands behind his back, he again turned and considered them.

"You fear something," Marco said without thinking.

Gaze sharpened, Roman thinned his lips. "You *anak'd* me?"

Hot lead poured through his gut. *Anaktesios*, the act of drawing in the scent from another being, was strictly forbidden within the Citadel. Hunters should not fear their Brethren. "No, sir." But the lie of it … "Not intentionally." He inclined his head. "I beg your mercy, Master."

Booted feet moved away as the master went to the windows overlooking the valley below. "I'm surprised you could detect it," he said quietly, the admission forcing Marco to eye Rico, who seemed just as intrigued. "I have long mastered my feelings, but …" His gaze never left the valley. "You both heard when the scout was located, the masters wanted to pose a response. Now that the crescent has been found, they're convinced of Dolon's demise and Symmachia's responsibility for his death."

"Death? We know this?" Marco started forward. "We—"

Roman lifted a hand. "Nothing is known. Not definitively." His expression turned grave and dark. "But neither is Dolon the first hunter to go missing."

Not the first? "Who else?"

"A handful." His head lowered, a wake of grief roiling.

Scents came whether Marco bid them or not. And this was so strong that Rico surely detected it as well. That meant …

What? What did it mean? His mind wouldn't follow the facts, though that was what he'd been trained to do—pursue truth. Justice.

Roman turned and focused on Marco. "We must find out—quietly—why they would do this." Those weighted blue eyes remained on him. "You're going to Cenon. The girl will be there."

Marco started. "How—"

"Go," Roman barked, then clenched his jaw and more softly said, "prepare."

Now? With all this happening?

"Is that wise?" Rico asked, edging forward.

It seemed a silent duel ensued between his master and advocate, neither speaking, nor moving. But the scents …

Curse the reek!

"Marco," his master at last said, "to Cenon."

Gritting his teeth, Marco bowed his head.

"And while you're there …"

The pause grew so long that Marco shifted.

Roman's expression sparked with meaning and ferocity. "You are our best hunter. I care not for rank or years at the Citadel or on Kynig. You *are* the best, Marco." Razors had nothing on the intensity in his master's gaze. "Go there. And *pay attention.*"

Marco's receptors were infused with the master's subtext. The words were more than words. They were instruction. Warning.

TSC *MACEDON*

"What've you got?" Tigo scurried up behind the steel shipping crate that hid them from the security detail.

"Five guns on the tube, which they're about to load in the transport."

Tigo noted the other team—225. Baric wouldn't have an Eidolon team monitoring a crew member in that tube. Definitely had to be the Kynigos. "I commed the—"

"Excuse me!" Dr. Knowles's tenor voice rang through the bay, followed closely by the thump of her approach. "*What* are you doing with my patient? I demand he be returned immediately to—"

"This ain't your problem, Doc. Go back to medical," said Arkin Cleve, one of the meanest soldiers on this ship and Tigo's sometime competitor back at the Academy. The guy had a vicious streak and an even worse thirst for retaliation.

"Is she *always* this stupid?" Jez growled.

Tigo surged forward.

"That's a mistake," Jez warned as she caught his arm. "You do this and your career is on the line. For *her*? This is not why you're here."

Surprise lit through him with confusion. "This isn't about *her*, Jez. It's about right—"

"Open this at once," Knowles's demand reached across the bay. "Perhaps being a hired gun, you are—"

"*Academy* grad, ma'am." Pride dripped from Cleve's voice. "Top ten in my class."

"Then I'll grant leniency because you've been brainwashed. But this?" She motioned to them. "This is wrong. This patient was removed from my care without my authorization." She aimed a channeler at the pod.

"Don't do that, ma'am." Cleve drew up. "Put the device down. Now."

Tigo rounded the large container as if taking a light stroll through the bay.

Come in charging, he'd just amp Cleve's tension. He heard Jez and Diggs behind him. Rested his hand on his weapon.

"Ma'am," Cleve barked. His body language warned things were quickly escalating. Too quickly.

"Ah, Dr. Knowles," Tigo called. "Here you are."

Cleve jerked toward him, his weapon coming to bear. The four with him did the same.

Laughing, Tigo raised his hands. "A little tense, gentlemen?"

"This bay is off limits to all personnel," Cleve growled.

"Interesting," Tigo said. "I haven't gotten that wave." He smiled at Knowles. "Everything okay, Doc?"

"It is not." She kept working the channeler, and he heard one of the digital mechanisms on the pod hiss into the unlock position.

Cleve aimed at her. "Put it down, Doc, or I will be forced to stop you."

"Seriously?" Tigo said, moving between him and his target. "You're going to shoot the *Macedon*'s chief medical officer for ensuring the safety of her patient?"

"Not to mention inside a ship where arms fire could puncture the fuselage or disable any number of systems." Diggs planted his hands on the tactical belt. "That's some kind of stupid."

Tigo gave a lazy shrug. "Have to agree with you, Diggs."

The pressure of Knowles's hand landed between his shoulder blades. Surprised, he glanced at her and found appreciation, most likely for the intervention.

"I don't care what you think of my orders. I obey them," Cleve said.

Her hand fell away again and he heard the soft tap of her working the channeler.

"Commander Deken," another member of 225 spoke up. "I have Captain Baric on comms. He said you are to stand down and report to the bridge immediately."

"Sure thing."

Hiss-click.

A prolonged hiss ensued as the air pressure from the stasis pod released.

The moment hung in shocked silence for several long ticks, the 225 no doubt surprised she'd bypassed security protocols on the lock. Knowles seemed surprised, too. And Tigo braced, knowing all the dark powers in the 'verse were about to come to bear.

And they did.

Cleve snapped his weapon at her—as did his four men.

Oblivious to the danger she'd unleashed, Knowles rushed to the pod.

Not a moment to lose, Tigo slid straight into Cleve. At the same time, he sliced a hand at Cleve's wrist and palmed the top of the weapon. Flipped the grip and snatched it.

Jez and Diggs flew into action, shouting.

Cleve threw a right hook. Nailed Tigo in the jaw, clacking his teeth. His head whipped backward. He stumbled, but caught himself.

"It's not him!"

The words faltered in his brain, refusing to make the connection to the voice. To its meaning. Adrenaline surged and sped through his veins as Cleve produced a knife.

"Commander!" Knowles caught his arm. "It's not him—this isn't the hunter!"

Tigo straightened, still on edge. Not trusting Cleve to hold his stance. He blinked and met Teeli's eyes. "What?"

She shook her head. "It's not the hunter."

The lid of the pod hovered over a body ... a dead body. A Symmachian uniform. A *Macedon* crew member. Fifty-something male.

"I don't understand," Teeli said.

"Me either," AO growled. "What's an Eidolon team doing guarding a dead body?"

"What we do isn't your business," Cleve said.

"Captain Deken, you are ordered into custody of *Macedon* security to be delivered to Captain Baric at once." It was the smarmy guy again.

"No slaggin' way," Diggs said. "You can't—"

"Easy, Diggs." Tigo nodded at him. "I've got this."

To the side, Knowles swayed. Her face blanched.

"Doc?"

With a dismissive wave, she grimaced. "Just a little upset."

Even Cleve hesitated at the way her words slurred.

Tigo moved closer. When Cleve's cohort started to object, Tigo glowered and met Teeli. Left no room for propriety. "I know this was upsetting," he said. "You okay?"

A sheen covered her face. Very pale. "I ..." Her eyelids fluttered. She wobbled.

Tigo caught her shoulders. "Doc."

She clamped onto his bicep, bracing herself. Her touch again fiercely hot. "I ... just ... ressssss." Her legs buckled.

Tigo lifted her into his arms. Her head tipped against his chest.

"Commander!" Cleve objected. "You're under arrest!"

"Yeah, yeah." He stalked out of the bay. "I'll come—"

"*Now*, Commander," Cleve ordered. "You're ordered to Captain Baric immediately."

"Here," Diggs said, shouldering in to take Knowles. "I'll make sure she gets top care."

Irritated but powerless, Tigo relinquished Teeli's limp form.

"Move!" Cleve barked, ordering Tigo back to the present.

"Nice setup," Tigo bit out, forcing the 225 commander to shove him.

At his side, Jez touched his arm. Gave him a look that said everything she couldn't voice. She'd deal with this. Find out what happened to the hunter. Make sure Teeli was okay in medical.

With a nod that he understood, he let 225 lead him to the bridge. Or the brig.

Many lacked the imagination and passion to pursue a course that could deliver humanity to the next phase of their evolutionary progress. Those included the rule followers. Unmotivated by the opportunity to seize what hovered at their fingertips, they suffocated in lesser, more unpleasant tasks.

Zoltan Baric had never shied from hard work. In fact his drive and determination to see things through were how he'd so quickly earned the rank of captain and command of the *Macedon*. Both were a part of his destiny to press humanity past its complacent coma. There were costs, of course. And people hated him for that.

"The shuttle and package are away, sir."

Zoltan nodded to his XO. "Thank you, Commander Dimar." He'd done it. It'd been the trickiest endeavor by far. "I'll be in my quarters." He stepped off the bridge and climbed the four steps to his quarters, where he retrieved a secure channeler and sent a wave. He waited for an answer, amazed at the ease with which so much had been accomplished. So much that he'd expected to be opposed. Sure, there was the irritation known as Deken and a persistent fear that the Kynigos might return. For now, the hunters' departure empty-handed represented a major hurdle cleared.

The screen blinked on. "Go ahead."

"It's done," Zoltan said.

"Good. And you're sure about this one? It's a terrible risk—"

"I am—100 percent. The results with him far outweigh any to date. She was right," Zoltan said, feeling a heady concoction of giddiness and nerves warm his veins. "It *does* work."

Silence rattled the air. "You've sent him to the station?"

"Just moments ago."

"You'll follow. There cannot be any missteps, Baric."

"As you're aware," he said, determined to show he could not be pushed around, "I must attend the Launch Day celebration, but after—"

"Good."

As the secure communiqué ended, his comms chirruped. He sighed as he spotted the waiting comms. "What is it, Mr. Crichton?"

"Cleve and Dawes are here with Commander Deken, sir."

Baric released a longsuffering sigh. Domitas Deken had been a royal pain in his backside going all the way back to his Academy days, when the now-fleet admiral had been one of his instructors. Now he was shackled with the admiral's son aboard his ship. "Send them in."

"Aye, sir."

A minute later, Tigo Deken stood before him, a bruise reddening his jaw and cheek. The kid hadn't even crested thirty, yet he led an Eidolon detachment. As arrogant as they came. Bruised chin high, brown eyes apathetic and the left swelling, he stood with his hands behind his back. The security team had no injuries. But roughing him up changed things. Would beg questions. They'd needed this clean.

"You scuzzed this, Cleve."

"Sir?"

"The bruise!" Zoltan hollered, motioning to Deken. "How do I explain that to the admiral of the fleet?" He wouldn't admit how much liked seeing the punk roughed up—nice dose of humility. "Do you realize how that will go over?"

"The admiral should know that even his own son can't attack fleet officers."

"Attack."

Cleve nodded, his chest puffed.

"That's a mistake," Baric said quietly.

The major shifted.

"Lying to your captain is insubordination." He came off his desk and flexed his hand. "While I might resent that Commander Deken and the Two-one-five are aboard my ship and that relationship is tenuous at best, it is how this fleet operates." Curse him. "His record is pristine. Some say he's the best. Never failed a mission. That's how he got his team. That's how he got aboard the *Macedon*." Baric walked closer. Stared down the major. "And you want me to believe that he *attacked* you, yet he alone is the one bruised?"

Zoltan slammed his fist into Cleve's face. "Now there is evidence he attacked you."

YLONT CITY, ZHOSALL
PLANET CENON

It'd been a guess to come to Zhosall, the most accommodating country on Cenon. While the cities of Zlares and Klille were known for their deft trading and black markets, Ylont had open plains and a government desperate for people to work the soil, which drew immigrants and refugees. Though he appreciated working with his hands, Marco shuddered at the archaic beliefs of the Ylontians. It reminded him of Thyrolia. The stench of that plague-filled planet still stung, but more, the reason behind their health problems, thanks to Iereans.

Rolling his neck to shake the memory, Marco firmed his position in the towering tree overlooking the plains where the people toiled well past dusk, due to the close proximity to Pir and the cooling of the day. They had little on the heat he'd trained under on Kynig, but he could appreciate the later hours to reduce heat exhaustion.

It'd been his intention to remain in Ylont a fortnight. But this was a wasted endeavor. The girl would not come here. It was too barren of both land and opportunities. The futility of trying to discern where the girl would go when freed from Symmachia made Marco swipe a hand over his mouth.

His thumper pulsed behind his ear. He thumbed the implant. "Speak, Brother."

"How goes it?" Rico asked.

"Wind and emptiness. There is naught here but farms. This is not where she'll come."

"Were I within klicks, your anger would sting my nostrils."

"Not anger," Marco countered. "Frustration. I cannot fathom why the Citadel approved this hunt, or how iereas can know she will be on Cenon and when, yet do not have knowledge of her current location. This hunt is a mockery. It goes against—"

"Forget whom you serve, Marco?"

He huffed, reining in his irritation. "No." He took in the moonlit field. "The Ancient gifted me. I will hunt."

"Valerik and Palinurus send word to keep your receptors open."

He recalled the missing hunters. Was that the reason for all the mystery and warnings? "Understood," Marco muttered, not satisfied. Convinced something was amiss. Much like the "pay attention" admonishment from Roman.

"To the Decree," Rico said.

"And the hunt." With another flick, the comm ended. "For honor." Mood foul, Marco returned to the village. The thought of warmed, tart juice quickened his pace. It was an indulgence, but it helped him relax.

Rich heady scents of food and cordi—few among many but they called to him like a siren—met him as he stepped in the tavern. Seeking isolation, he closed his receptors and found a table at the back near the fireplace. Smoke and burning wood helped curb scents but also kept his back to the wall and his gaze on the door.

A plump, matronly woman approached with a bored expression, which didn't change even as she took in the Kynigos sigil across his nose. "What'll ye have?"

"Stew and warmed cordi." As she departed, Marco scanned the tavern and nearly groaned when his gaze struck the interested, painted eyes of a chatelaine. He shook his head and turned to his vambrace for intel reports on Zlares and Klille.

"What? Too good for me, love?"

Why must they insist? "I am under Decree," he said impatiently without looking up. Blessed relief came when the hostess returned with a steaming bowl and cup.

The chatelaine slid into the chair beside him, her bosom barely contained in her too-tight bliaut. "That didn't matter to your brother," she said with more than a little pride.

Pretending not to hear, Marco sipped the cordi and let it seep into his muscles and bones. The fruit was of little consequence, but the process of heating released vital nutrients. He lifted the utensil and scooped up meat and potato.

Her eyes hadn't left him. Neither had her scent, though he wasn't searching for it. To his dismay, *she* had not left him either.

Ignoring the unwanted guest at his table, he ate and mentally planned his next cities to explore, Klille and Zlares. Both equally as likely, but which would the girl seek shelter in? To know, he must visit them as he had here. In the jumper, it'd take an ora to reach Klille. Zlares three. So, Klille then.

A hand reached toward his.

With a thump, he pinned her wrist. Snapped his gaze to hers. "Cease!"

Coal-painted eyes flashed. Urgency speared her efflux. And fear, but not of him. "It was his." There was something in her hand. When he loosened his grip, she drew her hand back.

A very distinct shape rested on the table. A Kynigos monocle. The piece clicked onto a hunter's right-arm vambrace, ready to be detached and telescoped for searching great distances. He lifted the telescoping eyepiece. "The vambrace?" Which would hold the channeler that logged intel.

She held his gaze for several long ticks. "Hidden."

"Whose is this?" He staggered through the implications. A Kynigos without a vambrace. And her without the Kynigos. This was trouble, and she seemed to second-guess her choice to approach him. "You know well what I am, chatelaine. Answer me quick—"

"He was with me the night he vanished."

Vanished. "*Who?*"

Now she tucked her chin. "Polyeidus."

One of Valerik's hunters. Marco knew the man, had trained and broken fasts with him. But he had not been aware of his absence. "When?"

"Two weeks past."

Another one missing? Did the Brethren—

"Keep your receptors open."

"Pay attention."

Aye, they knew. He sharpened his gaze on the girl. "Where?"

"Zlares."

"He set you up." Futility marched across Jez's shoulders as she stood on the other side of the brig's electrostatic barrier. Her gaze shifted to his swollen cheek, reminding him of the instant Baric coldcocked Cleve. All to add to the trouble Tigo would face before Symmachian Command.

"Yeah, but for what? Why is he working so hard on this?" A new concern lanced him. "Two-one-five needs to watch its six. Don't give them a reason to ship you back, too."

Her eyes widened. "We should return with you. There's no reason for us to be here."

"No."

"Cleve and his goons are here. We can't justify our presence with another Eidolon unit on board."

"Yes, but we need to find out what happened to the hunter. We need to make sure the girl is protected." He drilled into her eyes. "You're needed here."

"*You're* needed here," she argued.

"Going back gives me a chance to get in front of Command, my father. Find where this trail begins."

She drew in a breath, dark eyes widening. "You think they authorized the machine."

"No way he gets all this tech onboard without someone back there knowing." He shifted his gaze to the side, knowing they were being watched. "But you need to be here, Sidra."

She balled her fists, lips compressed. "For wh—"

"The girl. The hunter. Whatever the slag is going on here. What happened in the bay—they were distracting us. So what did he do? Where's the hunter? We have to find out, Jez. You need to do that while they ship me back." He nodded firmly. "Understood?"

She gave a slow nod.

"He boards the *Damocles* within the hour," came the voice of Gans, the posted guard, speaking to someone they couldn't yet see.

"Go," Tigo urged her, not wanting Jez to draw undue attention to herself.

After a look filled with some expression he couldn't decipher, she huffed and started for the passage. At the juncture, she stopped and eased aside, glowering at Gans as he escorted Dr. Knowles to the cell.

The thrumming of the barrier evaporated and the lock disengaged. "Make it quick. They're retrieving him in fifteen." He held open the door.

Knowles glanced at Jez, then entered with a medical kit. "I am to tend your injury." She indicated the built-in bench. "Sit."

The door locked behind her and the static shield thrummed once more.

Seated, Tigo noted Gans and Jez watching. He slid his gaze to her, silently ordering her to leave. After a second, she complied. Somehow, she always knew what he was thinking, which made her a class-act first officer.

Knowles bent over him, aiming a penlike instrument at his cheek.

"Where I can see him, Doc," Gans growled.

She rolled her eyes and shifted aside. "You Eidolon are all alike, getting into scuffles and needing to be glued." The distinct odor of high-strength medical glue hit him seconds before the stinging.

He winced.

"Keep still," she murmured, "so I don't seal your eye shut, too."

In her gaze, he found no admonishment or reprimand. Only alliance.

Hovering over the box and head down, she adjusted something. "He's already put her in that chamber," she whispered. "I don't know—"

"Doc—"

"Gans," Tigo spoke loudly. "I heard the captain would be on the runner with me. That right?"

Teeli's gaze flicked to his, hopeful.

"What's it to you?"

"Just nosy."

"Don't get any ideas," Gans grumbled. "You try anything and they'll float you."

As the guy continued on about the trouble he'd serve up cold if they tried anything, Tigo whispered to Teeli. "Keep her safe. I'll talk with my father."

She applied a salve to speed the healing and sooth the fire of the glue. "What if he won't listen?"

"He will."

Eyes swollen and burning from days of crying, Kersei dragged herself to the corner, limbs trembling. She had not realized crying could be so exhausting. But this … it wasn't just crying. It was … more. Slumped against the wall, images blurring in her periphery, she stared across it. Knew better than to close her eyes for long or that initial sequence—the crushing, shrieking terror—would again rake her soul.

Never had she imagined a cruelty this horrific. She learned on the third day—or was it the fourth?—that if she stared not *at* the images, but *through* them, she could will her mind to find safer—

Oh. There was Adara. Her sweet little face. Frozen in time. In death.

Remember her in life! Remember! She must. For she did not want her family relegated to ashes and brittle stillness forever. Adara. So lively. Belly-birthed laughter and carefree chatter. Once she had danced down the field back to Stratios, slashing and twirling with the practice sword Kersei had used to spar with machitis.

"You spoil her." Darius's words rang clear, strong. So much that Kersei lifted her head. Looked around, expecting to find him. And she did. Just not in person. He was there on the wall. His face handsome and framed by rustling sandy blonde curls. Matted with blood as he lay amid the ruin. A straight nose at an odd angle. Square jaw. Attractive, the youngest son of the medora had taken after his mother's side. Bright blue eyes, however, belonged to his father's line. And they were frozen as they stared forever up to the heavens.

He blinked.

She jolted, gaping at his likeness. *He blinked?* The screen shifted and changed to one of his guard. Also dead. Forever frozen in time here.

"Just hold fast." Darius again. The time he'd saved her when Bastien spooked and took off in a dead gallop for the cliffs of Kardia. Terror swept her. A cold breeze. Shouts lost in the wind. Kersei gritted her teeth. The javrod snatched from her hand, wrenching her shoulder. She screamed in a very girl-like manner. Something hard punched her chest. She went flying. Landed. Air knocked from her lungs. The world went dark.

His voice warbled. He touched her arm.

Kersei clapped onto his person.

"Hey!"

The world shuddered.

The face before her transformed from one of concern to anger. From Darius to— "Oy, you all right then?"

She shook her head to clear her thoughts. Saw the close-shorn head scowling at her. The guard. "What?"

"You were screaming."

I was?

"So go quiet with that because you're scaring the medics."

She looked to the open door, to freedom. But then his broad back filled it and once more, it closed. A hiss slid through the chamber. And only in that tiny second did she realize the deafening noise clogging her ears—silence. The walls were blank.

Which meant—requeuing.

"No no no."

Timbers roared to life. Groaning.

Sobbing, Kersei covered her ears as the remindings began all over again.

VOLANTE ORBITING STATION, SYMMACHIA

Shackled like a criminal as the *Damocles* docked on the orbiting station, Tigo was led by 225 off the light cruiser toward the suspension bridge that connected the docking arms to the main hub of the satellite. White arches served as supports for expansive windows that afforded a pristine and unencumbered view of the Kedalion Quadrant.

Disembarking first, Baric eyed them over his shoulder. "You know where to take him." With that, he left.

Spying the small gray blip in the distance, Tigo hesitated. Tryssinia. No doubt Teeli was working hard to protect the Droseran girl. What would it cost her? He hadn't considered that before. Willfully, their kiss invaded his thoughts. How she'd responded … The unpretentious, sensible chief medical officer had all but said she wouldn't look at him twice. But that kiss contradicted her words.

"Get moving."

A jolt through the cuffs reminded Tigo of a more pressing mission: his own freedom. "Unnecessary," he said to Cleve, whose now-broken nose added to his sneer.

They entered the receiving area, a massive immigration way station clogged with hundreds seeking shelter after Balasi Quadrant had been hit hard by a star-gone-supernova. Kedalion was their best option, since Herakles and

Amphion were farther out.

As members of the Security Forces and Tertian High Council, 225 escorted Tigo past the weary souls and long lines—earning boos and grumbles—to a side vestibule. Scanned and cleared, they boarded a military transport and anchored Tigo near a portal with a view of Lycurgus, the nearest moon.

"Shuttle Five Five," radio chatter filled the cabin where the team sat on benches, "you are cleared to land at Dock Alpha Delta Three Three Four One."

Alpha Delta? What in the black were they doing heading to the Coalition headquarters? "That's a mistake," he said quietly to Cleve, trying to warn him. Because while Tigo might rub a lot of people wrong, he was the son of the fleet admiral and well-liked by most of the admiralty.

But Cleve's gaze sharpened, the words apparently taken as a challenge. "Says you."

"I know my father. If he gets wind—"

"Shut it!" Cleve tapped into his channeler—was it Tigo's imagination or did the major look nervous? Maybe worried Tigo was right? Soon came the blue glow of a response, and the arrogance returned. Was Baric already in the hall?

Docked, they disembarked down the sterile corridor. Bay doors whispered back and delivered them to the south entrance of the atrium. Awe struck him every time he saw the gilt arches of the hall winging up a hundred stories high to catch the glorious gold orb. The powerful design symbolized their sun, Melanthius.

A hard yank on his arm spiked pain through his shoulder and wrist. When Tigo stumbled, Cleve growled and pulled harder.

Enough. Tigo planted a foot. Clasped his hands and rammed them at the major's gut.

Oof! Cleve stumbled, but caught himself. Snapped up his weapon.

Weapon aimed at his head, Tigo winced at the jagged darts of fire from the cuffs.

"*What* is this?"

The familiar bark drew Tigo up straight as he turned to Cleve. "Tried to warn you this was a mistake, bringing me here."

"Explain yourself, Major!" Domitas Deken, epaulets glinting with his rank and experience, stalked beneath a row of arches. Lips flat, chin tucked, he spared not an ounce of his outrage. "Why is Commander Deken in shock cuffs?"

"He's under arrest, sir."

"Under arrest." His father's gray eyes blazed. "So not convicted."

Cleve hesitated, realizing his misstep. "Not yet, sir."

"And what does Article 51.987 of the Code of Justice state, Major?"

Now Cleve lowered his head. "Any officer charged but not convicted of a crime must be treated with the same respect as one not charged, save the appropriate internment and military escort."

With those flat lips and annoyed, hooded eyes, his father made his anger obvious. "Then why is Commander Deken in cuffs and paraded like a convicted criminal?"

"I—"

"Would you be treated so poorly after all you have earned and attained, Major? Release him! Do we not owe each other more respect than to yank an Eidolon commander around like a dog on a leash through halls we hold sacred?"

"Captain Bar—"

"I'm taking custody of Commander Deken."

Chin down, Cleve worked to contain his humiliation as he freed the cuffs, never once lifting his gaze.

"Tell Captain Baric to report to me immediately." Admiral Deken pivoted, his gaze finding Tigo's for only a second. "With me."

Rubbing his wrists, Tigo kept his ego in check, knowing his own dressing down was coming. Falling in step behind his father, he noted how those epaulets only magnified the man and the weight he carried as admiral of the fleet. Though his hair had grayed, there was no loss of vigor or acuity. Domitas Deken had earned his position because he was the best.

And his son? Well, there was a reason Tigo had been assigned to the outer reaches of Herakles.

TSC *MACEDON*

See through it, not to it. See through it, not to it. Kersei repeated the mantra over and over as the images spliced her thoughts. Adara once again ran the stone steps of the house, her laughter reverberating through the dark passages.

Why are they dark? They're never dark.

It's night.

No. It's day—see? The window shows daylight.

Kersei shifted on the thin mattress that served as a bed. Her mind wobbled a bit, as if she were falling. She jerked, but realized she was sitting. How could she fall while sitting? Just for good measure, she leaned her head back against the screen wall. And saw Ma'ma swirl in her gauzy coral dress, looking over her shoulder at Kersei.

No, not me.

Ma'ma turned and saw someone. Spoke. The words seemed to fight their way past the billowing smoke and howl of the wind. "We trusted you. Why would you do this? How could you?"

The sharp words seared the courage from Kersei. *I didn't. I didn't do it, Ma'ma.*

"The dagger of your guilt is there in your hand!"

Kersei glanced down and saw the blade resting in her palm, a gift from Father.

No. Not a gift. This blade … it was familiar. Etched. The blade serrated. Arcs.

Steel melted into black arcs and snakes, which crawled up her arm. Her breast beat the drums of panic. Breathless, she hiked up onto her knees on the cold stone floor of the hall. "No, Ma'ma. It wasn't me. I didn't—help me!"

The arcs dug into her skin with painful barbs. Infused her flesh with heat. Crying out, she clutched her arm to her chest.

"If you had given one thought to the rest of us!" Lexina's chastisement snapped through the imaging.

"You're a bad liar, Kersei." Darius.

"I'm not." Tears blurred her vision as she tried to remind herself this wasn't real, but the room jarred again. Like it was trying to get away from her terrible, murderous heart.

I'm no murderer!

See through it … see … The walls aflame. Timbers crackling and popping in surrender. She'd done that. Killed them all.

She gripped her head, fisting clumps of thick black waves, and curled in on herself. "No!" she screamed. "It wasn't me!"

Beams fell. Screams shrieked, and she joined them.

For a deprivation chamber, the Engram wasn't depriving Teeli or the girl of the terror. Teeli told herself to turn off the feed, stop listening, but doing that felt as calloused as the security officers standing over the girl's torment with those flat expressions.

A thought stole into Teeli's mind. She snatched a steel canister and stalked toward the chamber. She cleared the corner, and glowered at the two security officers.

The one on the right—Hankin—straightened, hand going to his stunner. The other drew up behind him, watching her approach.

Adrenaline and dread speared her stomach. "I want to see her." No, *want* wasn't relevant.

"Sorry, Doc—"

"I am the chief medical officer on this ship, and as such, I am not only responsible for the care of the crew—"

"She's not crew," Billings countered, his gaze dark.

"—but also for anyone brought aboard." She huffed, her heart trying to climb out of her chest. "Open it. Let me do a wellness check."

"Sorry, Dr. Knowles," Hankin said with a cockeyed nod. "I respect your concern, but this door stays locked under Captain Baric's orders. You'll have to—"

"Do you understand that as chief medical officer, I have authority over what happens in my medical bay?"

"You do, ma'am," he said with a nod, "but not to give or countermand our orders, and while this chamber is in the bay, it is not classified as medical."

Implacable. She fisted the wand, working her options. Wondering … Could she take them? She felt desperate enough.

"I think you were about to give a patient medicine," Hankin said, his gaze drifting to her tightly fisted hand. A message that he knew what she was thinking.

Wetting her lips, Teeli nodded. Took a step away. Then flung back, arm flying up on its own to stab his shoulder with the wand.

Instead, she found herself spun around, face slammed into the wall, arm restrained. She whimpered at the pain radiating through her shoulder.

"I like you, Doc. You care." Hankin's voice never elevated. Never changed. He was the epitome of calm. "That's … different out here in the black." His breath huffed against her face. "But if you try that again, I can't promise I'll let it go next time."

"Oy! What's going on?"

Hankin stepped off and Teeli righted herself, smoothing her coat and erratic heart rhythm as she lifted her chin. "I will hold you both responsible if that girl has any deterioration in her health, physical or mental."

"Doctor?" Lieutenant Sidra sidled up next to her.

Stretching her shoulder, Teeli gave the security detail another glower and started walking.

"Doc."

She stopped at the security officer's call, and when she faltered, she felt the lieutenant's touch at her elbow. Teeli did not want to look back, but …

"Thought you might need this." Hankin held out the sedative wand. Her guilt hung in the air between them.

The lieutenant grabbed it and followed Teeli back to her office. Shut the door.

Teeli dropped into the nearest chair, only then realizing how much the adrenaline dump had drained her. She rubbed her face.

"Did you try to drug him?" Jez asked with a disbelieving laugh.

"I was desperate," she admitted with a rueful smile. "The girl screams and cries all hours of the day. She's losing her mind, and I'm losing mine watching her. This should be considered psychological warfare." She shuddered. "I can't take it anymore."

The lieutenant squatted and rested a hand on her knee. "Let the Two-one-five help."

Teeli looked into the gold eyes of Commander Deken's first officer and saw a lifeline there. "How?" Dare she hope?

"Give me time to talk to the others. We'll figure something out."

"Why?" Teeli fought a yawn. "Why would you risk … everything?"

"Because the commander asked us to." She lifted a thin shoulder in a shrug. "But mostly because it's wrong. That girl isn't guilty." She jutted her jaw toward the monitor. "Tell me everything you know about that machine."

QRIMONT, SYMMACHIA

House arrest sounded nicer than it was. About to climb the walls, Tigo paced. His father had deposited him almost four days ago when they'd arrived from Volante. He refused to hear him, refused to even stay with him, opting instead for his quarters at Command. Tigo spent that time trying to hack a data channeler to no avail. His father had been prepared, right down to the security officers at the front door and the servant's entrance at the side of their home.

After a good workout, Tigo resumed his efforts with the channeler. He had to get a comm out. Tonight was the gala. Then he'd stand before the tribunal on Baric's trumped-up charges. Well, mostly trumped-up. It didn't surprise him, really. Baric needed grounds to get Tigo off the ship—at least, that was Tigo's guess. Whatever was going on with the Engram, he didn't want Tigo figuring it out. Which was all the more reason to dig. He growled at the circuit board and running code on the screen. He'd never been skilled with tech like Diggs, but he hadn't failed the courses either.

Hearing the unmistakable voice of his father outside the door, he powered off the channeler and moved to the bay of windows.

The door hissed open and his father stormed in, saw Tigo and stopped, his brow furrowed in suspicion. His gaze fell on the channeler on the table. He huffed. "Just can't leave it alone, can you?"

"Dad, I—"

"That!" His father pivoted on him, eyes ablaze and lips tight. "Is your mistake."

Tigo took a step back, this anger too familiar. He had to placate him, be submissive so he'd listen.

"'I' should never be the first word out of your mouth after all you've done. Categorically ruining your career by disobeying orders—"

"Dis—I was *following* orders!"

"—and striking a Coalition officer."

"I—" He snapped his mouth shut.

"What have I always told you?" his father demanded, then flapped a hand. "I don't have time for this."

"You never do," Tigo growled. "Not for me. But this isn't about me. That isn't why I'm here."

"You're here because Baric filed charges against you."

"They're using it, Dad. They're using the Engram."

Something flickered through the admiral's stony expression. His gray eyes bored through Tigo's defenses. Then he started toward the hall.

"Did you hear me?" Tigo followed, furious. "There's an Engram on the *Macedon*. They're using it. First on the Kynigos Krissos sent me after and now on the Droseran girl. Neither had a trial nor any judicial process—and they weren't part of the TSC, so how in the black is he carrying out a punishment on them?"

Flinging open the closet door, his father was growling. Then he stopped short again. Glanced back. "Kynigos?" His eyebrows rose in fury. "Drosero?

You went to Nine!"

"On Krissos's orders to retrieve the hunter. He never told me—"

"No!" His father stuffed a hand between them. "This isn't happening. We can't do this. I can't—I *must* remain impartial."

"Impartial?" Tigo balked. "Wouldn't want to be swayed by facts now, would we? I mean, the truth can get emotional. Or how about the fact your son is being set up?"

"Enough! I am late." His father's shout prowled the slick walls as he emerged with his uniform. "Save that story for your tribunal."

Futility pulsed through Tigo. "Baric is using the Engram," he repeated in exasperation. "How are you not hearing me say that? You voted it against it, Dad. At least on that we saw eye to eye. That girl won't last in it!"

"Stop."

"Why? Am I bothering your conscience? Or do you even have one anymore? This is a crime against humanity! It's cruel—"

"Enough!" His father's chest heaved, then he grabbed shoes and started for the door. "The case against you is significant, Commander Deken." The admiral always resorted to ranks when he didn't want to deal with hard truths. "Your mother would be ashamed!"

When his father stormed out of the residence, Tigo hung his head. That had not gone according to plan. But his father had acted as if he hadn't heard. Or maybe, he had … but …

Augh! But what? He's the admiral of the slagging fleet! Why wouldn't he want to know about this? Rubbing his knuckles, he worked the details he knew.

Fact 1: Krissos had given him orders to drop to Nine. Extract a fugitive. One he never revealed to be Kynigos. After a fight, they returned with the fugitive.

Fact 2: Baric took custody of said fugitive without authorization.

Fact 3: Baric has possession and utilization of an Engram chamber and placed the Kynigos in said chamber.

Fact 4: A girl found adrift on a stolen corvette was—by Baric and without a uniform Code trial—determined guilty and placed in the chamber after the Kynigos had been removed.

Fact 5: The Kynigos went missing from the *Macedon.*

Fact 6: Baric set up Tigo to take the fall by reporting him to TSCn Command for violation of the Codes and entering a noncompliant planet's orbit without authorization.

Fact 7: His father set the tribunal date for after the Launch Gala.

He wandered to the windows that had a spectacular view of Kaj's mile-wide waterfall. With a sigh, he dropped his forehead against the glass and groaned. He couldn't get the pieces to come together. He was missing something.

Movement in the courtyard three levels below snagged his attention. People milling—no, working. Serving staff. Tables lined with flowers and silver trays.

The Launch Gala. Right here.

If he could get down there ... he could talk to councilmembers. Maybe get them to hear him out. What if they were all like his father and closed their ears? No, there had to be *someone* who would listen. But how could he get out when his father had placed him in lockdown? He paced beneath a stifling sense of futility.

His channeler buzzed. He flicked his wrist and saw the IDent code of the caller. Surprised at the range, he tapped his comm, opening the line. "Doctor."

"Yeh, no."

He started. "Jez. How—"

"They're blocking your comms, so Diggs got some friends to bounce our signal around the whole boiling 'verse to reach you via the doc's IDent."

"Probably because I'm under house arrest here."

"So he listened, huh? Such a loving father, yeh?"

"It's scuzzed." But she wouldn't be calling just to shoot the breeze. "What's going on?"

"That guest you wanted me to look after?"

The Droseran girl.

"She's not doing well."

The wad of frustration in his gut bloated. "I can't do anything from here."

"Soon she won't even know her name."

Tigo balled his fist. "I'm under house arrest," he said again, turning and walking the perimeter of the living area. "I face the tribunal in two days."

"I'm not sure you'll have a guest to come back to."

"What do you want me to do?" he growled, hating the violence in his voice but unable to prevent it. "I'm locked in!"

She scoffed. "Never stopped you before. You're there for a reason, remember." Jez ended the transmission.

He cursed and thumped the wall. The first day, he even tried the dumb waiter—which made him dumb. He'd grown a bit since he'd rode it down at ten years old. But he couldn't do nothing. Couldn't let that girl suffer. He wouldn't be able to defend her or make his case in the tribunal because he'd be sealed in a soundproof box, his microphone only turned on when they deemed it time for him to speak. It made for a streamlined process, but made it harder to make your case when someone could silence you on a whim.

He snatched up the channeler and considered it again. Tapped it, light from the windows flinging up in his face from the way he waved it. He considered closing the curtains.

Wait. Balcony. He hurried to the sliding glass panel and swiped it. Nothing happened. As expected. But what if … Tigo pried off the casing and hotwired it, sending a crosscurrent that popped the circuitry. A definitive *schink* rattled the glass door.

Tigo grinned. Using brute force, which he had plenty of, he slid back the door. Hope pulled him onto the stone terrace where he glanced over the rail. And snorted. Security—posted directly below. He bit back a curse.

Yes … *below.* But not above.

He craned his neck back and looked up. The balcony overhead—did the senator still live there? She always was soft on him. Tigo raced back inside, changed into a uniform, and returned to the balcony. He toed the rail, careful not to kick anything off and have a rock tap security on the shoulder. On the rail, the concrete pillar at his back blocked the view of him. He thanked his Eidolon endurance and strength training as he jumped to catch the upper ledge. Dug in and hauled himself up, cringing when he heard the scrape of stone against his uniform. Didn't need to get written up for disorderly appearance.

He climbed over the edge. Turned to the window and stilled.

Senator Rasmussen stood in her living room with a wine glass in hand, gaping.

Tigo fastened a smile on his face. "I locked myself out. Can you let me through?"

She rolled her eyes and allowed him inside. "You really expect me to believe that lie—again?"

Tigo could not keep a serious face.

"But go on," she said with a wave. "I know there's no stopping you. I heard every tale from your mom."

Tigo bent and kissed her cheek. "No wonder you were her best friend." He hurried to the front door.

"Tigo."

He turned as he tugged it open. "If you want answers, ask Acrisius."

"I will kill you for this, man!"

Teeli looked up from the nurse's station, where she was signing off on a script, and saw two of Tigo's Eidolon storming the hall. *What in the 'verse?* Her heart skipped a beat—not at the man's bare chest smeared with blood, but at the only reason that really could have brought them here: they'd found a solution. She tucked her work aside. "What is going on?"

"Fool cut me while we were sparring," Rhinnock said.

"Guess you forgot to block," the older man shot back.

Jez was behind them, and when the two were about to go to blows, drawing the attention of security, she stepped between them. "I need to know if this will exempt him from duty."

"If I get pulled, he's going down." Rhinn glowered at Diggins.

"If you think you're big enough."

Before Teeli could comprehend it, the two were shoving and punching each other. Startled screams broke out in the corridor. Jez tried to separate them, but … couldn't. The two rolled and shoved, knocking over equipment.

"Help us!" Jez shouted.

And the two security officers were there, prying the men apart. Each held back an Eidolon and aimed stunners at them. Teeli sucked in a breath. The Eidolon hesitated, considering the security officers.

"You realize I'm trained to disarm wannabe cops like you," Rhinn snarled.

Jez slapped his chest. "Oy! Stand down!"

Teeli shuddered, but movement past the chaotic scene caught her attention. She almost reacted at what she saw—the larger, older Eidolon they called AO emerged from the Engram with the girl curled in his arms. She held her breath, afraid they'd be seen.

"Thank you, Hankin," Jez said with a lot of emphasis. She turned a glower to her two buddies. "Move—down to the bay."

Would his father have guards there, too? Hesitation held him fast as he palmed the access panel. The door slid aside silently. A dank hall stretched down the fourth floor. Tigo made for the nearest elevator. He stepped in and hustled to the main level, just outside the gathering hall. At a series of double doors, hundreds of officials and officers were making their way inside.

Hesitating—but not long—Tigo suddenly wanted to pray to the god his mother believed in. This was a lot of brass. A lot of ways to get caught. Yet he made his way through a double-door entrance with nothing more than a nod from the cadets standing sentry. Like with any high-risk infiltration, he assessed possible exfils and means for distraction or cover. This was why being in space benefitted him—the youngers didn't recognize him.

Scanning as he swam the sea of uniforms and gowns, he searched for robes and the ridiculous elliptical hats the High Council members wore, supposedly designed to represent the Kedalion Quadrant. To Tigo, they made the wearers look like their heads had been stretched, warped by too much time in space.

At a refreshment station, he eyed the prepared drinks. Then the bartender. "Pure cordi?"

The man curled his lip as he reached for a glass.

"Still stuck on your fruit juice, I see." The sultry voice belonged to Alestra Galt, stunning in the long black gown of the dress *As* with its bolero-style jacket and epaulets that marked her a lieutenant colonel.

Tigo shrugged. "Old habits." Did she know he was basically a fugitive? Was that why she was talking to him?

"Guess you missed the part where they are supposed to *die* hard."

The bartender delivered the glass of thick liquid with a grimace and Tigo inhaled the tangy spiced aroma. He sipped and started away from the stand.

Alestra slid her hand into the crook of his arm. "So. House arrest again, eh? More old habits?"

He fought the urge to stiffen. "Like you said, I forgot they were supposed to die." He eyed the snug dress. "You look good after popping a kid."

She rolled her eyes. "That was four years ago, Tigo."

Oops. "Compliment still stands."

Smiling, she shook her head as they glided around the crowds. "So, why would you be here? Looking for trouble?"

"Yes, and if you see him, let me know." His pulse thumped his ribs hard when he spotted his father, but Alestra guided him in another direction. He frowned at her, but she never broke stride or smile. By one of the marble pillars, she swirled so they faced the throng. Her expression went … strange.

"You okay?"

"Not in a long time." She let a long pause settle between them, fat and familiar. They'd been friends for years. Things had gotten romantic once, but they both decided it wasn't for them. "Aren't you going to ask me to dance?"

"Won't Calvin kill me if I do?"

"Cal's been dead for twelve months."

He jolted. "*What?*" Man, he really had to get his head out of the black.

A shadow passed through her expression, but in a blink, it was gone. "So? Dance?"

Wondering at that shadow, Tigo took her on a turn around the floor. It made sense—would make him less conspicuous and enable him to get a pulse on this crowd.

Her eyes hit his. Filled with meaning. With … knowledge. And fear. So much fear. Then her gaze skipped away, restless. "When I saw you enter," she said just loud enough to be heard over the din, "I felt hope for the first time in ages."

"Hope?" Tigo snorted. "I think you meant dope."

"Well, that was understood." Though she smiled, there wasn't one in her words. Or the tense way she held his hand. What was going on? "So much has changed." She looked at the voltcuff. Then him. "Obviously not you."

"Hey, someone has to keep Marine Security Forces on their toes."

"Any special ladies?"

Where had that question come from? "Aren't all ladies special?" And why did Jez's face invade his mind's eye?

Alestra laughed. "That's my Tigo."

"I have to talk to Krissos. Or any of the Council about …" Telling her would make her complicit. It was more knowledge she didn't need with a kid to provide for.

"This is a bad time, Tigo."

"What I need to talk about—there's never a good time."

As the song ended, he saw General Gilpin and for the first time since he'd set boot on Symmachia, he thought he might have a chance. Gilpin had always been tough but reasonable.

Alestra caught his arm. "Be careful, Tigo."

Something in her voice pulled him back to her, concerned. "What's wrong? You've been—"

"Things are … happening. A lot has changed since the *Macedon* deployed." She watched the crowd until her gaze finally settled on the councilmembers.

Her green eyes came to his. "Sometimes, what we scientists discover during exploration isn't what we thought."

"Alestra—"

"Haven't you ever wondered why Command sent a *battle cruiser* to Herakles?"

The rote answer rang in his head—to represent the Council and show an unwavering means of defending the quadrants so the reluctant would feel safe and join the alliance. "What're you saying?"

"You know well what I'm saying," Alestra said in a low voice. Her gaze shifted over his shoulder. "And if you want to stay out of the brig, I suggest you duck out of sight."

He tensed. And quickly made his exit, slipping around a column and drifting into another group, which enabled him to catch sight of Commander Bedth and his goons storming toward Alestra. "Where is he?"

Tigo hated that he had left her with trouble, but she was more than capable of handling it. As for him, he navigated his way to the front dais. Toward Krissos.

Musty. Damp. Sweet, sugary—by the table, probably cakes. But too recent. He closed his eyes and probed for the older lingering scents. There, subtle but ... insistent. Spices. Yes, that would suit a hunter better, since most of their meals at the Citadel were prepared by a Sargosi chef.

"I shouldn't be doing th—"

"Shh." Marco snapped a hand at the lodge worker, silencing him. Angling his gaze down and to the side, he shifted to where an old wooden frame held a tattered mattress. A far cry from the firmer ones in more upscale accommodations. But this? It suited a hunter used to the simple Citadel provisions. Luxuries clogged the mind with comfort. Dulled instincts and training.

He pressed a fingertip to the blanket. Closed his eyes again and drew in a long, testing breath. Many scents here. The more recent patrons. A couple of females. Mostly male. But where ...

He moved to the bedhead. And smiled. The *vestigi,* a remnant only the most skilled could detect, of Polyeidus mingled with that of the chatelaine who'd given Marco the monocle.

"If they find out I let you in here—"

"They will not. Unless you reveal it." Marco pivoted toward the employee, but when he did, a strange, unusual scent whipped out. He glanced over his shoulder, searching.

Marginal. Nearly gone. Clinging to some remnant in this room. What was it?

"The room is already let. All are, and my boss will be very angry if he knows you were in a room let by someone."

All? Marco's investigation gave way to curiosity. "All are let? I've never known the Lower District to be heavily patronized."

"It's the Elysium."

Marco frowned. What did the coliseum have to do with crowds?

The manager winged up his eyebrows and thrust a hand toward the towering edifice in the distance. "The Caucus for Intelligent Expansion?

Only the largest gathering of politicians and representatives to talk about Symmachia's influence and impact. There've been riots and parties the likes of which none of us have ever seen, especially among the Thyrolians. All in a rage over the loss of business for their shipwrights."

Marco peered out the window to the Elysium perched on the hills. Its metal silvery-white façade glared down on the lessers and the business center.

Voices came in the hall.

"Stay here. If they see you ..."

When the worker rushed to the door, Marco took to the window. Eyed the shutters lining the hotel's exterior plaster wall and leapt. He caught the edge of one and pitched himself to the left, down to the next level, then eyed the distance to the cobbled alley. With a swing, he vaulted sideways. Landed with his knees bent, feet apart, instinctively *anak'ing*.

A commotion lured him into the alley, where there came a pounding of hooves. Horses. Here in Zlares? One of the largest, busiest space ports in the quadrants? The combined cadence of the riders proved thunderous and drew Cenoans from homes and shops as the cannonade of riders continued through the city. The greater surprise came in the attire and the blonde hair of the riders. They were not local.

The gray-blue stained leathers and white shirts set them as a sect.

"Droseran," he breathed, the realization pulling Marco along with them. Assessing.

Heavily tanned and brawny, the contingent moved up the main street with confidence and a compelling presence. What were their thoughts about the girl—his quarry? Were these men the reason the iereas knew she would eventually be here?

When they turned the corner and slipped out of sight, Marco cut through a smaller street and jogged up to a fountain. He slid into place as the three front riders approached. At the center, the leader wore a leathered cuirass and double baldric that formed a bold X across his chest. Rows of braids, silver-white and dyed gray-blue, were tied back. His beard also bore the silver-gray pattern. A calloused hand held a loose, casual grip on the reins. The other hand was fisted and rested on his leg. The man was sure of himself, a fighter. Notable were the mounts—no need for them on Cenon, so the procession was a message.

Again, Marco considered the double baldric. Stained white, studded with silver and securing the man's large sword to his back and a dagger at his hip, the X was glaring. X for Xanthus. So Kalonican. While all within the armies of Kalonica were machitis—warriors—there were different general types. Stratios were trained primarily in hand-to-hand. Xanthus on mounts. The Plisiázon of the south were swift and silent on their feet, cunning and ruthless in protecting the border against the blue raiders.

Droserans. At the Caucus. Intriguing!

Staying to the shadows, Marco eyed the man on the leader's right. Same double baldric, but silver and without ornamentation. His beard was thick and tightly trimmed. The leader's eldest son, no doubt. Hair more sandy blond than white like the others, he wore braids that melted into the beard and the rest hung wild.

Wild. Aye. Good word for this one. Strong ridged brow and a gaze that bordered on fury and apathy at the same time. He enjoyed this display of their people.

Marco refused to break eye contact, forcing the Xanthus warrior to look away as they passed.

A thump just behind Marco's earlobe pulled him from the procession. He depressed the spot and angled down an alley.

"You're on Cenon."

Marco hesitated at the voice of the master hunter, who rarely thumped him. It was the responsibility of his advocate to monitor him. Why did Roman sound perturbed? "Scouted Ylont earlier this week, but it was a waste—save the chatelaine who gave me the intel on Polyeidus."

"And mentioned Zlares."

"Aye. I checked where he lodged and caught his vestigi but nothing else."

"Why would he be there? He had no Decree."

"Maybe he knew someone was hunting him. It's busy here." Marco broke into a trot, his muscles tight from the tension on the street. "Good place to hide."

He caught a low-slung rail and hauled himself up onto a rooftop. Sprinted to the next building and did the same, rising with each one until he was nearly at eye level with the Elysium roof a few blocks north. "I just encountered the Xanthus."

"That—" Roman fell silent. "How many?"

"Roughly a dozen that I saw. Here for the Caucus." Marco spied a temple spire and started for it. "Did you know of it?"

"It is of no consequence to us."

"If the Xanthus are here—"

"A coincidence."

Nay. The large stone blocks lining the wall of the temple proved easy to scale, and Marco perched atop the spire without breaking a sweat. He stared down at the Elysium, taking a mental inventory of the arrivals. "I'm sorry, Master, but there is no such thing. Not on a hunt."

"Aye, a *hunt*, but you are not hunting the Xanthus."

He eyed the throng in the temple courtyard. "I am in the right place. I can sense it. Perhaps her accomplice is here. There are Thyrolians and Okariens."

"Give care. Many among the Caucus do not approve of the Brethren."

The stern glare of the Xanthus first son hit his thoughts. "Understood." He unhitched the monocle from his vambrace. Peering far below into the crowds, he skipped the green-hued Okariens, who had drawn a crowd of onlookers. To the Cyroxians. To the …

Heat flared across his arm. He focused on the red and white robes dusting the road. "Why are iereas here?"

"It is an Ierean temple."

"*Defunct* temple. Zlarens ran them out long ago. It is now a place of commerce." His arm grew warmer. Balling his fist, he tried to ignore it. "This …" He blinked, beads of sweat squeezing from beneath his armor. It was getting hotter. Harder to focus. He growled.

"You well, Marco?"

White-knuckling through the explosion did nothing. "Aye." He gritted his teeth. "I must go." He tapped the thumper, ending the transmission. Dropped back inside the small landing of the tower spire. Fell against the cold stone. Worked the vambrace buckle.

As he lifted it, the fire receded, making it feel as if there'd been a cool breeze. A faint blue seeped through the black mark beneath his sleeve, which sweat stuck to his skin. He ran his hand tentatively over the arcs and lines as it again gradually darkened.

What the mark meant, what significance it held, had been lost when he was brought to the Citadel, where boys replaced familial sentiments and memories with training and Codes. Flexing his hand, he wondered at the timing of the heat. Just when he'd seen the iereas. Again. Coincidence?

There is no coincidence in the hunt.

TSC *MACEDON*

"He'll be livid."

"When isn't he? Besides, he has to find out first." Teeli glanced through the small window of the alembicus to the dark-haired girl who lay unconscious, her body receiving vital nutrients and antibiotics since they'd pulled her from the Engram. The airtight neural network snaked cannula, IVs, and nanites into her body, keeping pathogens out and the healing nanites contained. "But even with that fast light craft the captain took to Symmachia, we have at least another week before their return."

Running scans and tests through the alembicus, Teeli studied the results. Prayed she had not waited too long to remove the girl. When she was satisfied she was in healthier form, she entered the code. A schematic of the girl's body showed a million-plus tiny dots vacating her body and seeping into a tube running along the perimeter of the medical capsule.

"Vitals are stable and strong," Zilla reported.

With a nod, Teeli entered another code. Palmed the security panel and finalized the protocol. "She'll be awake within the hour." Exhaustion gripped her as she considered what the girl's state of mind would be like after all that trauma. "Let me know—"

The room tilted. Pain hammered her temples. Teeli gripped her forehead, tripping into the alembicus. Weakness claimed her limbs, ate at her focus.

She needed to …

The thought fled her grasp. What was she doing? She squinted, staring at the gray hull of the alembicus. Great Flames, her head hurt.

"Doctor?"

Someone was standing in front of her. Someone … *Don't I know her?*

"Dr. Knowles?"

She blinked and with it, her thoughts stabilized. "Zilla."

"Yes?"

Oh good. "Zilla, we need …" Her hand rested on the alembicus. That's right—the girl. "Commander Deken …" Why was it so hard to think?

A look of concerned puzzlement crossed Zilla's face. "They arrested him and took him to Symmachia. Remember?"

"Right. I know." How could she have forgotten? "I meant his first officer."

"Lieutenant Sidra."

Jealousy pangs struck Teeli, which was absurd. The commander was a ladies' man, but the way he looked at his first officer … "Yes." Lieutenant Sidra was the right choice. "I'll wave her." She looked at the capsule again. "Notify me when she's awake."

"Yes, Doctor."

Teeli returned to her office, thinking of the young Eidolon who had taken the girl's place—to avoid sensors alerting Baric and so Kersei could get rest and treatment. She was thankful and relieved the fight had not been hers alone.

Teeli reviewed scans and notes on her other fifteen patients. Authorized the return to duty for two officers, denied one still battling Thyrolian sickness, and then sent the summons for physicals for other crewmembers. A smile hit her—Commander Deken's name was listed. Like a fury, the memory of their moment barreled over her. She rested her forehead on her desk and sighed, allowed herself to relive that one tiny moment of happiness. The warmth of his touch. His strong arms. His groan when he'd caught her mouth.

And yet—he'd *pretended*. All of it? Was it really just pretense? It felt like … more.

"Hey." He hung in the doorway now. The light combat armor molded beautifully to his muscular torso. "I can't stop thinking about us." He unhinged his chest plate armor. Dropped it on the chair. Grinned. "Thought we could finish what we started."

Teeli came to her feet. Stumbled. Relieved he hadn't given up on her. He tugged her tight against his chest. When had he taken off his shirt? Warm and teasing, his lips traced her jaw and neck.

Thunk. Thunk.

"*Hellooo?*"

Teeli jerked upright, the dream vanquished. Tigo gone. But not the tingling that clung to her. The form in the doorway took shape. "Lieutenant Sidra."

"Sorry to wake you, Doc." She was smiling. There was no way she could know the dream Teeli had just experienced. "You asked for me?"

On shaky, adrenaline-heavy legs, Teeli stood. "Shut the door, please."

The lieutenant complied. "Is the girl okay?"

"Yes, relatively," Teeli said with a sigh. "Thanks to you and the Two-one-five, she's getting rest her body desperately needed. The poor girl hasn't had a quiet moment since she found out about her family. She hasn't even been allowed to grieve, instead enduring the horrific images of her family's deaths." She brushed back her hair. "But this may all be in vain since we will eventually have to put her back …"

"Those images," Jez said with her lilting accent, "are brutal. I'm not sure Esq can handle that regularly."

"Nobody can—which is why I'm so determined to figure something out."

Teeli stifled a yawn as her comms intoned. "Yes?"

"Doctor, she's waking."

Teeli met the lieutenant's gaze. "I'm on my way."

"Did you need something?" Jez asked as reached for the door handle.

Head clearing, Teeli lifted her flex screen to carry with her. "We may not agree on some things, and you may not like me—"

"What I don't like is the way you distract the commander."

"—but Commander Deken trusts you, so I do too." *The way I distract him?* She eyed the woman, curious about that comment. Was it jealousy? Did she know he'd kissed her? Under pretense, but still … "Your assistance with this situation more than convinces me to trust you. I hope you'll extend me the same courtesy."

As if coming to a decision, Sidra motioned with her hand. "We can't pull her out all the time. But we are working on something."

"Walk with me," Teeli said as she stepped into the hall. "You say that wound looks infected?" she said as distraction as they swept past the security detail outside the Engram.

Jez flashed wide eyes at her. "He's saying it is. I'm not convinced."

"It's likely not infected—it wasn't deep enough." She laughed as she led Jez around the corner and into the room with the alembicus.

Teeli glanced at the data on the flex screen and nodded to Zilla. "The numbers indicate she's surfacing."

"Surfacing?" Sidra asked. "Her eyes are open."

Teeli hurried forward, surprised when brown eyes followed her around the pod. She tapped in the sequence to open it. With a hiss and expel of chilled oxygenated air that rustled the girl's dark curly hair, the top parted, the halves receding into the base.

"Hello," Teeli said quietly, activating the translator in the flex screen, and heard her word repeated in the girl's tongue. "How are you feeling?"

Kersei's eyes widened. "I-I can't move."

"It's counterpressure," Teeli explained and gave the translator time to work, "responding to your suit. The magnets are in the sleeves of your medical gown. I'm afraid they were necessary since we weren't certain what your state of mind would be when you awoke."

"How did I get here? I-I don't … I don't remember … only …" Her chin bounced, eyes reddening with unshed tears. "I-I beg your mercy. I-I …"

Distraction would be the only way to keep the girl calm. "Kersei, are you hungry?"

She blinked, a tear slipping free. "I ... I don't know." Her stomach rumbled loudly.

Teeli laughed. "Well, your stomach does." She nodded. "I'm going to release the counterweights."

"You sure about this?" Sidra asked warily.

Teeli smiled. "Kersei, this is Lieutenant Sidra. She'll assist you once it releases. You can trust her—she's very *capable*." She paused, looking between the two until certain the girl and the warrior understood her meaning, then cancelled the magnetic field. "There."

With a grunt of relief, Kersei lifted her hands and rubbed her wrists.

Lieutenant Sidra helped her sit up and step out of the pod. The girl slid off the hard surface to the floor and wobbled slightly, using the alembicus and the officer for support.

"There are clothes for you there," Teeli said, pointing to the pile. "The partition is set up. Go ahead and change. We'll get you a food tray."

Wonderment filled young brown eyes that, Teeli guessed, had seen little and yet hoped for much. What was it like to live on a planet without technology? She guided the girl behind the screen, then turned, cancelling the translator and looking inquiringly at Sidra.

"She's like a child," Sidra said. "Ignorant—"

"*Innocent*," Teeli corrected. "I prefer to say she's innocent since she is intelligent but hasn't yet learned the hard truths we are so familiar with here in the black."

Kersei stood behind the screen, staring at the lavender-gray jumpsuit. So much like the short gown she now wore, the weight of the material leaden against her hopes. That suit meant she'd go back into the room with the pictures of her dead family. She dropped back against the wall. Felt a tremor race up her spine.

"Kersei? Are you okay? Do you need help?"

Covering her mouth, she fought the urge to cry. To scream. No ... no, she couldn't go back in there. She wouldn't. Digging her fingers into her palm, she gritted her teeth. She had to get out of here. But she couldn't. Who would help her? With her family dead, she had no one. A strangled cry forced its way up her throat.

A shadow loomed to her right.

Kersei jerked left, straight into the wall. Crashed against the screen, which toppled. "No! No! Leave me be!"

The lieutenant held her palms out and said something Kersei couldn't understand. Then a strange voice said, "Easy. I'm not here to hurt you."

The pharmakeia appeared and spoke. Again the voice came, translated. "Kersei, what's wrong?"

"I can't—" She tightened her mouth and fought the tears. "I can't go in there. I can't watch them die again. I can't."

The lieutenant drew closer, her dark brows knotted.

"Don't!" Kersei growled, feeling cornered.

"Kersei, listen to me," the pharmakeia said, "I need you to put that suit on because …" She sighed. "I am trying to help you, but if you wear different clothes and go back in the room, they will know I took you out. And…"

"If they know the doctor helped you," the lieutenant said, "she will lose her job, and nobody will be able to help you."

Kersei didn't want the woman to lose her job, but *she* would lose her mind if they put her back in there. "I cannot … I cannot see the creature anymore nor their empty faces."

The two women exchanged a glance.

"What creature?" the pharmakeia asked.

Kersei slumped on the floor and hugged her knees. Tears came greedily. She just wanted to go home. Just wanted to run into Father's arms. She'd be that daughter he wanted, the polite one in dresses and coils. Whatever it took. She'd do it, just to see his smile. Hear his laugh. Prove that they weren't really dead.

Someone touched her shoulder and Kersei jumped. Blinked up at the lieutenant, watching as she folded herself on the floor next to her. The pharmakeia rushed away as a knock sounded somewhere.

"Please do not make me go back," Kersei begged. It was unladylike and shamed her. But she … just could not.

"Your father was a warrior, yeh?" the woman asked.

Kersei considered her—what was her name? Lieutenant Sidra?—then gave a slow nod. "He is." She lifted her chin. "I refuse to believe those images are real. They cannot be dead."

Lieutenant Sidra shifted, her eyes frank. "I am a warrior, too—in the Marines." She was swathed in an unusual material that seemed improper for the way it molded her waist, hips, and breasts, yet nobody seemed surprised or astonished. "Sometimes we have to make painful sacrifices in skirmishes to win the greater battle."

Kersei studied the woman. Her words hollowed out the last vestige of courage she possessed. "You want me to go back in there."

"For now."

Kersei tore her gaze away, unable to bear the thought of reliving all that again. "They are not my memories. I did not do it. I should not have …"

The woman touched her arm. "We have a plan, but we need you to do this." She nodded toward the pharmakeia, who had returned. "Dr. Knowles is your biggest ally, Kersei. Trust her."

Tears burned and defied her command to die. She broke into sobs, and for the first time in what felt like cycles, she felt arms encircle her. Hold her. Kersei cried into the warrior's chest, realizing how very far from a warrior she had become.

ZLARES, CENON

"Symmachia goes too far!" a voice boomed from below.

High up in the rafters, Marco crouched and peered below to find the source of the objection. The Elysium had been sectioned into more than a dozen boxes, marking the groups by countries and worlds. Nearest the front were the Xanthus with the smallest contingent, yet they occupied much time in the debate.

"It is not merely Symmachia," the Xanthus declared. "But the Kynigos."

What was this? The words packed a punch that made Marco waver. Drosero held a limited accord with the Citadel. The Brethren were not allowed to accept Decrees to hunt on Drosero or for them, but they could pursue a fugitive should they go to ground on the planet.

A man in an orange headdress shaped like a half sun spoke from the main dais. "On what grounds do you blame the Kynigos?"

Ah, an ally for the Brethren. Good.

"The entolis of Kalonica have seen ships slipping into our world without permission over the last cycle, Mr. President."

Cycle—a whole year. And for this, he blames Kynigos?

"Are you so well versed with aircraft, Xanthus, that you can identify the craft belonging to the Kynigos?" the president asked in a monotone voice. "And what proof have you that a Kynigos piloted any of those crafts?"

"We have this!" The leader lifted something into the air.

Too far up to see what the Xanthus elder held, Marco detached his monocle and peered through it. He drew in a sharp breath. How had he come by a vambrace? First the chatelaine in Ylont had Polyeidus's monocle, now this Xanthus had another Kynigos's vambrace. Why were hunters separated from their most critical gear? The only way a hunter would allow that was in death.

Anger speared him, nearly had him descending to the floor of the Elysium to defend Kynigos honor. But then alarm trilled. This … this had implication. Far beyond what he could defend or question. It meant someone knew the value of the vambrace to a hunter. If a hunter discarded the gear, it was most likely to avoid being tracked through the embedded channeler. If not, then harm most definitely had come to whoever owned that vambrace. The Brethren must be warned.

"Elder Ares," the president proclaimed, "I appreciate both your anger and your outrage, but as the Kynigos are not present to defend themselves—"

"Not present?" the first son responded. "There is a hunter among us. Ask him."

Oh no. Roman would slaughter Marco for this.

"Show yourself, Hunter," the first son shouted, looking up.

He could not. Roman said to tread carefully.

"There, in the rafters."

Cursing his carelessness, Marco pushed to his full height on the handspan beam. He stepped into the air and dropped—catching the curtain that draped a support column loosely in hand and foot and descended.

A flurry of surprise erupted as he landed with a soft thump and released his Kynigos cloak at the same time. He flared his nostrils to draw attention to the sigil on his face, then turned to the Xanthus. "You seek me, Machitis?"

The first son pointed at him. "See? He wears one."

Marco stalked to the front, forcing himself to stay calm.

"What is your purpose in this hall, Kynigos?" the president demanded.

"What else?" he asked with a shrug. "A hunt."

Gasps rippled through the crowd, and every man and woman with reason to hide flung wild, acrid fear scents. Curse the reek! He snapped closed his receptors.

"You hunt here, in Elysium?" the president balked.

"A Kynigos hunts wherever the quarry flees." He pulled his gaze from the dais back to the Xanthus. It took a dozen paces to reach them. "The vambrace. May I see it?"

The first son hesitated, a sign that forced Marco to open his receptors and accept the man's efflux. No fear—save a modicum, probably concerned Marco would steal the armor. But there was also an undercurrent of anger.

"Go ahead, Bazyli," Ares said.

Reluctantly, the son extended it.

Marco accepted it, the signature's vestigi rubbed into the rhinnock plating very distinct and familiar. Dolon. He studied it, wondering anew what had happened to the hunter.

"Well?" the elder Xanthus growled.

Marco angled his own vambrace to Dolon's and scanned it, knowing he must notify the Citadel at once. "I must beg your deference for a moment. Please—where was it found?"

"On the Heights," Ares said. "Near the southwestern boundary between Kalonica and Hirakys."

"Southwestern boundary." Marco squinted at the elder, then to the warrior with long, white hair and broad shoulders who stood behind the Xanthus. "Prokopios lands, is it not?"

The elder's face reddened. "How do you—"

Marco quieted him with an uplifted hand. "The accord allows us to retrieve fugitives that violate your airspace. As such, we are versed in your lands and people to keep interference as slight as possible."

"Aye," spoke the white-haired Prokopios, "but is it not also written that on Drosero you must have permission from the realm on which you *retrieve*?"

"It is."

"And yet we received no notification," the Prokopios elder said. "Have you an explanation?"

Marco turned over the arm guard. "I do not, but since a hunter is never without his vambrace, I am concerned for my brother and will inquire at once with the Citadel."

"Excuse me," the gravelly voiced woman intruded. "But this is not relevant to the Caucus on Symmachia. We must continue."

"Hunters have too much power," someone shouted.

"They are as crooked as the Symmachians."

As the objections morphed to epithets, Marco met the elder's gaze. "I would speak with you privately." He lifted the vambrace. "Can we—"

The elder snatched it back, his anger roiling.

Crowds grew raucous and the din amplified with the high ceilings. Sensing the tumult aimed at him, Marco relented, resolving to find the Xanthus later. He rolled his cape and vanished into the crowds.

Avoiding Bedth and his men took longer than Tigo hoped, but he still found his way to the front and stood off to the side among waiters preparing drink trays. Clustered at the front were all sorts of trouble, dressed as generals and admirals. If he went up there …

There is no choice.

"Excuse me, Admiral," Tigo said to Krissos, who stood surrounded by uniforms. "May I have a word, sir?"

The man turned a deadly glare to Tigo. "I thought you were under arrest, Commander."

"Of which I would like to speak to you, sir. Your order—"

"My order?" He sounded affronted.

"Yes, sir. You sent me to Drosero to retrieve a—"

"I'm sorry, Commander Deken," Krissos scoffed, "but I have no knowledge of—"

"You waved me." His breath struggled up his throat. "You sent me there, gave me the drop numbers."

Krissos shook his head and furrowed his brow. "You have this order?"

Tigo scowled. "I wouldn't have dropped without it."

"Show me."

Something curled in Tigo's gut at the admiral's demand. Snapping his gaze to his channeler, he felt a terrible tremor race through him. He knew what he'd find, but he hoped against hope that his prediction would be wrong. Desperation and fear forced him to look. To scour the files. No record. He swallowed as he flashed a look at the admiral. "You had them removed."

Krissos barked a laugh. "Son, I have no idea what game you're playing at, but this is over. You broke a dozen intergalactic laws and treaties with not only the Droserans, but the Herakles Quadrant."

"Sir. *You* waved me on the *Macedon*. We spoke—"

"Enough." He flicked his hand as if Tigo were a gnat. "You have always been a loose cannon, and we've put up with it because of your father and because you *were* a good officer. Until now."

"Nothing has changed, except your order," Tigo barked. "Do they know? Do they know what you're hiding?"

"Commander Deken," came a calm voice—Vice Admiral Acrisius. His dark skin was shadowed with concern.

"You're not going to get away with this!"

Krissos shoved into Tigo's face. "*Stand. Down*," he hissed. "Or I will have you removed from house arrest and placed in the brig, Commander."

Anger strangled, even though he felt a hand on his shoulder. "Do they know about the Engram?"

"No," Acrisius said, as if warning this was the wrong path. Wrong time.

Humiliation and the truth of what was happening on the *Macedon* forbade him from listening to that voice. "The Council voted against it, yet you're using it. On Droserans and Ky—"

"Tigo!"

Void's Embrace! *Now* his father appears? But he would not be dissuaded.

"Tigo, c'mon," Acrisius said, tugging him away as his father stormed toward them.

"Admiral Acrisius, I've always respected you. If you saw what was happening on the *Macedon*—with that—*augh*!" A vise-grip on his bicep nearly brought him to his knees. He swung around, narrowly pulling his punch.

Security detail, led by his father. *Slag me.* He pivoted to Krissos and the other council members watching mutely. "So, this is what we do now? When an officer of the fleet engages in human rights violations, uses an Engram, we drink to it. Dance. Pretend it doesn't exist. Blame it on the commander."

"The Engrams?" Admiral Ahron guffawed. "They were destroyed when we voted the machines down two years ago."

"Tigo, you have always been passionate about protecting people," Rear Admiral Emesyn Waring crooned. "Unfortunately, you have never been able to pair that with good sense and responsibility."

Tigo glowered at Krissos. Pointed at him. "You waved me. Ordered me to Drosero."

"Get him out of here!" his father bellowed.

The detail swarmed. "Every one of you will be held accountable!" He was hauled up off his feet. "They're using it. On Kynigos. On Droserans."

Sizzling fired through his shoulder blade. Colored his world gray and ... warbly.

Boom! Boom! Boom!

Tigo rolled and fell. He hit the ground hard, brain scrambled. Confused. Disoriented. *Where am I?* Looking around, he noted the gray-on-gray décor. White that pinched his corneas. Not the *Macedon*. Home.

Right … the gala. Everything came back in a rush—the confrontation with Krissos, Acrisius, Waring, and his father. But after that … nothing. He braced against a wall as the room acted like it was in zero-g. Swam. Tilted. Rotated.

Voices drew him out of the grunge. He tilted toward the ajar door. Shuffled closer. Why were they shouting? Two shapes stood in the foyer. He blinked a few more times before the fog receded.

Tigo caught the door and jerked it open fully, only to catch the lithe form of the woman as she left. His father pivoted and bolts of thunder flew from his mouth, pounding Tigo's ears.

"Stopstopstop," Tigo growled. "I can't … when you shout, I can't hear. It's too painful."

His father stormed toward him, shoving Tigo back inside, and slammed the door. "Painful? You want to hear painful? How about your son humiliating you in front of all of Command and the High Council when he accuses them of human rights violations!"

"What else would you call it?" Tigo growled. "The Engram—"

"By the Void, would you stop—"

"It's there!" His world tilted. Heel of his hand against his forehead, he steadied himself. "Why won't you even check into it? I know we have our differences, but I have always done my best as a member of the Symmachian Marines. Always. You know that." He pressed his palms together. "Please— just look into it."

"The Engrams were destroyed, just as Ahron told you," his father barked. "I orchestrated a tribunal, where you'd get your chance to sway the Council, but now you have every slagging one of them believing you're out of your mind."

"Have I ever lied to you?"

"Yes."

"About things that matter?"

His father hesitated, eyeing him and finally—maybe—listening. "You had it in you."

Tigo frowned.

"If you'd spend half the time on your command and honor as you do with getting women into your bed—"

"*What?* I haven't—"

"You were seen in a heated kiss with the chief medical officer on the *Macedon*."

Despite his guilt in that instance, Tigo had been off duty and it hadn't been a real kiss. *Yeah, try explaining* that. "I know it's been a while since you ran mom off, but kissing doesn't mean *sex*. Or maybe you've taken a refresher course with"—like a bolt of lightning, he saw the woman's shape and wondered—"Waring? You're sleeping with *Waring?*"

His father's backhand flew hard and fast, sending him reeling. Tigo crashed against the wall, his jaw throbbing.

"Do not *ever* speak to me like that again!"

Tigo drew himself up. Though his head was still gooey from whatever they'd dosed him with, he forced himself to stand. Realized he didn't know the man before him. "Not a problem."

His father's chest rose and fell unevenly.

Tigo moved toward the door.

"Where are you going?"

On leaden feet, Tigo walked out of the residence. "Reporting to the brig. At least they'll be happy to see me. And it'll be … quieter."

TSC *MACEDON*

MEET ME IN THE SUPPLIES CLOSET OUTSIDE THE #4 MEDBAY DOOR.

Teeli frowned at the message, then glanced down the passage leading to that location. Past the security detail. Jez had a reason for summoning her, and that made her heart race.

"Everything okay?"

She jerked toward the voice—Zilla—and the room spun. She pinched the bridge of her nose until the dizziness subsided. "Yes. I think …" She gave Zilla a smile and started away. "I'll be back."

Trying to act normal when she was spiraling with anticipation and adrenaline, she moved purposely down the passage and turned left. When she did, two different corridors presented themselves. But no people.

Wait. Why was she looking for people?

She glanced at the floor. Tried to remember why had she come out here.

Fear trembled through her, stirring dread.

"Doctor? You all right?"

She looked up into the warm gold eyes of … "Sidra."

"Yeh." Wary, she glanced around. "Has anything happened with the girl?"

Teeli frowned. "No." The girl in the machine. Kersei. Why must every thought be such an effort? "Why? Have you heard something?"

The lieutenant smiled. "Come on." She backstepped and then walked a dozen paces down the hall before opening a door. The supplies closet.

Teeli hesitated, growing uneasy. "Lieutenant, what …"

Sidra tugged her arm and pulled her into the closet. Shut the door. "Sorry, didn't want to risk being seen."

Teeli shifted, stiffening at how close the racks were to the door, leaving no breathing room. "I thought this space was bigger." It was a dumb thought in the scheme of things. Her mind was succumbing …

The lieutenant walked to the back, stepped around a shelving unit—no, *disappeared* behind it, calling for Teeli to follow. When she did, she was stunned to find an entire separate room. Long and narrow, it seemed to stretch the length of the medical bay. At the far side were the older Eidolon officer, Tigo's communications officer, and— "Kersei." It wasn't the mine plague numbing her mind now. It was shock. "*How?*"

Jez smiled and nodded to the comms specialist. "Diggs found a way to reroute the circuitry in the wall of that chamber so it's undetectable to the system. The walls are all in sections, so we created a track for one of them to pop back and open without disrupting the screen. Closed you can't tell."

"In one day? You did all that in one day?" Teeli balked.

"Nah. We've been working on it since the commander left." Jez shifted toward the girl. "We've been pulling her out for most of the day. One of the Two-one-five stays with her at all times."

"This is amazing."

Another long smile from Sidra as she turned to the girl, who stood nearby. "I have a surprise for you." She reached behind Teeli.

Kersei drew in a breath, her expression dark, tangled, no doubt, in the horrible memories from the chamber.

"It's a good surprise," Jez clarified.

Something flew at Kersei. Her mind registered the object. She stepped back with her right foot and caught the rod, hands automatically sliding to the hold she'd practiced so often. She sucked in a breath as the familiar weight of wood in her palms awakened something she hadn't felt in weeks. "How …?"

Jez bounced her shoulders. "You were pretty obsessed with me being a warrior, so I looked up practices for your clan."

Kersei brushed back a dark curl. "Entoli."

"Come again?"

"We call it the entoli." She eyed the long stick, not quite the same length as a javrod, which was good, considering the smaller space. "My people."

"Thought they were Stratios?"

"The Stratios are my entoli—my … clan." She turned the rod, stepping into the dance she'd performed hundreds of times. The drills. *Darius shouting, "Lighten your grip. Widen your stance."*

A sorrowful pang struck her. She drew up her shoulders. Closed her eyes. Fought the tears, fought to push out the images from that awful room in the—

"Augh!"

Her eyes flew open. She saw an attack. Another javrod. Coming high.

Kersei countered, finally seeing the older man—AO—attacking. She slid her foot back for balance. For traction. The impact of the rods rattled down into her arms. "There's not much room here."

"Enough to pin you," he said.

Challenged, she swept the end up and another thwack resounded through the confined space. Followed through, which brought the tip down and under—and right into the opposing rod.

She hustled back a few steps and brought the rod to waist level, evenly gripped. Then charged with a flurry of strikes. Alternating angles and strikes. Releasing the energy from her hands into the weapon. Then rotated with the right side swinging down, then arcing up.

AO stumbled back with a beefy grin. "'At's it, pet."

"Sorry, sir?" The ensign screwed up his face, looked at the black glass, then back to Tigo. "I … don't have those orders, sir."

"You need orders to take someone into custody?" Tigo grunted. "What's it take to find somewhere quiet to sleep off stun drugs?"

"He's with me."

At the female voice, Tigo pivoted, surprised to find Alestra Galt there. A shadow farther down the passage captured his eye. His heart skipped a beat. *Mom?* No, not possible.

"You look like you've seen a Nephesh, Tigo," Alestra crooned.

"I—" He glanced at the corridor again, then shook himself. "Aren't you late?"

She gave a brittle laugh and waved at the brig officer. "Ignore him." She gripped his arm. "This way, Commander." As they rounded the corner, she snorted and threaded her arm around his as she had at the gala. "Really, Tigo. Melodramatic looks better on Cleve or Krissos."

He craned his neck, searching for whomever he'd seen. Needed to verify that it wasn't … *Don't be an idiot.* Mom fled Symmachia years past. He shrugged, realizing he'd waited too long to answer and felt Alestra's stare. "Hey, whatever it takes to get someone to listen."

"Always were one hungry for attention. What? Did your mom not pay enough attention to you when you were little?"

"Beg off, Alestra."

She considered him. "I guess that hit a nerve."

"My nerves are wobbly after being stunned at the gala."

She pointed down the hall. "Walk with me. I need to share something with you." They walked a few minutes before she sighed. "Baric called an emergency tribunal last night after the gala."

Tigo stopped short. "I'm scuzzed."

"He wanted to have you removed from both command and duty, court-martialed as well as banned from Qrimont so you could not wrongly influence students at the Academy."

"How does the High Council have anything to do with my career?"

"Because you violated treaties with your incursion on Drosero."

"On Kris—" He threw up his hands. "It's my word against his. I have no proof."

"But you do have allies, Tigo," Alestra said quietly. "Allies who presented potential evidence that could prove your innocence—"

"Seriously?"

"—or guilt."

"I am cursed."

"It was with this evidence—"

"Wait. What evidence? The wave with my orders for the drop vanished."

She inclined her head slowly. "It did. But on the wave servers, there were 935 waves at the time you claim to have received that order. However, when matched with individual waves, there were only 934. So that could be the wave you purport came in."

"No purporting. It came." He angled to her with a frown. "And they bought that? No details, just an extra wave?"

"There is also an ensign who claims he was tasked with consolidating incursion data for Drosero. Naturally, this person is under protective custody, but this information was enough to convince the Council to give you a proper trial and not rush to judgment."

Tigo let out a long breath. "Do I have you to thank for this?"

She smiled. "One of many."

"Then thank you."

"Maybe don't thank me yet."

"Why?"

"Because you have to go back to the *Macedon*. And play nice."

"You mean play dumb."

"Well, that was understood."

He snorted, then shook his head.

"Haven't you wondered," Alestra said quietly, falling silent as an officer swept past them, then continuing, "why all this weird activity around Drosero?"

Tigo slowed, his sluggish thoughts churning. "You're saying ..." It hurt to think.

"You pulled that Kynigos. And then the girl was discovered adrift."

Tigo frowned. How in the 'verse did Alestra have this information? "But she wasn't anywhere near that hunter. How could she know anything about that?"

"But she wasn't alone—or so she claims."

"How do you know all this? Seriously—this is all classified."

She rolled her eyes. "Which is why you shouted it for the world to hear last night."

He groaned and rubbed the back of his neck.

"Done arguing semantics and protocols?" Alestra leaned in. "Ready to figure something out and *not* be Baric's pawn in his little coup?"

"Coup? What are you—"

"The machine is going to break that girl, and that simply cannot happen."

"Because?"

Imperiously, she sniffed. "Is your humanity lost, Tigo?"

He glowered. "Would I be in this mess if it was?" He folded his irritation away. "I just want to understand why this girl is important." A thousand thoughts ricocheted, including the fact that this officer of the fleet knew about the Engram being used. "I feel like I'm missing key pieces on this chess board."

"Oh, there are missing pieces all right."

"But you are holding more of them than I am." He turned to her in confrontation. "Give it to me. Tell me what I'm missing. Why am I risking everything—"

"This isn't about you!" she snapped, then pulled herself straight. "There are far bigger things at play than you. We got you out of that tribunal—"

"We?"

"—for one reason: return to the *Macedon* and protect that girl. Get her away from Zoltan Baric."

TSC *MACEDON*

"So—you have no technology where you live?"

"No." Grateful for the universal translator Jez had brought and helped Kersei tuck into her ear, Kersei looked up from the thick stew to the others gathered in the hidden room. At the best of times, the space felt more like a secret passage at Stratios than something on a ship, yet with all the team here during the shift change, as they called it, it felt even smaller. But that was okay. They were helping her. And when they were here, she was safe.

"And you don't miss it?"

"How could I miss what I have not had? And I could never miss the technology of that room." Kersei shuddered, then glanced around. "Here it is cold, it smells funny, the lights give me a headache, and you do not even use water to bathe."

"Baths waste too much water," the one called Diggs said as he tore open a dried fruit packet. "Tascan ships can't carry enough water or purify enough wastewater for a complement this large to bathe."

"Tascan?" Kersei said, wrinkling her nose.

"It's a short version of Tertian Space Coalition," Jez explained.

Kersei nodded. "Well, there is nothing as luxurious as a warm spring-fed bath." Tingling danced along her inner forearm. Inwardly groaning, she gripped the edge of her sleeve and held it in place, afraid the others would see the brand.

"I can't imagine life without tech," Jez said. "I don't think I could live without my phase pistol or being able to wave someone."

"Wave?"

Jez smiled and pointed to her ear. "Implants that help us send voice messages."

"Curious. I'm not sure I would like someone else's voice in my ear—'tis strange enough with this translator." Pursing her lips, Kersei forced her mind from her arm. "It is not so terrible on Drosero as you might think. We are quite content. In all earnestness, I would not want to live like this."

"I guess that means she won't marry you, AO," Rhinn taunted, earning a slap to the back of his head.

"Well," Jez said, her accent somehow soothing. "You have not had the best introduction to Symmachian life."

"*Is* there a best introduction?" The heat. Accursed, worsening heat.

"The Falls at Qrimont," AO offered. "I'd start there. Nothing like that."

Kersei dragged her arm from the table and pressed it to her stomach.

"Or the tech center of Rhianta. That place is amazing," Diggs said. "There's a large research facility with the most advanced technology in all the Quads."

Kersei's eyes burned as pain pulsed.

"They're making headway with FTL," Diggs said.

Jez widened her eyes. "Where'd you hear that?"

"On the shell. Apparently they're testing somewhere."

"What're you doing listening to the shell?" That must be bad with the way Jez barked at the man. "That's enough to get written up."

Diggs pursed his lips but remained unaffected. "Have to stay ahead of our enemy, don't we?"

"What enemy does Symmachia have?" Kersei asked.

"Yitans," Rhinn said with a sneer.

"They're just on the outer belt of Balasi and disgruntled with refueling times." Jez shook her head. "Can't really count them."

Rhinn shifted. "Hir—"

"Nor Hiregna." Jez nudged her food tray and folded her arms on the table. "Asteroid destroyed a quarter of the planet. Wiped out a third of the population. They blame Symmachia for not intervening."

Again, Kersei blinked. Heard the words. Struggled to process them. "How … how are you to have intervened?"

"Nukes on the asteroid, blow it to chunks." Rhinn grabbed bread.

"Only," Jez said, "it was too late by the time they detected it. Detonating weapons would've proven disastrous to the other planets."

Fist balled, Kersei tightened her stomach and leg muscles. Her thighs and buttocks. Anything that might … possibly … stop the pain.

"Iereans."

"Iereans are a religious sect. They have no alliances."

"If you believe that, you deserve whatever they do to you." Diggs shook his head, then lifted his chin. "Thyrolians."

Jez grunted. "I'll give you that one."

"Who … who are … they? Why are they your enemy?" Beads of sweat trickled down her face and spine. She trembled beneath the fire in her brand. Her flesh would melt, like those images of her family and entoli in the reminding chamber. Their skin burning … she could smell it now. She was going to be sick. "Please …" *Oh Ancient, it burns!*

"Hey." AO was on his feet. "Something's wrong—"

"Kersei?" Jez rushed to her. "Kersei, you okay?"

The smells. The blurs. The fire. The shrieking creature.

"Get the doc!"

"No slagging way," AO said.

"There's nothing to help her here."

"Distraction," Jez said to Rhinn and Diggs as she pulled Kersei upright. "Back into the chamber, so—"

Kersei screamed. Shoved backward.

AO caught her. Lifted her from her feet.

Flinging out her arms, Kersei railed. "No! No, don't put me back." Clarity swept in and she fought them, wishing for a javrod. Wishing for— She sucked in a breath. The heat … the heat was gone. Cool air wafted over her. She brought exhausted eyes to Jez. "I'm … I'm better."

"You sure?" Jez asked, scowling.

"She doesn't want to go back in the tank," AO muttered.

"Neither would I." Jez studied her carefully, slowly. "But … I think she's okay."

Forcing a smile, Kersei took a shuddering breath. She would do anything in her power to stop from being put back in there.

"Doesn't matter what she wants," Diggs said. "We got trouble."

They all looked to the man working feverishly on a flat, black thing.

"What?" Jez asked.

"She has to go back—now."

"No," Kersei breathed.

"There's a detail accessing the chamber now."

Jez swung toward the hidden door and depressed it. "Kersei. Hurry. If they see you're not there, we're done."

Terrorized by both thoughts of entering and never coming out again, she stood frozen.

"C'mon, pet," AO said. "We won't let them leave you in there." His touch was fatherly, his voice firm but gentle.

"I'm stalling them, but it won't last," Diggs warned.

Kersei took a breath and shoved her way into the awful room, passing the woman, Esq, who had held her place. Darkness clapped on her as she dropped and lay on her side. Alone. Shut off. The images were playing. Screaming. Fires burning. Wisps of that creature.

Light exploded from the other side.

Kersei lifted her head as two guards entered, activated the magcuffs in her tunic, which yanked her fast to the floor, then two more guards and an iereas entered. Fear struck a hard, hollow chord in her chest.

"Bring her!"

19
ZLARES, CENON

"The Xanthus have Dolon's vambrace."

Rico looked tense. "How did they come by that? Think you they have him?"

"It's impossible to know for certain," Marco conceded, "but I am inclined to think not. I sensed no discordance. Only concern and outrage."

"That outrage could simply be because Dolon was on their planet."

"Granted," Marco said. "But wrapped around the scent was confusion and concern—confusion of finding the vambrace but no hunter."

"I will trust your receptors, since I could not be there."

"It reeks to sit here and not be hunting when the girl is yet unaccounted for. Let me know if the Citadel wants action."

"They do not," came Roman's deep voice as he entered the room behind Rico.

"Master."

Roman palmed the table and stared into the camera. "Your presence at the Caucus unsettled some local officials."

"Only those with something to hide would—"

"So under the Articles of Preservation of Peace and Cooperation—"

Oh no.

"—I've accepted a Decree on your behalf."

Marco jerked. "No hunter may be bound by two Decrees simultaneously."

"Except," Roman said with a wag of his head, "under the Articles. A rare exception, but to allay concern over your intrusion into what should have been a peaceful—"

"Intrusion? I remained hidden—"

"Until you didn't." Disappointment creased the master's brows. "Regardless, this is not punishment, but to protect your Ierean Decree and your need to remain on Cenon. High Lord Kyros anticipates the girl will be there within a fortnight."

Again Marco frowned. "How can he know that and not know her location?"

Roman stared back, expression stony. "Unknown."

It was impossible not to feel like a pawn. "Master—"

"I know well your thoughts for they mirror my own, so waste not your breath nor mine on this any longer." Roman had always been curt, but this bordered on severe. "You will secure a fruit smuggler on Cenon named Jubbah Smirlet and remand him to the Zlaren authorities."

Zlaren?

If they already knew the location of the fugitive, why hire a hunter? "I will lodge the hunt with—"

"Cenon is already aware."

CHRYZANTHE STATION, ORBITING SICANE

An icy finger traced Kersei's spine. Though she had little concept of time nor a visible sun to mark the days, she knew it had been days since the guards had pulled her from the wretched room, escorted her to a ship, and set off for this ... place. Deferential silence had marked the trip from Baric's ship to this orbital satellite, as they called it—a strange name for something that looked like a giant metal flower dangling against a black nothingness. What unsettled her most was the presence of the iereas. Her family died shortly after iereas showed up at Stratios. Would she now die, too?

Once docked, the guards had marched her to this room and locked her in. Her view on the *Macedon* had been nothing but cruel images of death and terror. Here she had windows lining an entire section of the room ... yet, somehow, she still felt closed in, for there was nothing but a large vast, hollow expanse of space and the "petals" of this metal flower. She had no bearings, no landmarks to sort her location. It was as if she floated in a black sea on the darkest of nights.

Was the chill from this new place or something else, something ... worse? A foreboding? At least here, she would no longer be held in that horrific chamber, forced to watch her family die over and over.

Such a strange place, this satellite. It had a series of circles held by long arms that jutted from the center, where arcing bands of steel rose from an outer shell, then dove into the center, as if holding the inner edge together. Thereby reminding her of the many-petaled flower.

Life was starting to feel like a sparring match in which she didn't know the rules. First her family's deaths. Then Uncle Rufio and that shuttle. Next the big ship with memories not her own burned into her mind. She had found friends in Lieutenant Jez and AO, but now she was ripped from them, too, and thrust into the cold black.

"What do you think?" The masculine voice pulled her around. In a dark red uniform, Captain Baric stood just inside the door, arms folded. Blond hair threaded with silver defied one to guess his age. Somehow, he did not seem as severe as he had the moment he'd pronounced judgment on her.

However, she was not fool enough to think him a friend. "About what?"

"It's nearly complete." He nodded to the windows. "The final ring is ready for assembly."

Only then did she see the last, empty brace. Kersei studied the strange circles. The braces. Massive metal arms moved, attaching a long tube to the waiting brace. "What is it?"

"I call it the *Chryzanthe.*" His chest puffed. "Years of inspiration finally come to life."

Why build something like this in the middle of space? "What is its purpose?"

"Consider it the gateway to the universe."

How did one make a gateway to a universe? And why, when the Symmachians already had means to travel through space?

Captain Baric eyed her and touched one of her black curls. "With all this hair, it's a wonder you are ever cold."

A shiver tremored across her shoulders. Froze her, sensing his ill intentions. "Why am I here?" she finally braved, feeling sick.

"Because I asked for you."

ZLARES, CENON

Locating Smirlet in government records had been way too easy. Even though he'd avoided a transportation tag, the man had smuggled fruit. That meant he wanted to *sell* the produce. Which required a bin or stall, or if he were adept at his illegal trade, a shop in the main commerce center. That cost too many *sols*, though. And too many records. Which left one option: the small vendor stands.

Glad to avoid the many scents plaguing the commerce center, Marco strode to a bar on the main square. A petite woman accepted short-order requests from patrons, while another tended bar.

He sat with a view of the lattice-like wall stuffed with wines and bottles of other liquors. Beyond it, a row of produce vendors. Of note was the third stall on the right. Wrapped in linen and head shorn close, the man was heavily tanned. Much time in the sun. With produce.

White hair tipped with blue, the Thyrolian bartender faced Marco. "What can I—" Fear drenched her efflux. Then in rushed loamy disgust.

Marco met her gaze. What did she fear so much? "Cordi, please. Not warmed."

She swallowed. Nodded. Turned, her gaze sliding to the market and her scent tingeing with cypress. Concern. As she prepared his drink, she skated glances to the market. Then came the quiet tap of a vidscreen. Her right hand prepared the cordi. Her left worked the screen. Sending a warning?

Marco almost smiled as he sipped his drink. Now, he had only to wait for the message to hit Smirlet's channeler. The fugitive would flee, betraying himself and his guilt.

A crash sounded from the cluster of stalls. Wall curtains flapped aside. A man darted from stall to stall. Panicked. Doused in balsam. An easy efflux to track.

Smirking, Marco lifted the cup and met the woman's gaze. "Thank you," he said, referring to more than the drink. After finishing it off, he set down a *bezant,* more than enough to cover the cost. Rolling his shoulders and craning his neck, he locked onto the odor spiraling through the market. Navigated around patrons. He broke into a jog, unfurling his cloak, which wafted the earthy efflux.

A bristling woman stopped. "What in the 'verse is—" Seeing Marco's sigil, she snapped down her head.

Smirlet's efflux strengthened as Marco gave chase. Yet with each step, the scent grew strangely ... *soiled.* Blurred, the way vision is sometimes affected.

Marco slowed and glanced at the wall above his head. A vine snaked along the mortar between the bricks. Chamomile. He snorted. His quarry believed this a means to losing the hunter? He traced the bricks then bolted forward. Toed the wall of a house. Vaulted to the right. Tic-tacked to the ledge. Then lowered into a crouch. Spindly branches of anemic trees lined the footpath below, struggling to conceal him. Rotating on the balls of his feet, he searched the narrow path between wall and row houses for his quarry. There, behind a cardamom bush.

A twinge of pity spirited through Marco—Smirlet was not clever enough. He slunk along the plastered ledge until he looked down on his target, who wore a black hat down to his ears, but tufts of stark white hair glared in the darkness.

Freeing the webbing gun, he slid his thumb along the warming switch. It'd heat the webbing strands, so once they made contact around the fugitive, they'd solidify into a near-iron cocoon.

A breeze tussled the man's hair—not truly white, but a soft, bioluminescent blue.

Pausing, Marco now understood why Cenon wanted this man removed from the streets. After a plague wiped out most on their planet and the disease spread to other planets in the Quads, Thyrolians were widely blamed and hated.

Marco landed with a soft thump near the man.

Strangling his cry, Smirlet leapt back, stumbling. Gaunt eyes. Sallow complexion.

No webbing, Marco decided. Holstering the gun, he held up a palm. "On your feet, Smirlet."

"Y-you're the hunter." Smirlet's voice cracked. Fright, aye, but also because of the damage done to his vocal cords and lungs on Thyrolia.

"I have no desire to harm you. Come quietly, and—"

"My bound." His eyes went glossy. The glow in his hair seemed to brighten, something Marco had never seen before. "She's with child."

The bartender—was she his bound? He had detected no pheromones to indicate she was pregnant. "No lies or my compassion dies."

"You c-can truly *smell* us." There was a curl to his lip, a smack of pepper to his efflux. Anger.

"Would that I did not. I care not that you have slept in a stale flat with rats or that you ate khorian root—"

"How—"

"Enough." Marco swiped a hand across his mouth. "Easy or not, Smirlet? How will you have it?" He flicked the webbing gun into display. "Webbed or Walking?"

"W-walking."

CHRYZANTHE STATION, ORBITING SICANE

"The daughter of Nicea cannot be bound to the Kalonican prince!"

Kersei jolted, the memory bleeding into her mind of the red-robed iereas rushing down the black halls of Stratios Hall. Timber falling. She shuddered. Through the narrow panes in the door, she caught sight of a red blur.

Iereas. The realization hurried her to the doors. As if anticipating her intent, the barrier whisked open. Kersei froze, expecting Baric to enter. Only the open, icy corridor waited. To the far right, the red robe fluttered around a corner.

She hurried after it, glancing back to be sure *she* wasn't followed. Or discovered. Ahead, a glimpse of crimson spurred her on. At the next juncture, she pivoted—and froze. The iereas stood mere feet away! She whipped back, realizing he had been waiting for a door to unlock. She beseeched the Ancient not to be discovered. Waited a few more heartbeats before peeking around.

The corridor sat empty. Light bloomed beyond the doors that had swallowed the iereas. Kersei moved closer, worried they also would open at her approach.

Through the glass, she saw the iereas standing over a long gray box of some kind. It reminded her of the pod she'd woken up in, the one Dr. Knowles said had nanites. Top panels slid away from this pod and revealed a sleeping man.

He looks dead.

Her heart thundered.

The iereas tapped a square of some kind, and riffled the hair of the encased man. Why would the dead need air? And that strange mark on the man's nose and face—it was familiar. Memory of the men on the *Macedon* when she'd first been captured—those men had a similar mark, didn't they? From the floor came two big metal arms that hoisted the box upright.

Another man in a gray jumpsuit appeared with a small device. He aimed at a depression in the wall. With a definitive *thunk* that Kersei felt in the hall, the box went dark. She strained to see what was happening.

Light suddenly exploded through it.

The dead man jerked violently. Arched his spine. His head thrust back. Eyes wide.

He wasn't dead, then. Unable to breathe or move, Kersei watched. Felt the agony writhing through his face. It was terrifying, hollowing out her stomach.

Something touched her shoulder.

Kersei screamed—and jumped right into Baric. She shoved herself against the wall. "Wh-what are you doing to him? You monster! Who—"

His hand flew fast and hard. Struck her face and sent her stumbling backward. She gasped, cheek and eyes stinging.

"How did you get out?" Hand to her throat, he pinned her to the wall with a strangling grip.

"I-I don't … know," she squeaked. "The doo—"

"Stay out of matters not your concern! Sneaking around this station is forbidden!" He lifted her, his acrid breath forced into her nostrils. "You will learn not to anger me." With that he moved away. But the vise on her throat did not ease.

How? He released her, yet she still could not breathe. Sharp pricks stabbed both sides of her neck. Cold metal choked her. Panic drummed a cadence in her temples. Her hands snapped to her neck, but a strange vibration rang through her hand and arm. Kersei cried out.

"Give care, Princess," Baric said. "That's a grappling collar. It hooks into your spinal column, sending a tendril up into your brain."

Shock stilled her.

"*What* are you doing?" With a cold whirl, an iereas appeared in a rage. "What have you done? You fool!"

Tears escaped. Slid down her cheeks. Desperation and fear drove her hands to the collar again. More shocks. She didn't care. "Take it off!" Thrashing, she was desperate to pull it off. Smelled her hands burning. She growled, glowering at the monster who'd put it on her.

Something about the iereas warred with her alarm. But the collar—it was hard to breathe.

"I wouldn't do that, Princess." Baric's boiling tone was so superior. Cruel. "You only injure yourself further."

"Get that off her," the iereas demanded. "You cannot—"

Baric punched the priest backward. "This is *my* station, Theon. You will not tell me what I can and cannot do."

"Remember well who positioned you, Zoltan Baric!" The iereas stood straight. "What you have been given"—he motioned toward the room—"can be stripped away."

The captain looked into the chamber. "You know the consequences, if you do that. The cost. Tell me, will she be happy? How will you answer—"

"Do not question me, Symmachian! This is far above your shortsightedness and arcs." Theon stabbed a finger at Kersei. "You touch her again, you strike me again, it is all gone, Zoltan."

A quick repetitive thump carried through the corridor, soon delivering guards.

"Secure her," Baric snarled. "Lock down her quarters. Nobody in or out."

Thick-muscled guards grabbed Kersei and hauled her away. As she was dragged around the corner, she caught a few more words.

"This was a mistake," Theon said. "She is not here just for your pleasure."

ZLARES, CENON

"I might not have enhanced smell, but I know you stink rotten."

Steaming cup to his mouth, Marco slowly found her gaze over the rim. Smirlet's bound stalked to his table in the sparsely populated café. He set down his drink.

"You got some nerve," she growled, "coming back here after what you done." Her scent wasn't the only thing betraying her intention—the hunched shoulders, the balled left fist. Tight lips.

Even as he came to his feet, he reacted as her arm extend, a steaming slosh of liquid sailing out.

Marco rolled his left hand to her wrist, nailing it a fraction too late. Hot liquid seeped under his forearm plating. Searing hot. Even as the pain registered, so did the clap of silence that struck the café. He held her arm. Her gaze.

Wide, frightened blue eyes. Anger bottomed out of her scent, yet her muscles stayed taut. Poised to strike like a viper. She knew the penalty for assaulting a Kynigos.

A tall shape slid into the confrontation. "I'm sure the lady meant no harm." Touch feather-light against Marco's shoulder, the man spoke with calm assurance that brooked no argument.

The audacity to step into a conflict with a hunter—to show no fear, but rather compassion for the woman who attacked him—galled Marco. Yet ... the man's boldness held no disrespect, which forced him to consider the newcomer. Silver hair, tied back in a queue, framed a heavily tanned face. It was hard with the artificial light and the moonlight to know for sure, but it seemed he bore a scar across his brow. He wore leathers, mail, and rhinnock armor. Droseran—Marco had seen him ride with the Xanthus and confront him at the Caucus.

"Oh, I meant plenty, all right," the woman argued.

The man angled his shoulder toward her, a move that placed his torso directly over the grip Marco held on her. "Your customers are waiting, Baytu."

"There a problem here?" came a stern, nearly mechanical voice.

The Droseran lifted his gaze to the courtyard entrance where two officers stood, batons out and thrumming. "A difference of priorities, Constables. I'm sure it will be resolved without incident."

The constable in the lead looked to Marco. "Master Kynigos, what say you?"

"That I am no master, and"—he eyed the woman, feeling the sting beneath his vambrace—"if this conflict is worthy of your time, then Zlares is safer than I heard."

Nervous chuckles skittered around the market.

A nod with more uncertainty than assurance had the constables resuming patrol.

The interloper shifted back as the woman yanked free from Marco. She spun away and returned to the bar, using it as a barrier.

Returning to his seat, Marco looked at the man. "Not many would brave interfering when a hunter is involved."

"I seek peace where it may be found."

He raised an eyebrow as he removed the left plating. "And how goes that search on Cenon? At the Caucus there was little found and less created."

The man jutted his chin with a hint of a smile. "It *was* you."

Flesh still pink from the scalding liquid, Marco used a table linen to dry his arm, rotating his wrist to test for tenderness. Tonight, he would need to re-oil the armor and apply a salve. He tested the buckle to ensure it would hold.

Toying with glowering at the man to make him leave, which normally worked, Marco decided it would have little effect on this one. "Sit, if you will."

No hesitation as the man lowered himself to the chair.

"Have you a name?" Marco secured the vambrace on his arm.

"Ixion Mavridis."

He bobbed his head and lifted his cup. "Plisiázon." Stalker.

"You know me?" The man rued Marco's nonchalant response.

"*Of* you," Marco corrected. "Your leathers are distinctly Droseran."

"You can purchase this style here."

"Mm. But not the scent. Drosero tinges woodsy. And your arm bands"—the man shifted his right shoulder and the red leather—"identify you as one of the Five."

"I'm impressed you know so much about my world."

Marco hefted his drink in a toast. "To hunt effectively and with as little disruption as possible, we learn culture and customs. Do our best to respect them."

"And the woman?" Spine against the back of the chair, Ixion tilted his head. Palms on thighs. Shoulders squared. He was used to being in charge. "Is that as little disruption—"

"I was not hunting."

"But you were. Earlier." He was far too comfortable in his challenges.

It was hard, but Marco restrained his annoyance. "I held a Decree." What did the man seek from this conversation?

"For the woman's bound."

Trying not to grimace at the lukewarm cordi, Marco wanted to leave this man. But the efflux spiked—a floral middle note with a woodsy one. Grief— loss of a loved one. Curious. He turned his attention to the Droseran. Not surprised to find the man studied him as well. "Ask it."

"What?"

"The question that lingers in your eyes. What do you seek of me, Ixion?"

Though the man pried his gaze away and studied his hands for a moment, he eventually returned, "You are young."

"Most would not call one who reached twenty-and-seven cycles young."

"To a man of fifty and two"—he nodded—"young."

"Have you family on Drosero?"

"As you said, I am one of the Five. The Prokopios are my family."

"Have you a bound?"

That strange scent sailed again and twitched the muscle beneath that scar. "No."

Though Marco wanted to probe, wanted to know if the man had ever had one, he would not cross the lines of propriety. "And the Stratios?"

The first crease appeared in Ixion's brow. "What of them?"

"What know you of the attack that leveled their hall?"

"Only that my medora and brother are dead, along with two hundred of the strongest machitis to walk the kingdom."

"Brother."

"Not of birth," Ixion conceded, "but of loyalty. Is that not how hunters relate to each other as well?"

Marco hesitated, unsettled by the intrepidly calm efflux from this man. This was no casual conversation. "Why are you at my table, Ixion?"

"I beg your mercy?"

"Look around you, Droseran." Marco sipped from the drink, not having to motion to the handful of people still in the courtyard. "Twenty citizens in this square, an additional twelve workers along the perimeter. They keep well their distance from me. Yet you …" He motioned to him.

"They fear you. I do not." Earnestly spoken. With bravado and experience.

"Perhaps you should reconsider."

"I have done nothing to deserve being hunted."

Until two weeks ago, that was enough. But this hunt for the girl changed things. The Iereans said she was innocent and had to be found.

"You asked of the Stratios," Ixion said quietly. "And why I am here with you."

"I take no bribes nor can I—"

"I would not stain myself with such a request," Ixion said, offense rank. He didn't shift in the chair, but his gaze squirmed. "There are … rumors."

There always were.

Ixion leaned forward, intensity amped. "It is said that one of Xylander's daughters survived."

Was the Droseran testing him? "How is that possible? Streams show the stone hall leveled."

"I have seen the ruins myself," Ixion growled. "That is why we are here. To search for answers."

"You seek answers on *this* planet? From me?"

"Considering the Caucus, what better place to search?"

"Drosero? Your people eschew techno—"

"There were reports across the northern lands of a craft in our skies. Droserans may avoid technology, but we are not ignorant." Ixion seemed affronted. "This is not the first time Symmachia has invaded our skies and lands. But it is the first time they have attacked."

Marco lifted an eyebrow. "Give care, Droseran. Remember where you sit—a Symmachian-allied planet."

Rubbing his hands together, Ixion sat back. "We are told they have Xylander's daughter."

"And the Caucus affords you cover to talk with those who might have word of her."

"It does."

"Why come to me with these things?"

Discerning eyes held his as Ixion tightened his lips. "You let a room."

Marco laughed. "Aye, lest I sleep on the ground, I must."

"A hunter moves on after webbing." He glanced over his shoulder. "Baytu's bound is in jail. Yet here you sit."

"Transports only run every—"

"You have your own scout shuttle. Docked at Citrion 5."

That knowledge went too far. "Speak your piece now, for my temper is short and my patience thin."

"We want our daughter back. She is being held on a ship."

"You know much of me and my business, yet you speak of things in which I cannot interfere." Marco drew in a breath and let it out. "Since you are so well-informed, you also know that the Brethren have a tenuous alliance with Symmachians. We cannot hunt on their ships."

"Then you *are* hunting her."

Indignation sparked at the way this man attempted to entrap him. "I state only the Codes that guide hunters." He stood. "Good rest, Droseran."

"Please. I—"

Marco stalked from the courtyard, anger his only ally. He had been foolish to entertain the Droseran and the idea that anyone wanted anything other than a favor or revenge. And to have the man attempt to coerce Marco into violating his oath as a Kynigos—

He stopped short at the stench in the air.

Ixion rolled around Marco, his calm ruffled at last. "In earnest, I only—"

Claxons rang through the city. A siren wailed as a constable's speeder whipped overhead. Trouble—that's what Marco had detected.

"It's close," he muttered as blue and white lights hit a building across the market square.

"That's our lodging!" Ixion broke into a run.

Irritation tempted Marco to turn around. Return to his room. Forget this happened. Concern and curiosity carried him after the Droseran. Across the square. Crowds thickened as they closed in the chaos. Constables nudged onlookers back and established a safe perimeter.

"Kynigos." With a deferential nod, the constable released the magnetic barrier for Marco.

Though not on a hunt, he entered and made his way toward Ixion, who—with his silver hair and height—stood out among the gathered. Fierce expressions mingled with reeking scents. Grief. Anger. Fear. Outrage.

Marco eyed the Xanthus, pairing expressions with the roiling scents. And immediately noticed who was missing.

"… was dead when we returned."

"Who?" Ixion demanded.

"Ares," the first son said. "Our father is murdered."

"Compassion is a violent weapon in the right hands. Always be the advocate, Tigo." Renette Ukat-Deken told Tigo the day he took bullies to task over a girl on an obstacle course. They'd beaten him bloody.

He could still hear the lilt of her accent after all these years. He'd followed her sage advice more recently, too. A girl at the Academy defied all odds, bested the best of the expected Gauntlet winners. Candidates hated her for it. Tigo caught wind of her times and had her assigned to the 215. A black eye, a fractured rib, and a split chin later, Jez Sidra joined his team.

Tigo missed the wisdom of his mother, the elegant woman who had convinced the fast-tracking Domitas Deken that it was his honor to her marry her. After Mom left six years ago, his dad had been saddled with a very headstrong son. It was a loss for them both.

His mind buzzed, tripping back to Qrimont. The shadow in the corridor behind Alestra. The ache to find his mother was so strong, it defied reason— she could not be there. Would not be there.

Restricted to quarters in the Eidolon bay upon his return to the *Macedon*, Tigo waited in agonizing boredom for Baric to sign off on his return to duty. The attempt with the Council had done nothing for his case to protect the girl. Now his every move would be controlled by Baric and monitored by Command. So far there had been nothing but silence. For days.

Tigo pressed his knuckles to his aching brow. Gritted his teeth. It was like they were all avoiding him, avoiding this publicity nightmare.

Or they're hiding something.

Which was exactly what Alestra seemed to suggest. But how was he to get Kersei off the ship if he was locked up?

A chime sounded, alerting him to a visitor. The door hissed aside and revealed—

"Teeli." On his feet, Tigo flinched at his use of her first name. "I mean, Doct—"

"Enough formality." She entered with a wan smile. "They said you had returned, but I wasn't sure."

"Why's that?"

"You hadn't come by. Now I see why."

She *wanted* him to? "Really?"

"To check on Kersei Dragoumis, I mean. Of course." Her face reddened. "How is she doing?"

A frown flickered through her dark complexion. "She's gone. They removed her from the Engram and from the ship."

Tigo started. "When?"

"Days ago!"

Where could Baric have sent the girl? He hadn't been on the same light shuttle back to the *Macedon* as Tigo. Is that why he hadn't heard from Baric— he wasn't on board? "Why would they take her away?"

"I don't know. To hide their nefarious actions? To let her die without us knowing?" Teeli lifted her shoulders—and around her clavicle peeked a mean bruise.

Instinct rose. Tigo lifted the collar of her tunic, assessing the injury. "What happened?" Didn't look like a punch. But even as he peered at the green-and-blue merle of her skin, he saw her eyelashes flutter. Noticed her intake of breath.

The last fortnight of confrontation with his father and the Council washed away. Reminded him of his particular gift. Violent compassion. And Teeli Knowles needed it right now. He slipped his hand up her neck and cupped her face.

Her wide brown eyes came to him. Then she angled away. "I'm nothing. It's okay."

He snorted at her mix-up. "Want to try that again?"

She hesitated, then wilted. "You know what I meant."

Mine plague. Tigo knew bruising was one of the stages. *Advanced* stage. "Are you in pain? Can I do anything—"

"No. To both." She flinched a weak smile. "You are kind to ask, but I am here over a different concern." She eased onto the inches-thick pad that served as his bed, resting her arms on the narrow table in front of it.

Tigo joined her.

"When the captain of a battle cruiser can take people from their planet and do as he pleases," Teeli said quietly, "where does it end? To what authority do we appeal about the Engram and his handling of downworlders?"

"Normally, I would say the Council, but they wouldn't listen. They tried to blame me for everything. I'm half expecting civilian charges to be brought against me at some point. A scapegoat."

"There must be someone who holds them accountable."

There was a whole lot of "personal" in her expression and posture. He wouldn't argue the point that he was the one responsible for extracting the Kynigos. Did that make Tigo complicit? And the rear admiral? Who denied involvement.

"You said you were going to speak to your father ..."

He hated letting her down. "He punched me." After that, he felt powerless to stop ... whatever was going on. Powerless and angry.

"So what will you do?"

"I'm a grunt, Teeli. I don't have the weight to put behind my guesses and that's all we have right now. So, until something changes, I put boots on ground and do what they say."

Teeli drew back, looking hurt and confused. "I thought you believed in stopping him—or at least finding answers."

"I do! But I'm not in command. I'm—" Only when she stood did he realize he was shouting. "Sorry." Running a hand over his head, he rapped his fingers on the table. He came to his feet. "It's like I have all the components of a rail gun but can't assemble the weapon I need." He thought of Ahron and ... Alestra's charge. "Something"—he fisted a hand—"something is going on. I just don't know what. I've never been treated like that. My dad and I rarely see to eye to eye, and Alestra hasn't given me the time of day in years, but—"

"Alestra."

"Yeah, she was really great, but—"

"Was she." Teeli stood.

Tigo frowned. "Yeah." What was that about? "She ..." Wait. Was Teeli jealous? Her tight expression—still beautiful but angry. Interesting.

"You know what? Never mind." At the door, she pivoted. "I don't know what happened to you at Qrimont, but you should just go back."

Defenses up, irritation amped—though he had no idea why—Tigo squared off. "Yeah? Why's that?"

"Because you left your decency and compassion there."

"You have no idea what I went through! Handcuffed and led off the ship, escorted like a criminal through the very halls where I once held my head high. Humiliated before the Council, tased and hauled out of the gala by security, and punched and rejected by my own father!"

Teeli tilted her head and furrowed her brow. "People are being tortured and dying—*On. This. Ship*—and you're worried about your insipid *pride*?"

"I told you they wouldn't listen," he shouted, pointing to his bruised jaw. "I'm being investigated. I got the only answer they intend to give. What else do you want from me?"

"What *would* I want from a spoiled officer's son who's had everything handed to him?" Her lip curled in disgust. "I mean, it's not like he has the ability to influence the leadership of the whole slagging Tertian Space Coalition!" Her voice pitched. And stabbed him in the heart. "A man who wears a uniform that promises to protect those unable to defend themselves—like Kersei Dragoumis!"

Talk about handing him his manhood on a medical tray. And she sounded just like Alestra, telling him to help the girl.

"That man I knew. That man left two weeks ago. But this"—she drew her hand up and down him—"this cocky piece of work standing before me …?"

"You don't know two bits about me or who I am, Dr. Knowles."

"You're right." Her breathing was ragged. Chest rising and falling unevenly. "I don't."

She whirled and the door whisked open.

Jez stood on the other side, wide-eyed gaze drifting between the exiting Knowles and Tigo. Finally, she turned back to him. "Lover's quarrel?"

He stomped to the small galley and retrieved a glass. "What d'you want, Jez?" He poured water and drank it, nerves buzzing.

"You do realize everyone on this deck heard you yelling at her?"

He slammed the glass into the sink, shards splintering in backlash. He gripped the edge of the counter. He just couldn't win. No matter what he did. "Have you no pity for me?"

"Rarely."

He leaned against the counter. "You need something?"

"Been thinking over what you said when you first got back, about your dad dating Weary Waring."

He hesitated and glanced at her. "Is this about me and Laryse again?"

She snorted. "You know it was a mistake, I don't need to tell you … again."

It'd been a fiasco and he seemed to make a lot of those. He waved a hand. "So, Waring and my dad?"

"If your father is in bed with Waring, then we have little chance of stopping a civil war with the Kynigos when they find out about that hunter. And they will. They always do. I swear they can smell across a galaxy."

He dropped onto the thin couch pad and bent forward. Elbows on his knees, he stared at the floor. "I really thought he'd not only hear me out but help—do something. Ask around." He cradled his head. "Instead, he backfisted me, then I got shipped back here." He rubbed his hands over his face. "Things are so scuzzed, Jez."

With a sigh, she slid onto the bench next to him. "When the slag hits the intake, people get stupid."

"But the *people* I was so sure"—he stabbed his steepled hands at the floor—"would do something … Baric taking me in like that, voltcuffed …"

"You make it hard on yourself. Harder than it needs to be."

He met her gaze, confused. "What?"

"You go in there, balls to the wall—"

"Because it needs to be done," he said, incredulous.

"Yes, but those in Command prefer deferential treatment."

"You mean butt-kissing."

She breathed a laugh. "*That.* That right there is my point."

He couldn't help but smile. "And that is why I keep *you* around. Diplomacy is not my strong suit."

"I don't think it's *any* suit you own. What was it you told AO when we were on Rhianta and that official was screaming we'd ruined his campaign? That diplomacy just ate up O$_2$ and—"

"—bloated politicians." He gave a sheepish shrug. She knew him. Knew what he'd say.

Now she laughed. Did she have any idea how pretty she was when she let loose? He wasn't sure the last time he'd seen her laugh. Had she always been that beautiful?

Like an eclipse, her expression darkened. "Don't."

"Don't what?"

"That look you give women. Don't do that to me." She stood up. "And I can't believe I'm going to say this, but whatever you did to Knowles—"

"*What look?*" He came to his feet. "*Did* to her? I—"

"I know you, Tigo Deken. You love women. Most people don't get that it's just a thing you do." She motioned toward his door. "Commander Deken opens a hatch and every woman in the room breathes *you* in." Her lips stretched taut. "Knowles—she gives you that look, too, but she's sick."

"Why, because she likes me?"

"No." Jez touched her forehead. "The mine plague. She passed out again while you were gone."

"What? How?"

"She was fierce upset about something in the medbay. Next thing we know, she's falling. AO caught her. They checked her out, but … It's worsening. I don't think she has much time."

"*Don't* mention that anywhere," he growled. "Dimar or Baric finds out and she's on the next transport to Tryssinia to die like the rest of them. She's too good for that."

Jez took a step back. Eyed him. "You *do* like her."

"It's not that." But wasn't it? "I care for her. But I care about you and AO—"

"Don't tell him. He's liable to plug you."

"I don't mean that. I …" Knowles was a complication he didn't need. Didn't want. But … *I care what happens to her. A lot.*

"She's *dying*, Tigo. Don't crush her when—"

"Yes. She's dying." Scuz, that hurt to say. "And I won't let her die alone."

Jez stared at him. Slipped out of hyper-reactive attitude and drew in a heaving breath. "This is about your mom."

"Wha—"

The door chimed again.

"What is this? Volante Port?" He huffed. "Allow." This time, when the door whisked open, Tigo froze. "Benjt."

Commander Benjt Crichton looked relieved, but then stiffened at Jez. After a nod to her, he spoke to Tigo. "Meet me in the Eidolon bay in ten."

"Kind of busy," he sniped, allowing his bitterness about being confined to quarters to soak his tone.

Glancing down both directions of the corridor, Crichton balled his fists. "Thought you wanted to do something about the Droseran girl."

"Kersei."

She faced Darius, laughter and light filtering around them. Old irritation at his superior tone tugged at her.

No—that was him, tugging her black curls.

She pulled free. "Treat me not as a child, Darius."

"When you behave as a woman, I will treat you as one."

"That is a very male thing to say, you boiled-out prince."

"See?" he said in that grating tone again. "Epithets do not become young ladies."

With a growl, she swung the javrod.

Darius leapt back like some preternatural creature. Landed easily in a fighting stance, his rod perfectly balanced. "Harness your anger—"

"Have you only talk to spar with?" She arced the rod overhead and aimed for his head. Their wood connected, clacking and vibrating in her palms.

Gracefully, Darius ducked and glided forward. Before she could move, he had her waist. Lifted and pinned her to the ground. Her javrod bounced free. Kneeling beside her, he crammed his javrod across her neck. Grinned down with his blue eyes and sweaty dark-blond hair. "You're a wild, passionate creature, Kersei."

"Who will best you one day," she vowed.

He helped Kersei to her feet and pulled her close. Shoulders touching. Eyes locked. "Everything I have is yours, Kersei. Ask what you would—"

"I would have your defeat."

Handsome, flirtatious Darius smiled back. "Upon payment of a kiss, my lady."

Ugh. Must he? She shoved him back—only this time, the field behind him opened into a great black chasm. Flames roared and surged.

Eyes bulging, Darius drifted back … back … Reaching for her, yet finding only more distance.

"No!" As she grabbed for him, the fire of the black void caught her. Snaked up her arm. Seared. "Augh!"

Kersei jolted upright with a piercing scream. Light bloomed. Disoriented from the nightmare, she sought the light's source only to find her brand glowing. The fire in the dream had not been the explosion, but the accursed brand! Grinding her teeth, she yanked back her sleeve and stared at the strange marks. Overwhelmed, she slumped against the bed. Tears fell—both over Darius and the growing fire of this mark. Crying made her throat tighten.

No. Not the crying. The collar.

She touched it, feeling more a hound on a lead than human when a jolt slapped her fingers.

The fire grew more intense, more demanding. Desperate for relief, she pushed off the bed and hurried to the small water trough along the wall. Thrust her hand beneath the tap. Water trickled out. Though it sizzled and hissed, she found no relief.

Just like life. Her parents and sisters. Her world. Life. Even Darius. Now Jez and her team—AO. All taken from her. Locked on this insipid metal trap in space. Heel of her hand to her head, Kersei battled the futility of tears. There was no point.

She lifted her gaze to the glass. The only sense of not being closed in came by looking at the other half of the circular rings and the black of space. She hated it here. She would have grass beneath her feet and the sun upon her face again.

Escape. Get out of here.

And go where? How exactly was she to escape a space station? She knew not their technology nor … anything. It was just … empty out there. She had no ship, no ability to drive one. They wore suits when working on the metal flower, telling her it must be hard to breathe out there. So how was she to escape? Everything about space seemed cruel and painful. And cold—the air, the buildings, the people.

The man. The man in the pod.

His plight and what they were doing to him cut her pain by half.

"Will you whinge and whine? Or will you seek strength where it is to be found?"

After drying her arm, she shuffled to the windows and peered out at the persistent black. "Okay, Father," she whispered, sliding down her sleeve, "where is strength to be found here?"

Through the glass, across the expanse in the middle of the satellite and through a window on the other side, she spied a glimmer of light. The iereas—Theon—hurried out of where they'd held the man with the strange mark. In the fraction of a second that the door was open, she spied Baric with another man, both studying something on a wall. A picture. What were they looking at? Who was the other man? How had he gotten on this station? Could she escape when he left?

Menacing eyes probed her, and with a start, she realized Baric had spotted her. Face tight with anger, he glowered.

Kersei backed up. Thought to spin away. Not have to look at that malevolent expression. But she had never backed down. She was Stratios. She lifted her jaw. Besides, there was nowhere to go.

"I see your vanity," his voice crackled into the room, his mouth moving on the other side of the satellite. "It is why you were chosen long ago. And it is why you are here now. But since we can't have you growing arrogant in that strength ..."

An explosion of pain stabbed her neck and spine.

Irritation mounted among the 215 when Jez and Tigo led Crichton into the Eidolon hangar. Tigo felt the weight of his failure on Symmachia compound as he allowed the commander on the sacred ground of 215's bay. Especially when Crichton was joined by Commander Dimar.

"Afternoon, Commander." Tigo slid an accusatory glance at Crichton. "Wasn't expecting more company."

"Yeah, maybe you're lost," Diggs suggested as he, AO, Rhinn, and Esq closed up ranks. "In case you missed it, this isn't officers' quarters. It's the Eidolo—"

"Deken." Dimar strode to Tigo. Looked him in the eye. "This'd better not be a mistake."

"Not sure what mistake—did you lose your way, XO?" See? He didn't punch the guy in his face. Wasn't that diplomacy?

"Crichton and I agreed this was best handled by someone other than Baric's loyalists."

The 225.

Well, Tigo wasn't going to beg. "Too eager" looked a lot like stupid.

"Get grunts to do your dirty work?" Rhinn growled.

"Easy," Tigo warned his team. Not showing the proper respect due an officer was grounds for reprimand, and he did not need to rack up any more. He held Dimar's gaze for a long time. "You wanted us to listen. We're listening."

Without further comment, Dimar angled his channeler to Tigo, who hesitated, then offered his own. "Send," Dimar said. A beep sounded as the communication transmitted. "Don't access that until I'm back on the bridge. Fifteen minutes." Sweat beaded on the XO's lip and brow.

"You look scared, Dimar."

"You will be, too." Expression tight, he pivoted and stalked out, with Crichton walking backward as he gave Tigo a firm nod.

Once the bay doors ground shut, Tigo couldn't help but look at his channeler.

"In the corvette?" AO thumbed toward their transport, which had been repaired in Tigo's absence and sat ready for duty near the bay doors. The *Renette*'s communications were secure, but only from lower ranks and civilians, not from Command. And if Dimar had something this valuable …

"Esq."

"Yeah, boss?" she said.

"Still got that black-market channeler?"

She swallowed, knowing full well she should have ditched that by now. "Yeah."

"Get it. Meet us in the *Renette*." He climbed up the rear ramp.

The others claimed seats in the small galley. A minute later Esq bounded in and handed him a channeler with its blue paint heavily scuffed. This model had become obsolete nearly a decade ago, so it had no access to the Neura—the new Symmachian satellite system. "I disabled its ability to relay waves," Esq said. "Thought we might need to contain whatever he dropped."

"Good." Tigo selected the data from Dimar and transferred it to the old device.

He eased onto the seat beside Jez and accessed the file. The screen went black. Then flared to white. Slowly, the camera compensated and focused.

"Looks like some type of lab," Jez said, leaning forward. "That's a medical pod."

"Heavily altered," Diggs noted. "It's the hunter."

"Check it." Rhinn pointed to the upper corner. "There's Kersei."

Sure enough, the Droseran girl was hovering in the background, outside the room, looking in. Like she wasn't supposed to be there. But … "Where is this?"

"Not the *Macedon*," Jez said.

In the feed, Baric loomed behind her.

"Wherever he went, he has them both," Tigo muttered.

"No surprise," AO said.

"No." It just complicated things. A lot. The screen went black, and the team stared at one another, thinking.

"Why'd Dimar give that to us?" Jez asked.

AO shrugged. "Not like we can do anything."

"We don't even know where they are," Diggs muttered.

"Commander," Jez said quietly and nodded to the device.

He lifted it and was surprised to see movement. He wound the video to the black. "Slag me," Tigo hissed. "It's not a blank screen. It's stars."

"A UAV?" AO echoed Tigo's forming thought about an unmanned aerial vehicle. "Fly by."

"How …?"

A large metal arm swung into view.

"What in the 'verse …?"

"A satellite," Rhinn grunted. "A big one."

It continued, the arm growing. Consuming the drone's field of vision. The angle changed, revealing several circles, lined up one behind the other, with each one smaller than the previous one.

Diggs muttered an oath. "That's not a satellite."

Tigo eyed him.

"Saw this in some … reading I did."

Jez lifted an eyebrow. "Reading, as in breaking into TIA servers again?"

"Don't need secure servers for that," AO cut in. "That's all over the shell. It's what Tertian Intelligence has been working on for the last two decades."

Diggs nodded. "He's right. They call it the *Chryzanthe*."

"What's it do?" Tigo asked.

"Wormhole."

"No scuzzin' way," Rhinn scoffed. "Thought they gave up on that after the slag-storm on Nape five years ago."

Nodding, AO went grim, lips tight. "That time the ship they used to test it vanished and the station blew up." He stabbed at the screen. "But this is different—the Nape facility was on the ground. This is in space. I don't know how it's there and nobody knows, but that's what that station does."

"But where?" Jez said. "We can't do anything if we don't know where."

Silence clobbered them as they sat staring at the channeler, thinking through the ramifications, the possibilities … The thought that Baric was in charge of this worried Tigo, that he had the hunter and girl there confounded him. If it generated wormholes and was functional … they had to get to the girl—now.

"The stars," Diggs announced, motioning to the old channeler. "Map the constellations." His dark eyes probed as he ran the video back and then forward. "Look, this is Narelle-26 there."

"Got it." Jez opened her channeler.

"No!" Tigo barked. "This stays off wave until we know more."

"Pretty sure …" Diggs continued, "here's Mikallia 7—yeah, that's Fiona's Bow."

"Wait," Tigo said. "That means …"

"Herakles."

Jez peered closer, pointing at a blue dot. "Is that …?"

"Drosero," Tigo groaned. "That's why Command's been pushing so hard to colonize."

"And that's how we found the *Renette* adrift," Jez suggested. "*Macedon* has been monitoring the whole region between Drosero and Sicane because of the *Chryzanthe*. It must be orbiting Sicane."

"Yes, but how'd Kersei end up on the *Renette* in the first place?" AO asked.

"Kersei said her uncle was with her," Jez reminded them. "She swore by it. What if she was right?"

"It was empty when we opened it," Rhinn countered. "Except for Kersei."

"Maybe they jumped ship," Esq said. "Left her there to die."

"She was knocked out—maybe someone boarded the corvette when it was adrift."

"That's a stretch," Jez said.

"Everything is a stretch! Either way," Tigo mumbled, "if we can't get the girl or that Kynigos back—"

"We may never."

His channeler beeped again. "He sent me another drop."

"Is Dimar a total dimwit?" Jez growled. "He'll be tracked."

Tigo slipped the data to the old device and then erased it from his channeler before opening it.

A mechanized voice came through. *"What you're going to see defies explanation. This is why I'm risking my life and yours to send it. Something has to be done. I don't even know whose uniform I'm wearing anymore. This is a live feed video from moments ago. Do something. Please."*

Tigo frowned and felt the scowls of his team as the video switched.

"What the—" Diggs breathed.

The lab with the altered medical pod appeared again. This time, a willowy person in a pale blue lab coat glided around the pod.

Glided was the wrong word. In fact, the whole way that person moved—

"Is that zero-g in there?" Jez asked.

Suddenly, the person spun.

And Tigo froze. Couldn't move. Couldn't process.

"What is that?"

He couldn't answer as the … *thing* turned back. Accessed the pod, revealing the unmistakable face of the Kynigos.

"By the Ladies," Jez said. "He's … *white*."

As in no blood in his veins. Tubes and lines flowed in and out of his body.

Then he lifted from the pod. Stood—no, floated like the thing working on him. "What in the Void is that thing?" Tigo muttered.

Baric appeared from the side, dragging—

"No!" Jez cupped a hand over her mouth.

Dark curls in disarray, the Droseran girl—Kersei—thrashed, her face etched in terror as Baric dragged her closer.

AO grunted. "C'mon, pet. Give him—"

Kersei stabbed her elbow into Baric's gut. Then backfisted him. He stumbled back and she darted forward—straight at the camera, as if she were seeking refuge in it—but then her face contorted. She arched her spine, revealing the silver band around her throat.

"Son of a—he collared her!" Jez cried.

Diggs shook his head. "What a sick—"

"Let's go," AO growled.

"Say again, Corporal?" Tigo understood their anger. But they had to be smart.

AO punched the codes to close the bay doors. "Using the stars from that wave, we know that station is orbiting Sicane. That means we have four hours to put together a plan."

"No slaggin' way," Rhinn said. "I am not going over there until we know who's in charge and what that *thing* was."

"I know you're short on brains, Rhinnock, but that's what we in the 'verse call an *alien*," AO growled. "An *alien* life form with intelligence we don't have. Somehow, they're using that hunter …"

"Whoa." Tigo stood. Held the bulkhead. "Hold up." Things were hitting nuclear too hard, too fast.

"Commander, you're the first to go save a damsel in distress."

Eyeing Rhinn, Tigo felt like he'd suited up with a malfunctioning O_2 snake. They were right. Something had to be done. And it'd been handed to him. Violent compassion, right? "Jez, file a departure—anything that will look routine."

Though she gave the barest of hesitations, she moved to the cockpit.

"Diggs, get 'er ready."

But Diggs was already on Jez's heels.

"I can't believe this," Rhinn said. "This …"

Tigo huffed and glanced around at his team. "We're Eidolon, tasked with readiness on land and in space for the protection and preservation of *humanity*. Baric and that alien are colluding against a Kynigos and a civilian, and that's probable cause. So, if you want to stay behind, disembark. Now. No harm. No foul."

"Scuz that," AO said. "Suit up. Let's take her for a spin."

Tigo gave a firm nod. "Suits to dark—no record of this. We do not need a repeat of the Drosero fiasco."

CHRYZANTHE STATION, ORBITING SICANE

It was bad enough for her arm to burn, but now her neck? Tears slipping free, Kersei lay on the floor, unable to move after the electrifying shock and a pervasive chill that drove daggers of ice into her veins.

"Pleasant?" Baric stood over her. "That was the smallest dose."

She wanted to speak, kick him, but her body wouldn't respond.

"You probably feel cold. The collar taps into your spine. It essentially freezes your nerves." He sneered, eyeing the willowy creature. "You'll recover use of your limbs first. When you do, stand and cooperate. If you do not, we'll increase the … motivation. Are we clear?"

If she could just spit …

"Whyyyyyy fight what yooooou cannot defeeeeeat?" a hollow voice intoned.

"Xisya is right. Why fight it?" That stupid smarmy smile again. "Unless you want to end up like the hunter."

Kersei's gaze shifted to the man suspended by cables over the pod. Terrifying. Glowing. White, translucent skin. Though he wasn't moving, though he spoke no words, his horror, his pain roiled through his now-glowing eyes. Somehow, she heard his screams. His torment. It twisted and squeezed her heart.

Oh Ancient, have mercy!

"On your feet, Princess."

Her body defied Kersei, lifting her from the ground as if on its own, positioning her to face the lithe creature with its—*her?*—unnaturally long face and stretched eye slats. Little mouth to speak with. No ears. No hair.

The thing came toward her. "I am awarrrre"—her words echoed in Kersei's head like a magnificent gong—"that my appeeeeeearance is staaaartling. We have noooo use of hair in our worrrrrld, and grrrrrravity is less strenuuuuous on our bodies."

The explanations did not help. "W-what are you?"

"I am a Khatriiiiiiza," the creature said in that nauseating timbre.

Kersei's mind thrashed against the frightening being and had the idea to flee. She swallowed. "How can I understand you?"

"The collar," Baric said. "Not only does it limit your movements on the *Chryzanthe*, but it injects a molecule that allows you to both hear and understand Lady Xisya." He focused on the alien. "We must finish. Our timetable is short."

Xisya glided forward. Somehow, though she barely had a mouth, it seemed she smiled. For some reason, Kersei felt herself relaxing, despite the part of her that demanded she scream. The Khatriza put a hand on Kersei's shoulder.

"She must not remember," Baric said.

Head tilted to the side, Xisya's expression didn't change.

Relief rushed through Kersei—then a violent sensation of falling …

"She will not reeeeemember this."

Some smells Marco couldn't ignore no matter how hard he tried. They demanded action, honor, justice. Such was the scent of murder. It clung to the perpetrator like no other.

Yet what was he to do when that scent led him to someone who could upend the very tenuous peace keeping the quadrants in check?

Tucked in the shadows of a bar, Marco knuckled his mouth, watching the man drinking to excess. He believed he'd gotten away with his crime. There was truth in that—Ares was dead. And as of this minute, the murderer was not in custody.

Nor would Marco take him in. He could not. A thin loophole of the Kynigos Code. There was a reason for the Codes and hunting only by Decree. A hunter delivering his own justice could destroy the system that had been in place since space flight first came to Kynig.

Yet the death of Ares had to be connected to what happened on Drosero. A medora and two powerful leaders, all set against Droseran colonization, died within months of each other. And the girl—was she a casualty or a contributor? The Iereans, who were even less politically inclined than Kynigos, were adamant of her innocence.

With a belch, the killer stumbled out of the bar and into the busyness of the city.

Marco exited and went in the opposite direction. Turned left and sprinted to the end of the street. He tic-tacked up the corners of two buildings, gripped the ledge, and hauled himself onto the rooftop. Hustling across, he ran in a crouch. He slunk along the edge and spotted the killer trudging up the winding road to a well-lit café, where he bought a pint of warmed cordi. Marco used the moment to capture a vid. With that shiny piece clearly visible on his shoulder. The man downed the drink then headed to a small building attached to the chancellor's residence.

Well, well. What was this?

Marco's mind ran a dozen different courses, most leading to one conclusion: the chancellor was in bed with Symmachia. But these days, who wasn't? Except Drosero. Though, he'd wager his living someone on Drosero *had* bedded them. It would explain much.

He again grabbed a capture, then waited until the man went inside before skipping across rooftops to the historical district, a quiet neighborhood populated by ergatis, the working class. Perched on a turret, he peered across the alley to a hostel and the upper-level flat. The Droserans sat on the rooftop terrace, talking.

Their voices were quiet but there was no mistaking their angry scents. Silver-haired Ixion was talking to the eldest son of the murdered Xanthus, who no doubt would assume leadership of the clan. An argument rose and escalated, though Ixion sought to quell the rising tempers. A quarter hour later, the Xanthus left and Ixion alone remained on the terrace.

What drove this man? How could he—

"Did you have need to speak with us or do you just like to watch?"

Marco felt a grin. "The view from here is better." He must give care not to be overheard regarding this endeavor. So he took a running start and leapt over the alley. He hit and rolled into his shoulder, then came up straight. He pivoted to face the Plisiázon.

"Have you heard of doors, Kynigos?"

Marco noted he did not call him master this time. "And windows," he said. "Too civilized."

Ixion gave a smirking nod. "Why do you spy on us?"

"You have a channeler?"

"I am Droseran."

"Not what I asked." Marco held his gaze.

Ixion lifted one from his pocket. "It has been useful while here."

Marco took it, tapped it to his vambrace and delivered the images. He held it out and said, "What you do with this is your own business."

Ixion glanced at the screen, then raised his eyes Marco, none pleased with what he saw on that image.

"Look at his right shoulder." Another scent came from behind. One of the Xanthus had returned.

Wariness held Ixion fast before he slowly glanced at the screen. Then tapped to zoom in. A storm filled the man's eyes. "That's Ares's sigil."

"A trophy, I'd wager. He was last seen entering the chancellor's residence."

Ixion's gaze snapped up. Darkened.

"You accuse the Cenoans, Kynigos?" The voice came from behind.

Marco stepped to the ledge and inclined his head to Ixion. "It is your knowledge now."

The first son charged forward. "Why are you afraid to hunt this man down when you know he killed my father?"

Ixion held out a staying hand to the Xanthus. "Peace, Bazyli. He delivers a great gift."

"Gift—"

"Would you prefer he not assist us at all?" Blue eyes pulsed with meaning as Ixion watched Marco. "Because that is his only other option. To maintain his honor, he must remain neutral in affairs like this."

With a nod of appreciation, Marco stepped back. Over open air. And dropped.

CHRYZANTHE STATION, ORBITING SICANE

Kersei awoke with a start. Her head ached as if she'd run the gauntlet. And been thrown a thousand times by Bastien. She groaned and pushed off the mattress. Touching her temple, she looked around, confused. When had she returned to her room?

She snorted. This wasn't a room. It was a prison.

"She will not remember ..."

The voice, so strange and icy, felt like a threat. Who ... who had said that? And what wasn't she supposed to remember? Missing thoughts clung to the shadows of a dark hall, their mournful cries screeching in those empty corridors.

"How do you feel?"

Sucking in a breath, Kersei swung around, the room upending. She tilted. Fell off the bed with a yelp.

"Sorry." Baric rose from a chair nearby. "I did not mean to startle you." He extended a hand to help her.

She eyed it. Knew she shouldn't accept anything from him. "Why are you in my bedchamber?" Some memory, some *thing* lurked behind a thick curtain in her mind.

"She will not remember this."

But she did. And did not. Yet she must. She groaned. Touched her forehead again, straining to recall.

"You fainted," Baric said blithely. "The effects of space. Your body isn't used to it. Eat so you can remember—"

"Yes." She must remember something. But … "Remember what?"

His gaze sharpened. Lips went taut. "I said, so you can regain your strength." He picked up a small roll from a tray she hadn't noticed.

Is that what he'd said? Then why had she thought … An urgency to recall something sped through her pulse. Of great importance.

Baric touched her hair.

Scowling, she leaned away.

He grabbed her by the neck, a sensation stabbing the back of her skull. "You are mine," he hissed.

She nearly choked, disgusted with him so close. "I am no man's."

"I warned you not to anger me." He jerked her forward, his mouth on hers. Hands going places no man's should.

Kersei writhed, a strangled scream clawing her throat. Fear struck an uneven chord as she fought his grip. He spun her. Slammed her against the wall, pinning her between his weight and the cold wall. Smothering fear squeezed the air from her lungs. Froze her as his hot breath spread over her neck. She tried to shove backward, but he was unmoving. His grip in her hair tightened, prickling her scalp with fire, as he tugged her against him. Mouth wet as he kissed her neck and jaw. It reminded her of cows when they stretched their long, slimy tongues to take treats.

Do something, she ordered herself. If she did not, what innocence she had left would be torn away. Training and instinct had her reach over her shoulder and clutch his collar. Kersei let her full weight drop, pulling his head forward. Right into the wall with a hard thunk. She slipped free and leapt back.

With a growl, Baric rounded, cupping his forehead. "That's going to cost you."

Heart pounding, knowing she had nowhere to go, Kersei mentally searched for weapons in the room. Nothing. She saw nothing. *Oh Ancient, help!*

Baric lunged at her.

She whirled around, grabbing the chair.

His shoulder slammed into her. Pushing her to the floor. Her chin hit hard. Chattered her teeth. His full weight fell on her. Pinning her. Pawing at her clothes.

Panic drumming, she elbowed him—and he laughed. Turned her. She felt the crushing angles of his body. Fought and growled. His attempt to disrobe her provided an opening. Kersei stabbed her hand into his throat.

He gagged, groping for air.

She caught his arm and yanked hard.

The captain's head cracked against the floor, stunning him. He swayed and careened.

She leapt up, tripping over the long cloak. Scrambled to the door. It wouldn't open. She had to get out. Over her shoulder, she saw him come to his feet, face contorted in fury. Something moved behind him. A shape. Looming outside the window.

Kersei sucked in a breath, startled at the dark shape. A ghoul. She blinked and now there was nothing. But there had been something. *Someone.* Floating in space?

"Can't distract me that easily, girl. You owe me."

She backed away, searching again for a weapon, anything to fend him off. She bumped a table. Heard the water pitcher falter. She reached for it.

The captain lurched again. She curled her fingers around the handle and brought it down on his head. It shattered with a resounding crack. Glass and water whooshed, sending water and blood cascading down his face and neck.

Baric stumbled. His eyes went unfocused as he slumped forward, but she skidded sideways and let him fall—right onto the shard of the handle. He growled and arched back. Blood seeped over the floor. On a knee, he staggered. Pushed himself up.

Blood and boil, would he not stay down? She darted away.

He followed, but his steps were uneven. His gaze black with fury. "I will take everything from you."

Throat constricting, Kersei spotted a floor lamp. Shuffled back to it, sure not to take her gaze from him for long. He saw what she intended, his gaze bouncing between her and the lamp. She had one chance. Kersei threw herself at it. Gripped the metal pole. Jerked it up and aimed at his head.

It stopped short, the cord anchoring it.

He grinned at her failure. Stormed forward.

She snapped the other end at him. The brace frame thumped his head. While it didn't take him down, it did free the cord from the wall. She felt it give. Felt the freedom. And cracked the base right at his temple.

Baric dropped like a wet rag at her feet. Shuddering through her own frenetic breaths, she saw his chest still rising and falling. Alive. Meant time was short.

Where are you going to go, you idiot? The door won't even open! Her mind was flooded with images—the man in the bay. And … something shadowy there. Something terrible. Dangerous. But her mind refused access to the threat.

Get out now. Remember later.

But how did she get out? The collar controlled where she could go. She should hide his body behind the long sofa. Hooking her arms under Baric's bloody form, she hefted him up and dragged him behind the couch.

At the sound of the door hissing open, she dropped Baric and snapped straight.

Guards entered. "Sir, we—" They froze, their gazes falling on the captain. Weapons snapped up. "Hands! Hands now!"

Kersei's panic renewed as she lifted her arms. "I … he tried to—"

"On the floor! Down on the floor," a guard shouted as he stalked into the room.

Furious and defeated, she went to a knee, trembling.

A strange whistle sounded in the hall. Then a thump.

The guard closest to her spun and darted out. He saw something and took aim. A bright light struck his chest. His armor sizzled and he slumped to the glossy white floor.

On her knees, Kersei stared, mute. Confused. Scared. Was it the creature? Had she turned on everyone?

The shots were coming from the direction of that room where the man with the strange facial mark had been suspended with cabling. Climbing to her feet, she hesitated. If she went out there, she had no way to defend herself. She should hide. Yet her feet carried her to the corridor.

A loud, angry noise grated through the station, slowing her. That, and the realization that she had no way to get off this place. That Baric would come to in a rage. But maybe he'd die—it was a horrible hope.

She stepped outside and glanced back in the direction from which the shots had come. Seeing nothing, she threw herself to the right. And collided with an armor-clad body. She screamed.

The man caught her. Hooked her waist.

Kersei erupted in a fevered fight against him.

"Easy, easy, pet!" The tinny voice reached through her wild panic. Stilled her. "Better," came the voice with a mechanical echo. "You okay?"

Startled, she looked over her shoulder at the black helmet. "AO?"

He set her down. "You okay? Got holes we need to patch?"

"What?"

He motioned to her clothes. "Cloak's bloody."

She glanced at it. "Oh. No." She blinked, glancing around, trying to get her bearings. Unsure at first where the blood had come from. "It's Baric's."

"You did that?"

"With a vase, then a lamp. I ... I don't know if he's alive."

Grinning, he turned. "Can we give her a medal?"

Another suit was there, working a large, oval door. "Let's get out of here first."

"Jez." Relief rushed through Kersei.

"Princess, suit up."

"Here." AO handed her a suit of some kind. Then motioned. "Might have to shed that cloak."

She was already removing it. Stepped into the suit and secured it, surprised at how heavy it was.

"Let's move, people," came another voice. "Guards made it through the barrier."

AO helped her with the helmet. "Since you don't have a thumper, you'll need the snake." He bent sideways as his hands worked to secure it. Then he put something on her wrist. Tapped into the device. A tube slid around her face, making her stiffen. "Let it do its job. You'll be able to breathe, as well as talk and hear us."

Cold shot through her sinuses and she sucked in a breath, which made it sting. She winced, then blinked. "How did you find me?"

"Little birdie," AO said and tapped the top of her helmet. "Good?"

She nodded.

"Let's move!" AO led her down the corridor. But she slowed, feeling like she was forgetting something. Feeling like she should go in the opposite direction.

"Move!" Another suit jogged up from behind. She didn't recognize the face in the helmet. Was this the leader? The one Jez called Tigo? "Hey. Is the Kynigos here?"

Kersei struggled not only with the heavy, awkward suit, but the images assaulting her. Terrifying, painful images. She tried to grip her head, but the helmet ... "Wait," she whispered. Glanced back.

A strange symbol.

"She will not remember this."

Cold pinch at the base of her neck.

Blurry figure—shape warped by confusion.

Glowing.

"Nose bleed!" AO barked.

Screams.

Floating people.

The man.

"Eyes are rolling," Jez said. Arms wrapped Kersei. "What's the snake's O_2 level?"

Symbol.

Tap-tap. "Kersei. With me?"

Oval, elongated head. Stubbed chin and mouth.

"Kersei!"

Man. Half circles on his nose.

"Ker—"

Screams.

Cold. Dark. Black.

With the girl hooked over his shoulder, Tigo hoofed it back to the bay, grateful for the suit's power assist. Clear of the airlock, he launched and aimed for the scout hovering a league out. It'd been the only way to reach the rings without being detected.

But getting Kersei off the station should've been harder.

A pulse beam seared past him, narrowly missing his suit.

That's more like it. "Taking fire!" Using heel thrusters to rotate, Tigo wheeled and drew his weapon. He had a precarious time managing direction, defensive maneuvers, and protecting the girl. Whatever happened to her just before they launched—he hoped she wasn't dead.

AO and Jez adjusted their trajectory to cover him, returning fire on the *Chryzanthe.*

Freed to get to the scout, he swiveled back with another boost. Five hundred feet now.

"Augh!" came AO's grunt. "Bloody—"

"Save your breath!" Jez ordered. "Get to the *Renette.*"

Tigo looked back.

AO was tumbling, his suit venting oxygen.

"Move, AO. Now!"

"You might be ugly," Rhinn said as he covered their six, "but you're our kind of ugly. Get to the *Renette*, old man."

With that, AO rolled and aimed in Tigo's direction.

Tigo sailed into the rear bay of the *Renette*, gaping and waiting for her crew with Esq anchored to assist as jumpmaster. She hooked a line on the girl's suit, then his, and slapped his shoulder. Tigo magged down on the deck, grateful for the firm magnetic lock as he steadied his precious cargo. "On board," he reported. "Plus one. Pull it in, Two-one-five. Let's dust this place."

AO clambered on board next and scrambled to the front, where he grabbed sealant for the tear in his suit. Until the bay door closed and they repressurized, he needed what was leaking.

Tigo secured the girl into a rack and turned as Jez thumped into the wall, grinning at Rhinn behind her.

"Go, Diggs! Go!"

He thunked in beside Jez, grabbing a clip to hook in.

The door was closing and the scout coming around when a pulse beam carried its perfectly placed shot right through Esq's helmet.

"No!" Tigo lunged for her.

She flipped backward, then hung limp, floating from the anchor.

24

ZLARES, CENON

Rest eluded Marco, though he lay on the bed with eyes closed. Especially when he detected a familiar signature. He peeled himself off the mattress and squinted at his advocate. "What brings you to Cenon, Rico?"

"You won't like it."

Wary, he didn't dare try to guess. But hadn't he already? "Tell me."

"The girl will be arriving soon."

On his feet, he lifted his vambrace. Opened the Decree and stared at the timer. "Could be two weeks and—"

"She'll arrive on a transport shuttle in two days."

Marco scowled. "How do you know this?"

Rico huffed. "High Lord Theon visited the Citadel. You've not met him, but he is next in line to become Supreme Lord on Iereania. When they asked me to bring this news—"

"Wait." Marco tried not to pace, but his body insisted. "Why are you here? Why didn't you just thump me?"

"Because I also bring a reprimand."

Marco gritted his teeth.

"Interference with political matters is strictly forbidden." Rico leaned against the wall and folded his arms.

How in the 'verse did they know he'd provided intel to the Xanthus? "Since when is murder a political matter?"

Rico sniffed. "You know well what the death of Ares means. That's why you provided aid."

"No aid. Just—"

"Just a video of the murderer entering the chancellor's residence."

Curse the reek! He had wrongly trusted Ixion. "Does a man have no privacy?"

"A man, mayhap," Rico shrugged, his long light brown hair curling along his neck. "But a Kynigos? Not while Decreed."

Marco sat and pressed his fingertips to his forehead. "I cannot pretend to understand what is happening in the quadrants. Everything is upside down, and for me to be tethered to *priests* …" He heard the revulsion in his own words.

"How is your arm?"

He scowled. "What has that to do—"

"Theon asks."

Anger churned. Coiled and constricted around Marco's throat. "It is of no concern to anyone but me."

"I sense your desperation," Rico said quietly.

"Sense?" Marco sneered. "Or smell?"

"Does it matter?"

Nay, it did not. Except they were not supposed *anak* one another. Yet *anaktesios* was as natural to hunters as breathing. Even with this, his advocate had made a trip for intel that could be passed via vid or thumper. "What else brings you?"

Rico's expression shifted. "Urbain was on a diplomatic mission to Thyrolia …"

"What happened?" Had he fallen ill, as many had when too long on that diseased planet? Or had something more nefarious gone down?

"Shuttle was found docked, empty. No sign of him, and his vambrace is no longer waving his location."

"So." He grunted. "You travel here and risk your own life."

"The Citadel believes we should change our patterns, be less predictable. What better way than to visit my favorite mentee?" He stood. "Come, let's sup."

"Is that all you give thought to—eating?" There was more to this.

With a lecherous grin, Rico said, "Not all. We could seek out a chatelaine."

"Nay," Marco growled, stalking out into the early morning as Rico's laugh followed. "Let's eat." He set out for his favorite café, the one in the market where Baytu Smirlet worked. He chose the seating that left his back protected and a clear view of the market and all who entered the fenced-in café.

"In earnest?" Rico asked as they sat down. "Have you not more refined tastes, Brother? We are Kynigos."

Marco *anak'd* the area, then, confident things were serene, let himself relax so he could enjoy his meal. "Quick service and decent food."

"Decent! Bah." Rico flung a hand in the direction of a more expensive establishment on the corner of the square. "There you have refined food and attentive service."

"At twice the cost."

"Can I take your order?" Baytu's words were curt, her efflux as well.

Rico sensed it, stiffening and glancing at Marco.

"Cordi and the roast melt with fried potatoes." He kept his gaze neutral, letting his advocate know there was no danger from Baytu.

"I'll have the same," Rico said, returning the menu he'd never looked at. "Oh, except no cordi. Give me whatever lager you have." He folded his arms as the woman left and narrowed a gaze at Marco. "What happened with her?"

"Jubbah Smirlet's bound."

"Ah."

"She's not a fan."

"And you chose this place to eat?" He sniggered. "You have strange taste, Marco."

"She is aware of who I am and what I am willing to do. She may not like me, but she will serve me expediently and with little harassment."

"That efflux is harassment enough."

He gave a cockeyed nod. "Granted."

"I know the real reason you eat here," Rico said, settling back. "The cordi."

Baytu delivered their drinks and Marco tipped his glass at his advocate. "To the Decree."

"And the hu—"

"Attention. Attention." The word was repeated in a half-dozen languages, drawing their gazes to the massive screen mounted on the tallest building and hovering over the square. Maximum reach for Zlares. "It is by the order of the Tertian Space Coalition and Symmachian Command that a warrant is issued for the immediate arrest and return of dangerous fugitive Kersei Dragoumis."

Marco lowered his glass to the table, staring at the image they'd posted of the girl, glittering in digital glory for all to see. Dark, spiraling curls. His heart thumped as he shifted his gaze to Rico.

Who wasn't watching the display. But Marco.

"You knew," Marco muttered. "How? How did you know about this?"

"Kyros informed us there would be increased efforts to find the girl. They'd learned that this bulletin would go out."

"They learned it would?" Marco scowled. "Then it was planned."

"Mayhap. I think it's playing the alerts on a planet-progressive status."

"So the farther from wherever she was kept, the later they're played."

"Our guess," Rico agreed. "For Kyros to know about this means she was being held somewhere close to her homeworld or Iereania."

Marco growled. "It also means—if they are looking for her—that she is no longer with the Symmachians. Right?"

"So it would seem."

Marco ran a hand over his face and sighed. "They're making my hunt more difficult." Then he grinned. "I will capture her as she lands and remand—"

"Remember, she cannot go to Iereania until the appointed time."

He scowled again. "What am I to do? Web and *store* her?"

"Just make sure she stays alive, then get her to Iereania."

TSC *RENETTE*

The great support beam crashed down with a mighty roar. Flames leapt away, then rushed back in to consume it. Screams reached out, vain pleas for rescue. Ma'ma—her pale blue gown splotched with blood. Lexina, her head oddly twisted. Flames rushed toward Kersei, roaring, laughing. Screaming. Taunting.

"Augh!"

"Easy."

In a cold sweat, Kersei shuddered. Glanced around. "Jez."

"Yeh, it's okay, love. You're safe now."

A chill traced her spine as she relaxed. "I'm s-s-so cold."

"That's the sedative wearing off." Jez touched the panel over her. "This should warm the tube."

Sure enough, heat rippled over Kersei, aware now of the contraption that held her in place. "What …?"

"You blacked out. To travel, we had to strap you in," Jez said. "Your vitals were dangerously low." She gave Kersei a speculative glance. "What's in your neck?"

Her hand flew to the collar, but it was gone. "You got it off?"

"Diggs is good with tech, but I was talking about the implant."

The words threw confusing images into Kersei's mind—a strange dog-face woman with a hollow voice. And a symbol. The captain trying to rape her …

"Hey-hey-hey!" Jez warned. "You're going to crash again if you don't calm."

Wrangling her thoughts and pulse under control, Kersei reminded herself she wanted to be more like Jez. The epitome of calm.

"Teeli just docked," came Tigo's voice. "She'll be here in ten." He appeared and hovered over Kersei. His handsome features wrinkled in concern. "How you holding up?"

She glanced at Jez, but decided to skip her emotional wellbeing. "Where am I?"

"Docked at Cyrox. A Symmachian way station."

Her eyes widened.

"Easy," Jez said. "Keep your heart rate down until we figure out what that thing in your neck is doing."

"That … they put it on me—the collar."

"Yeah, collars we're familiar with," Tigo said with a grunt. "But the umbilical in your neck is new."

"She—" Kersei stopped, thinking. What she? "*They* did it on that station with rings."

"Yeah, figured that out."

"Think it's a tracer?" AO asked from behind the commander.

"Or a kill switch," Rhinn muttered.

"Oy!" Jez scowled at him. "Enough."

"Kill switch?" Kersei balked. "What does that mean?" A question without sense, for its name alone betrayed the meaning.

"Wouldn't put it past them," Rhinn said.

Tigo shoved him toward the rear. "Watch for the doc."

"I …" Kersei hated the whine in her voice. "Can they do that? Kill me, all the way out here?" She wasn't even sure how far they were from the station. "I can't—why is everyone trying to kill me?" Hot tears crashed down her face. "I just want to go home. I want my father and—"

"Calm down," Jez said, with a growl, "or I'll put you under again."

"Doc's here," AO's gruff voice announced.

"Teeli," Tigo said as the doctor slipped into view. "Thanks for coming."

"Not easy getting a pass with the captain gone, but I told Dimar I needed to see a specialist." She inclined her head to the bay. "What do we have?"

"Did a scan." Jez pointed to a screen on the wall. "Any idea wh—"

"What in the 'verse …?" Dr. Knowles slipped on gloves and leaned closer, squinting at Kersei's neck.

"We were hoping you could tell us."

Silence amplified the hum of the machines around Kersei. She closed her eyes and tried to tell herself it was okay. That she would be fine. That things would work out.

But she saw a man. That man in the tubes.

"Kersei?" Dr. Knowles sounded worried, forcing Kersei to look at her. But she was studying at the panel. "That's better." The doctor's expression went from taut to a near smile.

"We extracted her," Tigo explained, "and she went rigid, her nose started bleeding, and she was out."

"I'd say so," Dr. Knowles agreed. "This"—she drew her finger to one end of a silver line in the image—"is her temporal lobe, which affects short-term memory. But whatever this is, it goes through the cerebellum, which affects her coordination and equilibrium."

"Why?" Jez asked.

"Can you remove it?" Tigo asked at the same time. He shrugged when both eyed him. "If he's tracking ..."

Dr. Knowles looked worried. She studied the imaging. "I am not sure I can remove it. I've never seen technology this advanced." She turned her gaze to Kersei. "Do you know who put this in you?"

"A woman." Wait. What woman? "I ... I don't know. Maybe it was the captain." Her mind was like a child's painting—chaotic and blurred.

Brow furrowing, Dr. Knowles lifted Kersei's eyelids in turn and peered at each eye. "Do you feel like you've forgotten something?"

Kersei frowned. "Yes ... I keep hearing a woman say, 'She will not remember this.'" Saying it awakened thoughts, memories. The voice she'd been hearing—it *was* a woman.

"And you don't remember?"

"No ... yes." She sighed. "Pieces—things that make no sense. A man. A symbol. This strange ... creature."

"Do it," Tigo said. "We have to get her on a shuttle ASAP, and she can't go with that thing in her head."

"Even if I do this," the doctor warned, "there's no guarantee how its removal will affect her or if she'll remember what she's forgotten."

"Please," Kersei pleaded. "I don't want it in me. The feelings I have about it, the vague memories are ... terrifying." Tears stung her eyes again. "Do it."

"Just know there are no guarantees." With a nod, Dr. Knowles looked to Tigo. "Okay, let's prep her."

Running rooftops, Marco trained rigorously. Burned off his anxiety and his thrill—the hunt was most invigorating when engaging the quarry. And, according to the intel Kyros passed down, Kersei Dragoumis would arrive today. Since he had no idea the hour or the transport delivering her, he finished his predawn workout, cleansed, then planted himself at a café within sight of the port. The weeks of platitudes and frustration would prove whether or not the iereas could make good on their promise.

Anticipation wound through his veins as another ship unburdened itself and passengers filed out. He flicked open his channeler and holo'd the girl's image, which he'd lifted from the galactic-wide bulletin, even though her face was burned into his mind already. A mass of curly black hair. Petite, but athletic. One by one the passengers disembarked. Still no quarry.

As two more ships set down in the concrete port, a vidscreen sprang to life and again announced that fugitive Kersei Dragoumis was wanted by Symmachian Command, the Tertian Space Coalition for theft, and Droseran Authorities for murder.

Marco groaned. They were either poorly timed or perfectly timed. The two new ships emptied passengers by way of long, metal umbilical stairs. He hated transports. He'd never board a flying city—too many scents, too many overlooked regulation violations. Though the first, a luxury liner, probably held every possible comfort desired.

Bruised and battled, a short-range salvage/transport vessel settling at the far dock intrigued him. *She's on that one.* He wasn't sure how he knew. Just did. Workers unloaded cargo from belowdecks as a shipwalk telescoped from the stern. A queue of tired passengers soon spilled out, markedly less wealthy than those from the luxury liner, now delivering the elite, *evengis*, by pod from the uppermost level. Nobility. *Always above the rest.*

In a hunt, they all webbed the same. Hard. Patience thinning, he ordered himself to remain put.

There. That was her.

A hooded jacket, fastened at her small waist and hanging to her knees in an arc, concealed her face and hair. Black pants—tactical, at that—were an odd choice and drew attention, just as her efflux did. For him, at least. Her gait seemed awkward. Uncoordinated. Why was she so pale?

Clinging to the shadows, Marco stayed out of sight, yet closed in to familiarize himself with her efflux. First, he processed the fear and panic. Her signature slowed him, forced him to take it in. Appreciate the unique combination. Strong, slightly sweet with a dark, musky-earthy aroma and layered with a milky-warm tone. Strangely calming. Yet, there was something else …

What? He angled his head, homing.

Urgency flared from another direction, distracting Marco. Shifted his gaze, squinting as he sifted what assailed him until he found …

He spotted the white hair tipped with blue bobbing through the crowds, rushing the port, and growled. "No," he muttered, knowing well the intent of Baytu Smirlet: Revenge. Against him. How did she know he hunted the girl?

Pitching himself into the air, he aimed at a ledge across the alley. He caught it and toed the plaster wall. Fingers gripping the stone tight, he peered down the length of his body to the lower ledge, then shoved backward and dropped. Caught the next one. And the next. Swung to a fire escape. Hooked the last rung and silently deposited himself on the street.

He broke into a jog, dodging people, electric footpaths, and crafts zipping down airlanes. Deft at navigating crowds, Marco slipped up behind Smirlet's wife before she reached the port queue. "Do not interfere with my hunt."

She stiffened, her neck stretching, body going rigid. "She's a child."

"I will not warn you again," he cautioned. "The mark of an interferer is difficult to overcome."

"Difficult," she spat at him over her shoulder, "but not impossible."

He should not ask, but he must. "How did you know I hunt?"

She laughed. "I saw you and that other hunter when the bulletin came across. Then when you started heading for the docks—she is here, and I was right." Her eyes narrowed. "I will not let you destroy another family!"

The woman was far too perceptive for her own good. He must make Baytu understand her precarious situation. "If you are marked for interference, will the magistrate declare for or against your husband?"

That shifted her efflux from furious to desperate. Her lips parted, hesitating. "You wouldn't." But her scent warned she knew he would.

Marco inclined his head. "Leave off. This is not your concern." Warmth trickled through his right forearm, distracting.

"Look at her," Baytu balked, indicating to the girl in line. "She's terrified."

The roiling scent of his quarry was indeed rank. "Fugitives usually are."

Large brown eyes watched those around her as others in the queue provided papers. Did she have the necessary documentation? He couldn't let her get arrested. That would unnecessarily complicate things.

"As are the abused and wrongly accused."

He needed to move closer to monitor the girl's progress through security. "Stay clear. Last warning." With that, he rolled around her to find a safe distance until the girl cleared the checkpoints. No need to draw attention, especially with her wanted by more than the Iereans. He had to protect not only his hunt, but her, the quarry, to ensure a successful hunt and his honor.

Intensifying heat in his forearm shot sweat down his temples and neck. Hand fisted, he struggled against the fire until his arm shook. Training and fortitude mustered to stop him from growling.

Red blurred around him. "I must speak with you." Deep, dark eyes bored into Marco. An iereas.

Reek! "The Decree is set. Leave me to—"

"She's in danger," the short, stocky iereas said, and his efflux affirmed what he spoke, stilling Marco.

"From Symmachians or local authorities?"

"Both." The iereas nodded. "As well as a self-seeking, soon-to-be-supreme lord."

Marco stopped, recalling his advocate's mention of one such iereas. "Theon." He considered the brown-eyed man with tight ash curls. "One of your own."

"He may be an iereas by trade, but not by heart." The man wet his lips. "Theon is given to his greed and lust for power. He does not follow the Ancient or the Ladies."

Intriguing. "What do you want of me?"

"There are many who wish the girl returned to Symmachia." Ferocity glinted. "Kyros sends word—that *must* not happen."

Marco frowned. "Why do the one-verse advocates want her back?"

"We are not sure, save that returning her would prevent the fulfillment of prophecy she is tied to."

Gritting his teeth pulsed pain across Marco's jaw and neck. "Prophecy."

"Protect her until—"

"Protect!" Marco barked, shaking out his burning arm, irritated. "Nay, Iereas. You misstep. My Decree—"

"You cannot hold her without impugning your character and honor, according to your own Code. And you cannot release her to the wilds of this quadrant without endangering her life to the Symmachians." The iereas was too shrewd. "Watch her. Protect her, if necessary. Secure her only when necessary to bring her to the temple at the appointed time."

Marco hissed, convinced the fire in his arm was directly connected to the iereas before him. "Release this curse you placed on me." He had said the same words to Kyros.

Without moving his head, the iereas glared down Marco's arm then drew his gaze back up. "Timing is of the essence, Master Hunter. Shed your ego and do what you know is right."

Alarm and fear crackled in the air, strangling his quarry's efflux.

Marco blinked, refocusing on the docks. Scent thick with panic, Baytu was looking at him, eyes wide—she had made it to the girl. At the far end of the line. As authorities questioned the Droseran girl, her dark eyes widened. Their aggressive stance and demeanor bespoke the danger she found.

"No," he hissed, shifting around the iereas.

"I ... you don't understand ..." Her voice was soft like a gentle breeze yet urgent, luring his attention to her yet again. A pink flush crept into her nearly porcelain-white skin. Was it embarrassment? Or anger? An inhale told him a little of both. She was the daughter of a warrior, after all. Her hollowed-out cheekbones and the dark circles beneath her eyes surprised him. She appeared frail—but she was Stratios. A fierce, strong race.

"This is not ego," Marco mumbled as he erased the distance to his quarry. This was honor. He accepted their Decree. Now he hunted. By the Codes. "I will not fail."

Be strong, Daughter of Stratios, he willed her. *Give them no quarter.*

"You don't have the appropriate documents," the guard flung the papers back at her.

Something flashed in her eyes.

Ah, there. Marco smiled inwardly as her indignation rose to the surface.

"I cleared for transport before the *Kai-Tee* left port, yet you now hassle me over documentation? How is it my fault that your people don't do their job correctly?" Her full lips pulled into a tight, straight line. A dizzying blend of panic and desperation churned into anger.

Yes, this was definitely Kersei Dragoumis.

He had found her. He just hadn't expected her to be so ... compelling.

ZLARES, CENON

"No papers, no entry. Cenon makes no exceptions."

Terror gripped Kersei, making it impossible to breathe, and she secretly wished she no longer had the earpiece translator that told her what trouble she'd wandered into. "But—"

The uniformed man waved to someone over her shoulder, and she glanced back, stricken to find a security officer working his way toward them.

"Please," she pleaded. "I beg your mercy." She'd awoken on the salvage ship wearing a long coat and clutching a letter from Tigo, which said she had everything necessary to make her escape. To go hard and fast and never look back. Never had advice suited her so well. She remembered now. Everything she'd seen. The creature and the marked, tortured man.

"What's that?" someone behind her asked in a thick accent, tapping her coat. "In your pocket."

Kersei glanced there, surprised to find a thin black leather folio. Where that had come from, she couldn't say. She drew it out, confused.

The border agent snatched it. "Slagging ergatis wasting my time."

"Hold up there." The security officer had arrived at Kersei's side. "She looks like the fugitive from the holo-alert."

Kersei sucked in a breath as the customs agent squinted at her.

The security officer, a mean-looking man, grabbed her arm and tilted her so he could look in her face. "Sure enough. What's your name, girlie?"

Quick thinking and courage fled. Kersei opened her mouth but could say nothing.

"Let's take her to the magistrate," the customs man said. His two front teeth formed a V. "If it's my lucky day, I'll get a reward."

"Oy, *I'm* getting the reward. I noticed her."

"Sister!" A woman stumbled into Kersei, expression tight. She quickly seized the folio and glanced at it. "Erianne, did you not hear me calling?" She flashed a weary smile at the officers, then took both Kersei's hands in hers. "Sorry I wasn't here to greet you right away. Had to work late." She pulled Kersei into a hug and in her ear whispered, "Play along."

Stunned, Kersei didn't move.

"What is this hold up? What are you slugs doing to my poor sister?" She handed a yellow plastic card to the blue coats. "I'm Baytu Smirlet. This is my sister-in-law come to stay with me while my husband is away, she has." She nodded at the card. "Check it."

"She looks like the fugitive on the holo-alert."

"Are you blind? I've been seeing those vids all day long while I work. Erianne looks nothing like that fugitive, who is older and wicked."

Truth or lie, this woman was getting her out of a horrendous mess. Licking dry lips, Kersei darted a gaze to the officers, muttering between themselves and inspecting the credentials.

Baytu squeezed her hand.

"Where are you staying?" the customs man asked.

The woman sniffed. "Jexa district by the market. Rented flat. Not the greatest, but it keeps me dry. Most times."

He returned the card. "We might come for further documentation later."

"If you must." She nudged Kersei into the crowds around the busy port.

Kersei eyed the woman, Baytu. "Who—?"

"Just walk. They aren't the only ones after you," the woman warned. "There's a hunter, and if we see him, we run to the sewers."

Heat coursed up Kersei's arm, the brand burning as they left the docks. Though she tried to think, the flaming became too great. She hissed and clamped her jaw, forcing herself to walk ... one foot in front ... Sweat slipped from her nape and slithered down her spine, making her clothes and cloak heavy. Stumbling, she gripped the woman's sleeve.

"You don't look well. This thing is too hot for Zlares." The woman was pulling at her, making Kersei trip.

She frowned, then it seemed air finally found her. A breeze. She glanced over, surprised to see the thick coat folded across the woman's arm.

"There. That should do for now."

Kersei smiled her thanks. Somehow, past the dozens of people hurrying this way and that, past the strange vehicles that floated and darted down streets, she met the gaze of a man. Her heart skipped a beat at his piercing eyes—in shadow but she felt them all the same. Black hair hung in waves around his face and touched broad shoulders. Intensity rolled off him.

His gaze slid to Kersei's left and he slipped out of shadow. She sucked a breath and stumbled back. The mark! He had the same mark as the man on the satellite! The one being tortured. The ones on the ... her breath seized in her throat. Was it the same one? The one on Baric's ship who looked through the window at her yet did not see her?

"Oh no," Baytu whispered, fingers digging into Kersei's arm. "It's him. Run!"

A chase. So soon. It must be his lucky day.

He watched Baytu and the girl flee into the alley off the port, so he sprinted in the opposite direction. That alley had one exit, and if he hurried, he'd be upon them when they broke into the open. Even as he rounded Haru's bakery and flung himself up the hill street, he heard the warning of the iereas. Though dates and methods could be dictated regarding a Decree, it could not be altered once a purse was accepted. A hunt was not protection. He was not a dog to pupsit fugitives.

He tic-tacked a corner. Pitched himself up onto the roof.

Heard the slap of feet in the alley.

Baytu had been foolish to think she could outrun him.

Fear and shouts came from his left. The small, busy street with a bustling market. Marco glanced down among the tapestries and street-side cafés. Saw two red grunts stalking the vendors. Symmachians. No doubt looking for the girl, too. But why was she so important?

Marco trained his receptors to the right. His quarry. Heading straight into the arms of the Symmachians. He stood and leapt to the other building, frogged back and forth between the two until he landed with a soft thump in the alley. He straightened, unfurling his cape as he hugged the shadows.

Hard breaths rasped behind him. Acrid scents. He kept his back to them, knowing if the girl stepped out, she'd be seen.

Marco shifted into the open. Lifted a belt from the nearest vendor to feign distraction. Angled so he could see both the Symmachians and the women.

"Kynigos!" one of the brazen one-versers said. "What business have you here?"

Setting down the belt, he shifted so the Symmachians were forced to put their backs to the alley. "A hunt. What else?" He jutted his jaw at them. "And you?"

"R&R."

Marco smirked. "I would have chosen a better place for rest and relaxation.

Like the lakes of Antrouille. Or the peaks of Etau, but maybe your armor would rust there."

Glowering, the Symmachians took the bait—and the women hopefully seized the chance to get out of the alley. Even now, he detected the girl's signature, strong and clear, which concerned him until he realized Baytu's scent had faded. Had she left the girl? Surely neither had been that foolish.

He peered into the alley.

One of the Symmachians glanced over his shoulder. "What?"

Marco shrugged. "Rats."

"What, can you smell alley rats?"

"All rats," Marco said. "We do not discriminate."

ZLARES, CENON

"Wh-who was he?"

"A hunter. They are relentlessly cruel and effective."

"Hunter?" Kersei hurried with Baytu into a busy area with large, towering structures all around them. She felt closed in, trapped. "What does he hunt?"

"People—you!" Baytu snapped. "And thank the Mercies he didn't see us, or who knows where you would be right now."

"*Me?*"

"Yes, you!" She motioned toward a small building and ducked inside. Shelves lined three of the four walls and a brown cot was shoved against the far one.

"*Attention Citizens!*" In the middle of the market, an enormous face sprang to life, like dots of a whole image dancing in the air.

Mesmerized, Kersei watched from the hut.

"*This is an urgent communiqué. Tertian Space Coalition, along with the Droseran Council, seek the location of Droseran native Kersei Dragoumis.*"

Kersei sucked in a breath at seeing her own face hanging in the air.

"Get back!" Baytu snapped.

"*Accused of murdering her family, then single-handedly damaging and escaping a vital satellite, this fugitive is assumed armed and dangerous. Do not attempt to apprehend the suspect. If you encounter this suspect, contact Symmachian Command or your local authorities immediately.*"

Tugging the curtain closed, Baytu gaped. "Murder?" She scowled. "What do you get at, girl?"

Kersei held up her palms. "On my oath, I did not kill my family—or anyone." Was Baric alive? "Though I can give no explanation for what happened, I will find the answers and those responsible."

"So they *are* dead, your family?"

Grief tugged at her. "There was an explosion …" The images taunted her, threatening to overtake her mind.

Murmuring, Baytu shook her head. "What have I done? They'll never let him go now."

Seeing the woman's fear and hating herself for causing more trouble, Kersei hung her head. "I'll leave. You have done more than enough on my behalf. I would not put anyone in danger."

"I'm sorry," Baytu said, her brow knotted. "But … they have my husband and … I just wanted to get back at him."

"At your husband?"

"No, *that* hunter! He caught my husband and he's in jail now," she declared. But then her defiance wilted, eyes going glossy. "But if he finds I hid you, they'll never let Jubbah go."

The story did not make sense—if the woman's bound was in jail, did he not do something wrong? Yet … is that what people thought about Kersei, when that big sign declared her dangerous and a killer? "I beg your mercy. I will leave at once." That she had no place to go was of no consequence. Protecting this woman was. "Your help has been much appreciated."

Baytu's nod was small, grieved. She reached for the curtain, then stumbled back, hauling in a grating breath. "He's here." She motioned Kersei away. Grabbed a container of spice. "Dump this over yourself."

Blinking, Kersei drew back. "What?"

"He smells, that's how Kynigos hunt." With vigorous movements, she doused Kersei, then nudged her to the back until Kersei plopped on a dusty cot. "Stay here. I'll get rid of him and we'll figure out where to take you later. Understand?" Baytu left.

Fear pushed her into the corner. Pervasive darkness cocooned her. In a rush, terrible memories from that chamber swarmed Kersei. Strangling a cry, she shoved to her feet, unable to breathe. Movement beyond the curtain caught her eye. She inched forward to peer through the finger-width slit in the fabric and saw the large man stalk into an area with people enjoying meals and libations.

Hunter. Kynigos. So like the man with that creature.

Grievous thoughts tugged her back onto the cot, sprites of dust burning her eyes. Kalonica was not this hot, dry, and dirty. It was green and beautiful, filled with flora and fauna. She longed for lavish fields to ride Bastien—was *he* still alive? What of Darius?

Blood and boil.

The memory of him from the feed rose up. He lay there, eyes open in death. Hand reaching out. Fingers curled, as if seeking help. The memory tightened her throat. Pressing her face into the dusty pillow, she tried to hide from it, but the tears came. She cried hard, grief luring her from consciousness.

"Kersei! Why did you do this?"

"'Twas not me, Darius!"

"You are a bad liar, Kersei."

"No!" She jerked, but exhaustion held her captive. Forbade her from surfacing, waking. In the hollows of those dark torments, the emptiness that claims a sleeper swarmed her, bringing with it more terrifying images of her family's deaths. They were a part of her, the very fiber in every muscle, the hitch of every breath, every torment. There was no escape.

Palms on the counter, Marco fought the urge to laugh. The spices ... He marveled that anyone thought that really worked.

Baytu hurried toward him, her scent surprisingly clear of guilt and panic. "How may I help you, Hunter?"

"Cordi." He lifted only his eyes to her. "And my quarry."

Baytu tied on an apron, avoiding his gaze as she worked. "Have you lost her already?"

Games, was it? He waited quietly, the girl's signature clear and strong against his receptors—with that ridiculous covering of spices. Guilty parties tried many things to conceal themselves and others from the hunters.

She placed the warmed cordi on the counter.

Eyes locked on her, he reached into his pocket, retrieved an item, and set it beside the steaming mug. Though her eyes did not widen nor her lips part, Baytu saw it because panic stained her efflux. The Kynigos branding iron usually caused that reaction.

He met her gaze with apathy. "It was foolish."

"Leave her alone," she growled. "She has done nothing wrong."

"That is not for you or me to determine." He lifted the mug and sipped, relishing the spicy-citrus flavor sliding down his throat. "Had I not detected the Symmachians, you would have delivered her straight into their hands."

Understanding made her soften. "You protected her."

"I protected my hunt." He took another gulp—a little too hot, but entirely satisfying. "If my Decree had been ruined, so would my career. And you would now wear a permanent mark." He set down the mug. "In earnest, did you think I could not track you both?"

"She's not well," Baytu said—and there was no lie in her scent. "She was pale and uncoordinated. She has been through much."

Aye, her pale complexion told him that. Mayhap … she was best sheltered here—for now. How was he to play this, keeping tabs on her, yet not frightening the girl into fleeing? "Symmachians are on alert. Port security must have reported a possible sighting. Keep her hidden until dark."

"Do you jest?"

A bitter scent smacked his receptors. Marco jerked around and stiffened. "The girl."

Screams shattered the silence. Baytu gaped at the curtain as another mournful shriek ripped the air.

Marco started toward the shack, then thought better of it. "Wake her. She sleeps in terror."

27

ZLARES, CENON

Drenched in her heavy efflux, Marco stumbled from the café. The intensity disoriented him. Surprised him. It was fear—yes, and definitely terror. But there was something else. Something ... more.

It is not for you to judge, only to secure.

Though he removed himself from the square, he did not venture far. Could not with the hunt active, the girl so endangered. He stayed on the periphery, always reaching out for her signature. So much that it became familiar, even wanted. He liked it. The strength of it. The uniqueness.

Late that evening as the café was closing, Marco hovered on the edge of the square again. He lowered his head, letting his receptors work. Breaking past all the other scents, her signature with its calming tones tapped him on the shoulder and told him to turn around. His gaze let his receptors guide it ... across the seating area. To the shadow of the hut.

The girl stared back at him. Heat spilled across his shoulders as they locked in a visual duel. He dared not look away. And by the way she lifted her chin, she wouldn't either.

No. She was not a girl. Though she stood a head shorter than he, she was an adult. The unruly curls dancing over her shoulder, a mirror to the black tunic and belt she wore, accenting her diminutive waist. Aye, she had curves, but more importantly—mettle. Staring so boldly.

Moonlight haloed her dark hair as she drew a blanket over her shoulders, bunching her thick curls into a frame around her face. Where he expected alarm and fear there was only worry and ... curiosity.

Strange. Did she not fear for her safety?

Why am I still standing here?

No sooner had he wondered than he detected the Symmachians again. With a small shake of his head to warn her, he slid his gaze to the right. She must've followed, because her fear smacked him again.

"No," Baytu gasped, then hurried the girl back inside as Marco took to the rooftops.

Irritation and agitation spun thick webs through his mind, making his moves sluggish as he parked himself on a ledge and stayed there long enough to ensure the Symmachians did not find his quarry.

Once Baytu and the girl retired to her flat—not, he noted, the address she had given the customs agent—Marco returned to his room, detesting the great distance from the girl, which made it more difficult to detect her. Thoughts heavy, he skipped the door and launched at the wall, tic-tacking up the corner and grabbing the sill. He hauled himself inside but sank back on the ledge. Bent forward, he roughed his hands over his face. The slow breath he took didn't help.

What was wrong with him? He felt addled.

His vambrace thumped. With another thick intake, he flicked his wrist and released the breath as Rico holo'd. "Brother. Good news." If it was that. "And bad news."

"She is there?"

"Aye. Arrived on a salvage transport." Marco adjusted his vambrace, his advocate's image faltering as he pulled up a secondary screen. "The *Kai-Tee* out of Cyrox."

"Cyrox." Rico scowled. "How did she get there?"

"Unknown, but I'll look into it."

"Good. But be on guard. Two corvettes were detected on a course for Cenon."

"I feared as such," Marco muttered. "She was spotted at the port and the bulletins are looping frequently." He sighed. "This is too contrived, how they knew she was here. I would have answers."

"Aye, and I could well suspect where to find them."

Marco stilled at his advocate's tone. "What know you?"

Rico glanced over his shoulder before adjusting his camera angle and continuing. "When I returned after our visit, Theon was here again. Sought a private audience with Roman and Palinurus, after which Roman informed me the girl had been on the *Macedon*."

"And we were there! How did we not *anak* her?"

Rico shook his head, the thick braids rolling over his shoulders. "Unknown. An airtight container, mayhap?" He huffed. "But Theon was on the battle cruiser and Cenon shortly before the Caucus. And remember Kyros mentioned an iereas entered Stratios Hall before it went down. Why would a high lord be involved in this?"

"I would know as well. An iereas met me on the dock," Marco remembered. "Told me one high in the Order wanted the girl returned to Symmachia to prevent her from fulfilling a prophecy. Said I must protect the girl until it's time."

Rico harrumphed. "There seems to be a division in the holy order, and it is working in our favor."

"This Decree stings my nostrils. Something is amiss." And yet, he was beginning to understand ...

His advocate leaned in. "You think her guilty? That she killed her family?"

"I know not." Yet he *knew* she wasn't. A nuance in her bold, naïve stare haunted him, made him question that guilt. "There were things about her signature I could not process." So unique. Calming. And those eyes ... wide, dark.

Rico grinned.

"She's bold, too—stared openly across the market. There was no fear in her scent, Brother. She was ... confused by me."

"Confused? Or *attracted?* Many a woman has called you handsome, and I have seen her likeness. That could work in your favor." Rico shrugged. "A plausible scenario."

Marco chose to ignore the illicit suggestion. "It was as if she didn't know what I was. Also, the Droserans here are a concern." Fearless Ixion came to mind, as did revenge-prone Bazyli. "If they learn I hunt her, they will extend protection and that will complicate this hunt."

"You will sort it. Keep me posted."

As the holo swept away, Marco released the bindings of the vambrace and tossed it on the bed. Tugging the blade from his boots, he leaned against the plaster wall. He looked out at the city and dragged the blade over his rhinnock boot, a perfect sharpening stone. This hunt was proving disagreeable. Most were straightforward—get the Decree, complete the hunt. Not this one.

Dark, pleading eyes pushed into his mind. Before he could blink them out, he saw the girl—Kersei. Not in the black attire of today, but in a vision of white. The gown bared her shoulders, arms, and graceful neck. As she tipped her head back, melodious laughter wound around his mind, warm and soothing.

Marco leaned into the vision, as if his thoughts could become corporeal. The image grew stronger. Her smile faded and she lowered her head, breaking eye contact—and he felt the pain of that severance. A hand reached and unbound her hair. Raven curls ran over her shoulders like a river rushing beneath the moon's power. When she looked to him again, sadness—deep and mournful—consumed him.

Something ... *something* tugged at Marco's mind. Pain ... somewhere ...

He jerked and blinked, suddenly registering the black of night. Yet light exploded through his room. And pain—so agonizing! The mark burned with an unrelenting fury, as if jealous over his distraction with the Droseran girl now invading his dreams.

TSC *MACEDON*

Cleaning his weapon, Tigo kept a weather eye on the access door and stairs. They'd returned to the *Macedon* two days ago, fully expecting to be thrown in the brig after the encounter on the *Chryzanthe*. But nothing happened. They'd spaced Esq's body before returning to the *Macedon*, and logged her death as a terrible accident involving a faulty airlock seal. So far, no one had questioned the story, and crewmembers had even dropped by to express their condolences.

In the days since getting Kersei on the transport to Cenon, Tigo had had nothing but time to reflect and worry. He'd cleaned every piece of equipment in his kit. Told himself again and again that Esq would have had it no other way. That rescuing Kersei was the only honorable thing to do. But why hadn't the captain retaliated yet?

"Baric's driving me scuzzing mad," AO grumbled as he broke down his sidearm and reassembled it for the umpteenth time. "Why haven't they arrested us yet? Sent Crichton or Dimar to put one in our heads? What're they waiting on?"

"He's in control and knows we can't go anywhere," Tigo said. "This is what he wants—for us to get antsy. Make a mistake. Wants us—"

A door slammed behind the large gear container. Feet pounded.

Tigo snapped a look to AO, who jerked up his weapon. One set of boots incoming. Hurried. Intent. Hand on his weapon, Tigo angled to the side, thinning himself as a target.

The person rounded the corner.

"Jez." Tigo splayed his palm.

She heaved a breath. "He's going after her."

"Who?"

"Baric. He knows we sent her to Cenon. He's going after her."

Confusion swarmed him. "Why?" He shook his head. "She's just a Droseran."

"The people I heard it from—some who overheard it from a guard who overheard it"—she waved her hand, indicating the source was watered down—"said the girl knew or saw something."

"Saw *what*?" Tigo balked. "She was in that reminding chamber the whole time."

"She was loose on the satellite when AO found her," Diggs noted.

"Never did take a real good look around that satellite," AO mumbled.

Tigo eyed the corporal. Then Jez. Yeah, they hadn't checked out the satellite because they'd had one goal—getting Kersei out of there. What had they missed?

"So," Rhinn said with a lazy shrug, "whatever we didn't see that *she* did— it's gotta be big if he's going after her. Am I reading this right?"

"It's a scientific research satellite, according to the data on the Neura," Tigo said. "Last I checked, none of us were scientists. If we go back, what're we going to see that would mean anything or alarm us? How do we know if it's for wormhole creation or a massive lab to study the effects of life on Sicane without water or oxygen?"

Jez folded her arms and arched her eyebrow. "Kersei barely knew how to open doors here." She touched her temple. "So, what did she see—and we missed—that makes her a threat?"

"We're assuming a lot," Tigo said. His channeler vibrated. So did everyone else's. They glanced at each another, confused, then worry swam in deep when the ID hit their devices.

"Slag me," AO said.

"We are scuzzed, Commander," Rhinn muttered.

"Group up," Tigo said. "Let me do the talking."

A feed went live, throwing a face into the bay from Tigo's gauntlet. "Sir."

"Two-one-five, at ease," Admiral Deken said, shifting aside to reveal Admirals Waring and Ahron flanking him. "We're going to cut through the bull and get to the point: you broke into a top-secret research facility and removed … a package from holding."

Tigo felt the tension thickening as the team heard the admiral out, and heard Rhinn mutter another oath. He resisted the urge to shift his feet. But Tigo's mind snagged on who was addressing them. And who wasn't.

"While you may believe you were effective and stealthy," the admiral continued, his face one of Hermelian granite, "that facility transmitted all relevant imaging connected to your breach, insertion, and … theft." He nodded to the side, and their images were temporarily replaced with silent feeds.

"I look good in my drop suit," AO mumbled behind Tigo.

"Mine looks snug," Rhinn countered.

"Shut it," Tigo growled.

"Since there were no relevant orders dispatched to support these actions,

Tascan Command therefore has no choice but to charge all of you with treason, destruction of Tascan property, and theft of valuable assets and resources, as well as negligent manslaughter in the death of one of your own."

Tigo's heart slammed against his chest. "Sir—"

"Negative!" his father's voice boomed. "I will not hear anything you have to say. Every member of Two-one-five acted in gross violation of the arcs you wear and the oath you swore."

"Sir—"

"Do you deny making the insertion?" Waring demanded.

Tigo huffed a breath. "No, ma'am."

"Your fate is sealed, Commander Deken." Waring's jaw lifted—as if she'd finally gotten the long-desired vengeance against Tigo for hurting her daughter.

"It is the decision of this committee that you are all immediately stripped of rank, removed from duty, and will face court-martial here on Symmachia at such time as Command can arrange."

"There is no slagging way," Rhinn balked.

"Admiral," Tigo said, feeling like he couldn't get enough oxygen, "I understand your anger—"

"This isn't anger, Commander Deken," his father bit back. "It's regulations. The Two-one-five acted outside legal boundaries and violated not only a dozen Symmachian regulations, but also negatively affected intergalactic relationships."

"Fine," Tigo said, knowing he wouldn't get him to change his mind. "Punish me. My unit was only following my orders—leave them out of this."

"That's the problem," Waring spoke up. "They followed you. Violated orders just like you did. There was no gun to their heads." She gave a sharp nod. "So they will face the same consequences."

"It's really a shame how deeply this will impact all of your families," Ahron said. "You get an idea and follow through, but you don't think about what it'll do to your families."

"They threatening us?" Diggs hissed.

"I'll hate to see your father struggling beneath the shower of shame, Tigo," Ahron said, "when the wave hits about this. Or you, Mr. Diggins—last I heard, your mother was struggling to keep her job at the Academy."

Behind him, mutters and grunts wafted in the air, but Tigo lifted his jaw. Sensed it coming. Decided to head it off. "What do you want?"

Ahron smirked, then lowered his head. Waring stared hard at them.

His father glowered. "Retrieve that package you absconded with, then return to Symmachia so we can deal with this situation."

"You mean with the girl, Kersei Dragoumis." Tigo wasn't going to play the neutral game anymore.

"Yes, the one you captured."

"Didn't capture," Tigo countered. "She was in a stolen corvette that was adrift."

"We can argue," his father intervened, "and the waves hit, bringing irreparable damage to families and careers. Or you can deploy in thirty and get this done."

No. No, this could not be happening. He glanced at the others, detecting a similar dread, and realized each and every one of them felt trapped. Threatening families. Nice touch. He hadn't thought his father had it in him. Slowly, Tigo slid his gaze back to the holofeed.

"In case you get any ideas, you are being monitored. And you're not the only unit looking for the girl."

Tigo gritted his teeth. "How do you know you can trust us?"

"Because I know you care about your team. And if you want them to have a career after this, you'll get to Cenon and find her. Bring her to Symmachia. No other causalities."

"If her people discover—"

"Commander." His father's eyes brightened with anger. "The only way that happens is if you fail me—again."

"Understood."

ZLARES, CENON

He could not explain what drew him across the city at such a late hour, but Marco found himself navigating the square and monitoring the foot traffic before he could question it. She was, after all, his quarry. Not being aware of her movement and location would be negligent. He hadn't even made it out to the square when something in the air slowed him. Trouble.

Surreptitiously sweeping the area for scents, he tucked into the shadows. What was it? He angled his head to the side and flung open his receptors, *anak'ing*. As the courtyard of the trading square came into view and swaying branches made lights twinkle in the darkness, he waited. Lowered his chin. Trusted instincts and training that said something wasn't right.

His gaze slid of its own accord to the small hut behind the café where the woman worked. Surely she had not defied him again. Smirlet couldn't be that stupid, could she?

Aye, she could. Because she believed he had ill intent toward the girl and that acting against him gave her the moral high ground.

Marco gritted his teeth, rifling scents. Lifting his head and angling, he scoured for that vanilla and patchouli signature.

As expected, he snagged it from the warm winds—far to the left. Unexpectedly ... away from the café. He broke into a trot. As he erased the distance between him and her signature, instinct told him to get a higher vantage. He scaled a building and pulled himself up onto the roof. Running, he kept to the edge, *anak'ing* as he moved toward the river.

A boat, perhaps? Did Baytu intend to take the girl out of the city? Think that would keep her safe from him?

An explosion of effluxes yanked him on. Marco sprinted over the roof. Soared the distance between two, receptors drenched as shouts and screams tangled with the pheromones bleeding the night of its peace. A sharp change struck him. He shoved himself eastward. Skidded across a penthouse terrace. Toed the ledge and peered down.

Large and forbidding, a shadow moved through the night.

Several shadows. Two men wrestling women near a fountain encircling a flagpole. Not just women—his quarry! Anger shot through his veins when he realized they were heading for a private port. Toward ships. If they got them there ...

Not happening. Marco bolted across the balcony. Leapt at the towering pole. Clutching the rope, he used it to swing down the pole, breaking his speed and landing. The clanging of rope against pole invariably drew the attention of the men in red uniform.

Symmachian elite, Eidolon.

Brawny and ensconced in armor, one turned to him. Swung the girl around in front him as a shield, and aimed his weapon at Marco. Fired.

Diving, Marco felt the round singe his bicep. He rolled and came up behind a vehicle. He rolled again, taking shelter in the deep shadow of a wall and a line of trees. The faint yellow hue of the Eidolon's heads-up remained focused on the car.

Get high, he instructed himself and pitched at the wall. Dug his fingers into the mortar between bricks. Made quick work scaling it and prostrated himself at the top. Few people looked up.

"Let's go," the other Eidolon said. "'Vette's powering up."

He couldn't let them reach that corvette. Not with his quarry. They'd make her disappear. Flat against the ledge, Marco eased his webbing gun from its holster and switched it to pulse. Not as powerful as Eidolon weapons, but he didn't need power. Only accuracy. He aimed at the sensor on the nearest building and fired.

The Eidolon saw the shot, but not in time to deactivate his night-vision optics. Light exploded through the memorial square.

Rolling off the ledge, Marco threw himself at the brawny one holding his quarry. Booted heel nailed the chest of the Eidolon, who stumbled back and lost his grip on the girl. She scrambled aside as Marco dove into him, knowing he had to disable that helmet or he was as a good as dead.

A spark glanced off a nearby car—the other Eidolon had focused on him, too. He leapt into the air and spun, connecting with a roundhouse kick to the man's helmet, then using a stunner to fry the internal electronics and zap the guy unconscious.

Something punched him in the back, pitching Marco forward. A pulse blast, by the radiating pain and the scent of heated rhinnock armor. The aim must've been off or Marco would have another gaping hole in his back. He palmed the cobbled street. Swung his legs up and around, catching the Eidolon's.

The man anticipated it. Stumbled but caught his balance.

Yet Marco popped to his feet. Aimed his webbing gun at the helmet. Fired. The pulse blast splintered over the face shield, dispersing the charge. The visor cracked but held.

The Eidolon muttered an oath, slapped his helmet's temple. The face shield slid away, apparently disabled as Marco had hoped.

Speed was his only ally at this point. Marco swept in—and was struck by an armored backfist. His cheek screamed and nose screamed, blood warm against his upper lip, but he ducked and took the man's legs backward with him. The Eidolon slammed into the cobbled path with a resounding crack from the helmet. He lay unmoving.

Crouching, Marco verified the Eidolon were incapacitated, then searched for the women. No surprise—gone. But not her scent. He sprinted down a dark footpath between residential buildings. He scaled it and kept his movements random to avoid being targeted.

Rock spat at him.

Reek! He leapt to a balcony. Toed the rail. Shoved himself forward. Another punch to the spine slammed his gut into the next one. *Oof!* With a curse, he hiked up. Grabbed the ledge of the roof. With a shove of his toes, he thrust himself up onto the roof. He lay on his back groaning and wincing at the bruise already forming on his spine. Before they caught up—he wasn't sure they wanted the chase but he couldn't risk it—Marco flipped onto his haunches and *anak'd* for her signature.

"Quickly! This way," Baytu said, huffing as they ducked low under a bridge.

Kersei hesitated, the smells obnoxiously potent. "Are you sure?"

"With their armor, the Symmachians can't fit and the hunter won't be able to smell us." Baytu waved her on. "Hurry."

Heart in her throat, Kersei followed her into a very narrow passage. Water splashed her legs and face with a putrid, sticky film. Stomach roiling, she covered her mouth and nose but kept moving. The wretched Symmachian had touched her inappropriately, when—out of nowhere—the hunter attacked. Fast, he proved efficient in freeing Kersei and Baytu. Glancing back down the cobbled street to what was now a pinprick of light, she hoped he was okay. She'd seen the Symmachians shoot him. The hunter, however, seemed in possession of unparalleled skills with his flurry of strikes and violence. The Symmachian savages had technology and armor—it had been impossible to remove herself from their power. Had it not been for Commander Tigo or Lieutenant Jez, she would still be on that accursed metal flower.

One day on this planet and all she'd done was run for her life. Would there be no rest?

The tunnel spit them out along a small river filled with acrid waste that trudged heavily southward. Bile rose in Kersei's throat. Her stomach heaved.

Baytu scurried along a rocky bank. "It gets better a little farther up."

But Kersei couldn't hold it back. She vomited—a move that made her fumble. Her hands plunged into the thick, slimy filth. She whimpered, lifting her hands as the sludge plunked from her palms. Now she could not even wipe her mouth. Eyes stinging, she gagged, of a mind to believe she might never regain her composure if she remained here. "Ugh! What is *this*?"

"Waste," Baytu said. "Come from the drains throughout the city. It's amazing … what we endure … to stay alive."

Flapping her hands to fling off the excrement, Kersei wanted to cry. She sagged, searching for a way to clean up. Wiped her palms on a wall. Grimaced and groaned. Nose stuck in the crook of her elbow provided little relief.

Baytu stumbled. Then tripped. "Just … a bit … more."

"Are you okay?" Kersei asked, scrambling up the bank after her. Slowly, the waste lessened and somehow the water running past them cleared.

"Yes. Almost … there." Baytu crumbled against the wall. Slid down.

Kersei hesitated and considered the passage, wondering why they had stopped. Again, she wiped her palms—this time on her pants. She might forever feel the need to wash them after this experience. She used the back of her hand to shove back curls heavy with muck. "Why here? Can't we go somewhere … clean?" When no answer came, she glanced at Baytu.

The woman's head was down. Shoulders hunched.

"Baytu?" Kersei knelt, feeling a trill of panic. "Baytu!" She nudged her shoulder.

When her friend lolled to the side, she then arched her back and cried out, gripping her side, where a wound pulsed blood over her fingers.

"Boils!" Kersei gasped. "You are injured. We need help."

Several minutes were spent in moaning before Baytu shuddered. "Rest. I just … rest."

"You need a pharmakeia!"

Baytu's lips curled upward. "A *doctor*. You need … the right terms." She shook her head. "But no, no doctor. It's too la—not safe."

Too late. That's what she was going to say.

Training with the machitis as she had, Kersei knew when a wound needed the aid of a professional. And this was such. She glanced in the direction they'd come. "I'll go back. Find the hunter—"

Clapping her hand over Kersei's, Baytu growled. "No," she bit out. "He's not … friend." Grimacing, she released her as if it were too much effort to hold her hand. "Promise me."

"You could die!"

"Don't worry about me," Baytu said. "I've been through worse." She wiggled her hand into her jacket pocket, then held something out to Kersei.

"What is it?" A clear sleeve of some kind held two brown circles.

"If … we get separated"—air wheezed through her—"and the hunter is there, hide and swallow these tablets."

Kersei considered them. "What are they?"

"Herb tablets." Bloody fingers curled over hers again. "Promise."

Agreeing went against her own convictions, yet she would not stress the already-weak Baytu. "Very well." She must find help. "But you will be okay. Just a bit of rest, yes?" Somehow, Kersei knew nothing would be okay again.

As dawn crept into the horizon, Marco grew haunted that he could not find the girl. How was this possible? It would not bode well if his quarry was harmed or kidnapped. His work would be multiplied and he would be required to request help. It was not *dis*honorable, but neither was it far from it among the Brethren.

Irritation skidded through his veins, wrestling his thoughts. Because more than all that was the strange concern for the girl that consumed him.

Marco pitched himself at a fence. Hopped over it and trotted down the dank alley bordering the market district. He tic-tacked a corner, grabbed a window sill, and used it for a toehold to throw himself up to the next. Back and forth until he was sailing across rooftops, searching for her. For the white-haired Baytu Smirlet.

By the time the sun was high overhead, he paused on the spire of the cathedral, this time overlooking the Grand Terminal of Cenon's main port. Crowds swelled into long queues for transports out of the area. Children scampered around the small playground outside the terminal, which had everything from showers and cafés to shops and apothecaries.

Where was Kersei Dragoumis? That he held a Decree for her rankled—she was not capable of murder.

You know that by what? Her large, mysterious eyes?

He cursed himself. Hopped up, but something on the south side caught his attention. Tracking the men there, he pivoted on his heels, lowering into a crouch. Three men chasing another down the long, shadowed alley. More Symmachians? They were worse than Pir ants, biting and burning, leaving enormous welts.

Apparently their target had come from the terminal. Black unfurled, flapping on the wind as the target fled. A glimmer of red winked at him as the man ran.

Recognition hit. Marco shoved straight, his heart thudding. "Impossible." A Kynigos—not hunting but *being* hunted.

Alarmed, Marco jumped to the next building, landing in a shoulder roll and coming up. He detached the monocle from the vambrace and eyed the pursuit. With a snap of a small button on it, he captured an image, zapped it to Rico, then made quick work of walls, windows, and utility poles to reach the ground.

He broke into a sprint, pursuing the foot chase. He knew not what brother was on Cenon, but the Codes required he assist Brethren in need. Halfway down another alley, he felt his thumper. Thumbing it, he grunted.

"Marco, what is that?"

"Unknown—a brother, here," he gasped out between breaths as he palmed a large hover vehicle and slid over its hood. He landed, eyes glued on the dark forms breaking right at the end of the street. "Being chased."

Silence hung rank while Rico no doubt pulled logs. Grunted. "None of the Brethren are logged there."

"Aye," Marco huffed. "Yet he's here"—*pant … pant*—"in trouble." A door opened. He dodged it, rolling around a kid on a foot trolley. A dog leapt into the chase, racing with him down the road and barking. The mutt would draw attention, so Marco deliberately closed the gap between him and the wall, forcing the dog back.

The mutt stopped, barking its objection at being ditched.

"We're getting access to Cenoan feeds now," Rico said.

"Marco," Roman's voice boomed through the thumper. "This goes without saying, but in light of Brethren who have gone missing, do *not* lose him."

The thought, the warning, the relevance of what this could mean, fueled Marco's fight. He would not let a brother die on his watch. But even as he vowed that—he slowed. It'd been a few minutes since he'd seen them. "I … I need eyes."

"We can't," Rico growled. "Satellites are down."

"Convenient." Marco had to get vantage. Higher. Glancing around him, he weighed possibilities. A large recycling bot was scurrying through the city, several youth chasing it and spraying the hull with activist symbols. He swung around behind it and hauled himself atop the thing. He shut his receptors to the rancid odor emanating from the vehicle and eyed the skyscraper. It was taller than necessary yet tall enough. He ran forward and shoved off just as the recycler neared the building.

Slamming into the skyscraper nearly knocked the wind out of him. But he dragged his leg up and over the first apartment's balcony. Toed the edge and jumped, twisting as he did to grab the next ledge. Up to the next. Then another. One more. He stood on the balcony rail, peering at the city far below. Despite the vantage, he still couldn't find them. He skimmed the rail, hopped to the next balcony. Then another, all while monitoring the street.

A woman stepped out and screamed at finding him on her balcony.

Not faltering, Marco sailed to the next one. Almost to the corner of the building when he finally caught sight of the thugs chasing the Kynigos.

Relieved his brother had held his own, he bolted forward, reaching for the cord that hung from his belt, gaze bouncing from the chase below and the large satellite pole. From the last balcony, he shoved into the open air.

He whipped the cord at the pole. It hooked around the steel cylinder. He caught the other side, and used it to swing around … down. Even as the cord snagged and freed on the large bolts in the façade, he eyed the street below. Timed his release for the high-speed trolley barreling from the Grand Terminal.

Swung around one more time. Bucked himself into the air. He careened out. Feeling free. Invigorated. Determined. He slid his gaze to the Kynigos darting between two hotels.

Not that way! He'd be cornered.

Marco grunted even as he dove at the trolley, rolling onto it with his shoulder tucked. He came up running from the momentum of the free fall. He skidded to a stop, looking down at the Kynigos, who'd gone between the Sammarko and the Hoiloi. Those lined the river. It was a dead end. No way out.

Curse the reek! Marco eyed the river and bridge ahead. If he didn't time it right, he'd be taking a swim and that brother would be gone.

Three …

He eased his right leg back.

Two …

Tucked his chin and took two puffing breaths.

One.

He leapt, felt the cable of the bridge try to catch his sleeve. Landed in a roll again. Came up running—but too close to the edge. Felt his ankle twist. Heard rock crumbling beneath his feet. His right foot stabbed down, but he jerked himself up. Toed the plaster. Found solid footing.

"Marco?" Roman inquired.

"In … pur … suit." He sprinted around the corner.

"There's a speeder."

Speeder? They weren't allowed in the city.

But even as he neared the alley between the two hotels, he saw debris swirling up out of the brick well. No no no. "Inbound."

Before he jumped, he saw the sleek silver ship whip into the alley. He cursed as he landed. Rolled so he wouldn't break his neck or legs. Then pitched himself at the wall, hearing the near melodic discharge of pulse weapons. Smelled burned air. Felt it buzz his head. He ducked behind a large receptacle, but not before he saw two men carrying an unconscious, bloodied hunter to the ship.

"No!" Marco lifted his webbing gun. Aimed it.

Crack!

Light and glass exploded. Pain seared down his arm and he dove for cover, but came back up, firing. Refusing to lose another brother.

Scalding air punched him in the chest. Slammed him against the wall. Breath knocked from his lungs. Dropping to the side, he coughed. Tried to scramble, his limbs disobeying. Saw the craft lift and streak toward atmo.

"Augh!" Marco howled, fury tearing through him. Failed. Failed. He threw a fist into the receptacle. Flipped around. Slumped against it. Bent and gripped his knees. Let out another shout of fury.

Huffing, he swiped his thumper. "It was Oron. They got him." He saw the monocle on the ground. Lifted it—and dropped it, the metal still hot. Crouched, he eyed the piece, then noticed the green light. Still had a signal. Not caring for a minor burn, he retrieved it. Sent the transmission to the Citadel.

"Palinurus's lead hunter," Roman muttered.

"Yeah, and it wasn't a speeder," Marco said, thoughts weighted. "It was a Symmachian corvette."

"Not entirely surprising."

Marco wet his lips. Steadied his breathing, swallowing his pride. He had to come clean. "We have another problem." Saying he'd lost the girl as well wouldn't go over well; he'd look inept. "Last night the girl fled with the help of a local. Symmachians attempted to capture her. I intervened, but she and the local took to the streets." There was nothing to be done but say it. "The girl's missing."

"I'm disappointed," Roman said, his voice leaden. "Do you think they have her? Is that why you can't find her?"

Marco hesitated. "Doubtful, but not impossible."

"You must find her, Marco. She's … they *cannot* recover her."

Exhaustion pressed against him. "I will not sleep until I have her." Though his limbs ached from the life-and-death race moments ago, he pushed himself into a jog. "She will be found this day, I vow."

"To the Decree."

"And the hunt." Marco nodded, saying the last line with his master. "For honor."

He had failed twice in the last twenty-four hours, losing the girl, then being too slow to save Oron. What if his brother died? What if he was never again seen? He roughed a hand over his face. Why were hunters being snatched? They had no special ability other than heightened smell. There was their training, but anyone could hone that.

It made no sense.

He made his way back toward his room, intending to steam cajuput oil. The strong camphoraceous odor that smelled like hyacinth with herbaceous undertones cleared receptors and allowed a hunter moments of peace and relaxation. Time to think.

He rounded the corner and almost missed it—the attack scent. Shapes moving near the door. He vaulted back, hugging the wall. Peered around and saw two Symmachians at the hostel door. His gaze rose to the window of his room, not surprised to find more shapes flickering.

Reek. How did they know …? What in the 'verse was going on that hunters had become the hunted?

"Commander," someone called. "Major Shen reports they located his scout."

"Good," a lanky officer said, "tell them to ground it. We don't want him or her escaping."

Easing away, Marco kept his movements small, not wanting to draw attention. Once at a safe distance, he shot through the city, heading straight for the private port to verify they'd put a security lock on his shuttle. And sure enough, he found a corvette near his scout. Frustration choked him—but then he remembered what the Symmachian had said. *"... or her ..."*

The girl was still here. Somewhere. They didn't have her.

Hugging the river as he moved, Marco again swiped his thumper. "Symmachians are after me. They were searching my room and grounded my scout." Which was good, he supposed. Other than clothes and gadgets easily replaced, the Symmachians wouldn't find anything of use in the room. "Bonus is I heard them say they didn't want *her* escaping, so the girl is still here."

"Augh!" Roman's shout was followed by a thunderous crash. "I'm livid they're hunting us. I must talk with the premier and masters. Find that girl, Marco. There is clearly something going on that we aren't aware of. Get her and get off that planet."

Startled at his master's loss of control, something he'd never seen or heard before, Marco continued through the city, using back passages and cut-throughs as the shadows slowly lengthened. "I'll find her and a way off this slagging rock."

"Do it fast," Roman growled. "They're clearly several steps ahead of us."

"Agreed." Marco stretched his neck.

Oron taken. Symmachians violating dozens of Cenoan laws to kidnap innocents. Now, hunting Marco and the girl.

He'd never forget the moment she'd walked off that ship. Innocent. Attractive. Scared. Her signature that perfect blend. Loamy, sweet, and— "Spicy."

Marco stilled, head lifted from his heavy thoughts. He frowned. Angled toward to the right. Toward the river. *Her.* He hadn't just been thinking of her signature—he'd smelled it! He skipped into a light run, letting it draw him on. Lure him into the danger that existed with her. Closer to the waterfront. One side littered with dark, dank buildings that reeked of dampness. The other, pristine structures, no doubt owned by evengis.

Reeking, burning thing. Why now?

As fire crawled through his forearm again, Marco caught sight of a shape hurrying along the boulders of the riverbank. Relief rushed at him—the girl. She lumbered over the large rocks, sniffling. Dark curls whipping beneath the wind as she navigated the area. Alone—why was she alone? Then wide eyes lifted—connected. Shock spurted out of her, then panic.

"Be at—"

She twisted around, crying out—apparently catching her ankle. She shoved up the bank, scrambling toward the buildings.

"Peace." He huffed. Hated chasing her. Hated her being scared when he was the least of her worries. But no doubt Baytu had terrorized the girl with stories of him. Where was that Thyrolian anyway? Jogging, he followed her signature to a cluster of shops. "You have nothing to fear from me, Kersei." He stalked closer, ignoring what his eyes said and following his receptors. To the right. He angled around a table grouping. Saw her vanish through a gate.

Must these games be played? Annoyed, he trailed her. Walking—no need to run when her signature was so clear, strong, damp though it was and tinged with the odors of the sewer. He stepped past the gate into a surprisingly open and lush garden. "I am no threat to you," he called. "But you *are* in danger. Symmachians seek your life." He twitched his arm, trying to ignore the heat of the mark.

Again, that patchouli snaked out, wrapped around his mind, and held him fast. Coerced him to hold up his hands. "On my honor, no harm will come to you. Not from me." Branches creaked to the left. He glanced over his shoulder. "Where is Baytu?" he asked the limbs and leaves.

Grief assailed the air.

"Dead," he muttered, reading her scent. "What happened?"

Silence was the only answer, but her scent was moving. And oddly … fading. Yet not because of distance. It was … alarming. Marco felt a twinge of confusion.

A soft thump sounded on the far side of the garden. Compelled in that direction, he trotted over. Saw prostrate legs sticking out from behind a large stone planter. He darted around it and found her laid out. Hair a halo of black framing an unusually pale face. "Kersei!" Alarm sped through him, though he wasn't sure why.

No, he did know. Her signature was gone!

Disoriented by the vacuum created from the loss of her scent, Marco closed his receptors. Felt for a pulse—faint. She had no visible wounds, so internal? Regardless, she needed help—now! He knelt and scooped her off the ground.

The fire in his arm doused.

Surprised, he tugged it out and looked at his arm.

Fire leapt anew.

What majuk …? It mattered not. Though she lay before him, her signature was slipping farther from his receptors with each tick of his heart, scaring him. A strange feeling that.

Again he slid his hands under. Again heat ceased. "Madness," he growled and lifted her. He stood and turned, considering routes. Where? Where would he go without endangering her? She was a wanted fugitive.

He hoisted her into a better hold, tightening his grasp around her shoulders. Though she presented as formidable, she was small, light. Silky strands tickled his arm as he hurried. She released not a moan or twitch as her forehead lolled against his chest. The realization hurried him from the garden.

Glancing down, he started at how very white she'd gone. So still. Full lips nearly gray. Something primal screamed through him. *What* happened to her? Panic drilled him, still unsure.

"In the light, Master Kynigos," came a shout from behind.

Marco whirled, stunned to find the iereas from the port on his heels.

"Careful, careful," the iereas said, motioning for him to follow. "This way. We must be clear of the passage." The iereas shuffled down the street, glancing around.

"What is this, priest?" It was a good thing Marco had her in his arms or he would be crushing throats until he felt confident his quarry would not die.

"She hovers on Pir's edge." The iereas thrust a finger toward an open street, where late-afternoon sunlight warmed the bricks of buildings on one side. "There. Hurry." He was shuffling along, reaching toward Kersei. "What was given to her?"

"I gave her nothing." Except a fright. Under the direct light of the sun, even Marco felt better. But then the aroma registered. "I smell herbs," he said, noting the odor emanating from her mouth.

"Ah yes, I see." The iereas nodded. "Come. To my lodging."

They made their way to the historic district, where they entered a two-level cream-colored home. "The rooftop."

A boy on the cusp of manhood rushed ahead of them in the house, opening doors as they moved to a rooftop terrace.

"Duncan," the iereas said, "gather my kit and some water."

A cushioned chaise stretched beneath a long-armed umbrella, which the iereas swung away. "Here, here. In the sun to help boost her body's natural immunities."

Strength surged through Marco's muscles along with some odd, cool sensation. He went to a knee and gently placed the girl on the cushion.

Cradling her head with his hand, he saw a few strands of her hair caught on his vambrace. With care, he unwound them. Noticed dark lashes that dusted fair skin. Rosy cheeks—they'd been so pale in the garden. Pink-tinged lips— the sight of the change thrummed in his chest. He traced her cheek as he removed his other hand, surprised at what leapt through that simple touch and squeezed his gut. So fair …

With a jolt, Kersei screamed.

Marco stumbled back, fire and pain slamming him like that Symmachian pulse gun. Grateful for the tree he backed into, he gripped it, bracing to stay upright as the iereas rushed toward her. Breathing became a chore. With a hand fisted, he thrust it against his chest.

The iereas held the girl, quieting her with soothing words.

At least she was awake. And throwing scents at him again, though her signature wafted like a gentle breeze. Relieved at detecting it, Marco took a breath. Watched as the boy returned with a square leather pouch and a water pitcher. Recollection of the terror she spat when she saw him pushed Marco into the inner room, where he monitored as the iereas tucked something into her mouth.

Again she growled through a half-scream, arching her spine.

Heat pummeled Marco. He thumped against the wall. Tried to ease forward, but found himself pinned beneath her scream.

What is this? A curse?

The iereas rested his hand on her head, muttering. Then he lowered something else to her lips. *What is he doing?* Furrowing his brow, Marco leaned closer. The iereas poured water and the boy hurried past Marco on another errand. Alone with the girl, the iereas lifted her sleeve.

What manner of man would—

Marco hauled in a breath when he saw the twisting black arcs and lines on her forearm. *The mark.* She bears a mark. He'd known there were others marked by the Iereans. Yet it surprised him that she would have this, too. And so much like his own.

A low guttural moan wafted from her, and at some point, the boy had returned.

The pressure released in Marco's chest even as the girl relaxed. Stricken, he tucked his chin, taking a few measuring breaths. Swallowing. His gaze fell to her arm, now covered again. And his own arm—beneath the vambrace … Her pain. His pain.

When he lifted his gaze, he found the iereas staring up at him. Knew questions were forthcoming. Marco refused to entertain him with answers—of which he had none—so he presented his own question. "What happened to her—why was she in distress, near death?" He glanced up to the terrace, recalling the way the iereas had come flying around the corner.

The iereas shrugged. "It is but a guess, but I believe she was given a heavy sleeping concoction. All herbs, but unfortunately—"

"Nay," Marco muttered, peering up the stairs again. "I know well herbs connected to sleeping potions, but I detected an unfamiliar one."

"Bitter and tangy?" the iereas asked.

Narrowing his eyes, Marco frowned. "Aye, how—Who are you?"

"Sadira root—the herb, not me. I'm Ypiretis," the iereas said with a chuckle. "I should have known, given Kersei's connection with the Thyrolian woman. It's often used there, but their systems are inherently different because of the disease and the boosters they receive from childhood." He let out a long breath. "It essentially was shutting down Kersei's body."

"She has a brand."

The iereas did not respond, cocking his head. "You sensed her pain, did you not?"

That hollowness where her scent should've been still haunted him. "In truth, I detected *no* scent. There was nothing but—"

"I saw you stumble back. In fact, I believe what you felt went beyond your training. It wasn't something you could *detect*. It was more than that, right from the *adunatos* of the brand."

Enough. Marco would be rid of this company. He hustled down the steps.

"Master Kynigos!"

"Leave off, iereas. I have fulfilled my Decree." It was not entirely accurate, but he detested the weight of this hunt, the frustrations. The oddities

"Nay, you have not. Your Decree states you must deliver her to *Iereania*, not to me."

Marco stopped short, glowering. "Are they not the same thing?"

The man laughed. "I have been accused of looking like many things, but never a stone temple." Despite the mocking tone, the priest's eyes were grave. "Nay, you must see this through to the end. She needs your protection."

"This is a *hunt*," Marco ground out, his temples throbbing with rage. "Hunts do not entail protection!"

"Don't they?" the iereas challenged with a laugh. "I am sorry, Marco, but you cannot walk away from this one, no matter how badly you want to."

"I would never dishonor myself like that." Marco pivoted on his heels. "I will return for the girl after I retrieve my things. We depart for Iereania—"

"It is too soon! You must deliver her at the appointed time, not before."

Marco wheeled on the iereas. "She is safer on Iereania."

"She is *not*," the man barked, his chest rising and falling unevenly.

Fear. "You reek of fear, iereas," Marco noted, his own anger bottoming out at that revelation. "What do you fear with your own kind?"

"I cannot—"

"Ypiretis!" the boy hissed from the top of the stairs, his face bright with alarm. "The Symmachians are coming up the path."

The iereas jerked to Marco, his fear snapping into panic. "They cannot capture her."

Marco expected him to explain why, but no explanation came.

"We must get her off this planet," Ypiretis said. "You have a scout—"

"They locked it down. Only way offworld is passenger transport, but I know they will watch for me—they know of the Decree. If I am seen with her, they will intervene."

"I fear I have the same dilemma," Ypiretis said.

"Why would they be concerned with an iereas?" Marco wondered aloud, also noting the girl's signature was losing its more bitter tones, trending toward the sweet.

The iereas sighed. The skin tags on his cheek bounced as he hesitated. "No doubt when you were on Iereania and received the Decree, you ... detected certain underpinnings of discord."

"To put it mildly. The stench stung my nostrils." The entire temple had, but that was another matter.

A strange scent cocooned them as there came a severe knock at the door.

"Go, stay with her," Ypiretis said, nudging Marco back toward the stairs. "I will persuade them to look elsewhere."

The rank efflux sailing past the door warned Marco there was too much danger. "No, I have an idea." He started for the side window and peered past the curtains. "Get packed and ready. I'll find a way off planet for her. Be ready."

"What are you doing?"

Marco grinned. "Distracting trouble." He slipped onto the ledge of the window, glanced across the alley to the other building and with a decidedly loud grunt, thrust himself at the building. Caught a laundry pole, and jerked himself hard on it, the rattling noise filling the air. He swung himself up and around. Balanced there, he eyed the corner of Ypiretis's rented residence. Saw the first red boot step out. And leapt up onto the roof as a shout went up.

After an hour leading the Symmachians around the city, Marco felt a shameful measure of pride at being able to distract and eventually elude them. And he marveled at how far he could travel through the city and not lose her scent. Never had a signature been detectable at this distance. And that made him test just how far …

On the far side of the city, a good forty-minute run from her location with the iereas, Marco gave up trying to lose her scent. He refused sleep, sensing the situation too tenuous and the Symmachians too persistent to not be aware of the girl at all times.

Visions of those soft curls he'd touched but for a moment saturated his thoughts. Her dark eyes and those long lashes. The delicate weight of a warrior's daughter. He knew, somehow, that fire made up for her size. Strength she possessed in bulk.

Dawn snuck into the horizon and blazed its glory across the skies. Marco sat on the ledge a quarter klick off that still provided him with clear line of sight on the iereas's rented flat, thinking through his next steps. Figuring out how to get the girl away safely.

On the terrace where he'd laid the girl, he saw movement. He detached the monocle and checked it out. At a table, the iereas sat eating fruit and eggs with the boy, who delivered a pitcher of—Marco groaned. Was that cordi? A cruel taunt, and his rumbling belly agreed.

A swath of black blurred into view. The girl joined them, her chaotic dark curls secured back, but still wild about her small frame. She smiled at the iereas—but there was a wariness. An uncertainty. Mayhap even fear.

And you know this how? his conscience chided.

Because he could smell it on her scent.

Marco lowered the monocle, still startled with the way her scent clung to him despite great distances.

He must confess he found her beautiful. There was an innocence to her, equally matched with ferocity that made it hard to look away. Yet, watching from this vantage felt cheap and … wrong. What kind of girl finds herself wanted for the murder of an entire tribe? She was on a new world with strangers—that alone had to be disconcerting for someone who lived without technology. But one would not know it from watching her. It spoke to her mettle that she was standing upright after all she'd been through.

His arm itched and he glanced at the vambrace, catching the subtle hue of the glowing brand. No burn? Strange. That's when he saw the long black curl tangled in the clasp. He coiled it around his finger and yanked it free.

High-pitched shrieks in the sky drew Marco's gaze up. A corvette streaked toward the western docks, reserved for politicians and Coalition vessels. More Symmachians. No doubt coming for her.

He pushed off the ledge and caught a sill, then dropped to the ground and broke into a jog. He tapped his thumper.

"Marco?"

"Another Tascan corvette just hit orbit."

"They know *you* are there. *You* tried to stop them from taking Oron. Now they've returned for you. Marco, you must leave immediately."

"I think they're here for the girl."

At the end of the street, six or seven Eidolon rounded the corner, suited up, faces masked. Curse the reek! Were the savages everywhere? He pulled into an alcove.

"We're looking for a fugitive." An Eidolon spoke to a crowd gathered at a fruit vendor, his high-tech channeler springing the image of the girl into the air. "Have you seen her?"

"I need passage off Cenon." Marco backstepped, turning to run back to the courtyard, knowing Rico heard what had happened through the thumper.

"We're booking passage on the next transport," Rico said, then fell silent for a while. "Done. Details will tap your vambrace. Keep in touch every hour."

"Will do." Sliding through the shadows, Marco kept his receptors open, feeling as hunted as his quarry.

"Master Kynigos!"

Heat splashed his shoulders. He pivoted and stepped into a fighting stance.

On the other side of the road, the tall, silver-haired Droseran held up his hand in greeting as he broke from his people, gathered at the curb with their bags, and strode toward him.

"Ixion." Marco clasped the man's forearm and shifted to watch the Symmachians. But then the Droserans' bags and gear registered. "You are leaving Cenon."

Ixion nodded. "On a transport to Drosero by way of Thyrolia. Leaves in a couple of hours. Long journey, but it'll be good to be home." He glanced toward the other men. "Bazyli's bound is expecting their third child, and he would be there for the birth, not to mention that he must assume his father's role as elder."

Marco glanced at the grim-faced warriors. *This … this is the answer. Send the girl with them.* "Of course." She'd go—they were her people, were they not? One of the tribes. "I'm glad I ran into you, Ixion."

The man's smile faltered, hesitancy standing guard over it. "And why is that?"

"The daughter of Drosero."

Ixion drew up his chin, expression darkening. "What of her?"

"She's here in Zlares," Marco said. "Lodging with an iereas in the historic district."

"Is she why you're here?" Ixion challenged.

Commotion at the end of the street caught their attention. A large intercity shuttle wheezed to a stop at the juncture. Three red-clad Eidolon boarded, their mechanized voices ordering everyone to remain calm and stay where they were while they searched it.

"She is why *they* are here," Marco said, avoiding a lie about his involvement.

Bazyli joined them, his braids clicking as he bounced his gaze between them. "Is something amiss?"

"The Kynigos said Kersei is here on Cenon."

Bazyli started. "Where? Why would she be here?"

"Why is of little concern now. What is of utmost—is that." Marco nodded to the Eidolon. "They will do anything to get her back," he warned. "Get her out of here. Take her with you. She's with an iereas in a yellow house."

"How long have you known—"

"Go." He nodded, slipping back to the alley, eyes on the transport. "Do it now, or it will be too late."

Palms pressed to the cool, damp balustrade overlooking the Kalonican Sea, Kersei breathed in the salt air. Closed her eyes at the vigorous song of the waves pounding the rocks below.

Warmth pressed against her spine. A hand slipped around her waist and pulled her back. At that simple touch joy washed over her. Crashed into the horrible things she'd been through, and like the waves, shoved them out to sea, forever removing their power to torment.

Perfect. It was so perfect.

She rested her arm over his and relaxed with a shuddering sigh. When had she been this happy? Had it not just been yesterday she'd been terrified? Fleeing for her life? But he'd saved her. Brought her back home. He kissed the top of her head.

"Darius," she said softly, leaning into him. "I'm so glad you're alive. You're here. You saved me."

A deep rumbling laugh vibrated along her shoulder blades.

That didn't sound like Darius. She eased aside to peer up at him. She'd just caught sight of a black beard when he tugged her back against his chest. "No, stay." His breath was hot against her earlobe. "I need you, Kersei."

Definitely not Darius!

Thud! Thud! Thud!

Flames erupted around them. She leapt away, scrambling back with a shriek. Then she was falling . . .

Kersei landed with a thud. She blinked her eyes open, heart pounding. *Where am I?*

The bed was nice, but not where she'd stayed with—Baytu. Oh. Grief clawed her, remembering the woman, dead by the water. Kersei had stayed with her for a long time, bathed her face and hands with clean water from the river, not the sludge they'd passed through in the tunnels. But in the end, she'd had to leave her there, using stones to cover her body. Then things had gone . . . strange. She'd taken those tablets Baytu had given her when—

The hunter!

She looked to the window and saw the sun high in the heavenlies. She had napped longer than expected after breaking her fast with the iereas—he'd said his name was Ypiretis—and Duncan. Sitting on the edge of the bed, she thought back to the dream. She'd dreamed of Darius. His touch. His kiss. His voice.

Only . . . She touched her forehead. It wasn't Darius. The laughter was wrong. The touch . . . firmer. The voice, deeper. The kiss . . . wanted. Guilt harangued her. Should she have better accepted Darius? Could she have been kinder? More . . . willing?

Voices pushed into her awareness. She moved to the door, palming the wood so she could listen better. The low tones of men's voices carried up the stairs to her. Who could Ypiretis be talking to? Was he betraying her? Everyone else had.

"Get her. Now. It's urgent."

Feet shuffled toward the door, and Kersei leapt backward.

"Mistress!" Ypiretis knocked then pushed open the door.

With a yelp, she scrambled aside, surprised he would enter without her permission. But then, she wasn't on Drosero and he wasn't a sergius.

"Peace, child." The iereas smiled. "You are well enough safe."

"What is the matter? Who is here?" Kersei peered into the hall, but could not see the others.

"I fear you must leave," Ypiretis said with a grim smile. "Your people are here for you."

Cruel joke that. "You err, iereas. My people are dead."

"Sadly," he said, with a wan smile. "But other entolis were not lost." He motioned to the door. "Please, come."

Unsure of who waited out there, Kersei stepped from the room half expecting an ambush. For the men to be Symmachians. Or that hunter.

At the bottom of the stairs stood several men. Her gaze hit the pale blue eyes of Bazyli Sebastiano and one of his younger brothers. The sight shuddered a breath through her. Behind them stood Ixion Mavridis, of whom her father had spoken highly. A choked sob caught in her throat. She cupped a hand over her mouth, embarrassed at how their presence affected her. Relieved for familiar faces. It renewed the ache for her family, her father.

Bazyli came to her with an understanding smile. "Cousin." He spread wide his arms and pulled her into a hug. "Be at peace, Kersei," he said in his gravelly voice. "You are under our protection now."

She clung to him, afraid if she let go, he would vanish.

"We must leave, Mistress Kersei." Broad-shouldered Ixion inclined his head, which nearly touched the low ceiling. "Symmachians search for you."

At that, she started. "They have been … persistent. And cruel."

Bazyli looked to another by the door, who handed him something. He in turn gave it to her. "Your IDent card."

She eyed the card, saw the name. "I … this is not me."

"No." Pain skittered through Ixion's expression. "The name must not be your own to protect your journey home. For our travels, you will pose as my daughter, Isaura."

"Never thought I'd say this, but we thank you, iereas." Bazyli gave Ypiretis a curt nod, then fixed on Kersei again. "We travel now."

"Now?" Kersei flinched.

"Have you things to pack?" The younger man was remarkably like Bazyli.

"I …" Kersei glanced around. "I have nothing."

"Let us away," Bazyli said. "It is near time and we must find suitable clothing for her, so they do not question that she is ours."

Kersei allowed the men to lead her from the dwelling. They made quick work of the streets and dark passages until they finally directed her into a small clothing shop. Ixion handed her a piece of paper. "Find something, quick."

The paper, she realized, was money. She glanced around the racks of clothing, but the garments all seemed too … different. Colorful. She could not help but admire a coral dress with silks and ribbons. But it was not time for such attire. Moving around, she felt the pressure of the men. Felt strange—both protected and yet vulnerable. She knew these men would protect her as their own. But she could not help but wonder if they thought her guilty, too.

"Are you finding everything okay?" a woman asked.

Kersei smiled. "Omnir pants and a bliaut?"

The woman wrinkled her nose. "Too hot for that here, so we don't have many, but they're in the back corner there. Clearance."

With a nod, she moved in that direction, not sure what clearance meant. She found a muted mauve bliaut and black omnirs. Perfect. She had never preferred the frilly to the practical—that was Lexina. Pieces in hand, Kersei froze at the thought of her sister. Chewed her inner lip, trying not to cry.

"Want to try them on?"

Kersei nodded, swallowing her grief and refocusing on the task at hand.

A presence loomed behind her, and she flinched. "Be quick, daughter," Ixion said kindly, yet there seemed a violence to his words. "Our shuttle departs soon." He took the note from her and handed it to the woman. "She'll wear it out."

The woman frowned but shuffled away.

Ixion nudged her to a small closet. "Change and be quick."

Inside, Kersei removed the clothes that had been with her through sewers and terrors. She reveled in the softness of the bliaut and its long sleeves—so familiar. Like being home. Only, she wasn't. And she must remember that.

She stepped into the omnirs, very full and folded through the legs yet tight at the ankles. The sleeves of the bliaut were thin. The brand's glow peeked through, ominous and telling. Pain struck like a bolt. Startled by its ferocity, Kersei strangled a cry. Fisted her hand and held her arm to her chest. Gritted her teeth. Fought the urge to scream, to betray this nightmare. They must not know. Could not. Sweat slid down her back and chest. Down her temples. Tears pricked her eyes.

"Isaura."

Kersei straightened at Ixion's deep voice that reached through the door. "Are you well?"

"Yes, thank you," she managed, struggling past the fog of pain. "Just a moment." She squeezed her eyes shut. A whimper escaped as she hugged herself. Crouched at the door. By the Ancient it hurt so much!

"Isaura." He sounded more insistent, annoyed.

"I …" The ominous blue glow receded, taking the heat with it. She straightened, legs weak, and blotted the sweat from her face.

Several sharp raps came at the door. "Isaura. It's time."

With a steadying breath and one last glance at the brand, she tugged open the door. "I beg your mercy."

Something rolled through his expression. "You are well?"

She must give him a reason for her delay. "I am … now." She followed him out of the shop and into the street. "For the first time in a long while, yes. Thank you."

A smile creased his eyes. "It is an honor to see you safely home."

Her new guardian was older and had a presence about him that had others deferring to him, much as they had with her father. The violence of his words never left. When he spoke, he brooked no argument. Indeed, he was as handsome as he was fierce, even among the machitis—Xanthus.

"Let us be quick," Bazyli said.

They hurried through the sunlit afternoon. Though daytime, it seemed shadows skittered and leapt across the street, taunting them. Ixion and Bazyli stalked together, their gazes sweeping the streets. The young brother hung back with her. It was strange and comforting to be with them. Yet, she wasn't sure she would feel safe until back on Drosero.

"Have you heard," the younger asked, "of our father?"

Kersei glanced at him as another Xanthus fell into step with them. Where had he come from? "Nay, I have heard nothing …"

"Murdered here."

"Quiet, Galen," Bazyli hissed over his shoulder. "Not here."

Shock thumped her. "I beg your mercy. I had not heard. For your loss, I am grieved."

"We are here," Ixion announced as he caught her elbow. "I see the others. Stay close, Daughter."

It was a help, a means to get home, but somehow that term went crossways through her. But she set aside the annoyance and allowed him to lead, as any father would in a crowded terminal like this. They made their way toward another contingent of Droserans—a dozen machitis of the Xanthus entoli who, apparently, had accompanied Ares and his sons to Cenon. She reminded herself she was safer with him than in the market. Or with that hunter and his probing blue eyes.

She faltered on a step, but Ixion caught her. Steadied her. Thankful he could not read her racing mind or her thudding heart. He—the hunter!—was the one in her dream, holding her, kiss—

Impossible! She had never heard his voice. And he didn't have a beard.

"Symmachians," Galen muttered.

The word yanked Kersei back to the very real danger of their situation and the familiar red uniforms lurking about the terminal. She shifted away, worried.

"You are with us now. All is well," Ixion said, as if this were any other day.

"What if they see me?" she whispered.

Ixion drew her round. Cupped her face. Looked into her eyes as he drew up the hood of her bliaut, covering her hair. "Remember your iron, Kersei."

Iron. The courage of the Kalonicans. She drew in a shaky breath and nodded, appreciating his efforts to conceal her.

"In the queue," Ixion said calmly, guiding her to the other Kalonicans in the long line of people.

She looked ahead then back to the Symmachians—her gaze connected with a familiar face. Hauling in a breath, she froze.

On the entrance steps of the Grand Terminal stood Commander Tigo Deken.

Instinct ordered Kersei to look away, but before she could, she met Jez's gaze. The woman's lips parted. Her hand went to Tigo.

Kersei gave the barest shake of her head as Ixion stepped between them, severing her line of sight.

"Easy," he said quietly. "We're next."

Facing the ticket line again, she found they were indeed next. A glass barrier separated them from the booth, and Kersei used that reflection to watch Jez. Would they come for her? She thought Tigo had seen her. But then he took a step back. Tapped Jez and thumbed to the doors. They left.

Disbelieving, Kersei let out a breath. Confused. Relieved. He had to have seen her. Why didn't he come after her? He had helped her escape, so why would he be here at all? Orders? Had he gotten in trouble and now had to remedy that? What if other Symmachians found her here? She would rather be caught by Tigo.

Ixion drew forward, her only indication that they'd been called. Shoulders back as Ma'ma taught her, Kersei approached the booth.

The agent scanned their IDent cards. "Two tickets to Drosero." The agent's voice was monotone, but then he looked up. "Mr. Mavridis, you arrived here alone, yet you return as a couple."

Ixion angled his head. "There is a mistake—we are not a couple. This is my daughter, and yes, we travel together. Could there be an error in the log about the arrival?"

The agent went silent.

What was he doing?

"I'm afraid—"

Shouts rang through the Grand Terminal.

Kersei shifted to see—

Gripping her arm tightly, Ixion stilled her. Smiled at the agent and ducked. "You are right. I am sorry to say my daughter fled here months past. I have come to return her to our people."

The agent considered him, the story. Then Kersei.

"And it seems an uprising is starting," Ixion continued, glancing back to the doors. "Please clear us before the terminal is blocked and all bound for Thyrolia become enraged because we missed our shuttle to the transport and must wait another month. I would be aggrieved should my daughter have a chance again to flee."

The agent still wasn't responding.

Thuds resonated down the line of booths. Agents returned IDent cards. Gates swung open. "Approved."

In relief, she and Ixion hurried through and the gate jerked closed.

"Attention passengers of the Grand Terminal. On Tertian Space Coalition and Cenoan Transportation authority, a temporary halt in the processing of passengers for departure is now in effect. Please remain calm. We will work quickly to restore services."

Kersei kept pace with Ixion as they strode down a long concourse. Close to a hundred passengers made their way out of the terminal onto a gray path. At the far end, a ramp seemed to gorge itself on the bottlenecking crowd.

A familiar shape bobbed ahead, wading through the people. Those shoulders. The distinct manner of walking. Like he was perpetually stalking. Hunting.

Kersei stopped. Heart in her throat, she stared ahead, thinking of the pale blue eyes made fierce by the glower and the inked lines across his nose.

"What is it?" Ixion asked, hand at her elbow.

"I …" Why would *he* be here? *Was* it him?

"Kersei?" Ixion motioned up the ramp. "We are nearly there."

Jolted out of her thoughts, she shook her head. Continued into the shuttle behind the others. But she kept watch, as her father had taught her. Remained alert.

"We all made it." Bazyli climbed the ramp up into the belly of a small shuttle. "Jencir and Galen are at the back."

Ixion pointed her to a seat. "Buckle in."

Carrying a newly acquired ruck containing the few items he'd been able to acquire before the scheduled departure, Marco headed toward the terminal lines, his authority as a hunter enabling him to bypass the crowds. A mercy, considering the many stenches filling the terminal. Sticking to the walls, he skirted the circumference. Spotted two Eidolon stalking the crowds and tucked his chin, focusing solely on his goal. He could not miss that transport or Roman would scald his ears with remonstrations. If he lived to have his ears scalded.

Again, his mind skipped to the girl, to carrying her through the alleys. Barely heavier than his ruck, she ... That face. Wreathed in serenity as she lay against his chest. Hair caught on his vambrace.

Distracted, he barely noted the scent. Drew up—just as a wall of reinforced armor slammed him into the plaster alcove. Pinned him.

Anger shot through his veins. His hand went to his dagger as he pushed back against the bulk. "Unhand me, metal-neck." Though he fought the restraint, the armor strengthened the Eidolon.

"I know what you hunt."

The mechanized whisper startled Marco, hauling his receptors into singular focus. No attack scent. Just ... intent. He looked up into the blackened face shield. "I speak to no one of a Decree," he snarled. What did this Marine want? "What cause do you have to attack me?"

"Give her this. Keep her alive. Find out what she saw." The man slapped Marco's chest, and instinct had Marco clasp the gauntlet—and felt something pressed into his hand.

The Eidolon gave an extra shove for good measure, then stepped back. "Don't make this mistake again. Stay clear while we patrol."

Marco watched the retreating hulk. With the drop suit armor, the Eidolon was large. Powerful. Impressive. What was that about? He peered at what had fallen into his hand. Jewelry. Hers?

"Last boarding call for the *Kleopatra* shuttle."

The call ringing through the terminal yanked his attention to his goal—that transport. He glanced again at the Eidolon, now with his unit but staring back at him. After a long, silent moment and nothing more than a nod, Marco loped into a jog and cleared the security checkpoint. He hiked up into the transport. The hour-long ride to the Herakles civilian transport gave him time to think through the encounter with the Eidolon. And the piece in his pocket, now pressing into his leg.

Find out what she saw ... What did that mean?

An hour later in his quarters, he waved his advocate.

Rico shouldered into the camera's view. "You made it?"

"Indeed." Marco glanced around the quarters, which had a central living area with built-in table and bench, a bunk room, and an aerator closet for showering and daily rituals. "Symmachians got too close, forcing me to inform the Droserans that the girl was on Cenon. Her people got her onboard as well."

"Under their protection."

Marco inclined his head, knowing it had not been the best scenario but was the only option available at the time. He tugged out the necklace that the Eidolon had shoved into his hand. About to disclose the encounter, he wondered at it. At the cryptic message. Then pocketed it again, choosing to think on it more.

Disbelief curled along the edges of his advocate's jaw. He gave a stiff breath. "You've greatly complicated your hunt. The Droserans will not allow you to take her from them. They are downworlders of the purest kind."

"This transport is hardly the fastest ship in the 'verse. I have time to figure it out."

"No, I'm afraid not," Rico said. "We're recalling all hunters, regardless of Decrees." He nodded at the screen. "We'll send escorts to retrieve you—"

"No!" Marco faltered at his vehemence, then breathed out heavily. He needed to convince Rico that he should stay. "I was … confronted by an Eidolon. He told me to find out what she saw."

Rico scowled. "Saw where?"

"Unknown. If you recall me, I cannot get the answer." He leaned in. "Think, about it, Rico. This metal-neck got in my face and then left me free. After what just happened to Oron, I must risk this to remain here and find out what she saw." He smoothed a hand over his face. "The less attention I draw to my location—and hers—the better. Here I can easily monitor comings and goings, maybe find a way to talk with her. If there is an attack, the ship will go into lockdown."

"Which means you are trapped. And the girl."

"With a handful of machitis warriors and a Stalker." Besides, the only reason they'd send Eidolon to Zlares was if the girl had something of value, which meant they would want her alive. But what did she see?

"If you get into trouble on the *Kleopatra*, we're too far to assist."

"There are escape slips. I verified before boarding." But his mind was mulling options. Ways to finish this Decree without getting himself or the girl captured. "What of Revocation?"

Rico jerked, then glowered in a way that dug his eyebrows into his nose. "Do not speak such blasphemy! Do that and the Decree is lost. I am dishonored. Roman is dishonored. Is that what—"

"Peace, Advocate. I meant only temporary Revocation, should it become necessary to hide among the populace." He roughed the stubble on his jaw, not sure how he'd feel without his sigil. He might as well stand naked before the world. "If they are hunting Kynigos, we may need a way to conceal ourselves."

"No man of honor cowers or hides! It defies the Codes." Rico rolled his shoulders, shaking off the insult. "Never mention it again. That strips our very identity."

Chagrined, Marco dropped his gaze and his argument. "Forgive me."

With a long sigh, Rico leaned in, hands on either side of the camera. "Tensions are high with the loss of Oron, and now Apelles believes his prime advocate, Lidio, is missing."

Futility tremored through Marco. "*What* are they doing with us? It is not killings—that can be done in the street. Why kidnapping?"

"We are at a loss. Many have long been jealous of our abilities," Rico muttered. "Lie low and stand fast, brother. To the Decree."

Right. As if the sigil went unnoticed. "And the hunt, for honor." He ended the transmission and spotted again the dull glow of the mark.

Strange. Again? So soon. Why was it not burning? He turned his arm and released the vambrace. Caught around the hinge of the buckle was the strand of hair. Hadn't he removed that? Mayhap he'd only broken off a part. Or had there been more than one? To free it, he had to remove the gauntlet. When it came loose and he lifted the hair, heat shot through his arm.

He grunted, jerking at the assault. Hand fisted so tight, his arm trembled. Through the rail of pain came a thought: *replace the strand.*

Marco laid it on his mark.

The heat abated, though the mark remained bright.

Removed the hair.

Pain, fiery and cruel, bit into his veins. Darted up and down his muscle. So vicious. Seeking to consume.

He set the hair back in place, and the fire vanished.

What majuk is this? With a shrug—he must have all his faculties to protect her—he re-secured the vambrace over the strand. He recalled lifting her from the ground, which had also quelled the heat. What did it mean?

Disconcerted, unnerved, he staggered to his feet. Felt the walls closing in. Not enough space to stretch or work out. And he needed to let off some frustration. He left his quarters, staying alert. Bathed in pale gray, the corridor was caressed by subtle blue light at shoulder level. Though tempted to make for the cantina to drown his receptors in a million different scents and thereby dull the stress, Marco headed to the athletic area to accomplish that in a healthier way.

He skipped the weights and sparring rooms, instead going for the gauntlet arena, suspecting it'd be replete with ways to buffet his body. When the door slid open, he grinned at what waited. Half walls. Fences. Poles. No people.

Perfect.

He removed his waistcoat and tossed it aside. Tugging the clasps of his lightweight rhinnock vest and vambrace, he verified their sturdiness. Training with them made them familiar, an extension of his body, so there was nothing strange during a hunt. After a rigorous warm-up of sit-ups, push-ups, and stretches, he hopped the rail dividing the start line. Pitching himself over it several times made his muscles thrum. He did it two-handed. Then one. And backward.

Bouncing on his toes, he looked to where two walls met. Sprinted at the corner, then tic-tacked up and leapt to the side, where he caught a handhold in the climbing wall. Scaled it and flung through the air to a bar hanging over an emptied trough, that no doubt had been filled with some viscous substance during competition. He swung up and over, balancing on the bar using the balls of his feet. Where the spinning log supports met the wall, they created a ledge. Marco threw himself at it, but his brain ricocheted off the encounter with the Eidolon near the fountain, jumping from the wall to tackle him. Then carrying the girl. That pretty, round face. Silky soft curls tickling as he carried her to safety. And those dark lashes. Somehow his brain merged him getting her help with her standing in that hut watching him. As if she lay in his arms, peering up at him. Longingly.

He missed the hold. Landed and tucked to avoid injury. He cursed his distraction and came up running at the climbing wall, more determined to nail it. Scaling it like a monkey, he reached the top and perched there, annoyed with himself.

"Curse the reek," he hissed, irritated that he was wasting valuable training time. He planked on the floor. Lifted a hand. Held himself there until trembling threatened to make him face-plant. He shoved up and switched hands. Caught himself. Then battered the other arm into shape, relishing the pain. The reminder to keep his thoughts on the hunt.

With a running start, he threw himself at the parallel bar. After several momentum arcs, he launched out, twisting to the climbing wall. Snagged a finger hold, his toe stuffed on another so that he dangled sideways.

Light shifted in the outer corridor, allowing shadows to enter the bay.

Some trill forced Marco to hoist to the top and squat there. As he focused on the newcomers entering the arena, he was about to offer to clear out when his blood went cold. They might be out of the standard red uniform, but those were undoubtedly Symmachians. Worse—Eidolon as marked by the gold epaulet.

The weight of the javrod was gloriously familiar and comforting. Kersei tested it, her heart racing a little faster. Not because it was a weapon. But because … it was *her*. Her people. Their way. She flew through her routines, using a large padded pole for a target. Whirling, whacking, thrusting …

As she swept low, she sighted a tall, powerful man striding toward her. Intention in his stride. Strength in his posture. Challenge in his glare. Ixion set down no gauntlet. He spoke no words. But his javrod came at her.

Surprised yet pleased, Kersei hopped back, blocking. The wood was somehow different, and the blow rattled up her arms into her shoulder. She smoothed her grip as she'd been taught and used his over-strike to deflect. Popped to the head, then the knee. He parried, advancing, menacing.

She stepped aside, allowing his momentum to carry her in a circle, the clacks and fervor unlike any sparring before. Exhaustion tugged at her, but she refused to yield. Acute awareness rang through her that the machitis she had sparred with before *had* held back. Her heart began to beat a little harder—not with exhilaration. But with concern. Why was he driving so hard? Was he angry?

The sharp end of his javrod tsinged along her arm. She hissed and shoved backward, swinging her rod's broad end at him. And saw the mistake as soon as she did it.

He was angling down. Locked her javrod. Disarmed her.

Thwack!

The strike thumped her temple. Rattled her teeth. Swung her around. She lurched up—not scared. Furious and humiliated. Sweaty hair in her face. Temple stinging. Hands numb from the vibrations. She stepped back into a fighting stance.

He gave a nod. "Yes!"

She balled her fists.

"No!" He was on her in flash. Flung her around, her arm hooking her throat. Her spine against his chest. Breath burned. Lungs ached. "Master that wildness," he hissed in her ear, "or it will master you." He thrust her forward, sending her stumbling.

The man was vicious. The kindness she'd noticed before had vanished and in its place roared a fierceness she had only seen in her father.

She whirled, startled, eyes stinging. Scared. But angry, too.

He nodded to her javrod on the mat. "Again!"

Was he insane? She would not—

"I beg your mercy," he said, his ferocity unaltered, cocking his head, "I thought you Xylander's heir." He propped his javrod to the side like a walking stick. "Or are you telling me this is all he taught you. Tears and weakness?"

Breathing became a chore.

"Angry?"

She crushed the words champing to shred him and glowered.

"This a joke to you? They slaughtered your family!" he bellowed, face contorted. "Now they hunt you like a dog, and you want to be placated, pitied? Is that the stance of warrior?"

She lifted her jaw. "I—"

"You must *war*," he roared. "The enemy will not play nice. They will not come at you with etiquette and propriety, but with weapons and savagery. You are *machitis*! Give it to them first, Kersei. Do you understand? Remember what they did to your father, to our medora? The crown prince and your bound?"

She swallowed.

"Give the girl a chance to recover, Mavridis," someone said.

It was only then she realized fully with whom she had just sparred. Not the Ixion who acted as father, but Ixion the Plisiázon, the Stalker. No wonder the scar over his eye. No wonder the relentlessness of his attacks, the violence of his tone. Stalkers put the fear of the Ancient into everyone on Drosero. Some said their bloodthirst made them cross lines in defending the southern territories from the Irukandji and Hirakys.

Ixion inclined his head. "I meant no harm."

"No," she breathed raggedly. "Of course not." She shuddered her next breath. "I welcome your training and direction."

He strode forward, cupped the back of her head and drew their foreheads together. "You have fire in your blood, Kersei. Make it your weapon." After a nod, he started from the sparring room. "Good rest, Bazyli."

Braids swaying, the Xanthus elder shook his head, amused. "And you. Vanko Kalonica."

"Vanko." Ixion lifted a hand in the air as he stepped from sight.

Bazyli's gray-blue eyes met hers. "You are well?"

She touched her throbbing temple. "Aye. A good lesson. Hard, but good."

"That is where Ixion excels," Bazyli said, his rough edges softening. "And I cannot fault him for it. Stalkers have kept the borders safe for decades under his watchful eye."

Kersei looked to where she'd last seen the man. "Living so near Kardia, I have been sheltered from many dangers, I fear."

"Aye," Bazyli said as he came closer. "There is much your father protected you from. Your mother and sisters as well. As I and my father have done with our family."

She frowned.

"As the last of the Stratios, you will soon learn those dangers, but look not for them now. Rest, Kersei. Regain your strength and wits." He gave a cockeyed nod. "You'll need them. But right now—this very tick—if I do not return for the evening meal, my brothers and that Stalker will have devoured it all. Will you join me?"

Kersei smiled. Glanced at her javrod. "I will be along shortly. I would walk through how he disarmed me."

Bazyli winked. "If you figure it out, let me know."

"He disarms you?"

As he started for the exit, Bazyli snorted. "Ixion disarms everyone."

One day, she would be good enough that he wouldn't. She lifted the javrod and practiced her moves. "So, I was here. I'd just ... upsweep ... then he—"

Thud. Thump.

Kersei paused, looked over her shoulder for the source of the noise. Scanned the sparring room, but found herself alone. She shook it off. Back in position, she realigned herself. Bent her knees, shifted her weight to her right leg. Rotated the rod in a sweeping gesture. "Then"—she glanced at the mat, thinking—"he ... He what?" She repeated the move. Saw the broad end barreling toward her head.

Thud! Whoomp. Crack.

A loud crash erupted. The clang of metal and something hollow created a gong-like noise.

Kersei straightened. Blew the damp strands from her eyes. Stared at the wall where more thuds sounded. What was on the other side?

The obstacle course.

Perhaps someone was having bad luck.

But that sounds like ...

Curious and concerned, Kersei left the sparring room, a ding sounding in the hall, warning her to return the training weapon. "I'll be back," she muttered, slinking closer to the room marked ARENA. As she did, the commotion grew louder. The unmistakable sound of punches. A fight.

She peered around the corner. Blood drained to her feet.

Two men, one in a blue jerkin and one in tan, were attacking a third, who was forced to his knee because Blue had his arm twisted behind and up. But the victim rammed his elbow into Blue's groin. Kersei winced at the blow.

Blue stumbled back.

Tan surged forward. Threw a hard punch that spun the dark-haired man toward her. He staggered, sweaty hair fringing his face. All at once it hit her—his tunic, vest, that vambrace, the black hair. His blue eyes struck her. Widened for a fraction beneath the mark.

By the Mercies! *It's him!* The hunter.

She whipped away, heart crashing into her ribs. Heat washed through her. It *had* been him in the terminal. Why was he here? Why were they attacking him?

Someone moved behind him—Tan.

She drew in a sharp breath.

The hunter lashed into motion. Leapt into the air, spinning around and tackling Tan to the ground. They landed, rolling amid grunts and groans.

Blue careened after the Kynigos. Drew a weapon.

"Give it to them first, Kersei." Pulse roaring, she felt Ixion's words. Javrod tucked along the length of her arm, she sprinted forward, glided between Blue and the hunter. She spun, bringing her javrod to bear as she did. Her first form—temple, shin, groin—sailed out evenly. Each strike resonated through the wood, connecting with the unsuspecting man.

When he doubled and held himself, she swung around and thrust the rod back, straight into his stomach. Followed through, snapping the end down, then around and up, cracking the opposite end against his head.

She leapt away into ready stance again as Blue stumbled and tripped, groaning. Then collapsed. Pulse roaring and air clambering through her chest in ragged chunks, she lifted her gaze.

The hunter stood gaping at her as he protected his side. Blue eyes like the Kalonican Sea held her hostage. He took in her victim. Then her.

Self-conscious, she straightened. Felt a tremor of fear—Baytu said he hunted her on Cenon. And he'd pursued her through the streets. But then she'd awakened in the home with the iereas—was it because of him? Or would he now attack her here?

He retrieved Blue's weapon. "We should leave while we can."

We? "And go where?" She hesitated, not sure she should be anywhere with this dangerous man. Why she'd helped him, she couldn't fathom. Yet she had.

"Come! There is no time. If you are to be safe—"

"*Am* I safe with you?"

He hesitated and huffed. "You have nothing to fear from me here. For your own sake, come." He hurried to the door, then stopped short. She thumped into his back. He reached behind and caught her arm, shuffling them to the right.

"Wh—?"

"This way." His voice was deep. Assured. He guided her around, took the javrod and set it aside, then nudged her toward the rear padded foam supports of some obstacle. "Behind it."

"What?" Kersei hesitated. "No!"

But he pushed her into the dark gap.

Fear squirreled through her chest, recalling the chamber. The closed-in space, the images. "Stop. No—"

"Move. Go!"

No, she wasn't doing this. She pivoted to him. "I—"

His hand fell on her mouth. Not hard. But firm. "There are more." His eyes, so intense against the marks over his nose, drilled her. Waiting for her to acknowledge that she understood the danger.

It finally made it to her head. More attackers. She gave a quick nod and burrowed into the corner. When she glanced to the side, his spine was to her. He stood braced, facing the opening, his shoulders wedged in tight. Ready for the opponent.

Was it smart to be in a confined space? With a hunter? Well, she would not want for protection—as long as he wasn't the threat.

Kersei stiffened, realizing he was backing toward her.

He turned. Motioned to something.

She glanced over her shoulder, not yet seeing what he was indicating. He wedged in deeper, his chest close to her face, her spine crushed against the padded wall. Leaning forward, he touched rigging that anchored the climbing wall to a steel support. Nodded.

She frowned. What the boils did he want her to do?

He angled closer.

Air trapped in her throat, Kersei stiffened at the impropriety of the situation. At the audacity of him daring to draw so near. And the way her body betrayed her with an erratic pulse.

His breath was hot against her ear, throwing darts of heat in her stomach. His lips brushed her earlobe as he whispered, "Up. Climb."

She pulled in a breath. Face hot, she swam through the thick reactions back to reality. Climb. Aye. But climb what? Again, she eyed the brace. Several evenly spaced bars rose overhead. Ah. With a sharp nod, she palmed the wall.

His hands caught her waist.

The shock of his touch made her slip.

But his support was firm. She tried again and caught the upper bracket, glad for her omnirs, otherwise this would be most indecent. Well, *more* indecent. It would color her the harlot if they were discovered.

She reached for the next, the distance nearly the length of her body, but she pulled up. At the top, she had a clear view of the obstacle course—and the men. She flattened her stomach on the padding barely wider than her. The hunter eased over the edge without a sound, his maneuvering controlled and light. Though there was room for him, there wasn't room for propriety if they were to conceal themselves from whoever had come. When his arm hooked her waist, she started. Flushed at his nearness.

Shouts could be heard. Boots clomping closer.

Her mind was running its own obstacle course, wondering what Ixion or Bazyli would do if they found her here with him. A hunter! The thought pushed her gaze to him, surprised his eyes were closed. What was he doing?

Dark hair framed his face and fell along the arcs beneath his eyes and bridge of his arrow-straight nose. His lips were parted and relaxed. Stubble roughened the olive skin of his jaw. It would be futile to deny he was handsome. And … stirring.

His eyes popped open and he withdrew his arm. Kersei felt his gaze all the way to her toes as he traced her face, skidding from one feature—eyes, nose, mouth, hair—to another. A smirk touched his lips. Then it was gone. He withdrew his gaze, closing his eyes once more.

They lay in silence for what felt like hours, though she could not account for the time. It was strange. Awkward. Her thoughts bounced from the inappropriateness to the danger.

But was there danger? She had not seen or heard the men in a while. Long while. Minutes? Half ora?

She looked at the hunter, but he hadn't moved. It was amazing and yet aggravating the way he lay still as a large cat stalking its prey. Yet he wasn't *looking* at anything. Wasn't stalking.

Had he fallen asleep then? Her gaze strayed again. Found that jaw with a dark fringe of whiskers that hung thicker just below his bottom lip. The upper was curved. Not full, only firm. Taut. Recalling the way they'd grazed her ear shot heat through her again.

Kersei shook off the thought. It must be safe by now, she decided. She slowly lifted her head and eased to look over—

"No, stay." His hand slid around her waist and came to rest on her stomach, pulling her shoulder tightly against into his chest.

Shock stole her breath—both at his handling and the recollection of her dream, in which a man had said, *"No, stay."*

It was him. Not Darius.

That could not be. The man in the dream had a beard. And they stood by the ocean.

Yet … it *was* his voice. The same words.

No. No, it was wrong. All wrong. She didn't even know him. And he was inappropriate. Rough. Dangerous—he'd been chasing her on Cenon! Was he still hunting her, this a ruse or trap?

I have to get out of here.

He sensed her fear swell. Felt tension tighten the muscles in her back. Anticipated that she wanted to get away. Being this close drove him crazy, too. For different reasons. He could smell the determination roiling off the two who hid below, waiting him out—the danger they presented. He must do the same. As long as the girl didn't betray their position first.

Lying on his side, he eased his nose into the dark curls that had taunted him for the last hour. "Wait," he murmured firmly once he detected the two leaving.

Her lashes fluttered, but she stiffened. Didn't look at him. "They're gone," she mouthed.

True, but more were inbound. He gave a warning shake of his head, knowing this one had enough spitfire to defy him. So he indicated with a nod, and she craned her head slightly to the door seconds before the scents he'd detected manifested as Ixion and the Xanthus leader. They moved farther into the arena and he lost sight of them.

Panic flared through the girl's efflux. She tried to flatten her spine more, her fair cheek resting on the red pad. Her lips delicately curved in a firm line. Even the set of her jaw defined her spirit—twisted with the curls of black that hung everywhere. It was beautiful. So was the moment when she'd unwittingly thrown an attraction efflux at him. Which had nearly drowned his receptors and focus.

"You there," Ixion called.

Heart in his throat, Marco was sure they'd been discovered. There would be blood—his—after the machitis were done with him for being alone and with the girl in his arms, even though nothing untoward happened between them.

"Can I help you?" a new voice answered, washing relief through Marco—until he realized it was a Symmachian.

"I'm looking for my daughter." A pause. "This is her javrod. Have you seen her?"

"Earlier," one said. "She left with a man."

"A man?" Ixion growled.

"I'm going to notify security," Bazyli said.

"Yeah, well, Baru smile on you with that," one of the Symmachians said.

The scents soon rose with defiance, then faded out altogether. The men had left.

Marco relaxed. Let out a soft breath.

He expected Kersei to pop up and announce herself safe. But she didn't. She stayed his arms. Quiet and calm settled over the arena. They remained there a few more minutes, and Marco couldn't lie—his attention wasn't on some now-departed threat. It was on her. That delectable signature. The feel of her waist against his arm.

Nay, nay. This would not work. Marco slumped back, thought to roll to the side and catch the edge, but she probably couldn't make the drop without hurting herself. "You aren't leaving," he noted quietly.

Her dark eyes bounced to him. "I fear they think little of me already. I need not give them more reason to doubt me." She lowered her gaze. "I meant nothing about your honor."

"Why would your ... father think ill of you?"

"Ixion is not my father. He's my ... guardian."

Myriad scents ballooned around them, creating an ache for what she'd been through. He jutted his jaw. "Can you descend on your own?"

Without another word, she started down.

Marco rolled to the back edge, gripped it, then dropped. He landed a little harder than expected and grimaced through a spike of pain in his torso—a bruised rib mayhap. Arm to his side to protect the injury, he came around as she hopped the last few feet.

She saw him and started, looked at the top, then back to him. "How—"

"We should get you to safety."

Rubbing her palms, she gave a slow nod.

He hesitated. "That a problem?"

She lifted a shoulder in a shrug. "I ... it's just that you're a hunter." She glanced down, swallowed, and by the time she peered up, her fear scent stung his nostrils. "On Cenon ... Baytu said you were hunting me. You tracked me from the water's edge."

He tightened his jaw, not wanting to discuss this now or here. "Come. I'll walk you."

"I would have answers."

"Codes forbid me from discussing my hunts. We must go. It's not up for discussion."

Her eyebrows winged up. "I beg your mercy?"

"Beg all you like," he said with a smile and wink, then he sighed. "As I said before—you have no need to fear me here. Besides, I would not want any harm to befall you and be on my head, because one of your protectors would most likely then take it off."

Kersei snorted a laugh, the offense vanishing. "I fear you are right. Ixion presents a calm façade, but I believe there is a ferocity beneath it. The Plisiázon are notorious for their aggressive methods. My father admired him greatly." Grief doused her scent and she looked away.

Marco tested the air before they entered the concourse.

"Shouldn't we be sure they're gone?"

"They are." Marco hesitated. Frowned. "Know you how Kynigos hunt?"

"Smell?"

"There is no need to curl your lip when you say that," Marco said with a chuckle as he motioned her to the left.

"I beg your mercy—"

"Please, no begging."

"I am not *begging*," she defended herself. "It is merely an expression for seeking the pardon of someone offended." Her gaze was on him, and there was something … pleasant about it. "You already knew that."

Now Marco couldn't hide his smile as he headed toward the lift.

"You were mocking me."

"No." He eyed her. Then grinned. "Mayhap a little."

"May happen what?"

"No. Mayh—" He caught her gaze and saw the mischief sparking off green glints in her brown irises. Surprise held him fast. "Turnabout, eh?"

She hesitated, wariness crowding her pretty face. "In the garden on Cenon, when I grew ill … I awoke with the iereas." She tilted her head to consider him. "Was that your doing?"

He gave a nearly imperceptible nod. "I feared you would die. Knowing Symmachia sought you, I felt your safety was best guaranteed with the iereas."

He smelled her concern and fear. "Then I am indebted to you. Yet I know not your name."

"I am Marco Dusan." He smiled, an easy feat with her, and detected her stress lessen. "It has been a long time since someone teased me."

She smiled, then her eyes traced upward. "You have a nasty welt on your forehead."

"I've had worse," he said, touching the spot and wincing at the knot.

Quiet settled around them as they approached the lift, but Marco felt her unease grow—and it bothered him. "Where did you learn the javrod?" He palmed the access panel and the door whisked open, so he motioned her in first.

"I trained with machitis and sometimes managed to sneak into the aerios training grounds to spar with them. My uncle"—she hesitated for a moment as confusion infused her efflux—"thought it brilliant that his niece could hold her own—mostly."

She was a curiosity, this girl. "And your parents disapproved?"

"Ma'ma absolutely," she said with a laugh. "She was Lady of Stratios, so it was upon her to be an example for our women, and since Medora Zarek's kyria died, she also served as representative of the realm at certain state events. Propriety was her hallmark." She wrinkled her nose.

"Clearly, you did well with your training—"

"Oh, not near well enough. The day …" Her gaze flicked to his, drenched in grief. Then, wary, she looked at the door, as if willing it to open.

Marco thought of the necklace, wondered if would help. *No, too soon.* "I saw the vids on Cenon."

Her lips parted and she drew away. "Is that why you were chasing me?"

The tumult of her signature bothered him. "I don't believe you're guilty." He met her gaze, those wide brown eyes.

"How can you possibly know that?" the question was soft, roiling in both relief and confusion.

"Like I said—you don't know how we hunt."

"Then, please," she said with a twitch of her neck, "explain it to me. My father joined the medora for his annual hunts in the mountains—"

"No." Sniffing, Marco found her naïveté amusing yet bristled that she believed his gifts were something even her father could imitate. "Entirely different kind of hunting."

The door hissed open, and they started out, but two large shapes were waiting. Marco drew up sharply and stepped in front of her, ready to fight the men. Until he saw the severe, disapproving glare of Ixion.

Bazyli gave a shout.

Marco lifted his hands and stepped aside. "Good even—"

"You dare!" Ixion lunged, slamming him back against the closing doors. Jamming his forearm into his throat. "You will never—"

"Leave him!" Kersei balked, her voice pitched as she tugged his arm. "He was protecting me. There were two men attacking—please, Ixion. Please!"

Struggling for air, Marco instinctively coiled a hand around his knife. But forced himself to release, noting the man's silent fury. Assurances were needed here, not violence.

The glow of gray eyes warned that Ixion took action not debts. "This is true?" he asked, his pressure on Marco's throat unfaltering.

"Why would I lie?" Kersei asked. "Release him. Please. He was escorting me back to our quarters for safety."

"He is a hunter." Ixion leaned into Marco's throat once for emphasis, then stepped back but maintained the fist hold on his tunic.

Marco glanced to the man's hand. Assaulting a Kynigos just wasn't done. "It was my hope that our interactions on Cenon might convince you I meant her no harm."

Ixion frowned, eyeing Marco's temple. "She says men attacked."

"It seems to be all the rage, kidnap or beat a Kynigos. But," he said with a huff, straightening, "I fear she did not speak the truth."

Kersei gaped, her eyes bright with indignation. "I spoke no—"

"She saved *my* life, not the other way around." He smoothed his tunic and stabbed his fingers through his hair. "It gives me no pleasure to admit the attackers overwhelmed me. With her javrod, she delivered me of one, and I subdued the other."

"We will accept your account, but heed my words, Kynigos: keep your distance from the mistress." The man's gloved hand lifted from Marco's chest. Pointed at him. "We are grateful for your intel on Cenon, but do not mistake our encounters there for friendship."

The words stung more than Marco would admit. "I have no need of friends here." He took a step back. Eyed the girl, who was in good hands with the Stalker and kinsman. "I thank you for your aid, Mistress Kersei." He inclined his head and backstepped. "Good rest, machitis." He strode down the corridor, but smelled the danger pursuing. Anger. Revenge.

"Kynigos."

Wanting to be out of the girl's sight when this confrontation happened, Marco rounded the corner and pivoted to face the man.

Ixion's hand rested on his scabbard. "What is your business here?"

"I cannot discuss a Decree."

"If she is your mark, there will be pain unlike you have ever known. She is under the protection of the Kalonican crown." He gave a nod. "You understand my meaning, yes?"

"I thought Kalonica was without a medora at present."

"Test not my patience." Ixion's gray eyes darkened. "She is ours. Any attempt to harm or retrieve her will be met with all the fury I can muster as a Plisiázon."

"A threat?"

"Much more. Beseeching." A protective scent bled with anger and grief. "She has experienced enough pain this cycle. I will remove all threats to her happiness that are in my power to affect."

As Ixion hurried to catch up with the girl, Marco understood his meaning. He was all but *begging* Marco to show his hand. Let the men end him.

"It's decided. You will stay close to these quarters at all times," Ixion growled the next rise as they stood in the quarters shared by Bazyli and his brothers.

"The trip is long," Kersei objected. For the hundredth time. "I will go mad with boredom in this small space."

"It is for your own safety."

"I appreciate your protection," she said, trying not to sound condescending or ungrateful, "and all you have done for me, getting me off Cenon, sheltering me here, but—"

"Kersei." Ixion planted a hand on her shoulder and peered down into her eyes. Patience marked the life of a Stalker, who waited for the right opportunity to strike. Deliberate. Focused. "He is a Kynigos, a hunter."

"I am aware," she bristled, recalling the chase through the tunnels with Baytu.

"Nay, I do not think you are aware of the full meaning of what he is."

"In the sparring room men attacked him and were intent on the doing same to me, but he protected me until they left. On Cenon, when I"—she dared not mention the herb pill she'd taken, for she would have to mention that he was chasing her, which would not go well with these machitis—"fell ill, he hurried me to the safety of an iereas for help." She stretched her neck. "So, while I know the dangers of him, I know he means me no harm. Besides, it was only after you and Bazyli checked the room that we knew it was safe."

"Wait," Bazyli shouldered in, expression terse. "You saw us and didn't come out?"

Kersei swallowed.

"Did he forbid you? Hold you against your will?"

"No!"

"No, stay." His breathed words. His touch. His breath against her cheek that sent trills into her stomach. Those sea-blue eyes. His laugh and smile.

"You think he hunts her?" Jencir, the second-oldest asked. "Yet it was the hunter who told you her location. Had he not, she would have surely been taken by the Symmachians."

Kersei started at that. "He ... he did?"

"Aye," Ixion conceded, "he told us where to find you."

He saved me ...? "And yet you think he is a danger to me?"

"You are wanted by Symmachia. There are vids playing in the galley here for your arrest," Bazyli said. "He as much as admitted that he was hunting."

Heat flared across her arm, completely skipping the tingling stage. Oh no. Her mind scrambled back to the conversation. "But surely he is no danger to me—he has repeatedly protected me, not accosted me!"

"You are much hunted, so it is for your own safety that you remain in this suite," Ixion said. "Kersei, you are all that remains of Xylander and Nicea, and I would see you restored to what remains of your entoli and people."

She longed for that, too. But ... "I cannot remain cooped up here. Even at Stratios, the walls closed in on me." Her mind replayed the videos from the *Macedon.* The walls literally falling in. Her baby sister crushed. Her parents. Lexina. Darius ...

The room spun. Sweat slid down her spine.

"I am your guardian and I insist—"

"No," Kersei mumbled, gritting her way through another wave of fire. "You"—why was it so viciously hot this time, and burning so quickly?—"are not." She blinked, fighting for focus. "In earnest, I am grateful. But I must— augh!" Pain sliced like a sword through her bones.

"Kersei!"

Her knees buckled.

"To the bedchamber," Bazyli instructed as the room spun and the ceiling fell.

No. No, it ... Someone caught and lifted her. She curled against the fire. Felt herself falling. Flung out her arm. Saw flames dancing off it.

No. No, that was a memory—Myles. His arm on fire. He flailed.

She sobbed, checking her arm to be sure it wasn't on fire.

"What's wrong with her?"

"Get the pharmakeia!" Ixion ordered. "Kersei, where is the pain?"

"And you are sure they were after you?"

"No doubt," Marco said with a nod into the vidscreen of his channeler. "They nearly had me ..." Should he mention how he survived?

"What is it?"

"The girl," Marco admitted. "She intervened. Saved me with a javrod."

"*What?*"

Marco remembered being laid out, knowing he was outdone. "I was down. They had the advantage. Had she not struck, I may have been taken. I owe her a life debt." He recalled her voicing those same words.

"You don't know that," Rico said with a hefty warning. "You're a swift, shrewd fighter. I'm confident you would've eluded them."

The fear of what those men wanted, what they had done to his brethren had doused him. A feeling he was not used to. "There is also a complication. The Droserans came upon us as I escorted her back to them, and they assumed the worst."

"You told them you're hunting her?"

"I did not. But they assumed it. Threatened me."

His advocate ran a hand over his face and growled. "I'll speak with Roman. Get approval to retrieve you and the girl, so we can end this hunt."

"Too risky. It could draw attention to both of us. And, admittedly, I want more time to find out what she knows. Whatever it is, they're"—a sharp, foul scent pierced Marco's thoughts. The girl. *The girl's in trouble*—"willing to ..."

That odor. It was ... strong. Urgent. Like on Cenon.

"Marco?"

Something in him erupted. "I must go." He flicked off the vidscreen, grabbed his jacket, and darted out of his small quarters. He sprinted through the corridors, hauled onward by the rancid scent and the deep conviction she was in trouble.

Had the Symmachians gotten to her?

When he saw the dinner crowd waiting for the lift, he shoved into the stairs. Put his skills to work, going up two decks. Sprinted down the passage. Rounded the corner—and stopped short. Threw himself back. Huffing his breaths to calm himself, he mentally sorted what he'd seen.

The Droserans stood outside a room. Ypiretis was hurrying toward them with that boy.

What … what was going on? Droserans had been notoriously anti-Ierean for the last couple of decades.

A scream knifed the air.

Pained scent punching him, Marco held fast as the Droserans disappeared into the quarters. The iereas urged the boy ahead of him and just before crossing the threshold, he gave Marco an icy glare.

"What is wrong with her, iereas?"

The question warbled on a heat plume. Sweat doused Kersei. A wired-haired man sat in a chair at her side—and her heart thumped at the sight of Ypiretis. But she could not form words, instead moaning and pulling her arm to her chest. Curled in on herself to hide the brand. Desperate for them to leave her alone. And yet, out of her mind for relief from this pain.

He took her hand and drew it toward him.

Frantic that the machitis would see her brand, she yanked it back.

"Nothing is *wrong* with her," the iereas said gently. "May we have a moment?"

"Not alone," Ixion growled from the corner, arms folded over his leathers.

"I am an old man, guardian. An iereas. There is no cause for concern."

"There is always concern when Iereans are involved," Ixion said blandly. "It is said a high lord entered Stratios Hall before the walls came down on our brother. Seekers of revenge come in many packages. I have little reason and no desire to trust your kind."

Kersei remembered the high lord's arrival at the hall that fateful night. The commotion he caused. But wait—why had she not seen his image in the reminding chamber?

Yet … Ypiretis had helped her after the garden. Given her back to her people. Strangely, Kersei knew she must trust him. "Mavridis," she managed, finding her guardian beneath hooded eyelids. "Please. I would be alone with him."

"It will not be done," Ixion barked.

"Please." Kersei struggled to sit so she could make her point.

He unfolded his arms, concern etching his brow.

"I saw things. On Baric's ship, he decided my guilt and forced me to relive what happened to my family. Their deaths. Their blood. Their screams." She must convince him. "And though they burned the images of my parents' and sisters' lifeless bodies into my mind, I recall no priest among the dead. I would ask him why."

Shoulders still taut and hands fisted, he glanced at the iereas. Then nodded. "Door stays open."

She managed a weak smile as she propped herself against the wall on the narrow thin mattress, damp with perspiration. When they were alone, she braved the eyes of the elderly iereas.

"I cannot answer what you would ask." Near-black eyes glinted with a smile.

She eyed the boy in the opposite corner, who was a few years shy of her own nineteen cycles. "Who is he?" It was a tactic Father had taught her—become an ally, a friend. Then deliver the blow necessary to bring them to their knees.

"Duncan, my apprentice."

The boy went crimson and gave an awkward bob of his head. "Mistress."

With a halfhearted smile, she let her gaze drift to her brand, realizing the fire was receding. Though thick fabric and sparring cloth covered it, she rotated her arm. "You know of it?"

"Indeed, child."

She considered him. "On the oath I gave to my mother, I have never mentioned it outside our home." When it still stood. Heat tumbled through her muscles, plying a whimper from her.

"May I?" He took her hand and unwound the wrap, then slid back the fabric of her sleeve, revealing the glowing arcs, lines, and circles.

Fire leapt and surged, her stomach with it. Nauseating. Sweating. But lessening each time.

His expression shifted, and he flinched.

Panic started a marching cadence in her heart. "What?

"It's nearing fulfillment." But there was something scratched in his face that warred with his words.

"How do you know this?"

"He is also a mediator," Duncan spoke up, his voice soft but firm. "It's his job to research the brands and find their meaning. He spends weeks in the catacombs going over scrolls—"

"Silence, Duncan!" Ypiretis hissed. Sagging in defeat, he sighed. "It is simply my job to ensure the sanctity of the brands, that they and their hosts are preserved."

"Hosts? *Preserved?*" Alarm speared her, half at the words but also at the iereas's clear upset over what the apprentice spoke. "You know the meaning then? Please—I would know."

His gaze again fell to the brand. As he studied it, she too eyed the glowing, bluish hue that consumed the normally dark lines, then noticed his expression went quickly from concerned to grave.

"What?" she asked.

Ypiretis gave a weak smile and nodded to her arm, where the marks were once more darkening to black. "It's resting, as should you."

"No, you have given me no answers," Kersei balked, desperate for some understanding of her brand. "Why? Why does it burn and affect me so?"

Ypiretis hesitated, then patted her hand. "Some believe the brand is not merely the *touch* of the Ancient, but the *presence* of Him. A pure source in a corrupted vessel."

"Corrupted?"

"*All* are corrupt, child. Even myself." Kindness touched the edges of his eyes. "There was no offense intended."

The Ancient Himself … What an intriguing thought. She watched the blue fade, taking the fire with it. "If this is the Ancient, then"—she yawned—"He is … painful."

"He never promised His ways to be easy, only true and freeing—but remember that your perspective is particularly one-sided." He nodded to her arm as he struggled to his feet. "You know the pain, but not the plan or what will come to fruition."

Kersei relaxed against the pillow. "You grew concerned looking at this mark. Why?" She knew he would dodge again, and she was tired of not having answers. "Speak it, or I will rise from this bed—"

"In your condition, I seriously doubt that." He chuckled. "My concern is the amount of pain you are enduring—it is greatly elevated, even for this phase."

"Something is wrong?"

"I will seek answers. Rest well, Mistress."

Spotting Ixion in the other room, Kersei surreptitiously tugged down her sleeve. "Iereas," she whispered, pulling his gaze. "Between us. Agreed?"

He hesitated. Then nodded. "For now."

TSC *MACEDON*

His career was over. There was no way around it. Tigo stared at the gauntlet he'd removed. His gut churned. He'd set it to black, but there was a feed. It'd slagging recorded everything from the insertion—his vitals, what he saw, heard, and said. Including walking out of the terminal having clearly spotted the girl. Syncing it with the *Macedon* guaranteed Command would know exactly what happened on Cenon.

"You okay?"

The warm presence of Teeli Knowles filled his awareness and pushed him to his feet. He'd failed her. Failed the team. But she shouldn't be in the bay. "What're you doing down here?"

"Checking in. Things went bad, I guess."

He snorted. "They sent multiple Eidolon units to Cenon to recapture her."

"Did they?" Her concern flared.

He shook his head. "No. But they *really* wanted her." He bounced his gaze to hers. "Why? What did she see?"

"You mean what does Baric the Barbaric want with her?" Teeli let a sad smile touch her lips, then frowned. "You look scared."

"I sacrificed my career to get her off that satellite, and they gave us one chance to undo that damage, and we gave her a walk."

Teeli widened her eyes. "You what?"

"Let her board a shuttle to a transport."

"You regret it?"

"No." He grunted. "But I want to know why I'm doing all this. Why Esq is dead." He lifted his gauntlet. "Once I sync up, they'll know she was on Cenon, that my suit signaled a positive IDent, and I walked away."

"I'm proud of you."

He huffed and turned, but Teeli drew him back around. Her soft, caring words surprised him. Made him consider her, pull out of the hard crash-and-burn he'd been in for the last several hours. "Yeah?"

She looked pale, her skin blanched. Dark circles around her eyes. And yet, she was beautiful. Had a heart for the hurting and did her best to take care of her patients.

"Well, it might be the last thing I do as an Eidolon," he said. "I can't make sense of it. I wanted my dad to help, but not like this. His committee forced the Two-one-five to Cenon to find her. Threatened court-martial and enough footage to destroy our families."

She touched his arm. "I'm sorry. I feel responsible for—"

"No!" Cupping her head and peering into her eyes, he resented that this had affected her, that the fiasco had impacted any of them. "This is Baric's doing. Or Command's. But not yours." He thought of the kiss they'd shared. It seemed like eons ago. There were Codes of Conduct. He should obey them. For her. That made sense.

Until she shifted closer. With that look in her eyes. When her gaze hit his again with longing, he didn't care about Codes. He teased a kiss from her. She tasted like truth and rightness.

She curled into him, which drove him to deepen the kiss. She stumbled back against the locker and he gave chase. Her arms circled his neck and he tugged her tight against his chest, thrilling at the way she moaned.

"Tigo?"

He jerked at the incoming voice. Knew Jez would find them—but not for a few more seconds. He framed Teeli's face. Kissing her, savoring her. Not really caring anymore. He breathed against Teeli's ear, kissed her lobe, then found her mouth again.

"You here?" Jez called from the far end of the bay.

Teeli nudged him back, face crimson.

No, not her face. Her *mouth*. "Te—"

"Hey, Comman—" Jez rounded the corner, then slowed, looking between him and Teeli. Her gaze dropped, but not before he saw disappointment. Hurt.

The doc stepped aside. "I should go."

"No," Tigo countered and hooked her hand. "It's okay."

Jez sniffed. "If we weren't about to get our butts handed to us by the admiral of the fleet, I'd say suck faces all day long."

The title jolted him. "The ad—my *dad*?"

"Boarded twenty minutes ago." Jez flinched when she looked at Teeli—and so did Tigo. Her lips were darkening. Bruising?

Gut roiling, Tigo watched her go. Unable to abate the guilt or confusion. Worried for her. She deserved a better life. A disease-free life. He wanted to give that to her.

Jez touched her temple. "Listen … um, your dad is here. They …"

"Grav down, Jez," Tigo said, not caring about his father. "I'm worried about Teeli."

Another flinch. "I might've heard something. About her."

"What?"

Jez had never been one to hold back, so her hesitation unnerved him. And yet right now he had exactly zero patience.

"*What?*"

Jez let out a long sigh. "She's *very* sick, Tigo."

"Right. Mine plague. We knew that."

"No, she's in the final phase—*dying*. Another doctor came with your father to take over as chief medical officer. She's being removed from duty."

He pinched the bridge of his nose. He was whining about his career and Teeli was dying. Could the 'verse be any more scuzzed?

"I know you like her, but ... I'm guessing that kissing you actually *hurts* her. Like physically hurts."

He stilled, considering her words, her dark eyes. "You're serious?" Remembered the way Teeli moaned. Was what he'd mistaken for pleasure actually ... pain? Oh voids. The stain around her mouth—bruising. He muttered an oath, gripping the locker door. Didn't matter that she'd started the kiss. He knew better.

"Heads-up, en route," came Diggs's voice as he and AO rounded the corner.

"Okay, doc stuff has to wait," Jez said, all business again. A more confident look on her. "We got a load of trouble coming down about Cenon." She nodded to his gauntlet. "D'you sync yet?"

"I was about to when Teeli came in. We rode it black, but—"

"Yeh, they overrode it. Filmed the whole thing."

Even when he'd confronted the Kynigos? His gut churned. "Why ...?" His head hurt thinking about it. "They set us up. Again. We sync—"

"Yeh, don't." Jez snatched it, handed it off to AO, who stalked away. "Official story is that at twenty-two-fifty as we left Cenoan orbit, we experienced an electromagnetic storm that fried our tech. Gauntlets started shorting out—"

"All of them?" Tigo balked.

"—and wiped recs."

"They'll never believe it. There wasn't a storm and the corvette sensors—"

"Rhinn's already on that. Sensors will confirm."

Diggs curled a lip. "Maybe this'll tell them how we feel about the lies they've been shoveling down our throats about that girl, Baric—and what in the Fires the *Chryzanthe* is."

"Yeh, that's what I want to know too," Jez said. "It was large and mostly finished, so it's been in the works for a while. A long while."

Head spinning at the ruse the team had conjured, Tigo ran a hand down his neck. It was one thing to act outside their regs to protect an innocent, but lying and altering records ...

"You with us?" AO asked, returning with the gauntlet.

What choice did they have? Tigo nodded, his brain still catching up. "We need answers. Real ones." He eyed Jez, appreciating her tenacity and focus. "But why all this—"

"We have a whole lot of brass coursing down that lift right now," she said. "Can't say I know what it's about, but it's not good. And we'll get blamed."

"So why bother hiding what our scans—"

"They are *not* going to find her," Jez growled, her expression hardening. "They find her, they put her back in that thing, war starts, and everything we did—Esq—it was all for nothing. Something big is happening here. Bigger than us."

"No slag. But … what?"

"Nobody knows," Diggs said. "But that's why we got to rattle their hull. Get their attention."

Yeah, and they'd all end up at the bottom of tanked careers with possible brig time. For a downworlder they didn't know. Every one of these—Jez, AO, Diggs, and Rhinn—people he'd handpicked. The best. And he'd let them fry their careers? The team? For a downworlder?

"No," Tigo said. This was his fight. "I can't let you do this."

"Do what?" Fleet Admiral Domitas Deken clomped through the Eidolon bay.

"Dad—sir."

An obnoxious glow struggled out from beneath the vambrace stuck to his skin. Marco skated a glance around the galley, where tables and travelers littered his view. Swallowing the bite of meat pie, he pulled his arm closer. The illumination was barely visible, but he would not risk it being discovered. Not with her nearby.

Though garbed in men's clothing, head covered, and with a Xanthus escort of two—the petulant one and the more reasonable brother—Kersei ate in quiet. Her efflux told him this made her happy. No doubt being confined to quarters was enough to make even this small venture to the cantina seem an adventure.

Her gaze flicked to his, and after letting the connection hang for a few ticks, he lazily withdrew. He scooped more pie and lifted it to his mouth—only to sense innocent curiosity wash over him. Over his shoulder, he glimpsed a boy of six or seven staring at him from a table where he sat with his family.

Marco winked.

"Atep, look away."

"But I'm not afraid."

"You should be," the father groused.

"I'm not afraid, Father." The distant, childlike voice echoed in Marco's head. He swung his gaze away, the past tearing at his thoughts. Where had that boy in the memory been encountered?

The mother held the boy at arm's length as she broke into tears.

"No more," a voice declared as a large hand clicked a sensor back into a vambrace. Unmistakably the master hunter.

Marco stared at his own armor, the memory so large, so real … yet so far from his grasp.

Gold cords.

He frowned. What hunt was that, and why could he not recall more? For Roman to be present, it must have been one of Marco's early hunts, when he was green and needing instruction from the master.

Her signature sailed over him, yanking Marco's attention back to Kersei. Her escort wasn't at the table, which surprised him. He scanned the cantina and found one in a queue for desserts but could not locate the other. Marco's gaze bounced back to the table—and right into Kersei's eyes. It seemed she was considering something. Mayhap coming over to talk to him. But were she caught …

He gave a surreptitious nod. Now. Now was the time for the necklace. When she glanced away, he quietly stood and retrieved the necklace. Then rounded the room and came up from behind on her left, his gaze never fully leaving her Xanthus escort, who was busy choosing sweets.

He glided past Kersei as she peered over her right shoulder and searched his table, then—apparently not finding him—looked toward the rear of the cantina. Giving him the perfect opportunity to deposit the necklace on the table in front of her and make a quick exit.

Even as he reached the corridor, the cool waft of her surprise hit. He kept moving, down past the entrance to the cantina, where the sticky stench of anger flared.

Marco sidestepped the blur that came at him. Caught the shoulder and pinned the man, finally noting the face. "What fool tactic, ambushing me from the side!"

The youngest Xanthus had arrogance roiling off him and clearly felt in charge. "I am Galen Sebastiano, third-born son of Ares of Xanthus."

Marco curled his lip. "Would you have a trophy?"

Irritation pinched the pup's eyes. "What are you doing here? You were told to stay away from her!" Did he yet use a razor?

"Am I to also not eat while on this voyage?"

The pup hesitated as he looked over Marco's shoulder.

Sensing Kersei's approach and not wanting to compromise the gift he'd left, Marco nudged Galen back and stepped away. "Give care, pup. Next time I will not tolerate an attack."

Galen shifted. "As Mavridis warned—keep your distance. She is under the protection of her people now."

A sneer slid into Marco's mood. He could not help but toy with this pup. "Her people." He let it hang for a second. "The Stratios are dead, are they not?"

"Kalonicans," Galen snapped. "We are all Kalonicans."

Marco pursed his lips. "And as her people, where were you when she needed aid?"

Galen started. "I—we—the entire realm was searching for her. Praetor

Rhayld gave orders to find her and those responsible."

"You bore me, Xanthus." Marco pivoted.

The pup had the gall to grab at him. "You're hun—"

Catching the wrist with his left and bracing the pup's shoulder with his right, Marco forced the arrogant pup to his knees. A move so fluid and fast, he didn't react. And Marco found himself staring at the elder brother, Kersei now behind him. "What I do does not concern you. Interfere and be branded a traitor."

"We are not under your la—"

Marco twisted Galen's arm in one direction. Pulled in another. Not a lot. Just enough to …

"Augh!"

He released the pup, avoiding Kersei's gaze, though he could do little to not detect her signature, and stalked down the passage. Ixion stood at the corner, his scent quiet and calm. Jaw lifted. Expression terse. Wasn't that always the look of the Stalker?

"The pups are out of line, Ixion."

Hand pulled into her sleeve of the tunic, Kersei gripped tight the treasure he had planted on the table. At first, she'd only seen his broad, square shoulders as he passed through the door. Disheartened that she hadn't a chance to speak with him, she'd glanced down—to the necklace Adara had slipped around her neck that fateful night. Now tears stung as she wound her way through the ship to the quarters with her escorts.

"He needs a lesson in humility," Galen growled as they entered the lift.

"To teach that, you would have to learn it," Jencir taunted his brother. "He did nothing untoward."

"Did nothing?" Galen balked. "He nearly wrenched my sword arm out of socket."

"If the Kynigos intended you harm, you would be harmed," Ixion said in a cool, unaffected tone. "What I would have is the answer to why the mistress was alone. You were both tasked as escorts."

Though they voiced reasons—Jencir had gone to relieve himself, and Galen was getting desserts for Kersei, none of which she'd asked for—it did not matter. There was no right answer. Just the clear truth that they had both failed to do as charged.

What were they worried about? Marco meant her no harm. He returned Adara's necklace. Where had he gotten it from, though? She'd discovered its absence when she had awakened in the medical bay on the *Macedon*.

Back in the quarters, Kersei marveled at the other representatives of Kalonica who gathered. They were embroiled in a heated discussion over what had happened at the symposium on Cenon.

"We cannot let this go unanswered," Elek of the Trachys said. "They murdered our brother!"

"Be at peace." Bazyli sounded tired. Looked tired. He wore his hair with beads woven into the long plaits hanging down the sides of his face. A thick beard was both sandy blond and gray. Skin weathered by wind and sun, he seemed to bear Kalonica itself on his shoulders. "We will speak with the praetor upon our return. There is much to discuss—"

Kersei perked up. "Praetor?" Kalonica had not needed a praetor in centuries. "Who?" she asked from a low table near the door.

Bent forward on the hard sofa, Bazyli peered up through his thick brow. "Rhayld has stepped in until the council convenes after the Winter Solstice."

"Rhayld," Kersei murmured, thinking of the round-bellied, jovial brother of the more severe, austere Zarek. Darius had many laughs with Rhayld, often at him. It was strange to think a man with more laughter than logic could rule the kingdom.

"You should know, Kersei," Bazyli said quietly, "that we buried your parents and sisters with the honor they deserved."

Unprepared for the emotion in his voice and what pounded her, Kersei ducked. Chewed her lower lip. "I thank you."

"You should also know that some … were not recoverable."

Kersei frowned. "What say you?"

"Stratios Hall, as you know, was formidable. Its walls so thick …" Bazyli fell silent, leaving a gap for the chamber images to shriek through her mind. "Among those not recovered were Prince Darius, your uncle Rufio, and a handful of aerios, including Myles."

Darius not recovered? Confused, she thought of the images, searching for the faces of those mentioned. The thudding noise. Crushing of bodies. She squeezed her eyes shut. Buried her face in her hands and cried. They were gone. Truly gone.

Darius blinked. No, it'd been her imagination …

She felt someone kneel before her. Touch her arms.

"We grieve with you." Bazyli's words were soft. "We will find those responsible and return the pain they have visited upon us."

Swallowing the tears, she drew on courage her father so often commented on. Wiped her face dry. After a few sniffles, she nodded, grateful.

"But you should know that as elders"—his gaze was weighted with some burden—"we must question you about the events."

Her heart cracked a little. "Y-you think I—"

"Nay," he all but growled, his blond brow furrowed. "But we would hear your words. Know what you saw and heard." Earnestness marked his features. "I know it will be hard, so prepare yourself. We will talk soon."

Bazyli stood and faced the others, frowning at his youngest brother. "What has happened?"

"It's that boiled-out bloodhound," Galen railed.

"The Kynigos was in the cantina," Ixion added blandly.

Kersei's pulse tripped at the mention of him. She tightened her hold on the necklace.

"He nearly broke my arm! Slammed me into the floor—in front of everyone! I'll have his head."

"I'd like to see you try," Ixion scoffed.

"We should report him to the captain," Galen insisted.

"For what?" Ixion said, standing next to Bazyli. "Defending himself when you attempted to accost him?"

"Someone had to put him in his place!"

"Brother!" Bazyli barked. "Leave off this vendetta against the Kynigos. The laws in the quadrants protect them on a hunt, and we must act with discretion to protect Kersei."

On a hunt? Kersei shrank when she noted Ixion looking at her.

"They cannot be trusted," Galen warned

"What says that?" Bazyli asked. "Your wounded pride or your aching arm?"

Laughter rippled through the room.

"He has no honor!"

"That is where you are very wrong," Ixion countered somberly. "They are bound by honor. They will not cross those lines, no matter the cost. They are as fastidious about their Codes as are iereas and their rituals."

"You sound as if you admire him."

"Respect him," Ixion corrected. "A wise man would respect their dedication as well as their methods. Kynigos are quick and effective. Would that I had their training to pass to the Plisiázon. The damage we could do against the Irukandji …" He shook his head.

Soon the conversation fell again into dull talk about the Caucus. About boundaries. Bazyli and Ixion started planning exercises, and more than once the conversation returned to finding those responsible for her entoli's slaughter. Guilt plagued Kersei—she knew she should pay attention. She was the last of the Stratios. Things would be expected of her. But she wanted to leave. Get some air. Never had she been one to sit and stare at walls.

The machitis talked, devolving into an easy chatter as the afternoon passed, and, at last, Kersei found her opening. She slipped down the small hall and snuck out of the quarters. Hurried around the corner. Fought the urge to sprint for the lift. She must find the hunter and ask how he had come by the necklace.

She entered the obstacle arena, and though a half dozen worked ropes and the climbing wall, he was not there. Disappointment ached. She glanced down the corridor. Where might a hunter go? Was she foolish to look—

Clack! Clank!

Kersei jerked back to the arena to find the source of the loud, metal noise. In the far corner, two metal beams ran up into the rafters and had curves gouged out. A crossbar hung across the middle. And dangling from that bar—shirtless, muscles bulging along his triangular back and shoulders— the hunter. Forearms still protected by his armor, he wore black pants and empty leather holsters. He swung and popped his legs, hiking the bar and himself up a notch. Then another. Sweat glistened on his olive skin, as his sculpted torso quivering beneath the light. The power, the raw strength …

Clack-clank! Up another level. Effortlessly. Six levels. Then he swung under the high bar and sailed across to a wall. Narrowly, he caught the edge. Hauled himself up. Ran in a straight sprint across the wall the length of three or four horses—the same area on which he had held her close as they waited out the Symmachians.

He dove to a lower platform.

To follow, Kersei had to move out of the doorway and look up over the doorpost, the course cutting into the space above. As she twisted, she lost sight of him. She turned. Glanced around. Stepped back again to better see the upper wall. Where had he gone?

A blur dropped in front of her. Landed with a soft thump, bringing the woodsy smell of the hunter to her nostrils.

Kersei yelped, then covered her mouth. Straightened. Noted his smirk. The drip of sweat down his temples. "You knew I was watching."

Chest bare and writhing beneath tightly controlled breaths, he had no shame in standing before her as such. The light of the passage glinted in his pale eyes. Hair damp with sweat, he leaned in. Close. So close.

He reached toward her—to touch her hair? Her face. Why was her heart in a stampede?

Instead, from behind her, he retrieved a towel.

"Oh." Kersei cleared her throat. *Get on with it.* She held up the necklace, the chain dangling from her palm. "Where did you get this?"

He didn't put proper distance between them and his eyes never left hers as he wiped his face. "Know you what I am, Mistress Kersei?"

She huffed. "I care not what you are." She must have answers. "Where did you get this?"

"It was given to me, and I was told to return it to its rightful owner."

Confusion seared her confidence, her assuredness. "Who? Who had it? I haven—"

"Why is it special?"

Her determination wavered, remembering Adara's sweet little face. "It was my sister's. She gave it to me that … night." Only as she stood there, remembering the presentation, the laughter … did she realize she was yet again alone with this man. And this time, he was half unclothed!

"I am intrigued, Mistress Kersei." He toweled off and tossed it aside. "You come barging in here, knowing what I am and that I hunt, yet you do not fear me."

"I …" Defiance lifted her jaw. "How do you know what I'm feeling?"

He snagged his shirt and smirked that blasted smirk again. "I say again, know you *how* we hunt?" He threaded his arms through a tunic and pulled it down.

Though she enjoyed the sound of his voice and the lilt of his accent, with words broader, sounding more … rounded, Kersei bristled. "You asked that the last time." Right before Ixion barged in. She couldn't help but glance back to the passage. "You smell." She waited for him to detect her taunt.

He tossed her another smirk. "Smell is but a tool. A warrior does more than aim an arrow to take down a target." He raked his hands through his hair, then planted his hands on his belt.

"I concede." She held out her palms. "I do not understand how you hunt." She could not help but stare at the mark on his face—and how it had somehow shifted from terrifying on Cenon to intriguing here in close quarters. "What is your strength—besides arrogance?"

Surprise widened his eyes. "You think me arrogant?"

"I beg your mercy. That was rude of me."

He chuckled, a nice deep one. "Aye, but you feel it true all the same."

She wrinkled her nose again and shrugged.

"I am not arrogant, Mistress." He lifted his coat and started toward the door as he put it on. "Only confident in my abilities."

"Is that not the same?" Kersei trailed him into the brightly lit corridor, glancing up one end and down the other.

"You're scared."

She blinked. Balked. "No, I—"

"Scared he will find you again with me. And now you're anxious, afraid you've offended me."

Kersei stared. "How could you possibly know those things?"

A steward came toward them, eyeing Kersei, then the hunter. She watched him go, not sure where to place her eyes or what to say next. This entire encounter had been awkward, and the last thing she wanted was to return to the quarters to hear more politicking.

"The steward," Marco said quietly, drawing her attention back, "was jealous." He peered down the passage and jutted his chin. "And attracted."

She laughed, feeling heat in her cheeks. "I don't understand how you can know all those things just by smelling."

"I simply state what pheromones hang in the air."

"The what?"

He breathed a smile and glanced down. "On Drosero, you had a horse?"

Her heart tripped at the memory. "Bastien."

"And he could smell storms coming?"

She eyed him warily. "Aye." Then frowned. "You jest."

Shaking his head, he walked—no stalked—down the corridor. The man didn't know how to walk. He exuded so much confidence and authority, people deferred to him. "I can smell fear," he said quietly. "And any other emotion." He pointed to the lift and pressed a button as they waited. "In the obstacle arena before you entered, I could detect your signature."

"My what?"

"Each person has a distinct chemical makeup unique to them. Hunters can sort those." His gaze swept the corridor, then rested on her. "The more we're around a person, the more it's registered, if you will, on our olfactory nerves. We might forget a face, but we never forget a scent." A tone signaled the lift's arrival, and he motioned for her to enter.

Kersei hated these things—too much like the chamber on the *Macedon*.

She stiffened, but told herself it was okay.

A teen appeared in the doorway. "Hold u—" His gaze hit Marco, then he backed up. Palms out. "Go ahead. I'll wait."

The doors closed.

"He's afraid of you."

Chin tucked, black hair curling around his face and neck, Marco stared at the doors. "The guilty usually are."

"Guilty?" She frowned, amazed. "I can't imagine having people constantly afraid of me."

The mark across his nose somehow amplified his intensity. "I would hope not. You're an attractive evengis. It is not a life you should have to experience." The box whisked open and he indicated across an airwalk to a set of doors.

"Evengis?" she balked. Boils, she hated that word. "I am a warrior's daughter."

"Aye," he said, striding forward. "I saw evidence of that, too. Both—"

"Where are we going?" She stepped into the unfamiliar area, waiting for an explanation. And why in the world was she still with him? *Go back to the suite.* If they were caught together … She remembered the necklace, wanting to hear more of how it had come back to her.

"To see the stars."

"We're *in* the stars."

Smirking, he nodded to the gray doors with a question in his gaze. A playful question. As if daring her. The way he looked at her, the mark so fierce. Like his eyes. And yet not. The pale blue tones were somehow comforting.

No, assuredly threatening. He was a hunter, after all. A hunter staring at her.

Realizing he meant for her to take note of something, Kersei finally spotted a small plaque. "Stardeck."

He accessed it, and the doors surrendered to their presence. Pitch-black greeted them, and Kersei jerked tight at the confined space. The chamber— boils, would everything remind her of that thing? She would be free of it. The screaming amid the flames. Adara. Lexina. Ma'ma. Pain. Shrieks. Blood.

And he was there. Pushed right into her space. "Are you well, Kersei?"

Startled at her name on his lips, she opened her eyes. Released the tension in her hands, nearly placing them on his chest. "Y—" The word caught in her throat. She swallowed. "Yes."

"Come up the stairs. It'll be okay." His words were like water crashing over rocks, commanding yet reassuring. His hand on her back guided her in. Dots of light lined the stairs. With each step she climbed, darkness fell away—but not wholly, as the environment of the stardeck was decidedly peaceful with its low lighting and soft instrumental music. All curated to provide a serene experience as one gazed at the sea of stars.

A bar ran the circumference of the room and stopped people from touching the glass. Benches offered places to sit, think, and reflect. To the far right, cozy settees hugged couples.

Kersei strode to the bar, amazed at the view yet terrified of the height. Which wasn't really height. But how did one describe this? The expanse of stars reminded her of the gown she had worn to the last Winter Solstice ball at Kardia. Comparing the heavenlies to a dress made her laugh.

"What?" He eased back against the bar, crossing his legs at the ankles and staring behind her.

She refused to share her thoughts and have him mock her. "I could stand here a lifetime and still not wholly appreciate this view." It was impossible to see all the stars. To count them.

He turned. "It's amazing, isn't it?" But his grin beneath that ominous mark seemed such a dichotomy. *He* seemed a dichotomy as he pointed to the right. "Cenon."

She followed his direction and tried to find the big planet. "Where?"

"There." He leaned in, his chest against her shoulder. "The yellow one."

"It's so small!" She looked at him, startled he was so close. So handsome. The deep lines arcing his nose had barbs that swung upward. "Your mark," she said, then thought better of it. Glanced away.

"The Kynigos sigil," he said quietly, arms folded.

"Sigil?" She wrinkled her nose, thinking of the green aetos that served as the Kalonican sigil and the destrier for Stratios. "Why do you have it? To scare people?"

He snorted. "Its purpose is twofold: to mark our gift from Vaqar and to ensure no hunter ambushes a quarry. Our effectiveness scares them enough."

"And you question why I think you're arrogant?"

A deep chuckle. "Fair enough."

What was the mark like? Was it like her brand, the lines as much a part of her skin, or was it like scar tissue? Did it burn as her brand did? Only when his hand snapped around her wrist, startling her, did she realize she had reached out to touch the sigil. Locked in his gaze, she felt the pressure around her wrist lessening. Falling away. Giving permission.

Blue eyes beckoned her into his domain.

Her stomach fluttered as her fingers continued their course. Touched his warm cheek where the arc flung up over his nose. It wasn't raised or scarred.

So like her brand, except on his nose, which was arrow-straight, but not ... pretty. Not like Darius's. Marco's was stronger. Maybe it'd even been broken. And the planes of his olive face were well defined. Even his lips were ... nice. She recalled the way they'd tickled her earlobe when they'd hidden. Even now she felt the darts in her stomach. Wisps of his dark hair hung askew. Rugged. Handsome. So very handsome.

"Satisfied?" he asked, his voice husky, brusque.

Kersei started, realizing what she'd done. How she'd stared. *Admired* him. She jerked her hand to her chest and stepped back. "I beg—" No, he would taunt her if she begged his mercy again. "Yes." She shook her head. Pulled herself together. Pushed her thoughts back to where a proper young woman would have them.

The mark seemed threatening, yet it only made her curious. And maybe attracted her more than she'd admit. With his complexion and the deep hues of the sigil, it was all so ... dangerous. But not like ... "On the satellite when I saw the man with that mark, I was so startled. He looked so terribly white. And bloody, but that—"

"What man? What satellite?" His brow dug deep toward his eyes, and his intensity ratcheted, unnerving her. "What man, Kersei? A hunter?" Anger edged his words as he scowled down at her.

"I ..." She touched her forehead, surprised at his vehemence. Hated the way she suddenly felt scared—of him, of his reaction.

He shouldered in, head down as he peered at her through that dark brow. "The person who gave me your necklace said I should ask you what you saw." He inclined his head. "Please—tell me what you saw."

Searching his eyes, she wasn't sure if his words encouraged or dissuaded her from speaking of it. But he should know, shouldn't he? It was one his people. "I saw a hunter—well, I assume he was a hunter as he had that mark. They were doing things to him. I don't know what else you would call it save *torture*. I—Baric was ..."

"Captain Baric?" he barked. "So this was on the *Macedon*—"

"No. The other place. On the station."

"Start at the beginning."

"She saw one of the Brethren on the station where they held her prisoner."

Roman scowled. "You're sure?"

Marco filed away memory of her touch and nodded. "She recalled his sigil. Said he was bloodied and pale. Tortured, strapped into something like an upright table."

The master lowered his head, palms on the surface the held the camera. His jaw muscle flexed. "Did she recall what he looked like? Was it Dolon?"

"Unknown. The horror of it made it hard for her think or remember." Marco leaned in. "We *must* go for him. He may yet be alive—and mayhap they have the other missing hunters there as well."

"We will see to it," Roman said, but then his gaze rose again. "How did you come by this knowledge of hers?"

"She found me in the athletic center. Asked about the mark." Marco concealed the little jaunt to the stardeck and how her plight stirred something deep in him.

For several long, probing seconds, Roman stared through Marco. "Give care. This Decree—do not underestimate its importance. There are threats you must be vigilant against. She is attractive and innocent and sometimes that is the worst threat to a Decree."

Annoyed, Marco nodded. "Fear not. My intention is to stay close enough only to protect."

"Protect *yourself.* You can afford no mistakes." Roman angled closer to the camera. "What of your brand?"

Surprised at the question, Marco drew up. "It's … fine. What does that—"

"Very well." Roman breathed out heavily. "We will meet you when the *Kleopatra* docks at Cyrox. Be ready. You'll take her into custody then."

"Understood."

"To the Decree."

Marco nodded. "And the hunt." And together with the master, "For honor."

"In the lower deck, there are a variety of animals."

Kersei lifted her gaze from the book on her data pad. She had been fascinated to learn they could stuff hundreds of pages into something thinner than paper, and the little device had made the tedious days of travel more bearable. "Animals?" Anything would be better than the boredom she'd endured. In truth, there was an itch beneath her skin to get out of her quarters and find Marco.

Galen grinned. "Down in a bay," he said. "They're penned up and the crew lets passengers pet them." His eyebrow arched. "Want to see them?"

Kersei tossed the data pad. "Indeed!" She glanced at Bazyli and Ixion, who were watching a communiqué channel with some boring person talking about politics in the quadrants. For hours. "Will they allow it?"

"It has been well past a week since the encounter with the Symmachians or Kynigos."

Not quite … She tried not to swallow.

"And they are as bored as we are." He nodded to the door.

Again dressed in britches and a scratchy tunic, she pulled up the hood as they moved toward the door.

"Two oras," Bazyli called after them. "If you are not returned, we will come."

Kersei felt like she had escaped the *Macedon* all over again. They made their way down, and her heart sang—horses, sheep, goats, cows. She'd secretly hoped for a rhinnock or elephant, but they were too large, even for this transport. She spent a good deal of time near the sheep pen, where a wild dog had given birth to pups.

"She stole into the herd," a plump woman said as she wiped her hands on a heavily soiled apron. "Had no idea till we heard the pups shrilling." She motioned into the pen. "You can come in. Mum don't mind—in fact, I'd say she's grateful for someone to distract the litter."

Kersei hesitated but then forged ahead. Entered the pen and squatted to pet the pups. Lifted one into her lap. She sat against a wall, allowing the others to clamber over her. Admittedly, she was quite content, especially noting the way Galen grew antsy. Mayhap he would wander away …

"I'm going to check the mares," Galen said.

She nodded, but focused on the tiny paws and so-sweet puppy breath. She slumped onto the hay, laughing at the little snouts biting her hair. A man stood before the pen, and she sighed, knowing it was too much to hope Galen would stay gone for long. But when she met his eyes, she froze.

In all black, Marco winged an eyebrow at her. "I'm not sure who's more wild."

She felt color flush her face as she glanced around for Galen. "He'll see you."

"He has missed me more times than you."

Holding the pup to her chest, she considered him. Not sure what to say. A pup nipped at her necklace. Then another. They grew more frantic, and she decided to leave them to their mother for feeding. Exiting the pen, she brushed her britches free of hay and spotted Galen near the horses.

With Marco, she turned toward the goats and kids. So sweet and innocent. And a little crazy. They hopped on top of crates and meeeh'd their objections to this confinement. She laughed, noting a heap of alfalfa. She lifted a clump and extended it to a brown-and-black one. He took it greedily and chewed, his lopsided teeth seemingly large. "Hungry little thing."

"Not going to climb in with them?"

She laughed, noting the disparity of their height. She stood straight, but Marco had to lean on the bar to be at shoulder level with her. His hand was flush against hers and dark complected, calloused but strong.

He bumped her shoulder, bouncing her gaze to his. And something slid through his expression that somehow told her he felt this connection, too. But then he straightened and touched her shoulder. "Be safe, Kersei."

"What?" She drew up, realizing he was walking away. "Wa—"

"You gave me a fright." Galen's hissed, angry words struck her as he joined her. "You weren't with the dogs."

Bristling at his interruption, she squared her shoulders. "It is not my fault you were engrossed with horses and failed to pay attention."

It'd been but a touch. And yet, so much more telegraphed as their gazes connected. He hadn't meant to. He was a master of controlling his facial expression—indeed, he hoped he had. Because there had been a torrent roiling beneath him a week past in the Livestock Deck. He'd followed them down there, having detected her as they passed his quarters.

What he felt stirring around her forced him to avoid any further encounters, though he never allowed her signature to escape him. In the last seven days, they'd had brief encounters. She had shown up at the obstacle arena, and they'd chatted as he helped her learn some of the wall jumps, which amused him—both her tenacity and her clumsy attempts. What he did took years of training, and she believed to conquer it in an hour. But she tried. By Vaqar, she tried.

Alone in his bunk that night, he'd thought of the strand beneath the buckle. Her thick curls brushing his chin as he'd held her. That time on the stardeck he'd stepped closer—knowing better but drawn to her all the same. Recalled her cool, gentle fingers as she traced his sigil. Nothing had felt as wrong or as perfect as her touch. The way those eyes, brown like machi wood, skipped around his face, exploring his mark. Lips parted as if in question.

And by the Mercies—the scents roiling off her! Awe thick as fog. Attraction smothering his ability to think. Longing luring him closer. Fear keeping him in check. It'd taken everything he'd possessed not to move. Not to explore *her* face and those curls.

And in the Livestock Deck when their hands had touched? Reek, he'd nearly been undone by her warming signature.

He stretched his neck, rubbing his shoulder. Never had he come so close to breaking Code or his vow. He'd forgone chatelaines so his focus remained unaltered. Sharp. But his response to this woman …

This—*this* is why he avoided intimacy. It muddled logic. Distracted him. Good thought strangled to the point he nearly missed her mention of the Kynigos on the satellite.

Roughing his hands over his face, he groaned. Changed topics. Who was hunting the hunters? To what end? Kynigos were respected, revered on some worlds. Yes, there was a prejudice against them to an extent, some believing they had too much autonomy, but the practices and methods of the Brethren were strict. Rigidly so.

But to hunt us down?

And Kersei—Reek! When did he start using her given name?—had trouble nipping at her heels as well. All tying back to the Symmachian captain. What was Baric up to? Why did he so desperately want Kersei?

She saw the hunter on the satellite. Symmachians. Was that reason enough for them to pursue the girl—that she'd seen Dolon? Could it be that simple? And he had seen them snatch Oron from Zlares. Had they been the enemy all along?

Nay. It was not enough. Especially after the attack on her clan.

A scream pierced his thoughts. Drove a spike through his temple as he tried to come up. Fumbled to a knee beside his bunk. Groaning around the pain, he *anak'd* the scent.

Hers. Her signature. But wrapped up in an acrid scent. Balsam—panic. *She's in trouble. And close.*

Hesitating over the last time he'd rushed after her, Marco drank deeper of the efflux. What made it possible to detect her? Was she close? The thought pushed him into the passage. He scanned both directions. It was empty but her efflux prevailed. Where was she? He hurried to the right, convinced she was around the corner.

She was not. But the scent never wavered, so he continued following the scent. Let it lead.

Where are you?

He banked left past the cantina. A burst of woodsy and frankincense roiled together, yanking him onward. Anger with fear. His heart pounded as he sprinted. Angling to catch the scent where the corridor dead-ended.

Cool, conditioned air lured him right. He stopped, anger roaring to the fore at what he saw.

Halfway down, backed into a corner, Kersei angled aside from two men. Attackers who'd torn her sleeve at the shoulder, which she aimed at the two pawing her. Where were her escorts?

She hiked a leg up and slid in with the other foot, punching him in the gut. But the other pounced, scent coursing like weeks-old rot. Lust. He saw it. Saw it in their expressions. Tasted it in their scent.

Rage threw him at the wall. He toed it. Used it to launch. Only then did they turn—see him coming.

Colliding with them, Marco rammed his fist into the nearest face. Took both men backward. They collapsed like columns. A tangle of legs. Scrambling. He snapped a hand to a throat. Pinned him to the ground. Held him there and swung around, landing a round kick into the head of the other guy, who pitched forward and hit the bulkhead.

Holding the first one's throat, he stared down at the man and drew his fist back, ready to strike. "Come *anywhere* near her again and you will know my full vengeance."

The man nodded, face white.

Marco shoved off. Stood with fists balled. Reached out with his receptors and absorbed her pulsing fear and panic. He backed toward her, but glared after the two men scurrying away like vermin.

When the brigands were gone, another scent erupted behind him. Marco turned to Kersei, who slumped against the wall, her head down, face hidden by those curls. Her grief and fright assailed him. He knelt at her side. "Are you well?" Stupid question.

Tears staining her face, she hugged herself, wary, but she nodded. Barely.

He hated the fear dousing her signature. It wasn't dissipating. Which meant she was afraid ... of him. "There is no cause to fear me, Kersei. I am no harm to you."

A weak smile traced her lips. Her hooded eyes closed as a breath shuddered through her. Courage found, she slowly unfurled from the wall.

When she staggered, Marco cupped her arms. Slid an arm around her—for support. She dropped against him with a gush of relief. Gripped his shirt, her hot breath rushing against his neck as another breath shuddered. A small cry choked out. She seemed ready to crumble.

He homed in on her scent. There was still a lot of pain and fear. But now ... an ardent, beautiful addition: strength. The patchouli to the vanilla. It coiled around his mind. His heart. Made him tug her closer.

It was strange. And wonderful. Standing here with her in his arms. Reek, she fit so perfectly against him. Her head beneath his chin and those silky curls teasing his jaw again.

He firmed his hold, feeling strangely vulnerable in the hall. If seen, Ixion would demand his life. Or worse—that he bind with the girl, which meant Marco would have to surrender his honor, his cloak. He spotted a plaque on a nearby door. His heart thumped. Stardeck. He hadn't recognized the main-level access. Not the one he usually used.

Marco reached around her and palmed the panel. The door slid open. "Here," he said softly, guiding her into the dim interior. She settled on a bench hidden from the view of the lift and low deck chatter and he straddled it, facing her. Worried.

"You must think me weak." She had pulled up her hood again, hiding her hair, though curls still brushed both cheeks.

"Not possible."

Lifting her head, she met his gaze. Surprise. Pleasure. A smile. Then back to her hands—no her arm. Wasn't that one branded? "I ... wasn't feeling well."

He'd detected more than illness.

"My legs were tired, heavy. And I couldn't think around the pain." She sagged. "I fell, my hood dropped, and Galen ran for help. Then those men found me."

Pain? What would cause pain? Why he did it, he didn't know, but Marco welcomed her back against his chest, and she rested there with a sigh. Like relief. But more.

"You came around that corner," she whispered "And ..."

He knew what she hesitated to say and firmed his hold.

"You looked *so fierce.*" Her hoarse voice cracked. She rested a hand on his bicep, her face against his shoulder. "I thought ..."

It scalded him, what she left unsaid. "You were afraid of me."

She straightened and looked up at him, the chill air gaping between them. "No," she whispered. "No, I knew you were there *for me.* I saw you and feared for those men. Yet your rage ... it answered something in me. Spoke to me. For the first time," her voice was raw, "in many months, I *knew* I was safe." A tear slipped down her cheek.

Marco caught it near her lip. Met her gaze. Swept the curls from her face. Traced her cheek with his thumb. She parted her lips, a quick intake of breath.

Her scent was the lure. His heart the bait. He wanted to know the feel of her lips. To strengthen the connection between them. To answer what he detected in her signature.

"*... no room for mistakes ...*" Roman's loud admonishment forced Marco to break off. He looked away. Released her. "I ..." He stood and stepped back. "I should leave."

Kersei came up fast. Stumbled. "Please. Do not now steal away that security I so deeply need and feel." Her eyes were impossibly large and pleading. "Please, Marco."

His name on her lips—a poison to his willpower. He sagged.

She moved closer. "I ask only for the company of a friend and ally."

He pushed his gaze to the stars, struggling. If he looked at her, his resolve would crumble. "This ... It's ..."

"You must think me wanton." She turned away, her openness and vulnerability skidding back under her dark hair for shelter. And reek—there were tears again.

Misery forced him to close the distance. "Kersei, I—"

"No." She lifted a hand and squeezed her eyes shut. "You're right."

He wanted her. Wanted to know her better. "You are a daughter of Drosero. The mistress of Stratios. I am ... a hunter." The truth would come to light. And if she knew he hunted her, that he must web and deliver her to the iereas ... "There can be nothing between us."

Anger smacked him. Defiant. "But there is." She lifted her jaw. Looked at him over her shoulder. "Do not dishonor me with lies, *hunter.*"

Grieved by his actions, he gave a curt nod. The master had warned him to give care, to tread carefully. And he had failed. "Words well-placed, Mistress."

Desperation tumbled out of her efflux, and he realized that what he'd nearly taken from her, what she offered—had not been done lightly.

"But I must stand steadfast—there cannot be anything between us." He backed away. "Come, I will see you safely back to your guardians."

Disappointment clogged her efflux, but she complied. Gave a curt nod. They left the stardeck and made their way to the deck for her quarters. He perceived a rank scent and led her back via a different route. They turned a corner and she gasped.

Marco stiffened, but then realized her scent was not concern but excitement. He frowned at her.

"An artificial forest?"

"I don't think—"

She shoved through a door.

"Kersei, I—" He leapt forward before it could close, stepping into the thick air of an artificially produced tropical environment.

"It reminds me of the woods in Kardia," came her wistful voice. She ran her hand across a tree trunk.

"We should go," he said. He did not trust himself alone with her. "If we are seen …"

She wrinkled her nose. "Just let me look a little more. This is such a relief from the cold air and mechanical reality of this ship." Her gaze hit something behind him. She sucked in a breath and leapt aside, catching his arm. "They're here." Complexion pale, she hurried aside.

"You're sure you saw her?" Jencir asked.

"Yes," Galen said. "I think so."

Marco wanted to growl. This would not go well. He did not want any more trouble with the pup. "It will appear worse to hide and be discovered," he said softly.

She hurried down a path and took shelter behind a large frond. Though frustrated, he could not deny how it seemed she almost enjoyed this. The sprite of a girl beguiled him. Against his own better judgment, he crouched beside her.

"Hello?"

They made no sound and the two men veered in the other direction. A few more minutes and the door thunked shut. Marco monitored the fading scent. "They're gone."

She stood and a giggle escaped her.

"You enjoyed that."

"I confess I did. It reminded me of hiding from Lexina and even Darius when I was younger." Cheeks glowing with mischief, she shifted over a large rock to return to the footpath. But she lost her balance.

Marco caught her, steadied her. But his pulse went erratic, as he stared down at her small, round face amid the mass of curls. Her smile and sparkling eyes. Her willingness waxing soft against her scent. He bent in. Caught her mouth with his.

Kersei drew up.

He tested. With another kiss. Daring yet another when she didn't push him away. This one longer, sweeter. She curled into him with a soft exhale. Whorls of pleasure and joy trilled the air, forming a coil so strong and tight around them, binding them. He relished her scents—attraction powerful. Intoxicating. He knew she would be his undoing. And did not care.

Five long rises since Kersei had stolen away and seen Marco. The men were in the cantina, but she had claimed indisposition and stayed behind. Now she seized the moment and slipped out. She sought solace, and what better place than the refuge of the stardeck? Massaging her temples, she headed to the lift.

Only when she found the stardeck empty did she realize she'd hoped to find Marco there. Mayhap solitude was better. Things had been so excruciating. She ached for times around the great hearth with Father and Ma'ma, arguing with Lexina. Adara's sweet laughter. Boils, she would even welcome back Darius's lectures about how a proper lady behaved if it meant the past could be undone and her loved ones returned.

Air swirled and she felt … something. Warmth brushed her finger. A hand on the rail beside hers.

Relief rushed through her at Marco's presence. "How is it you always know when I am here?" She wiped away her tears. "When I am … distressed?"

"Must we again review my particular gift?" Gripping the bar, nudged his shoulder against hers. "You are well?"

"Aye," she sniffed. "I always cry like a baby when I'm happy."

"Strange." A smirk teased the edges of his lips.

Appreciating his lighthearted manner, she removed herself to the bench and smiled as he joined her. Forearms resting on his knees, he continued starwatching. And she continued Marco-watching. His hair was straighter but every bit as unruly as hers, with the way it dangled around his face and nape. She thought of the kiss they'd shared, eliciting darts of excitement once more.

Quiet wrapped them in a warm, comfortable silence. Not one that needed breaking. She breathed a long sigh. This was the first time since she'd stepped on the shuttle with Uncle Rufio that she felt … peace.

He roughed his palms together, reminding her of when he'd pinned the man in the corridor. What gentleness he now exuded evaporated when he hunted. The same hands had crushed her against him in the terraria as he kissed her. And at some point, he'd leave this ship, and her. The thought made her ache again. "Where will you go?"

"When?"

"After …" She motioned around them. "After wherever this ship takes us."

"We dock at Cyrox, a Thyrolian station in little more than a sabbaton."

Seven rises. Was that all they had left? "Is that where your hunt is?"

A weight touched his star-fixed gaze. "My hunt is where my quarry goes." He propped his chin on his shoulder and looked at her. "Have you given thought to which clan to join?"

She startled. "I had not thought to."

"You will need protection and fellowship. Ixion would be a good protector."

"A severe one." She wrinkled her nose. "Prokopios is too far south and too hot for me. And I wonder at his abilities if I am able to slip him well enough."

"He no doubt assumes you are *not* trying to slip him. That you are safe with the Xanthus."

"It is possible that I am too much trouble for him."

"Aye."

"No need to be so agreeable." Even laughing, she knew it would be too strange to join another clan or family. "He never finds me, yet you do."

By the way his cheek muscle seemed to ball up, she guessed he was smiling. She leaned a little closer and confirmed her suspicions. And with it came an epiphany. He *smelled* her *feelings*. He'd said as much, but she hadn't understood. Mercies—her attraction, her desire. It was … unsettling. This man … full of mystery and intensity. It felt like playing with one of the dangerous puffer moles. If one could but coax them from their burrows, they provided the perfect needles filled with sweet, sweet harkhul. Like honey but a thousand times better. Finding one had always been a game between her and Darius.

Darius. What would he think of all this? Of this man before her? Guilt rankled her.

Marco whisked to his feet, his long cloak rustling. Gripped tight the iron rail, his gaze on the constellations. "What are you thinking about?" His voice was quiet, flat.

She shouldered away Darius's name and memory, joining him. Part of her did not want to answer, yet she felt he needed—deserved—the answer. "What I lost in the explosion."

Marco still studied the expanse. "Who?"

Unsure she was ready to speak of it, Kersei hesitated for a moment. "My family, of course." *Be honest*, she chided herself. *He will know if you are lying.* The thought was startling. "Medora Zarek and his sons, Prince Silvanus and Prince Darius."

"Darius." His voice was rougher this time.

Kersei stilled, realizing he'd known she was thinking of Darius. "Yes." She pressed her hip to the bar. "I never dreamed Kalonica would not have a medora to rule. With three heirs, Zarek had a good succession established."

He frowned, glanced down to the side. "Zarek had two sons."

"There was another brother who died." Recalling the handful of stories Darius shared, she smiled. He'd had a little brother's hero worship for the eldest who'd been lost. "Few speak of or remember him since Darius and Silvanus could secure the throne." *Go on. Tell him.* "The night of the attack against my entoli, Darius had set petition for me."

"And you accepted?"

She scoffed. "As a daughter, I had little choice."

His gaze skewered her. "A good match, then?"

She shrugged, surprised at how her heart thrashed, not wanting him to think she harbored those feelings for a man she would never see again. "It was." But Darius was dead. She sighed, ashamed of the relief she felt. In the reflection on the glass, she saw movement and glanced down.

Marco's hand flexed and unflexed. Knuckles white.

Whatever had drawn out his anger, she wanted it to go away. She touched his hand, which seemed natural. Instinctual.

Marco's gaze shot to their hands, but he did not pull away. His jaw muscle flexed. And by the Ladies, he was so beautiful. Those brows eternally knotted and dark over his blue irises and ringed along the bottom with that dark sigil.

"Have I angered you?"

His eyes flashed with surprise. "No," came the begrudging reply.

"Then why—"

"You miss them."

There seemed a storm behind his words, but why? "Yes. Do you miss yours?" He frowned again. "My what?"

"Family." She stilled when he looked away. She touched his arm. "Mar—"

He caught her hand. Held it firm. The world tilted as he swung toward her, his moves lightning fast and intimidating. His scowl deep. "You do not know me, Kersei."

Startled, she gaped. Where had this come from? Where was the man who kissed her so passionately she could scarce breathe? "I would know you, Marco." She shook her head. "You are much changed from the terraria."

"I was weak."

She recoiled. "Is that what you call kissing me?" The question was not a fair one, but she would remind him. "Are you so fickle with your passions that you would abuse—"

"No," he growled. His breaths were ragged. Mouth in a tight line, he went rigid. That mark made him terrifying when he scowled. "You *do not* know me."

Fear squirreled through her belly at the way he threw his intimidation around. "If you mean to frighten me, you have succeeded." What was going on? "I am safe with you."

"No." He stepped back. "You are not." Marco drew up straight, his face washed of the moments-ago torment. "You will be safe now." Regret darkened his features, mixed with something she could not name. "Isn't that right, Ixion?"

She flinched as Ixion, Galen, and Jencir appeared from the shadows.

Ixion stalked forward, hand on his sword hilt, flanked by the others. "Have I need to challenge you, Kynigos?"

"The lady is untouched." Marco's gaze was apologetic and … raw. "There is nothing to challenge."

"You mistake me," Ixion said. "I did not refer to your attempts to seduce the mistress. I refer to your Decree."

Marco met Ixion's gaze, and a silent dialogue carried between the two men.

Anxiety tightened Kersei's chest. "I don't understand."

"Tell her," Galen ordered.

Dark anger roiled through Marco. "I speak of my Decree to no one."

Kersei started toward him but felt someone jerk her back. An action that made Marco lunge then freeze beneath barely held restraint. Which bothered her. She threw off the grip and shifted away, hating his severe expression. "Please, what is this—"

Ixion came to her side. "He hunts you, Kersei."

The ship stopped moving. Planets stopped turning. Heart galloping between painful breaths, she swung her gaze to Marco. Laughed, waiting for his denial. But instead only heard silence. Awkward, painful silence around which doubt crept in. "No …" Baytu had said as much, but he had been so different here. So kind, so … reassuring. "You hunt me?"

His gaze held the anger of admittance.

"No." Her heart strained for its next beat. Tripped her toward shame. "This?" She recoiled. Heard the shrillness of her own words. "*This* is why you—the terraria, here. You were—"

"*No.*" Now his denial held powerful vehemence. But he spoke no more.

Confused, hurt, betrayed, Kersei backed up. Shook her head. She'd been a fool.

TSC *MACEDON*

Confined to quarters!

Again. Still. For more than two weeks.

"Augh!" With a growl, Tigo flung his ruck against the bulkhead. It landed next to the door. He kicked the table with another shout, then dropped hard on his bunk. His father, the glorious fleet admiral, had confined Tigo until further notice and with threat of court-martials against the entire 215.

Fists to his forehead, he thumped his head. Again. There had to be a way to clear the team. Take the punishment for his decisions, their follow-through.

The familiar, faint whisper of his door drew his attention.

Teeli stood just inside his quarters. She gave him a coy smile. "Seems security protocols stop anyone from entering your quarters. Except officers, especially medical officers." With a shrug, she smiled. Then it slipped and she leaned heavily against the door. Thinner than he'd ever seen her, borderline gaunt, dark circles under her red-rimmed eyes …

Tigo sat up. "Teeli?"

She flashed a palm at him. "I'm slow, but I want to do what I can while I can." With what looked like painful, stumbling steps, she joined him on the bunk. "I've been ill, but I feel stronger today. Thought I'd come …"

Say good-bye.

The thought punctured his self-absorbed thoughts.

"Had a terrible realization last night."

"What? You should've married me a long time ago?" he teased, wanting to see her smile.

And she did—though it was wan. "You're the only friend I have."

Heartstrings tugged, he slumped. "Then you're pretty slagged, since I'm about to end up in a Coalition pen." He considered her. "How are you, really?"

"Do you mind?" She nodded to the mattress. "The walk down here took more out of me than I expected."

"No. Of course." He shifted to make room. Lying on his side next to her, he touched the bruise on her neck. "Looks like it's worse."

"I thought it would happen slower, too. The pace has accelerated. I'm not sure why. I've run tests. Tried … everything." She shrugged, her brown hair spilling over his pillow as she stared at the ceiling. "They brought in my replacement. I asked"—her gaze seemed to go distant—"them not to send me back. Let me die here. I don't want my family to see me like this."

"But surely your family would want you—"

"We thought I had defied the odds and escaped Tryssinia and wouldn't get the disease." She pursed her lips and shrugged. "Going back will just remind them that … maybe it's inescapable. What little hope my family has that spurs them to fight might die with me." Her face twisted as she fought tears. "I don't want to be the dark cloud that hovers over them."

"They'll find out. Eventually."

She threaded her fingers over her stomach. "I can't control that. But … maybe if they told them I died of something else?"

"*Lie* to them?"

She scrunched her nose. "Yeah, not my best idea." Her gaze went to the ceiling. "I just want them to hope and fight. I made it—I might not have lived long, but I left Tryssinia ten years ago. It can be done. And maybe if more leave, someone will find the cure."

As tears streamed down her face, Tigo hooked an arm around her head.

Teeli curled onto her side and quietly cried into his shoulder. "I'm scared," she whispered. "Is it okay to admit that?"

Wrapping his arms around her shoulders, he gently hugged her. "I'd be crapping my pants by now."

"I'm scared and alone." More sobs.

He firmed his hold. "You are not alone. I'm here. Remember—your friend."

She rolled her head to look up at him. "At least I've loved." Meaning telegraphed through her brown eyes.

The words sent a shockwave through Tigo. He cupped her face, gently kissed her. "And been loved."

"Remember me. Okay?" Through more tears, she kissed him, then burrowed into his arms. It was peaceful. Gentle. Loving. There was nothing carnal about it. He did what he'd felt he had to do from the start—give the heavy-hearted doctor a reason to smile. She fell quickly into a heavy sleep, and Tigo was glad for her to rest. This time with her reminded him what they were fighting for out here. What they really should be doing, not torturing innocents.

Teeli shuddered through a breath, her body relaxing more.

"It's been an honor, Dr. Knowles," he whispered against her ear before planting a kiss there. He closed his eyes. Listened to her steady breathing.

Tigo hiked through the facts of the last few months. Drosero. The girl getting picked up adrift in space. Baric putting her and the Kynigos in that chamber. Krissos had given the order to find the hunter. Hadn't told them who they were after. Just that they would know when they got there. Now he was playing dumb. Was he in on whatever was happening?

Was Baric still on that satellite? What in the black was a ship's captain doing on a scientific research satellite anyway? Why had he taken the girl there?

His door chimed, pulling him up. With care, he extricated himself from Teeli, relieved she didn't wake. He plodded to the door, kept the lights dim, and opened it. Stunned to find Jez there. "Thought we were confin—"

"Admiral wants us on the command deck." She nodded. "Tried to comm you, but didn't get"—her gaze hit the bed—"a response." With a growl, she slipped around him. "Tigo!"

"It's not what you think. She just came in to talk." He tried to get Jez's attention, but she'd gone pale. "On my oath, I didn't—we didn't. She was just tired. Fell asleep."

"Tigo, she's not asleep." Her brown-gold eyes went glossy. "She's gone. In the Lady's embrace."

HCT *KLEOPATRA*

Pain awakened her yet again. This time, however, the nightmares stitched into her mind were not from that wicked chamber but of Marco's betrayal. Kissing her one minute. Driving a dagger into her back the next. Him laughing and holding her one heartbeat. The next, pinning her to the stone slabs of Stratios Hall. Strangling her. Till she lay buried with her parents and sisters.

"You do not know me."

He had been right. They'd spent weeks on the transport together. Met several times. Laughed and enjoyed each other's company. A respite in the storm that had consumed her life. She'd felt happy. It ached. She ached.

Everything ached. She needed him. Wanted him, to be with him. Laugh with him.

"He hunts you, Kersei."

The vicious fire of the brand claimed her, seeping through her sleeve and especially bright in the unlit room. Sweaty and weak from the exertion of enduring the flaming, Kersei lay exhausted on her bed. Closed her eyes. Gritted her teeth, biting through the fire. Wished the Ancient to call her Beyond. Let all the terrible months vanish and her with them.

With a moan, she rolled onto her back and stared up at the ceiling. Fighting the heartache. She wiped the tears—and it was then she heard the voices in the main room.

"How do we know she's innocent?"

"Careful, Galen," Bazyli chided. "Your jealousies over her and the hunter cloud your judgment."

"I think her dalliances with this rogue are enough to make us question her character," Galen argued. "How are we to know she has not given herself to him?"

Shock pulled Kersei from the mattress and shoved her to the door. Wrapping her arms around herself, she stepped into the light of the room. "What say you?" she breathed, glancing from Galen to the other men with a tempestuous rage. "How dare you!"

Bazyli sighed, lowering his gaze, then eyeing his brother. "It is your charge."

The word lifted Kersei's chin as Galen came to his feet.

A tumult of irritation and regret flecked his Xanthus features. "Can you speak for your virtue?"

Ixion pounded a fist on the table. "Uncalled for!" His expression was angry and matched the furor in her chest. He motioned Kersei to a seat next to him. "That is not your concern," he said, pointing to Galen. "But there are questions, Kersei. We should broach it now."

Sitting straight, arms around her waist, she stared at the men. "And because I was talking with the hunter, you suddenly find me of ill repute."

"It is odd," Bazyli said slowly, his lips in a tight line, "that you would seek the company of the Kynigos and not your kinsmen. It arouses questions and concerns."

She swallowed. His words made sense, even if they stung. The irony did not escape her that the only person who found her innocent of what happened to her family was the one they claimed put her character in question. The one who hunted her. "Ask your questions then."

Ixion leaned forward, arm resting on his knee. "Tell us what happened. We have not had it from you."

For several long seconds, she merely stared at him, then shifted to take in Bazyli, Jencir, and Galen. Moistening her lips, she looked down, and began to relate the events that had brought them to this point. The celebration, Darius's petition, her father's acceptance—she left out her own views of the binding—the ceremony disrupted by the arrival of the iereas, then chasing her uncle down the hidden passages of Stratios Hall.

"Rufio," Bazyli repeated, braid beads clacking as he nodded for emphasis. "You are sure?"

"He is my uncle, largely responsible for my machitis training—of course I am sure."

He inclined his head. "Of course. I beg your mercy."

"How did you end up with the Symmachians?" Ixion asked, prodding her on.

And so she continued, chasing Rufio down that passage, his pushing her into the shuttle, the explosion … Throughout, her voice remained steady, her demeanor calm.

"You do not seem especially torn over this," Galen muttered.

"Perhaps because I have endured the deaths of my beloved family over and over for weeks. Perhaps because I can see the blood staining Adara's hair, and the brokenness of Lexina's neck. And Fath—" Her voice cracked, a sob thickening her throat. She turned her head away. "It has been seared into my mind. I am numb because they made me numb."

Galen lowered his head, but his petulance remained.

"Continue," Ixion again prodded.

Anger tremored beneath her veins—and that's when her mind awakened her to the fire in her arm. Why now? It was never a good time, but again, so soon? She resumed her story, the Symmachians, the reminding chamber, Tigo and his team … then Cenon. But the more she talked, the more the brand blazed. Excruciating with a speed and fervor like never before.

Sweat slid down her spine. She forced herself to finish the story, but the agony was violent and wholly distracting. Was she even talking still?

Bazyli came up. "Cousin?"

She looked to him, but it was as if someone had drawn gray curtains together, blocking him. A shout chased her into the fog.

"This is worse than the Matraxis 12 fallout."

Tigo refused to look at Diggs, who sat to his right, beside Jez at a conference table on the Command deck. Matraxis was one of his more notorious adventures. Diggs had been there through a lot of them. Too many. But this—this wasn't an adventure.

It was conviction.

He had one regret: that his team would get torched for following said conviction. And he was furious with them. With Jez. For concocting this story. They should've just let the debris hit whatever it hit.

"That doesn't look good," Jez murmured, pushing his gaze to hers, then following it past the glass wall between them and the bridge.

A stream of uniforms crossed the command deck, the pale blue instrumentation giving the circular space an ominous aura. At the center Dimar was engaged in an intense—and angry—conversation with Admiral Deken. The XO knew better than to show disrespect to the fleet admiral, yet he had no problem showing his dislike of whatever they were discussing.

Tigo surveyed the officers of the *Macedon*, as well as a few from Command. Waring—of course. If she was sleeping with the fleet admiral, it probably bought her a lot of benefits. He cursed when he spotted a third—Krissos.

"That's Lorcan," Jez said, her voice pitching.

Admiral Lorcan was the second-highest officer in the fleet, and it didn't bode well for the two admirals to be here.

"Scuz me," Rhinn muttered. "*What* is the captain of the *Argus* doing here?"

Next to the admirals, Captain Lasson Point with his wheat-colored hair and ruddy complexion wasn't anything to remember, but his cybernetic arm was. And Point was proud of the thing, forgoing the humanoid skin typically grown and applied to the implant. The way he swung it around, pointing at Tigo and his team—

Jez whistled. "He's not happy."

"Thinking we're in over our heads here."

That AO spoke the doomsday words pulled Tigo's gaze back to his team. Jez Sidra, beauty with a blaster, loyal to her last breath. Theodore Diggins, renegade who'd been all in from day one. A best friend, if that sort of thing still happened. Sevart Crafter, the only one who shouldn't be here—Rhinn hadn't really passed the final PT test, but Tigo signed off on him. Wanted the hardcore determination he saw in the brawny Napian. And that left Jaigh Eggleston, a.k.a. AO. The oldest, giving his final years to the fleet.

"No." No, they would not lose their arc-and-bolts. Not for him. He leaned in and tapped the table. "I want you all to—"

"Anyone hearing that strong wind?" AO gave an exaggerated look around, avoiding Tigo.

"Yeah," Diggs said. "Kind of a hot wind."

"Listen—"

Rhinn sniffed the air. "With a rancid smell."

"I mean it—"

"Yeah, we know," Jez said, her dark eyes flashing. "And so do we. This isn't about you, so shut up." When he widened his eyes at her insubordination, she gave a mock smile. "*Sir.*"

"This isn't—"

Click-hiss.

"Two-one-five," his father's voice boomed as the officers entered the room, trailing a wake of orbs and galaxies. Standing at the head of the long conference table, Domitas Deken took in each of them. His shoulders squared beneath his gleaming gold orbit, which identified him as the fleet admiral. The black-and-white dress uniform was severely out of place aboard a battle cruiser. But this wasn't about getting his hands dirty. It was about getting *215's* hands dirty.

He let out a stream of curses, then slapped both palms on the table. Glowered. "You are supposed to be the elite. The finest. Smartest. Swiftest." He bared his teeth. "And you can't capture a nineteen-year-old downworlder with no experience or technology at her scuzzing disposal?"

The revered and feared Domitas Deken on display for the world to see. Barrel-chested and one-point-eight meters tall, he struck fear into hearts. "How in the Void are we supposed to maintain control in this quadrant if our best and brightest are stupid and incompetent?"

Jez dropped her chin to her chest, lips tight. Face red. Nostrils flared.

Don't let him get to you, Sidra. He's more hot air than me.

His father broke from the arc of officers, which seemed as startling as the rings of Lycurgus breaking apart, and paced. Stalked and talked. It was one of his favorite tactics. "I'm wondering if any of you thought for one slagging tick that there might be things happening that you don't know about. If the sliver of a thought dug into your thick skulls that maybe—*just maybe*"—the veins in his temple bulged—"Command *might* know something you don't!"

Tigo kept his gaze on the table. He'd learned long ago it was best not to make eye contact. Not to react to the verbal assaults. But even with his head down, he noted Rhinn's balled fists. White knuckles. He slid his gaze up the chair to the sectioned panels of Rhinn's light-combat suit. Found eyes blazing with fury. With the barest shake of his head, Tigo warned him to stand down. *Don't respond.*

Hands slapped the back of Tigo's chair, jarring him. His father stood over him—and Rhinn was glowering at the admiral, who squeezed Tigo's shoulders. "And one would think that the elite, the brightest and best, being led by the fleet admiral's son, their commander might have a brain in that brain bowl." His dad knuckled his head. "But then—that'd be too much to ask, wouldn't it?"

His father returned to his officers, this time trudging behind Jez and AO. The red sash stretching from one lapel to the other hung so stark against the black-and-white jacket. "For the man in charge of a half-dozen trained killers to actually *think* through his actions. Figure out when technology breaks, when fugitives flee, how to succeed at his mission. Bring home the mighty victory for the fleet." He lifted his hands.

Fueled by conviction they'd done the right thing, Tigo met the admiral's gaze. Kept his expression neutral. Okay, he couldn't muster neutral, but disgusted was close.

His father lowered his fists. Straightened his jacket. Then planted his knuckles on the table, pulsing his anger and displeasure down the lacquer to Tigo. "Clear. The. Room."

Somehow Tigo knew that order did not include him. So he remained straight, but noted Jez's hesitation before she yielded.

When the door hissed shut, his father barked, "Window, darken." The glass separating them from the bridge went black, like his father's eyes. "*Why* is there a coroner retrieving the body of the former chief medical officer from your quarters as we speak?"

Tigo lowered his head. "We were talking—she wasn't well. She fell asleep... I thought."

"In your bed?"

"Nothing happened. But I doubt you'll believe that."

"You're scuzzing right!" his father bellowed. "You've ruined the lives of more people than I can count, Commander! Your team, every slagging one of them—Esqueda won't be going home at all, and Sidra, Diggins, Crafter, and Eggleston will be escorted back to Symmachia, court-martialed, and sent to Glatrille."

Tigo punched to his feet. "You have no cause to do that."

Teeth bared again, his father growled. "I am the admiral of the fleet! I can do—"

"That's your flaming banner, isn't it? You're like an Academy bully throwing around that orbit! Abusing power—"

"At least I'm *using* the power given me, while you sit on your—"

"They were only following my orders. Ship *me* back." Tigo wasn't going to let his father win, not this time. "Send me to Glatrille. I'll do the time."

His scoffed. "You expect me to believe they were only following orders?"

"I'm their CO. They obey my orders. Just like we obey yours. And Krissos's." The words were deliberate, targeted to break this charade. "Speaking of— where is he, Admiral? What is the *Chryzanthe*?"

"Scuzzing black void!" Frustration pushed his father's head down. "Why won't you let it go and just do your slagging job?"

Tigo noticed something about his father's rage. There was a lot of it. Too much. Yes, his father had been notorious for throwing that orbit around. But most times, it'd been without words, having the ability to walk into a room and effect change just by being there. What was with the shouting and railing? Had Tigo really hit a nerve that hard?

"I'm giving Two-one-five one last chance."

Tigo started, confused. "Chance? To do what?"

The admiral flicked a channeler clip down the table. "She's on a civilian transport, the *Kleopatra*. Find her. Bring her back."

Of all the … The girl. Again. "Why? You sent me to Cenon—"

"And you failed!"

"—and now to this transport. *Why* is this girl so important? You said it—she has no technology. No experience. And yet we're throwing all our resources after her? This doesn't make sense. And if you saw what was on that satellite—what Baric—"

"Dismissed."

Three ragged heartbeats struggled in the silence after that order. Tigo couldn't believe it. There had to be an explanation. "Dad—"

Eyes like his own latched on. "*Dis. Missed.*"

Unbelievable. With a cockeyed nod, Tigo gritted his teeth. "You can't silence the truth, *Admiral*. And I'm going to find it. I'm going to find the truth."

"She always said you'd be the death of me."

Mom. Tigo drew up straight. "You didn't deserve her, and you don't deserve to wear that uniform."

HCT *KLEOPATRA*

Marco stood on the suspended bridge overlooking the corridor leading to the Droseran quarters. Her absence created a thirst in him, a hunger to see her. To make peace with her. Days had passed and in two more, they would dock on Cyrox. But now a strange rage radiated through the air from her, and it worried him. He debated inserting himself in some way to learn what angered her. Besides him and his hunt.

"Marco."

He turned, surprised to find Rico and Roman approaching. "Master." Inclined his head, rifling possible reasons for them to be here. "It is an unexpected pleasure." He nodded to Rico. "Advocate." He was irritated to find the three iereas behind his brethren. Two in black-and-red robes—high guards. Protecting none other than— "Kyros."

What was the master hunter doing with the high lord? The thought of these two conspiring twisted his gut. "The Decree—"

"Come," Roman said quietly. "We must confer." He stalked away, and the entourage fell in step behind him, leaving Marco to follow. To wonder what in the reek was going on. He entered his quarters, crowded with so many bodies. Roman talked in low whispers with the high lord. The sight was disconcerting.

"Marco." Roman rubbed his jaw as he turned. "I'm sure our arrival is unsettling, but there are matters we must attend."

"Would a holo or wave not have sufficed?" Marco asked.

"Not this time." Disappointment leached from Roman's scent. Since hunters knew to conceal their feelings among each other, this was intentional. He had not failed the Decree yet, so what was this about?

High Lord Kyros glided closer, his red overcloak swishing heavily.

"Master Marco."

The serpent speaks.

"There is but one master here," Marco corrected.

"Of course," Kyros crooned. "It is said you are ingratiating into the life of the girl with amazing speed." He angled his head. "Is this hunt satisfying?"

Did he jest? Marco looked to Roman, who refused his gaze, so he holstered his annoyance. "Hunts give honor. Not pleasure." Prickly distrust pecked at his neck and shoulders.

Kyros and Roman shared a long look before the high lord lunged at Marco.

Pulse jammed, Marco fought to reconcile the serpentine iereas with the viper-like strike that caught his neck. Training shoved his hands up. Weight yanked them back down—master on one side and advocate on the other.

Shock coursed through him. "What is this?"

Powerful Roman shoved him back against the table. Pinned him as two guards secured his legs. "Be quick," he barked at the iereas.

"What is—*Master*?" Confused, he sounded pitiful. "Release me!"

"Be still, Marco."

He met Roman's gaze. "How could y—" He strained as the high lord swiveled around to his right. Took his arm and jerked it down. Marco growled against the insult. The humiliation. If he could just get free, he'd drive the iereas's nose through his skull. Rico stretched over his bicep as another iereas held his fist. Drew up his sleeve. Tugging at his vambrace buckles stilled Marco.

What in the …? His mark again? "What are you doing?" he demanded.

Kyros removed the plating.

"Release me!"

"What do you see?" Roman asked, peering over his shoulder.

"I don't—" Kyros chuckled. "Ah. Yes."

Through the sea of arms and bodies restraining him, Marco watched the high lord lift something from the armor—the strands of Kersei's hair. Then held a palm over Marco's arm.

When the brand started to glow, Marco gaped. "What majuk is this?" With the glow came fire. Roaring, angry. "By the Fires of Pir—"

He gritted his teeth and dropped back, sweat sliding down his temples. Steeling himself against the torrent, he refused to cry out.

Kersei. Think of Kersei. Holding her in the bay, the sweetness of her attraction. The lilt of her voice … her kiss …

Searing, boiling— "*Augh!*" He bucked but they held him. There would be no mercy. No fighting through this. Throwing his head back, he howled. Tears demanded freedom, fleeing his eyes in a tempestuous race against the fire.

Remember Kersei. Innocent eyes. The glorious scent drew him like a heelti moth to the—*flame.*

Pain! Vicious, vengeful. Enough.

"I vow"—the excruciating pain made it hard to speak—"on my oath." Marco growled, then whimpered and refocused. "Release me, or I will end you." Another shout turned to a whimper.

Roman loomed and pressed Marco's shoulder to the table. "Do not fight it. I know you do not understand. But trust me." He pushed against his shoulder again. "*Trust.*"

A volley of fire ripped through him. A long, guttural cry burst from him like a daemon-possessed and -tortured soul. With each tick, the agony increased. He bellowed. Shook. Cried. Thrashed.

"No more," he gargled the words. "No more. By Vaqar—please!" He sounded pathetic. Swirling nausea and dizziness made him want to retch. Retch and die. He slumped, unable to fight the pain. Feeling as if his flesh had melted away. His bones incinerated. The agony so extreme, he could no longer feel. No longer hear. No longer see. He dropped into the abyss.

He awoke in a sea of black. Blinking, Marco tried to regain his senses. Every limb and muscle ached as if trampled by a thousand rhinnocks. When he moaned, the throb in his head bounced back at him. He cringed and rolled onto his back, registering the hull of his quarters.

Whispers carried from somewhere. A tick later, Kyros hovered over him.

Marco's arm flew up. Caught the man's neck. With a curled lip, he begged the Ancient for permission to snap this iereas's throat. "I will kill you." But his arm trembled.

"Marco, release him!" Roman's command did not assuage his thirst for blood.

Strength failing, Marco shoved the high lord back. Propped on his elbow, he strained to make his body cooperate. Dizziness swooned, then faded. "What is this?" he hissed, looking to his advocate and master. "My own Brethren conspired against me."

"We did not," Roman said.

Marco slid off the padded bench, knees nearly buckling before he dropped heavily onto a chair. "You say that after pinning me to this table like a stuck pig and letting *him* levy some curse against me."

"It isn't a curse." Kyros rubbed his throat as he sat nearby. "Since we last talked, have you recalled more about when you received the brand?"

Why should he tell this madman anything?

"Trust, Marco," Roman insisted.

Time swept back twenty-five cycles when a small boy gaped up at the towering master hunter. The boy … *Me. I was the boy.* Why did he remember now, but not at the temple? "This is madness," he whispered, shaken. "Bowing to an iereas. I have a hunt! A Decree to fulfill. Release me to her."

"To *her*?" Roman repeated, cocking his head. "Or to the hunt?"

"Of course the hunt."

Kyros pushed forward. "Be assured, there will be no further extrications of the flame. Unless you again force my hand."

Scowling, Marco shoved his hair from his face. "*How* have I forced your hand? And what is this? A lie? Did you not tell me at the temple that the burning was not you?"

Impassive, Kyros sighed. "You discovered the hair of the Dragoumis child stays the fire." He looked grave. "How long have you had the strands tucked beneath your armor?"

"Vambrace," Marco corrected. In earnest, he did not want to answer. But the master prodded him. "Since Cenon."

Rico muttered an oath and turned to the door.

Kyros gave a long, disapproving shake of his head.

"He didn't realize the ramifications," Roman said. "He would not have continued, had he known."

"Known what?" Marco demanded.

Kyros leaned on the table. "Have you noticed the child's arms are constantly covered?"

"Space is cold."

A smile played on Kyros's lips. "Has it ever occurred to you that perhaps you are not the only one suffering the brand?"

"Many bear the stain of your order." The barb had worked well on Ypiretis, and Marco enjoyed using it again.

"You are not surprised," Kyros said. "You *knew* she bore a brand. How?"

"Better," Roman bit out, "is how you came to have her hair in your vambrace."

Marco refused to feel guilty for the discovery. "On Cenon, she was in danger and unconscious. Under the direction of Ypiretis, I carried her to safety and saw the brand. Her hair snagged on the buckles."

"It was an unfortunate discovery on your part," Kyros said. "Had I not intervened, you would have killed her."

Marco jolted. "Never!"

"By shielding yourself from the burn, you ... diverted the power of the brand, forcing Nicea's child to endure twice the energy, for lack of better word, that the brand was designed to harness."

"No. This is wrong," Marco argued, his mind refusing to process the words and implications. The connections. The ... insanity! "Why would my brand affect hers? What savage burns marks into children for a prophecy?"

"Savages?" Kyros chuckled. "Give care, Marco. It is the Ancient Himself who selects the Chosen. And be sure, the brands are not burned—they simply ... appear." He pressed his fingertips together. "And why it affects you? Simple—you and Nicea's child share two halves of the same brand. After you left Iereania, we researched ancient texts to learn of its attached prophecy and fulfillment. This is a powerful one in its scope. Too much for one body, so you were designed to share the burden."

Two halves. Same brand. How ... insane. Yet ...

It makes sense.

The times she'd burst into pain—her scent slinging through the air at him. And because of him, she'd endured more than twice what she should have. He nearly killed her.

"You have discovered how to stall the pain, but you must never do it again. She cannot withstand another attack. As it is, Ypiretis has gone to great lengths to subdue the fire and limit the damage."

Damage. The word haunted Marco. Made him feel miserable. He stared at the arcs and lines on his arm. Thought of Kersei's. Grieved the pain he'd caused her. "Does she know?" His words were strained, cracked by the enormity of it.

"That you share a brand? No. Her mother raised her to fear the brand, to hide it, and as with you, the prophecy connection is withheld to protect both the host and the fulfillment."

Chosen. Why would the Ancient choose him? Marco reached for his vambrace, wanting to hide the mark and his shame. "She should be told. I sense her fear and panic every time the brand burns."

"It will become marginally bearable as you again share this burden. As the brand nears its fulfillment, the power to be unleashed will grow. Remember, you are tasked only with her protection." Eyebrow arching, Kyros considered him. "I advise you not to share this knowledge with her as yet."

"Why?"

"How would you feel upon learning the other half had a pain-free ride at your expense?"

Marco swallowed. "She is stronger than that."

"You should guard your thoughts and actions with regard to Kersei," Kyros warned, "or you risk shattering the prophecy."

"I have not failed a hunt, nor will I now."

"When faced with the beauty of a Lady, men are weak, Marco." Kyros's steel gaze hardened. "Do not tamper with her virtue."

"I gave my word." Fisting his hand, he glanced at the mark, anything to distract from the fact he had been weak where Kersei was concerned. His feelings for her were strong. They need not know that. "What is the prophecy?"

Kyros hesitated.

"We are marked and cannot know for what?"

The high lord rose. "Deliver her to Iereania. Once there, you'll understand."

Clarity struck. At long last, he *did* understand. "This! *This* is why." He raised his forearm. "This brand is why you paid for a Decree with me. It's not a hunt. Never was."

A hover gurney bearing the body of Teeli Knowles glided out of Tigo's quarters under the direction of the new medical officer, Yukiko Durlaa. Hands tucked in his armpits, Tigo waited outside his door, his father's words still scalding his ears. He leaned his head back and thumped it softly against the bulkhead, disbelieving the nightmare his life and career had turned into.

Jez, approaching from the lift, paused and saluted as the gurney passed her. After the hall cleared, she leaned one shoulder on the wall beside Tigo, facing him. For a moment she said nothing, just scuffed the toe of her boot against the rubberized flooring, bumping Tigo's foot each time. When she finally spoke, her voice was subdued, almost disappointed. "You do not understand your importance, your purpose."

"My importance, apparently, it to scuz everyone's life." He shoved himself off the wall and entered his quarters, wincing at the antiseptic smell. Moving to his locker, he retrieved his ruck. Some purpose—to make colossally bad calls and get his team sent to the brig or demoted. Or discharged.

"You may have ruined everything—"

Tigo snapped up, silencing her. "I think we already figured that out—or did you miss the part where the admiralty promised court-martials?"

She turned those gold-brown eyes on him, and he hesitated at the sadness emanating from her as she slowly shook her head. "You don't understand."

His lip curled. He understood just fine. Why was she crawling down his throat anyway? She'd agreed to the Cenon mission, orchestrated the call to let the Droseran escape. She'd hidden the gauntlet intel. And now she was throwing him under the afterburners? "Scuz off, Sidra!"

Her eyes widened and her lips parted as she took a step back.

Tigo sighed, regret shouldering aside his anger. He pinched the bridge of his nose. "Sorry. This whole thing, now Teeli—"

But Jez walked away.

Slamming his locker shut, Tigo balled up his frustration along with his clothes and threw the whole lot into the ruck. Ten minutes later, he strode down the clanging iron steps onto the Eidolon deck. AO and Rhinn were already checking gear. "Diggs?" he asked as he joined them.

"In the 'vette prepping." AO straightened, using his shoulder to rub something from his eye. "Where's Jez?"

Tigo tucked his chin. "En route." He started for the *Renette*'s rear hatch. "Sooner we leave, the better."

"Agreed," AO said. "Didn't much like the way the admiral stuffed silence down our throats."

"Don't much like how he's okay with ripping people's brains inside out or secret stations working on throwing worms across the void of space." Rhinn lifted his gauntlets and ruck, then trudged into the ship.

"We have no proof of that." Tigo stowed his gear then hit the comms. "How we doing, Diggs?"

"Just completed preflight before your loud self showed up," Diggs's voice came over the ship's comms. "Where's Jez? Don't see her on board."

"Admiral on deck!" an unfamiliar voice barked.

"You have got to be kidding me," Tigo muttered, peering down the ramp into the bay, where his father and guards marched toward the *Renette*. "Any chance we could lift off *now*?" he asked quietly into the comms.

Diggs sniffed. "Not even a remote one. No clearance and no Jez."

Tigo released the comms as the rear hatch darkened with the brawn of his dad. He forced himself to attention. "Can we help you, Admiral?"

Domitas Deken stepped up into the corvette, but shifted aside as Jez wedged past, hurrying to stow her gear.

"*Renette*, you are cleared for launch," flight deck announced.

"Copy that, *Macedon*," Diggs responded.

Tigo gave his father a cockeyed nod, telling him time was short.

"You left this in your quarters," his father said, handing him a gauntlet.

Surprise tugged at Tigo. He snatched it and tossed it on his jump seat. "We're ready to deploy, Admiral."

"I came here to reiterate to all of you the importance of what you're doing."

"We're Eidolon," Tigo said. In other words, they knew importance.

"Drop, shop, and crop," Diggs, Rhinn, and Jez said in unison.

His father nodded. "You'll meet resistance on the *Kleopatra*. There are Kynigos there as well as standard ship's security, but TSC has jurisdiction over spacecraft in the quadrants, so board and secure. You'll know what to do."

"All the way, every day," AO said, snapping into his seat. The *shunk* of locks attaching to his mech-suit vibrated against the hull.

His dad's gray eyes bored into Tigo. "You have your mission."

Anger wove through his chest with barbed tentacles. "Had it before you came down here."

"Just … you'll know what to do."

"Already do—starting with closing the hatch and sealing the bay." Hands on his tactical belt, he returned his father's expression.

Until he didn't.

Something shifted. Something was … off.

"Make me proud, Two-one-five." As a chorus of hoyzahs rang through the confined space, Admiral Deken again looked at Tigo, then to his chest. "You'll know," his father said again with a nod to him. "You'll know what to do." His lips tightened. "No matter the cost—do it."

"Caught it the first two times, Admiral."

"Tigo," Jez's quiet reprimand didn't touch his anger.

His father nodded to the team. "Good luck. May the Ancient be with you."

The Ancient? Since when? Tigo didn't trust himself to move as his father exited the corvette. Once the admiral was clear, he pivoted up to the jump deck. "Rhinn, lock it down."

"Yep." He secured the hatch, then locked into his jump seat.

Weary, Tigo eyed Diggs. "Get us out of here." He leaned back as the umbilicals slid down and attached. He retrieved his helmet from the overhead rack and put it on.

"Opening bay doors in three …"

Tigo took a deep breath and felt the hiss of his O_2 line.

"… two … one."

His gauntlet was … tight. Short. He checked it, then clearly recalled stuffing his gear in the ruck. Both gauntlets. As his fingers coiled into a fist, the move that synced the armored glove to the suit and his comms, he realized the problem: this wasn't his gauntlet.

"Tigo." A vidscreen activated, splashing his father's grainy image over the face shield. "I know we've had our differences, and you've taken exception with the Engram, as well as the endeavor on the *Chryzanthe*. You were very angry with me, and it was quite surprising—"

Muttering an oath, Tigo reached up to release the helmet locks.

"What's wrong?" Jez asked.

"—which is why I'm trusting you with intel that will destroy me if you fail. Or destroy Symmachia if you succeed."

"There are five fast-attack crafts on an intercept course with the *Kleopatra*." Rico stood, his hands planted on his hips. "They'll be here in less than two hours."

Hours after the confrontation with Kyros, Marco pulled to his feet in the galley of the scout that had delivered the Brethren. "Then it is time."

His advocate neither moved nor spoke.

By the Mercies, he had no patience this rise. "Speak your mind, Rico."

"I would speak to you of your attraction to the girl." Rico was soon shadowed by Roman's broad frame filling the passage to the stairs, challenge set in his expression.

"What of it?"

"Are you ... involved with her?"

Marco moved past his brethren, lifted his vest, and slid it on. "There has been a significant ... connection between us. You know me, Brothers. Dalliances are *not* my weakness. But Kersei"—he found himself nodding—"is."

"Her virtue—"

"Intact," Marco snapped. "I have more honor than that."

"Then you are prepared to accept Revocation?" Roman asked.

Marco stiffened. "Nay, but has it not already been decided?" He hefted his forearm in meaning.

"The brand does not mean you must sacrifice your honor." Rico's gaze sharpened. "And do not assume because you share the brand that you are meant for one another."

"I assume no such thing."

"And is she willing to give her love?" Roman asked.

Despite the kiss ... "No." Marco hung his head. "She ... she learned of the Decree. Walked away from me."

"For your sake, be glad she will not have you. Regardless," Roman said, "this will complicate securing her."

"Aye, but I hope to convince her to come without trouble." He eyed his master. "After this prophecy is complete, what are my options?"

Touching his thumper, Rico hurried from the cabin.

"Your attachment to her is very strong," Roman said gravely. "Do you think it possible to abandon that once this brand is dealt with?"

"Master?"

"If the girl were to have you, would you choose her?" Roman seemed to probe his very *adunatos*. "It is possible to return to the Citadel—but only if you renounce her."

Marco had no grounds to think of a future with a woman who, at the moment, would not even speak to him. But he could not easily walk away from what she'd awakened in him. "If I am granted life when this over, I would want it with her."

"Large words from a man who would not even indulge a chatelaine."

"I want no leftovers. Only Kersei." The words startled him. So did their vehemence.

Roman glanced down. "I'm disappointed."

"She calls to me. I feel—" Glimpses of the past, of a woman and man in a large sitting room with a roaring fire taunted him. *Yes, that.* That's what he wanted. With Kersei. A home. A life. A family. Strange, as a hunter, those had never been his goals.

"I will wait until you are both delivered to Iereania. Until then, this conversation?" Roman said. "Never happened."

Rico charged back in. "Now—we have to go. There's a corvette minutes out. Not sure why we didn't hear about it sooner."

"Probably cloaked," Roman said.

"Well, it's about to dock and we don't have the girl."

"Let's go."

"We need to get her off the ship," Galen said.

She had walked away from Marco three days ago, and the empty void in her had only widened, cultivating bitterness and anger. She was tired of men deciding her fate.

"We heard you the first four times," Bazyli said. "The facts haven't changed—we have no ship or means to purchase an early departure on another vessel, nor is there one leaving early enough to alter this course."

"Perhaps we can barter passage—"

"Galen, this is not a station with shuttles leaving every ora. It's a transport vessel, designed for those who either cannot afford their own or choose not to own one."

"Perhaps it's time for us to reconsider that stance," Galen grumbled.

It was the first thing he'd said that Kersei agreed with. But she would not voice that now. Though the last flaming had weakened her, she stayed in her quarters for the solitude after Marco's betrayal. She lay in her bed, propped on the meager pillow as she listened to the men argue in the common room.

"Galen," Bazyli said. "You are out of line."

"Brother—there are two more Kynigos on board now as well," Galen exclaimed. "We know what this means!"

A gentle knock on the door frame ushered Ypiretis into the room, followed by his silent apprentice. He handed her a bowl. "Warmed broth."

Cupping the bowl, she blew over the top as a shadow filled the doorway.

Bazyli hung just inside the door. He was a rugged sort, a man of the wilds. "How do you fare, Cousin?"

Betrayed. Used. Manipulated. Broken. "Better, thank you." She sipped the broth and felt it sink right into her bones.

"We beg your mercy for the stress our questions caused you," Bazyli said. "We did not believe your guilt, but we had to hear it from you. There still may be a conclave back on Drosero, but you can count us as allies."

"I am relieved and grateful." She finished off the broth, noticing he had not left.

Something twisted in Bazyli's expression. "You should know that my brother seeks to set petition for you."

Weariness crowded what little strength she'd regained. She tried to hide her annoyance. "I ..."

"Because Xylander is dead," Ixion spoke up, appearing behind the younger man, "we must discern how that would go before Galen can pursue that course."

Which meant she had time. "I confess, since the deaths of my loved ones are so fresh, I cannot bear the thought of a petition."

Bazyli nodded. "Agreed. It is too soon, as I have told him."

A commotion outside pulled Bazyli back to the main room.

"Rest, child," Ypiretis said. His apprentice had sat on the floor and was busily crushing more herbs. "Your body—"

"Bazyli! They're coming!"

"What—"

"The Kynigos are coming for Kersei!"

Storming through the cantina—the shortest route to her quarters—Marco shouldered into the hunt. Which wasn't a hunt. But if he didn't get this over with …

Frantic movement and startled yelps cascaded as chairs scraped floors. Mothers yanked children close. Murmuring rose as men braved to see who the Kynigos sought.

Flanked by his advocate and master, Marco closed his receptors to the chaos and focused on the only signature important to his Decree: Kersei's. Panic splashed the patchouli and vanilla.

"She knows," Marco said to the side. He could only pray she'd come easily.

"Good," Roman muttered.

A horde of scents assailed the passage. Confrontation. Anger. Protection. But he had no idea what to expect. He couldn't pretend to know what would happen on Iereania either. Both situations set his teeth on edge.

"Prepare," Rico warned.

Rounding a corner, Marco slowed. Thirty paces separated them from a half-dozen armed machitis crowding the narrow corridor. Rigid postures spoke of readiness to defend that which was theirs. At the front wearing leather baldrics stood Ixion and Bazyli. Strategic placement. Protector and kin. Both had a reason to fight for her.

At the far end of the passage, a cluster of ship's security were being held at bay by more machitis. A claxon sounded, warning of danger to the ship's passengers.

Since he held the Decree, Marco edged ahead of his brethren. Considering the official confrontation, the battle lines drawn, he must start with a proclamation that would be recorded by all three vambraces. "By Quadrant Law and governing statute Fifteen Forty-Eight of the Kynig-Tertian Accord, as well as the alliance forged among the planets of Herakles, the Kynigos Brethren are authorized to receive Decrees, hunt—"

A shape emerged from a side door, Kersei's scent spewing distraction.

"—and web a fugitive across the four quadrants. By this authority do I,

Marco Dusan, a third-order hunter, approach. I am under Decree to secure Kersei Dragoumis and deliver her to Iereania."

"We will defend that which is ours," Galen shouted.

"Silence your tongue," Bazyli barked to his brother, then thrust his chin and gaze to Marco. "I speak for those gathered in defense of our people. We are Droserans and are not obligated to any interplanetary regulations or Decree."

"Understood, however, you are not on Drosero," Marco countered, keeping his receptors on the hovering scents. Jealous anger spurted again and he glanced to the young one.

"Your quarry is to be my bound."

"I think not, young pup." It felt good to relegate him to a lower position. Marco narrowed the scope of his receptors as he focused on the Xanthus elder. "I respect your people and believe neither of us would have bloodshed."

Wary, Bazyli gave a nod.

"Therefore, I would make you aware that Symmachia has dispatched five fast-attack vessels, which are on an intercept course for this transport. One docks in moments. We both know who they pursue."

"How are we to believe your words when you come like this?" Ixion said, motioning to the Brethren gathered.

"Says the Stalker with a half-dozen machitis at his back. Tell me—think you I would come unprepared?" Marco said, glancing around to the warriors. He nodded to Rico, who adjusted his vambrace and threw a holo image of the radar scans with the inbound ships. "Corvettes. Fast attack and each carrying a complement of six to nine. Some, if not all, are likely to be Eidolon."

Murmurs rippled through the crowd.

"Droserans—Kalonicans have lost much since the Stratios slaughter," Roman spoke loudly. "Are you prepared to lose more? And for what?"

"She belongs to us."

"That is not in question."

Bazyli was unyielding. "We protect our own."

Marco understood the mettle of the warriors and where Kersei had gotten her stubbornness. He lifted his head, searching the throng for her thick black hair. "Mistress Kersei," he called out when he failed to locate her but could sense her signature. "You have been in the custody of Symmachian warmongers once. Would you prefer to remain here to be captured by Eidolon or Marines, who will no doubt return you to Captain Baric? Or would you be safely delivered to Iereania by me and my brethren?"

"You are good with words," Bazyli muttered. "She will not go."

"Strategy has always been his strong suit," Rico said. "Me not so much. Hand the girl over and no blood will be spilled."

Tension ratcheted. A scent flew from behind.

"Defend!" Marco stepped into a fighting stance.

"Stop!" Kersei's voice erupted amid the warriors. "There is no need for this."

"Get her out of sight!" Bazyli's face turned deep red against his blonde hair.

"The girl has the sense to come peacefully," Marco said. "Release her to us, and this will be over."

Galen inched forward, his brow set in a deep furrow. "We will *not*."

Rolling his shoulders, Marco lowered his chin and glared at the warrior. "You are outclassed and outbattled, pup. Stand down before I am made to embarrass you."

Galen lunged.

Stealthily, Marco glided forward. Hooked Galen's arm. Swung him around. Yanked him back against his chest, snapping Galen's short blade to his neck in a strangle hold. "Cease!" he growled into the man's ear. "Or I will end you."

"Stop! Please!" Kersei shoved through the crowd, her panic flooding Marco.

"No, Mistress." Several tried to stop her, but she wrenched free.

Reaching the front, Kersei stilled behind Ixion and Bazyli as her gaze hit Marco's. Grief warred with anger. "Please, Marco." Her use of his name was intentional. Plying his weakness—her—against him. She stepped into the open and held up her palms. "I am here. There is no need for anyone to be harmed."

"Kersei!" Ixion shouldered closer to her, challenge in his posture. "You will not take her, Kynigos."

She turned to the man. "I must do this, Ixion. There can be no more lives lost when I have the chance to prevent it. Had I the opportunity to save my father and mother, my sisters, our royal family—I would have readily laid down my life." She raised her head. "The choice this day is mine. To prevent needless bloodshed. I make this choice willingly."

Reluctance silenced the Stalker.

Without hesitation, Marco pushed Galen into the machitis and held out his hand to Kersei.

She swallowed, flexed her fingers, then slowly advanced toward Marco. The air reeked of anger and disgust from the warriors. He took her arm.

Galen dove forward again.

Quickly, Marco tucked Kersei behind himself and squared off. Rico's and Roman's shoulders hit his, forming a barrier. Sealing her off from the Xanthus. A scowl dug into Galen's face as it washed crimson, gaze darting around, as if he might attempt to challenge them. Apparently, he wasn't as big a fool as that.

"She is a wise and fearless woman," Marco announced, his gaze sweeping back to Bazyli, then Ixion. "She will not be harmed."

"Swear it," Bazyli growled.

Ixion held his ground. "On your honor."

Marco clapped a fist to his chest. "On my honor." Already he felt his brethren drawing away from the machitis. He walked backward several steps, watching the warriors. Watching the pup, who would do something foolish. His scent reeked of it.

Kersei hesitated as the others progressed. Marco came up beside her as she glanced again to her clan. Sadness was the most wretched of scents, next to betrayal. When they reached the corner junction, Marco took another step toward the turn.

Rage blasted him. Thirst for blood.

He pivoted back.

"Galen, no!"

The pup was a howling blur.

Marco deflected the first strike. The second—catching his fist, twisting it up and away, leaving the warrior open. Marco drove a knifehand into the man's side. Then an uppercut to his face. Slammed him to the ground and punched again. The crack of his cartilage and the spurt of blood made Marco still.

Shouts went up, fury in the air.

"Fool. I warned you." Marco grunted at the moaning and disoriented machitis. "Be grateful I do not finish this as is my right." He thumped the man's chest with a light punch that knocked the air from his lungs.

Bazyli and Ixion ordered the machitis to stand down.

Marco rose. Glanced at the men. Shook his head.

Bazyli helped his brother from the floor. "He only seeks to protect her."

"She is no longer his concern."

They towered over her like the cliffs of Kardia. Black attire, black cloaks lined in blue—save the older hunter with a red lining and gold cords across his chest. They were forbidding and frightening as they hurried through the passages, people and ship's security diving out of the way.

"How is Galen?" Kersei asked as they banked down another passage.

"Bloody and humiliated," Marco said.

She eyed him, surprised at his curt tone and the unaffected way he described what he'd done to the machitis.

"Coming freely," he said to her, "I thank you."

"It wasn't for you," she bit out. "What I did was for my people, their safety."

"Admirable."

"I need not your flattery."

The older hunter glanced over his shoulder at her, then Marco, and she felt clearly his disapproval. She felt exposed, naked before these men, knowing they could unravel what she kept close to heart—the anger at Marco over his betrayal. The hurt. The fear. They smelled it all. No need for pretense.

"Form up!" the elder suddenly barked.

The hunters circled Kersei, backs to her. With their draping it felt more like a black pit. How surreal to watch them, see their gazes uniformly fixed on the corridor to her left though no one spoke nor a threat presented.

Soon there came the rush of feet.

"What grave do you dig this day, iereas?" a hunter asked.

Through a small gap between broad shoulders, Kersei saw the aged iereas and his apprentice. "Ypiretis."

"I beg your mercy, Master Kynigos," the priest said, huffing to a stop. "But you must come this way." He indicated back the direction from which he'd come. "They are here already."

The master hunter glanced at Marco, who nodded and reached toward Kersei. He then considered the iereas. "Show Rico where you saw the—"

"No, no." Ypiretis blanched. "That would be a terrible mistake. The mistress must be removed to safety immediately. It would be dire for them to capture her again."

"I agree." She thought of that horrific chamber. Forced to see her loved ones die over and over. Not to mention that person-thing on the metal flower.

"Mistress, your fear is rank." The master hunter was not even looking at her.

"So is what they did to me," she replied shakily.

Without so much as a nod, he shifted his formidable presence away. "Split up," he said, then faced Marco. "You know another route to the bay?"

"I know all routes."

The master hunter accepted the answer as if anticipated. "Go with Rico, take the girl. I'll distract the Symmachians. Get her off the ship, even if means without me."

Inclining his head, Marco eased back. Held a hand out for Kersei to move past him.

"To the Decree, Marco."

"And the hunt." Something twitched through Marco's expression.

"For honor," they said in unison.

Marco nudged her after Ypiretis, the other hunter sidling up beside Kersei. Her training, her father's lessons, warned her to stop at each corner, but the hunters barely slowed. She guessed they were trusting their noses, and she trusted Marco. Somehow. Though she hated that she did, her life depended on that trust right now.

"There can be nothing between us."

"Kersei."

"What?" she snapped, the burn of his crushing words too near, too fresh.

Marco glanced at her, brow knotted. "You're slowing."

She started, amazed at how grief had commanded her body away from him. Though she hustled a step, she glowered for good measure.

His hand came to the small of her back, guiding through a set of doors. "Be angry, hate me later. For now, focus on getting out of here."

Surprise leapt through her, along with irritation that he could know her so well.

"We've lost the priest and apprentice," Rico said.

Kersei frowned, looking ahead and wondering how that had happened.

The other hunter shoved into her with a hissed, "Back!" He forced them from a juncture.

Marco whirled, catching her arms and pushing her into a tight alcove with plants. Grabbing his arms for balance, she cringed, alarmed. Scared. His chest pressed into her face as he pinned her. "Quiet," he breathed and his pale blue eyes held hers until she acknowledged she understood. Palming the wall on either side of her, he tucked his chin and peered to the side at Rico.

Mercies, she hated this—the fear that Baric would recapture her, the uncanny ability of the Kynigos that defied typical skills, and that she must be here, cornered by the man she most wanted to detest right now. They had not been this close since the terraria. The change in him, the dissonance between man and hunter left her rattled. Feeling closed in—so much like the chamber—she shoved her gaze the other side, only to find a bulkhead there.

Breath struggled through her lungs.

Reluctantly, yet drawn like a magnet, she turned to him. The length of his hair, the sides dangling along his face and the back at his nape. Sideburns arced down to his jaw shadowed by light growth. His sigil. His eyes— evocative how they telegraphed so much. With his brow furled over them, he was so intense he stopped people in their tracks. He really used that sigil and his cloak to his benefit.

"Wait here," Rico said. "I'll scout ahead, try to find the iereas."

Marco nodded but did not release her or move.

Beneath his many layers … he was beautiful. And kind. When he laughed—his eyebrows lifted and brightened his eyes. Like a storm rolling away from Kardia and the sun emerging from the shelter of dark clouds. Much like her life. He had been that warm sun on her parched soul. And though she resented that he hunted her, that he had not told her, she understood the laws. Maybe. She wished he had let her in on it, but then he would have broken the Code. And that would not be honorable. She could grant mercy for that. Easily. The realization shook her, for she had harbored her anger for weeks when Darius had wronged her.

By the Mercies—what feelings she had for him! Was it love? An absurd thought considering they had known each other but weeks.

Marco shifted, lowering his gaze to her shoulder, which sent darts through her stomach. Because of course she had to think about the way he'd kissed her in the terraria. And just as she'd remembered, those brows lifted and gave her a glimpse once more of the sun. A smile teased the edge of his eyes and lips. Those generous lips.

Stop thinking about his lips! Kersei held her breath as his crystal-blue eyes darted around her face, as if looking for something. Hunter. He's a hunter. *Hunting me!* "What?" She'd meant it to sound annoyed, but it only squeaked out.

His hand slid to her waist and Kersei felt her body respond, her spine straighten. Her heart went erratic. Was she just a hunt to him? Just prey he found attractive, amusing? No, it was more. Had to be. It shamed her how much she wanted it to be more.

"You make it … difficult to concentrate." There was no admonishment in his husky words.

But they brought swift realization. "You detected what I thought?" She glanced to his mouth where a smile flickered.

His touch firmed against her hip. "Not thoughts. Scents."

She wondered if he would kiss her again—by the Fires, she wanted him to. Instead, he closed his eyes for a second, thinned his lips, and turned his head again to the corridor.

Right. The hunt. Of course. *You fool!* Kersei shuddered out a breath.

No. Not the hunt—Symmachians.

She cursed her idiocy. But that was his fault. He didn't have to be so … glorious. His hand hadn't left her hip, which speared heat through her stomach and up her into her chest. Made her pulse flicker like a candle beneath a breeze as she again studied his profile.

"Kersei," he hissed. Leaning his head down. "You must …" His eyes closed and he heaved a breath. "Redirect your thoughts. Please."

"Why?"

He turned, his nose against her cheek. "I cannot …" He drew her hip toward him, and she drew in a quick breath. She felt the prickle of his stubble at the corner of her mouth.

She struggled in vain to remember her anger at him. That she did not like him. Because she did. More than she had anyone before him. Never had she felt so alive than with Marco. And the way he crowded her, yet did not take his pleasure somehow proved … excruciating. Especially the kiss that lingered at the corner of her mouth, neither of them moving. She gripped his sleeve, seeking strength to avoid being swept away.

"Do you believe … what I feel for you"—his breath was hot against hers as he tasted another kiss—"is real. That … there is … no other."

She swallowed, her face hot. Nodded.

His hand slid to the small of her back, pulling her against himself. Swept her lips. Kissed her again. Growled. "This is not the time. Rico—" But his mouth was on hers again.

Slipping his hand to her waist had been for strength. To steady himself against the torrent of her emotions. Instead, it had undone him. Because beneath his thumb, he felt the involuntary contraction of her stomach in response to his touch.

Hand at her nape, he deepened the kiss, sinking into the drowning signature that so perfectly overlapped his. Nestled quietly in the shadows of a past he no longer remembered. "You fill a long-empty void in me." After a kiss on her forehead, he palmed the wall, told himself not to touch her again, to focus on protecting her.

Something shot through him, stabbing reality back into his faculties. Awareness. Alarm. He jerked back. Attack!

A shape flew at him. He flung his arm up, deflecting a punch. Coiled their arms. Hooked the man's shoulder and slipped under and behind him. Holding tight, he rammed the man's head into the bulkhead.

Kersei darted aside.

The man flipped—he'd been one of Marco's attackers in the arena—and sneered. Then whipped around, catching Kersei behind the neck.

Marco stilled, rage thrumming through him, seeing her in danger.

To his shock, Kersei grabbed the man's arm, then dropped her legs out from under herself, effectively slipping free. With the man clear, Marco drove a hard right into his face. Head snapped back. Whacked on the corner. The man slumped to the ground.

Kersei flew into his arms.

"Well done," he said. At the incoming signature of his advocate, he put distance between them where it belonged. The scent lingering in the air from him and Kersei was too potent to miss, so he knew chastisement would come. "What did you find?"

Rico glanced between them and huffed his disapproval. "Made it to the bay. The Symmachian corvette is docked two bays down from the scout."

Too close. Marco wanted to curse.

"We'll have to fight our way in. Once they spot our scout, they're going to try to lock it down," Rico said.

"We must move fast or more Eidolon will be aboard." Marco eyed his advocate.

"Entering that bay together ..." Rico shook his head.

"Mayhap split up as we approach."

"Aye," Rico said. "I'll come in by the main bay doors and draw their attention. The *Centaur* is powering up via remote start so you don't lose time. Come up from the stern. You know a route?"

Marco hesitated.

"The terraria," Kersei offered. "If we cut through there it'll bring us to the back."

"On the starboard side, aye," Marco agreed, then nodded to his advocate. "At the scout."

They clasped forearms then broke apart, heading in opposite directions. Marco motioned to Kersei, who skipped to stay up. They hurried through the terraria.

On the other side, he reached for the door handle and paused. Angled his head down. What … what was that? Something his receptors … A disorienting scent. One he could not align with …

"What's wrong?" Kersei breathed, her scent worried.

Marco shook his head. "Nothing."

"Tell me," she insisted.

"Trust me." He smirked, then eased the door open. Checked the passage, which ended a dozen meters to his right. "Come on."

They hurried through several hatches before seeing placards for the docking bay. Again that strange … scent. Which wasn't a scent. It was … He cocked his head to the side, closing his receptors to everything else. Homing in on that odd thread hanging in the air. Like an icy-hot current. Yet not.

Kersei caught his arm. "You're doing it again. What's wrong?"

"I don't know," he admitted. "It's … strange."

"Is it trouble? An ambush?"

Marco frowned. "Why would you say that?"

"I don't know. I just …"

Considering her words, he looked at the end of the corridor where a large opening gaped. The docking bay. Its bustling center was littered with maintenance personnel working on a shuttle's rear thruster. Two of the eight bay doors were open, a transparent membrane over each the only thing keeping the atmosphere from venting from the whole bay. The Symmachian corvette lurked in the sixth. Two berths from the scout.

Taking Kersei's hand, he edged closer, sliding along the bulkhead as they approached. Something definitely wasn't right. Where were Roman and Rico? He went for his dagger. Guided Kersei's hand to a strap on his armored vest. "Hold on. Stay close."

Her fingers dug around the leather band.

As he was about to step over the lip of the hatch, a shout sailed through the bay. Workers turned to the main bay door, where Rico sprinted across, two red-armored Symmachians in pursuit. Eidolon.

Sheathing the dagger, Marco lifted the webbing gun and swiped it to pulse. His gaze carefully traipsed the interior, ships, cargo … He stalked on, pulling Kersei with him. Weapon ready, he scanned. Wished for one of those helmets with heads-up readouts. But hunters opted against those because they diluted and sanitized scents. He startled as Ypiretis and the boy emerged from behind a crate.

"Ypiretis," Kersei said, as the priest's eyes widened at the sight of them.

"Easy," Marco warned, but Kersei surged toward the iereas. Marco tried to stop her, that strange—vacuous—thread exploding. He spun around, searching for the threat.

A blur of red dropped from above.

At the same tick Marco registered the threat, he shoved backward, into Kersei. "Run!"

The red-armored Eidolon collided with him. Knocked Marco reeling. He thumped his head. Steel vibrated beneath him at the clanging impact of the Eidolon's grav boots.

Shouts erupted.

Marco flared out his receptors. Assured Kersei was moving, he rolled, aiming his weapon at the red armor. Fired.

The pulse round thudded against the armor, then scattered over its surface. The Eidolon wavered. Didn't stumble. His accursed boots magnetized him to the hull.

Whipping to his feet, Marco noted the gold epaulet. This was a commander. He slid his webbing gun to hot. Fired. The shot sparked off the suit.

The commander rushed him, firing.

The blast hit Marco's gut, the impact stinging. The scent of singed rhinnock burned his nostrils. His knees buckled at the pain. He stumbled, but knew if he went down, he was dead. And Kersei taken. The commander's shoulder rammed his gut. They went back. Marco tried to twist out of the fall, but the commander locked his waist. Took him down. Air punched from his lungs.

"Mistress!" Ypiretis frantically waved her to himself.

Kersei fumbled toward the scout, tripping over her legs because she kept straining to see Marco. The Symmachian was on him. Punching him. The sight slowed her, then threw her back to help. She started toward him.

"No, Mistress!" Ypiretis caught her. "You cannot. We must get to the shuttle. Hurry."

"But—"

"He is a hunter, trained for this," Ypiretis said, urging her toward the thrumming ship. "If you go to him, his attention and efforts will be divided. You could be injured or get him injured."

"Master," his apprentice said, nodding to the front. "More."

Three additional Eidolon entered the shuttle bay. When they saw Marco's scuffle with one of their own, they sprinted to intervene. One helmeted head swiveled toward her. Kersei froze, then realized the trouble she'd aroused.

"Go!" Ypiretis shoved her around. "In now!"

She darted up the steel ramp, stealing a last-tick glance at Marco. Worrying she was doing the wrong thing. "Four to one. He can't—"

Ypiretis gave her an unceremonious shove.

Kersei tripped into the narrow opening but righted herself and kept moving. Duncan motioned her further into the steel embrace. The entry opened into a juncture. To her left, the same steel that led to large machines and various compartments. Straight ahead, another narrow passage with a door on either side. To her right large systems—engines? It was steamy and … mechanical. Stairs launched on both sides, arching over the largest caged system.

"Up," Ypiretis said.

Shouts. Shots. Grating deafening alarms made the small ship vibrate. Ate her courage. "What's happening?" she asked, gulping fear. "We need to help him!"

"There," Duncan said.

Kersei looked to a small wall-mounted screen that showed Marco—outside. He'd broken free from the Symmachian who had tackled him. Now, he stood behind a large crate, dodging shots from the other Eidolon. He fired a few rounds, then flung himself around. Swung up onto the crates.

"Is he crazy?" Duncan exclaimed. "They have a perfect bead on him!"

But Marco leapt into the air, vanishing from the screen.

Thud.

"He's on the ship," Duncan said with a laugh.

Hearing more thudding, Kersei's gaze rose to the ceiling. Heard sparks and angry shouts out in the bay.

Ypiretis shuffled into her. A loud clang reverberated through the ship as the bay door clanked shut.

"No!" Spinning, Kersei lunged at it. "You can't—why? He's still out there!"

He raised his hands. "It was not me, child."

Clanging abovedeck drew their attention. "Stairs!" She raced up the steel steps, the noise carrying loudly. Overhead, a panel jerked open in the ceiling.

She gasped and leapt away, heart hammering.

Booted feet appeared. With a growl, Marco dropped in front of her. He scrambled, reaching for the hatch. "Augh!" he clawed at his arm guards. "Shut it," he said, grabbing at his armor.

Lunging around her, Duncan made quick work of the hatch. Cranked it locked.

Kersei watched Marco, who frantically worked on his armor. "What's wrong?"

"Nanite pellets," he said. "Symmachians hit my vambrace. The buggers are eating through it." He nodded to the wall. "Behind you. The paddle. Quick."

She spun, but everything looked the same. Metal and square or rectangular. "I—"

"Here." Duncan plucked something from a small well. Threw it at her.

Whirling, she handed it off to Marco, who placed it against his arm. That was when she saw an ever-widening hole in the thick rhinnock armor. How was that possible? It ate through hide that was impossible to damage. Then through fabric. His flesh appeared.

"What in the boils …?"

Blood slid out amid Marco's growl. He twisted away, holding his arm against his legs as he angled the paddle. Pressed his thumb to a spot. A whine filled the air. Then a thump.

When Kersei looked back, Marco was rushing toward a steel wall. It whisked out of the way, allowing him to enter a compartment. She followed, amazed as he reached another door with only a few steps. Eyeing that much smaller space, she saw windows. A lot of panels and lights. Awe drew her closer.

"Snap in!" Marco flipped switches as he dropped into a seat. "This will be rough."

Snap in?

Ypiretis pointed her back and to her right, where she saw two rows of seats facing each other. She sat, distracted. Worried about Marco. "Isn't he inj—"

As soon as her weight hit the cushion, straps snaked out of the wall and hooked her shoulders. She sucked in a breath as a wider one encircled her waist. She looked to Ypiretis, who was reaching toward something that lowered from the ceiling. She glanced up and saw one above her. Following his lead, she pulled a steel harness over her shoulders and with it came a helmet and a clear visor. Something clamped her throat and she started to panic, feeling strangled—reminded of the collar Baric put on her. "No!" A hiss sounded in her ears. She whimpered, gripping the collar.

"Oxygen." The word sounded tinny, but it came with Ypiretis's reassuring gaze. "That sound means you have a solid seal."

Kersei felt her blood rushing like rapids. "Why do I need a seal?"

"For the launch sequence," he said. "And for safety."

"Undocked and heading for the doors," came Marco's deep, gravelly voice in her helmet.

Not sure what to do with her hands, she held the metal straps that cut into her clavicle. "Why will it be rough?"

"Because the Symmachians will not so easily surrender you."

"They'll shoot at this ship?"

"Look!" Duncan pointed at a screen showing the interior of the *Kleopatra*'s bay. "They're closing the bay doors."

Feeling trapped all over again, Kersei stared at the narrowing gap in the *Kleopatra*'s sides. "You sound so calm," Kersei balked. "We could be killed!"

"Have you so little faith in our pilot and the Ancient?"

In the latter, yes. In the former … no. But he was one man against *Symmachians*. Walls rattled. The floor vibrated. The ground seemed to sway—no! That was them. The shuttle was lifting.

"We have company," Marco said, his voice flat. "Prepare for hard burn."

"What …" The air in her helmet felt so cold. "What does that mean?"

"It will feel like a rhinnock sat our chests," Duncan said.

In earnest, Kersei did not like this. She gripped the metal harness tighter.

Ancient, help me!

The pressure on her body grew. Vibrated her as if someone shook her in a jar. Jerked her to the side as the ship tilted, wobbled, leveled out. Would the ship … explode? Come apart? What would she do then? This helmet was the only way she could breathe.

I'm going to die. She couldn't draw breath. Her chest—it hurt. Crushed. *I can't breathe.* She whimpered, tears sliding down her face. She would die here. She would. After all that. After losing—

"Kersei."

Father and Ma'ma. Lexina and Adara. Darius. She never felt for him what she felt for Marco—at least she had known that before she died.

I can't breathe. I can't breathe. It hurts!

"Kersei."

She blinked, expecting to see him in front of her, but he wasn't there. Aye, the helmet. "Marco?"

"It's okay."

"I can't breathe. It hurts."

"Easy, easy. It's … okay." His words took effort. No doubt he was suffering the same pain. But he was helping her. Talking to her.

"No … hurts."

"I'm here."

Her vision was closing in like a curtain drawing shut. "… s-scared."

"I'm … here."

At least they would die together. "I … love—"

Her world went black.

"They escaped."

Baric growled. "How did a Kynigos scout outmaneuver a Symmachian corvette?"

"Unknown, sir."

"Wave Two-one-five—"

"We've lost comms with Commander Deken."

Slamming a fist against a bulkhead, he cursed. "Find that scout!" He stormed back to the officers' quarters and entered his multi-room accommodations.

Two men rose as he entered, one wearing a blood-red robe, the other more relaxed as the downworlder he was. A third man did not rise but turned in the hover chair that supported his scarred frame.

"Why is the only effective person in this fight not on our side?" Baric groused as he stalked across the room to a cabinet, pulled out a snifter and an amber bottle. Uncapped it.

"He escaped?"

Dumping liquor into the snifter, he nodded. "With the girl."

"You swore to bring her back," balked the man in the hover chair.

Baric snorted. Tossed the liquid back. Swallowed hard. Then eyed the badly scarred man. The medical chair made him seem even more thin and pathetic. "I made you no promises."

"He did," the man pointed to the blue-and-red robed iereas.

"Ah, well." Baric lifted a shoulder in a shrug and arched an eyebrow. "Theon is not my problem."

"What are you doing to get her back?" Theon asked, his voice bland.

The door chimed.

"Enter!"

The door hissed open and in walked a galaxy. The admiral's orbs glittered beneath the office lights.

"Admiral Krissos." Baric slid the glass aside, knowing it was still frowned upon, though he had long ago shifted from a ship captain to … something else. He wasn't even sure what to call it.

"Take us to the *Chryzanthe*," Krissos said. "I've waved the Khatriza, and she says it's ready."

"I'm sorry," Baric said with a disbelieving laugh. "We just lost our only—"

"We can use it to jump to Iereania. Beat them there."

A sneer started in some dark corner of Baric's heart. "I want the girl."

"No!" The whiner struggled from the chair. "You *promised*, Theon. Promised her life for … "

"Rest, or you will not be strong enough to see this through." The high lord glanced at Krissos. "If we want Drosero, we must ensure the girl returns to him."

"No," Baric countered.

"Stand down, Captain," Krissos said. "You have the station. Your name will be written in the stars. That's what you wanted—a legacy. You'll have it. *Chryzanthe* goes online and you will be the golden child of Symmachia and Kedalion." The rear admiral moved to the sandy-haired whiner. Leaned into his face. "Realize that if this succeeds, we *own* you. Remember *your* promise."

Arrogance pushed up a scarred chin. "It's past time for Drosero to take flight."

"And you will answer to me," grumbled the thick-chested downworlder.

The whiner curled his lip. "You killed your own brother and nieces. When Kersei sees you, think not that she will grant you mercy."

"No," he said, "but I kept her alive because I knew she was the price."

"The price for what?"

"Your soul, Prince Darius."

Baric laughed, lifting his glass. "If I had known blowing up a clan hall would net us an entire planet to secure an intergalactic way station, I would've done it long ago." He tapped his thumper.

"Yes, Captain?"

"Set course for the *Chryzanthe*."

PSK CENTAUR

After the hard burn, Marco plotted their course and engaged the autopilot and artificial gravity. He freed the harnesses and leapt from the chair.

Darted to the midsection jumpseats, heart pounding. Kersei had stopped responding, as had her seat vitals.

Ypiretis was already rousing the apprentice.

Kersei was not. Blood dripped from her nose. He swiped her harness's control panel. Slid his hand to her neck as the dome released and the harness withdrew into the bulkhead. When she sagged, he laid her across the second seat. "Kersei?"

Nosebleeds were common, so he hoped that was the extent of this.

"Is she breathing?" Ypiretis asked.

"Aye," Marco said, scanning her. "Kersei, can you hear me?"

Lifting her from the seats, he could not help but remember the day in the courtyard on Cenon. He hurried down the gangway to the stairs, hearing the thud and detecting anxious scents of the Iereans who followed him. He swept into the medbay on the right. Laid her on the table. Activated the shield, which slid over her. Tapped his code in. Gel cocooned her body as the scanner started. He stepped back, planted his hands on his tactical belt.

"What's wrong with her?" Duncan asked.

"Nothing," Marco said, "I hope. But the scanner will confirm that."

"She's probably never experienced a high-g burn," Ypiretis offered, then glanced up and down Marco. "Maybe you should clean yourself up and put on a new tunic."

Marco scowled, then saw his arm. The nanites had eaten through the vambrace, the leather, his shirt … revealing his mark. He started. "Did she see it?"

"I don't believe so."

His gaze again hit the tube, unwilling to leave her.

"I will stay." Ypiretis's scent was too conciliatory. "The scans take a while, yes?"

Marco nodded.

"Then go clean up."

Recalling Kyros's admonishment not to tell her of their matching brands, unwilling to have her again angry with him, Marco headed abovedeck, grabbed clean clothes, then stepped into the sanitizing spray. He applied burn cream to his arm, snorting when he saw that the nanite pellet hadn't affected the mark. In the least. "Accursed thing."

With a new vambrace and clean tunic, he headed below and heard soft talking. He entered the medbay. Kersei was no longer ensconced in the scanner. The shield had gone down, and she'd drawn her feet onto the mattress. Held a hand to her head. The blood had been cleaned.

Marco went to her side, eyeing the scan report "How are you?"

She lowered her hand and groaned, covering her eyes again. "Duncan said I would feel like a rhinnock sat on my chest, but I think it got my head instead."

Marco smiled. "A headache is normal."

"You have one?"

"No," he conceded. "But—"

"He's not normal," Duncan said.

Marco arched an eyebrow at the apprentice. "I fly a lot," he explained. "Comes with hunting." He keyed the console, the medical table lowering. "Can you sit?"

She blinked, then tried to pull herself up.

Marco offered his left hand for an assist. "Your abdomen might feel as if someone punched you."

Grimacing, she agreed and allowed his help. Eyes closed, she went rigid, still. Hugging his arm to her chest. He doubted she realized what she was doing. Or her last words before she'd passed out. Or what that did to him. "Nauseated?"

"Mm-hm."

"Wait it out," he said, staying close. Glad she was comfortable like this. "No hurry." He angled in, his concern naturally for her safety, that she could tip over. If she did, she'd slump into his chest. It was a good excuse to maintain close proximity.

For several long minutes, she sat with her back to the priest and apprentice. Her shoulder nestled against his. Slowly lowered her hand—and his—to her lap. But she didn't let go. Not because of sickness. Her scent had shifted from the tumult of nausea flicking to concern. Worry. To … yearning.

So she *did* recall her words before she lost consciousness.

With her free hand, she traced his vambrace, and a new worry presented itself—had she seen the mark?

Ypiretis excused himself, his scent thick. Seasick, it seemed. But another scent lingered, putrid like garlic. The apprentice would do well to guard his jealousies.

"Duncan," Marco said. "Abovedeck—the galley. Get the mistress some water."

Reluctantly, the apprentice nodded.

"Thank you, Duncan," Kersei called to him.

The boy hesitated, glanced at her, then Marco, before hurrying away.

"He's jealous."

She smiled as she studied the floor. "There is plenty to be jealous of." She brought her gaze to his. "What I said … did he hear it?"

"I closed their comms during the hard burn to talk you down."

She seemed relieved. Then shifted and angled to slide off the tube. He eased away to give her room. On her feet, she remained braced at his side. "I was angry when I found out you were hunting me."

"You were rightly hurt."

Another flicker of a smile. "Yes, very."

He slid a hand around her neck, thumb sweeping her cheek and bringing her gaze back to his. "I regret the hurt I caused you. But what I … this … you …" Why could he not find the words?

She held his wrist. "Me, too."

From the shadows around the engine room, Ypiretis ached for Marco and Kersei to have the happy ending they were chasing. So well matched. He with his implacable character and experience standing over her diminutive form. Two halves of one whole, they fit together so perfectly. When Marco leaned down to kiss her, a gesture she welcomed, Ypiretis granted them privacy.

They were both strong. Both endured much. Sadly, that paled to what lay ahead. To the betrayals they would suffer. Bloodshed they must witness.

From the stairs, Duncan landed on deck and stopped short, staring into the medical bay. "*Blast* him."

"Mind your tongue," Ypiretis said gently. "Let's leave them—"

"We should interrupt," Duncan objected. "It's not right or appropriate. On her world, it's considered taking her virtue."

"We are not on her world. This world, I fear, is frighteningly new."

"She's too good for him!"

Ypiretis led the apprentice back up the stairs. "Mayhap, but she would not agree."

"What does she see in him anyway? He's all dark and scowl-y."

He laughed as they entered the galley. "They call that brooding, and most women find it irresistible."

PSK *CENTAUR*

On the small bridge Marco studied the route. Thought ahead to Iereania. What would happen there. The Decree ordered him to bring her to the temple. He hadn't realized before, but the Decree had been genius. Conniving Iereans. Having Marco bring her ensured they were both there at the appointed time.

He rotated his forearm, as if he could see through the vambrace. Was this why he felt so drawn to her? Why he could not think when he looked into her eyes? Whatever would happen on Iereania, he felt his days as a hunter were drawing to a close. If he wanted to pursue anything with Kersei, they must.

After the temple, she would return to Drosero with the Xanthus. He could go with her.

Me among downworlders? He would be bored. His sigil alone would earn him rejection.

Revocation.

The very word seared his heart. Separation from the only family he knew. Cut off from honor. A steep price. Was she worth it?

How could he even ask? Everything about her demanded his attention, his loyalty. Her scent lured him like no other. Coiled around his common sense and strangled it. He'd wanted to punch Duncan when the boy had spotted them kissing. His jealousy was a strong, almost painful note.

"You must tell her."

Surprised, Marco glanced to the side. Then back to the instrumentation. "I was told she must not be made aware until we are on Iereania."

"And you hate that."

"I have already hurt her too much." Marco gave a slow shake of his head. Then another. "I never want to smell that again." He watched the iereas drift closer and lower onto the only other seat on the bridge. "You saw us belowdecks, yet said nothing."

Ypiretis held his gaze.

That look ... "What do you grieve, Iereas?"

"There is nothing you miss, is there?"

He'd missed the ambush in hangar bay somehow. And it bugged him.

"What lies ahead of you is daunting. I will not begrudge you happiness when I know it may be the last semblance of it for you both for a very long time."

"You don't get invited to many parties, do you?" Though Marco teased, the words fastened onto his soul. Hung with warning and resonated so clearly, he knew the priest did not lie. He stared at the panels. "I've always felt life has been too easy."

"Meaning?"

Marco pursed his lips and tried to shrug off the smothering heaviness. "I was the prize pupil at the Citadel. Excelled at everything. Far exceeded goals and expectations. Hunting?" He scrunched his face. "Thrilling but easy."

"Was it hard being removed from your family, being made to start over in a strange place with nobody you knew?"

"It was a relief," Marco said, surprisingly able to recall the first day he'd entered the Citadel. "I no longer had to hide what I was nor pretend that I couldn't smell betrayal. I embraced it. The Brethren became my family."

"But what of your parents?"

Now he frowned. "What of them?" But he noticed they were not alone and glanced to where Duncan stood just outside the bridge, holding the damaged vambrace. He scowled at the boy. "What are you doing with that?"

"It's ruined, right?" Duncan shrugged. "Can I have it?"

That was the last thing Marco expected.

"Duncan, you cannot—"

"What need have you for it?" Marco challenged. "You are an iereas."

"Actually," he said with a chipper shrug. "I'm not."

"Duncan!"

What game did these two play at? Marco vacillated between irritation toward the pup for going through his things, and ambivalence—the vambrace had been destroyed in the fight with the Symmachians. The paddle had fried its circuits. It was of no use.

Duncan put it on his arm, and with it came a gleam that sent an eager, desperate scent into the bridge. He admired Marco and the hunters. It's why he wanted the vambrace. "Look," he said. "I could stitch some hide over the hole …"

Eyeing the vambrace, Marco could well recall as a youth how much it had inspired him. "I trained tirelessly for years to earn the right to wear a vambrace," he said. "Have you earned that?"

The boy stilled. "I-I can. I will!"

"Duncan, you are not a hunter," Ypiretis chided.

"I can be!"

No, he couldn't. Not without the *anaktesios* gifting.

"Duncan, to be a hunter, you must be able to detect things that are not readily noticeable to others," Ypiretis explained the way he would with a much younger child.

"I notice things," Duncan objected. "I noticed he was kissing her before you did."

Ypiretis lowered his head in a sardonic smile.

Marco began to understand … the boy wasn't quite functioning at full capacity. What ailment robbed him of his maturity and sense? "It is of no harm," he said. "Let me remove the channeler." He held his hand out.

Duncan worked to remove it.

And that's when Marco saw it. "Duncan." In the upper section of the vambrace there was a slit pouch. Peeking out— "Give it to me."

"I can't un—"

Marco caught his arm. His fingers worked the buckles with familiarity and speed. He pinched the small thing and drew it out. Round but set in an alloy frame, it was the size of his fingernail.

"What is it?" Ypiretis asked.

"A data dot." Much bigger than necessary, the housing simply made it easier to be handled. He dropped it into the *Centaur*'s dot tray. The system sprang to life and threw a grainy holoimage before him.

"Tigo."

At the sound of Kersei's voice, Marco glanced back. "You know him?"

"That's Commander Tigo Deken. He's how I got to Cenon." She came closer, her scent wafting with admiration, annoyingly strong. "He and his team also saw Ixion taking me off the planet but did nothing. Where did you get this?"

Marco stepped back and folded his arms—so he could see the vid better. "It was in my vambrace. He must've been the Eidolon who jumped me in the bay. Slipped it into my vambrace, I suppose." His mind whiplashed through the encounter. "He had more than one chance to put new holes in me but didn't. Then I incapacitated him and fled." It was the second time the commander had secreted something to him—the first, Kersei's necklace. Now this.

Was it because he had feelings for Kersei?

"Is he just talking quietly?" Duncan asked.

"The nanite pellet might've corrupted the dot." Marco adjusted the settings.

"*—ope you—something—can't …*"

Marco fiddled. Lifted the dot out, eyed it, then set it down again. Still the same glitching.

"I can." The apprentice pointed to the console.

With a rueful smile, Ypiretis nodded. "Duncan is extremely proficient with technology."

Hesitating, Marco glanced between apprentice and iereas. He removed himself to Kersei's side with a nod to the pup. "Go ahead."

Duncan slid into the chair and his fingers splayed over the instrumentation. "You think it was Tigo who tackled you?" she asked quietly.

"I don't know. He didn't really hold back, but he also didn't take opportunities." He snorted. "Should've known it was too easy to stun him. I think he's also the one who gave me your necklace."

Kersei started at that. "How did he get it?"

"The nanites did destroy some," Duncan said. "But here—"

"—let's hope I get this right. Contained in this dot is intelligence that is devastating to Symmachia. I can't explain what you'll see in this recording because I don't understand it myself. It is imperative you get this to your ... I choose you? Because you act with honor, something my superiors seem to have forgotten. Command is violently searching for Kersei for one reason: to stop her from talking about what she saw on the Chryzanthe."

Marco glanced at Kersei.

But she was pale. Her scent filled with dread.

"For the sake of time, I need to play the video while I talk." Footage of a series of concentric rings braced by massive supports.

"That's where I saw the other hunter," Kersei said.

At her bitter roiling efflux, Marco wrapped an arm around her shoulder.

"...what TSC calls a satellite is not a satellite. The Chryzanthe is an above-top-secret installation designed to bring about wormhole travel." He sighed. "And I've recently ... discovered"—he looked away, grieved—"that they have mastered it. To the grave detriment of your kind and with the dangerous assistance of an alien race."

Disbelief choked Marco as a room with a faint blue glow came into focus. Detriment of my kind? Is this why the hunters were vanishing? But ... What are they doing with my brothers?

Kersei gasped. "That's it!"

A steel chair with restraints held— "Dolon." His head had been shaved and lots of red marks pocked near-white skin. Marco felt sick.

A tall person with an elongated head stalked toward him, the movements contorted, wrong.

"It is through this alien that Symmachians have also discovered a newer but smaller benefit—concealing their scents."

Marco staggered.

"I will use this chemical when I attempt to slip this information to you, so you will know that what I speak is true. Baric and Command will stop at nothing to prevent word of this from leaking out. They intend to make their first long-distance jump soon, and I urge you with my life to stop them. Had Baric come by this technology honestly, I would have no misgivings. But the creature … I have …" His face contorted. *"They are using the Brethren as guiding beacons. It is a brutal, cruel fate, Kynigos. Stop them."*

Staring in disbelief and sick to his gut, the sight of Dolon with tubes in his nostrils, probes attached to his temples and shaved head, arching his back in a silent scream …

Fury spiraled through Marco. Breathing became a chore. He balled his fist. "Broke. Comm array is broken."

He blinked. Glanced at Duncan, whose fingers moved fast. "What?"

"It was broken," Duncan said, "but it's not now. I rerouted it through—"

The thumper pounded. He winced and tapped it. "Go—"

"Marco! Marco, where are you? We've been waving you for hours! You have trouble."

Panic took root. "We're en route," he said, glancing at the display. "I can see it now. Wh—"

The screen went hot, his system continually enhancing the image on short-range scanner.

"Slag me," he muttered as the object came into focus. "That's a Symmachian battle cruiser—the *Macedon*." He dropped into his seat. "Snap in! This will be fun in reverse!"

42

TSC MACEDON

Exultation rang through the deck as the disorientation wore off. Baric glanced at Krissos, then Dimar. Nervous laughter morphed to cheers. They'd done it. The first successful wormhole, tunneling from the *Chryzanthe* to Iereania. Victory was in their hands.

"XO, launch the Sentinel," Baric ordered.

"Aye, Captain," Dimar said as he doled out commands to the team that would send the Sentinel satellite out from the bay of the *Macedon*. It'd serve as a link point through which they could code in, allowing the wormhole to reopen so they could return to the *Chryzanthe*. In time, more stations would be built and the reach of the fleet furthered.

"Captain," Dimar announced, glancing at him, "long-range sensors are picking up a scout. It might be the *Centaur*."

Staring at the array with its orange and blue dots, Baric nodded. "Verify, and then when he's in range, target his engines and weapons." Disbelief tugged at his arcs, but with that came a heady, thrilling charge. They'd done it. Really, slagging done it.

Laughing, Krissos strode toward him. Slapped him on the back. "We did it!" He motioned to the fleet admiral. "We've even recorded the success."

"Sir, *Centaur*'s changing course," Commander Dimar announced. "Moving to evade."

Baric bounced his gaze back to the display. "He can't be that stupid. He's in a *scout*." But even as he said it, the craft swung around. "It's like stepping on a bug," he snarled. "Disable his propulsion. Engines if necessary, but don't risk life support or their lives."

"Aye, Captain," Dimar said with a curt nod. "Targeting propulsion. Firing pulse canon."

"Remember," Theon said as he glided forward. "Xisya wants that hunter. She says his gift is particularly strong. And I do not want that girl on Iereania."

"I don't need you to remind me," Baric growled.

"We get him," Krissos said, "and we skip to Xisya's world, bypassing decades, maybe centuries of travel? Trade, profit—unimaginable. We'll be unstoppable."

"Sensors indicate the *Centaur*'s main propulsion is down," Dimar announced. "They're on a steady course and speed."

Baric nodded. "Move to intercept and bring them aboard."

P S K   *C E N T A U R*

"I can't do this. I can't." Kersei stood frozen.

Marco held her shoulders. "You said you trust me, right?"

A nod, then a shake. "I can't, Marco. You don't know …"

"We have an ally on that ship."

"But Tigo said his life was forfeit by giving us that dot. What if he's dead?"

Marco hesitated. "I … I don't think he is."

"You can't know that."

"We don't have a choice." He drew upon that courage of the Kynigos, the sacred line of warriors who had fought for justice. "They disabled our propulsion. I have no way to get us out of here or protect us from them. But I have a plan."

"They're right over us!" Duncan shouted from the cockpit.

Thrumming wormed through the hull.

Marco cupped her face. "No matter what happens when they take us, remember to fight, stay alive. If we are separated, I'll find you. You cannot be hidden from me."

Her gaze went to his sigil and she nodded. Then, "No," she whimpered, catching his arms. "It was awful—they were awful. He touched me—and what if they kill you?"

His face darkened. "I need to show you something." He released her and made quick work of freeing the straps of the vambrace. Then slid his sleeve up. "See?"

She gasped at the brand. "Wha—how? I have one, too!" She scrambled to reveal hers. Then frowned at him. "You know, don't you?"

Nodding, he glanced sideways at her. "It means our purpose is together, Kersei. *Together.*"

Awe saturated her efflux. "I should be so angry with you right now." She shifted so her back was to his chest, her right arm aligned with his, the arcs and lines seeming to coalesce.

"*No!*" Ypiretis shouted.

Their skin touched. Hot and searing, white light punched Marco backward.

Kersei groaned, rolling onto her side, disoriented.

"Easy, Mistress," Ypiretis said.

"What …?" She sat up and glanced around the metal room. This one had bars on one side, but the rest was all too familiar. Cold. Hard. "No," she breathed. "No no no." No seats. Just the cold, vibrating floor.

"We're on the *Chryzanthe*," Duncan said.

"Where is Marco?" Panic thrummed. She whipped to Ypiretis. "His brand—why did you not tell me?"

"Some brands are shared burdens, Mistress, their meaning and power imbued by the Ancient too much for one body to bear, so the burden is … divided, if you will."

"But," she began, remembering Marco's smile as he showed her. "Marco knew."

"Only recently. High Lord Kyros admonished him not to speak of it with you."

"Why?"

"Fear of compromise, as there are some in the Order who would seek to thwart the prophecy's fulfillment," Ypiretis said. "Isn't that right, Theon?"

A large shadow slithered into the room just outside the bars. "There is a reason you were recused, Ypiretis. Long have you been a source of trouble."

"I would have it no other way."

Iereas like Theon were why her father had forbidden them on Stratios lands.

"Perhaps you could explain to the mistress why are you thwarting her relief?" Ypiretis spoke with a tone she had never heard in his gentle voice before.

"Relief?" Kersei asked.

"If the prophecy is not fulfilled," Theon said, "the brand will continuously and vengefully burn."

Kersei stilled, mortified.

Theon shrugged. "I cannot allow the prophecy to be fulfilled, for it will subvert all we have worked for with the Symmachians." The high lord was too vainglorious. "They have conquered wormhole technology, and that means we can proselytize other colonies and planets. We can spread the word of the Ancient—"

"Think you that we are fools?" Ypiretis hissed. "You have no interest in the ways of the Ancient. You have forsaken your calling for riches! The only reason you put her in that chamber—"

"Me?" Theon scoffed. "I wasn't even on the ship." But the leer in his words contradicted him. "You accuse me, yet *you* would break her. Put her through the prophecy's fulfillment, which will crush her."

Kersei couldn't breathe. "What?"

"Hasn't he told you, Mistress?" Theon asked snidely. "The process to fulfill the prophecy is not only painful but extremely taxing on the body." His expression flattened. "I have seen some hosts die to awaken their prophecy." He clucked his tongue. "Is that what you would have for these puppets of yours, Ypiretis?" His expression never changed as he looked down on Kersei. "You see? It matters not who you trust. They all betray you, child."

CHRYZANTHE STATION, ORBITING SICANE

Holding his hands and spine arched, Kersei swung around in a dizzy swirl. In a pale blue gown dusted with crystals. Laughing. He pulled her into his arms, the tickle of her hair soft against his mark.

She leaned up and met his gaze. "Marco—I never dreamed I'd be this happy."

Twirling, she was in the distance. Hadn't he been holding her? She turned and caught someone's arm. They stopped dancing, and her hands rested on her very round belly. With child! She lifted her gaze, painfully, slowly, and peered across the vacancy to him. "I beg your mercy." Her whisper reached him like a claxon.

A man—shapeless and undecipherable—stepped toward her. Arms encircled her waist. Led her away.

"Kersei!" Marco called after her.

"You were too late."

Marco froze. "No. Kersei!" He lunged. "Kersei!"

Metal clanged. Bit into his arms.

Buzzing at the back of his brain bored through Marco's thoughts, dragged him from greedy unconsciousness. His head swam. With a groan he forced his eyes open.

An efflux of rotten oranges assailed his receptors.

He recoiled, shaking his head to make sense of this. "What …?"

"They were right." The voice rang like the reverberation of steel cables when struck.

Struggling past the dissonance the sound created, Marco focused on the person before him. Blinked. Squinted. Oblong head. Nearly opaque eyes with a black horizontal slit. Like a goat's.

"You arrree gifted," she said, the voice vibrating in his head.

Groaning, Marco gritted his teeth and shouldered away. "*What* are you?"

She had an odd gait. Elegant, long strides, but then at the end, a surge of her neck made the whole thing seem awkward. As if she weren't used to her own legs. "With hiiiimmm, we can reaaacccch Kuru."

He groaned at the trill of her voice, which rattled his eardrums.

"Good," Baric said, stepping into the room with another man. One Marco didn't recognize. "The ship needs time to power back up. How long before you're ready?"

"Nooooooww that you arreee back, but a daaaay."

"Augh!" Marco gritted, the taste of her words metallic and painful. "Baric, I will kill you."

The captain laughed. "In that chair, I doubt you can do anything but breathe."

"Where—" His ears rang, but relief soaked him as the creature drifted away. "Where did that thing come from?"

"We found her shuttle adrift, life support failing on the outer rings of Balasi. She was near death." Baric sauntered over to him.

Half listening, Marco scanned the room, looking for a way to escape, something to use. Instead, he spotted a bearded man watching them, arms folded over a barrel chest. Behind him, a window framing a series of steel arms. *Metal flower.* He drew in a breath, remembering Kersei's words.

"Her people were being slaughtered by a savage race, the Draegis," Baric went on. "She escaped to find help. Promised to aid us in developing wormhole technology as long as we agreed to help her people fight the Draegis."

Marco glanced at her. "She has advanced technology, and you think Symmachia can help against an enemy slaughtering her people?" Though he'd closed his receptors to the foul odor, something about her shoved past that. Violated his senses. "You're an idiot."

"She could not do what she has accomplished without our help and providing her … fresh sources."

"You mean my brethren!"

"I do."

Marco growled. Thrashed against the restraints. "You metal-neck—you can't trust her!"

"She's been with us for the last two cycles and kept every word." Something akin to chagrin streaked through Baric's face. "It is an unfortunate necessity, the loss of so many hunters. Back on her planet, she had all the resources necessary. But here, our lack of development and supplies forced her to improvise. The discovery about Kynigos olfactory senses came almost by accident. Apparently, you're so enhanced that she can combine your gifts with her DNA to guide wormholes to safe orbits. We normal humans do not have as effective receptors—we die much faster. And without that guidance, we would end up plague-knows-where in this universe."

"Preferably the Fires of Pir."

Baric smirked. "I would feel the same way were I strapped into that chair and at Xisya's mercy. Have you had a demonstration of how much her technology hurts?" The man was sick, a sociopath.

Marco balled his fist.

Baric stepped back and indicated to the alien. "Go ahead."

"No," Marco growled, recalling the video of Dolon. "Baric!" It was useless to plead with that man. "I swear you will regret this."

Baric laughed. "Hear that, Rufio? He thinks *I* will regret this."

"Rufio." Marco's gaze shot to the older, barrel-chested man. The one who'd wrangled Kersei into the shuttle. Killed his own family and kin. "Kersei's uncle—when I get free, you will bleed a painful death."

With an efflux of shame, the man shifted out of sight.

Technicians approached and restrained Marco's head, a tight steel brace securing him. Tubes snaked into his nostrils. "No!" Panic warred as the tubes slid down his throat. A prick at the back of his head. "Augh!"

"Quiiiiiiet, Kynigos," Xisya's voice reverberated, "or this wiiiiiill be more painful."

O Ancient. Mercies. Ladies. Any being listening—help me!

"This is the fun part, Kynigos. She's threading her DNA into your brain," Baric explained. "Implanting memories for her to use against your olfactory senses." He tilted his head. "Did you know smell and memory are intrinsically linked? And that smell also has a sense of"—his eyebrows arched—"navigation."

An explosion of fire and ice shot through Marco. Stunned him. His brain wouldn't process. His body wouldn't cooperate. He felt as if he stood above himself watching. Silver. *Silver.* Cold, cold silver.

Then with violence, shrieking.

Marco thrashed. *"Augh!"*

A howl prowled through the ventilation to Kersei. In a cold sweat, she came to her feet, turning, looking up at the vents overhead. "What is that?"

"The worst, I fear," Ypiretis said, his expression grave.

"Marco." Kersei gripped the bars of their prison. "They're killing him!" Jangled them. It did no good, but she would climb out of herself listening to that. "Let us out!"

Sparks flew off the bars, flinging an acrid smell into the cell.

Palms stinging, Kersei drew back as a spark rocketed off the lock. With a groan, the door clunked open. What?

The guard pivoted toward the entrance, then stumbled back. Collapsed. Light dancing over his vest. Four red uniforms slid into the holding area, weapons tucked against their shoulders. They moved as one. Advancing without hesitation. The lead's visor cleared, showing the face.

"Jez!" Kersei breathed. "What are you doing here?"

"Saving you again." The woman broke from the line and rushed to them. "Hurry." They snaked out and Jez slid a vest over her. Planted something in her hand.

Kersei stared at the metal object. It was twice the width of her hand and as thick as a javrod. Fist in the air, Jez flicked her hand from one side to the next, then indicated for Kersei to do the same. She did.

Shink. Shink.

Kersei shuffled backward as two long shafts telescoped out from the part in her hand. A javrod. Of sorts. She grinned at the woman.

"Again," Jez said with a nod.

Kersei repeated the move and the shafts collapsed. "Brilliant!"

The woman smiled and indicated her to follow. "The *Renette* is waiting, but we have little time."

Ypiretis and Duncan were already a half-dozen steps ahead with the other Eidolon.

"Where is—"

Jez held up a hand, silencing her, motioning her past an open panel that led into an anemic, hidden passage. They were forced about every forty paces to hop over a steel brace. The walls grazed her shoulders, but Kersei focused on Marco, on going after him.

But it seemed for each step they took, there were another twenty. Her patience and mental focus were thinning. It was cramped. Hot.

"How much—"

Jez held up a fist and crouched. She glanced to Kersei, nodded, then hiked over Ypiretis and Duncan to the other Eidolon. They stayed there for several long, silent minutes. Just as Kersei's nerves got the better of her, there came the sound of boots. Her heart scampered away. She started to lurch up, but the approaching warrior's visor cleared.

"Go," he ordered.

Kersei started at the familiar face. "Ti—"

"Now!"

Light bloomed at the far end. The Eidolon rushed out and Tigo sailed past Kersei. When the compressed space released into an open area, Kersei slowed to a stop. It wasn't a bay as she'd expected. It was a lab. Just like the one in the video. In the metal chair— "Marco!"

Two shapes previously unnoticed pivoted to her.

Shock froze Kersei as she met familiar brown eyes. But her mind wouldn't process who she was staring at. Until he turned to leave.

"Uncle!" He could not escape. She had to stop him. How? The weight in her hand jarred her into action. With a flick of her wrist, she deployed the javrod, took a running start, and sighted him.

"Augh!"

Marco's shout spun her around—in time to see sparks fly off the nearby wall. Zip past her. She ducked behind cabinets and heard the clang of heavy doors behind her. She peered out, infuriated that her uncle had escaped. Why …?

Tigo and Jez were pinned behind a wall, technicians and security firing at them. Ypiretis cradled a wounded Duncan. She couldn't see the other two Eidolon. All that made it to her brain was Marco's thrashing body and the alien tormenting him.

Bouncing the rod in her hand as she pushed onto her haunches, she eyed Marco. If she moved into the open, she could get hit by security. If she didn't …

Kersei shot out, aiming hard and true as she'd been taught.

The rod flew. Sped across the twenty paces. Speared the alien, yanking her back from the instruments. Away from Marco. Skewered her to the wall. The shriek the creature unleashed distracted the security officers. Eidolon seized the advantage and converged, firing on their enemy.

Kersei shoved past the overturned carts and machines to reach Marco. Blood streamed from his nose, but his blue eyes went wild and locked onto her. "H-how do I get you out?" Hands shaking, mind racing, she couldn't think straight.

Shunk shunk shunk.

She glanced over and found Tigo at the console, punching the release on the steel braces. "Help him out."

Marco gargled, as tubes retracted from his nose and mouth. He regurgitated to the side, tumbling from the restraints.

With a leap, Kersei pushed up under him, her feet slipping in his vomit. He was heavy, but also struggling to not be. "Can you get your feet under you?" She wrapped an arm around his waist and hooked his across her shoulder.

After he spat, he nodded. "Go." The word was hoarse but firm.

They staggered and stumbled from the bay. With each step, Marco seemed to grow stronger, more assured. Ahead, Tigo accessed another compartment. They filed in and Kersei marveled at the bay of windows. This was familiar—this was what she'd experienced when Baric held her here. And it was also exposed.

"Move, move, people," Jez shouted.

Kersei looked to her friend and saw her waving them into a small tube-like arm. They staggered down the narrow space and right into a more open, but still-tight, area.

"Go," Jez said, hitting a panel on the wall.

Groaning, Kersei settled Marco onto a nearby bench. A steel ramp lifted closed. The floor shifted, then pulled. She dropped against the bench, startled, realizing they had boarded another ship.

"Everyone strap in," Jez ordered as Tigo lurched around them and disappeared into another compartment.

"Take us to Iereania," Ypiretis said.

Jez hesitated. "Why?"

"It's a safe haven and they"—he nodded to Kersei and Marco—"need to be there for the prophecy."

Jez looked at Kersei, and all she could do was nod. "Okay, that works since it's the closest planet other than that dead rock the *Chryzanthe* hides behind.

We might have a chance."

The ship whipped from one side to the other. "Hold on to your butts," a voice intoned over a speaker, "we are being pursued."

The next forty minutes were filled with maneuvers that turned her stomach upside down, then inside out. Kersei was convinced she would throw up—if she had had anything in her stomach.

Staying close to Marco, who wasn't quite himself yet, Kersei appraised him. "How do you fare?"

He sniffed and shook his head. "I don't want to think about it." He swallowed and rested his head against the vibrating wall.

A few hours later, Jez reappeared. "Prep the pods, Rhinn," she ordered one of the Eidolon. She then lifted a pair of black jumpsuits and tossed them to Kersei and Marco "Put these on, then inside."

Kersei stepped into the suit and zipped it, surprised at its weight. "What is this?"

"It'll mask your biometrics in the pods."

"Why pods?" Marco asked, though he was zipped up and waiting.

"Tascan is sending more ships after us. The pods will be harder to track and intercept."

"So a hard drop."

"Afraid so," Jez said. She pointed at the sleek black pod. "Step inside and anchor up. Pull the mask on and it will activate the oxygen and countdown."

She could do this. Had to do this. Kersei glanced at Marco, who nodded her inside. She stepped forward, but then caught the edge, bracing against the memory of the chamber. She turned and backed into it, her spine pressed against the padding. Connecting the anchors, she felt the gel forming around her waist and hips, holding her. From above, she reached for the mask, then had a thought. "I don't know how to drive it."

Marco was there, working the zipper that formed a pocket. He unhooked the mask and handed it to her. "Course is programmed. The drop will be terrifying, but trust the pod." He touched her face. "Thank you for the rescue."

Her gaze hit his. And internally, she sagged. Scared. Nervous.

"You'll be okay." Marco eased away and swung her door closed. "Pull the mask and put it on."

Eyes locked on him, she did as told and heard the compartment suck into a tight seal. He pressed his hand to the face shield. Then he was gone.

Without warning, the pod yanked her down. She sucked in a hard breath. Screamed.

Light flashed. The view shield went black.

Shaking violently, she was in a freefall. Yet … not just a fall. It was hard … like the way she'd thrown that javrod. As if the ship had thrown the pod at the surface.

Her head bounced and jerked, making her neck ache after what felt like hours in it. Hands on either side of the hull, she was desperate for some sense of control. But it went on and on. Her fingers and feet grew numb from the rattling. Panic clawed, realizing that she was in a steel coffin plummeting toward a planet. How would it not shatter into a thousand pieces?

TSC *MACEDON*

"Captain! They launched pods. At least four of them, sir."

Baric cursed, monitoring the pursuit of the *Renette* from the tactical station.

"Run biometrics and find that Kynigos." Krissos said. "Destroy the rest."

"No!" Theon said. "Lose the girl, we lose the prince."

"As if he can control this anymore."

"We need him on that planet," Theon said. "If he's there, then we have a pressure point."

"He's right," Admiral Deken grunted, joining them on the bridge.

Baric huffed. "Fine, locate—"

"Sir, biometrics are … flat," Lieutenant Wayton said from combat systems. "There's no one in them."

"What—"

"Sir, the *Renette* is veering off."

"The pods are a ruse," Krissos breathed.

Baric slid his gaze to the admiral. "Your son is good, but we're better."

"He's no son of mine," Deken said. "Gave up that when he started this fool errand."

"Dimar, disable the *Renette* and bring it back," Baric ordered.

"And the pods?"

Deken glanced at the radar. "They're too far and too small to accurately target at this range."

"Roger that, sir."

"How's the alien?" Krissos asked.

"She's healing. Amazing regenerative properties—that's how we saved the prince."

"Maybe we can patent that."

"Credits account not fat enough?" Baric asked.

"Never."

Baric snorted. "Theon, guess you need to get your prince and remind the girl who she married."

"You told that Kynigos about Xisya."

"What're you worried about?" Baric asked. "He's not going anywhere." He nodded to the helmet cam of the security detachment that would board the *Renette* and secure the fugitives. Another fifteen minutes and the hunter would answer to Xisya for that rod the girl put through her heart—if she had one.

The minutes ticked by and Baric ached for another glass of brandy. It'd been a long hard slog to reach this point. Having the end in sight was a relief, but they weren't there yet.

"Security has boarded the corvette, sir." Wayton glanced up, his jaw slack.

Baric rose from his chair. "What?"

"Sir," Wayton said, swallowing hard, "the corvette was empty."

44

IEREANIA

Marco groaned when the pod's door seal released. He stumbled out with one intention—find Kersei. The sun had set, the chill in the air evidence of the cooler season on Iereania and being farther from Pir. He stood and glanced around.

A thumping sound drew Marco's gaze behind him. Wedged in a murky swamp, one of the pods sat at an angle. Its seal hadn't released. He ran for it, the banging inside growing louder, more frantic. Kersei's panicked scent yanked him through the slogging muck. The view shield hadn't retracted, so she was in pitch-black.

Marco sludged over to the pod. He hit the release button, but nothing happened. "Hang on, Kersei!"

"Please …"

"Are you hurt?" He tried to break the seal.

A whistling sound filled the air. Marco glanced up at several small craft winging toward them. Symmachian corvettes. His heart thudded. Had Tigo's corvette gotten away?

Swamp splashing made him look to the left where Ypiretis and a still-injured Duncan fought to reach them.

"Seal won't release," he explained, "and we have trouble in the air." He flipped back a panel to access a palm pad. He pressed his hand there and rattled of a series of numbers and letters. Hissing, the door slunk free.

With a yelp, she shoved out—and splashed into the swamp.

Marco felt a flame lick across his arm. He glanced down, realizing Kersei did the same. They eyed each other.

"Now! Hurry!" Ypiretis barked, pointing to the bank where three iereas waited.

Marco reached for Kersei.

"No, no! Do not touch," Ypiretis said, motioning to Duncan. "Help her."

Irritated with the order not to help her, Marco stayed at her side as they pushed up the bank in now-sodden clothes to a waiting craft. Once they were all aboard, it lifted and whirred, speeding toward the temple.

"When we came for the Decree," Marco grumbled, "we were forced to walk the thousand steps."

"Two hundred," Ypiretis corrected. "The steps allow unrepentant hearts time to be worn down."

"Or grow more irritated and exhausted."

Ypiretis smiled, then sobered. "Time is short, so please be quick. With the Symmachians in orbit … Once inside the temple, you will each be taken to separate wings and prepared."

"Prepared?"

"Cleaned and clothed."

"High Lord Kyros is ensuring the chantry is ready," another iereas said. "We must hurry, for the sun is about to reach its zenith."

"It's beautiful," Kersei said, awe tingeing her words and scent.

Marco followed her gaze. The apex of the temple was a series of white stone arches that pointed to the heavens. Beneath the sun's caress, white glowed gold.

"It seems so … right." She glanced at him, then back to the arches. "All we've been through, all the terrible things … and we are here. Together."

"It's a great beginning." The memory of her with child—not his child—nagged him.

Kersei blinked. "Are you …"

He shrugged off the dream. "Mayhap it was for more than this prophecy that we were brought together."

"Only mayhap?"

"For me," he admitted, "it is much to even voice that. I am Kynigos—we do not bind."

She frowned and shifted to him. "Then how …"

It still pained him to think of leaving the Brethren, of Revocation. But being here, with her, he knew he had no other path.

"No." Kersei reached for him, but drew back her hand. "I could not ask you to leave them."

"You did not." He released her of that burden. "But I would do it." His heart clamped onto the truth of those words. "For you I would. Will."

She need not answer because her scent did that well enough, told him she was his. Her heart was his. Her smile rivaled the brilliant arches. "Marco—"

"We're docking." The door lowered and formed a ramp.

He turned to the opening and stilled. The craft had brought them up the high cliffs and leveled onto a wide plain where hundreds were gathered, tents erected. Banners waving.

Kersei gasped. "That's the Xanthus banner. And there, Prokopios." She hurried out, glancing around. "Are Ixion and Bazyli here?"

The iereas inclined his head. "The representatives of the Kalonican kingdom were brought here after the transport docked on Cyrox. They requested to be in attendance."

"For what?" Marco wondered aloud, then his gaze hit her. "To return you home after?"

"Milady," a woman said as she approached with a handful of ladies. "If you would come this way."

Kersei shot Marco a nervous glance, and mirrored in her dark eyes was the same reticence to be separated, fear of the unknown, of which there had been much lately.

He watched in irritated silence as they drew Kersei away from him.

"Marco."

He pivoted, stunned to see Roman stalking toward him. "Master?"

"Come. We will talk as you prepare."

Eyeing the banners once more, Marco hesitated. Something hung in the air—excitement. Wariness. Sympathy. It made no sense. Hustling, he fell into step, switching gears. "Have you watched the holovid?"

"Aye."

"The creature—I saw it. Baric delivered me to that thing and she hooked me up to the same machine." Phantom pains darted through his head. "It was unlike anything—excruciating."

Roman's glower still made Marco feel like a child, and yet there was a reassuring protectiveness that always anchored him. But as they stepped into the eerily quiet stone passages, that fell away. "Later."

"Later?"

"There are things I have been remiss in addressing." Roman used his long, powerful gait to stalk through the halls and up a flight of stairs. "Now we are rushed and that will make this more difficult." They rounded a corner and he flicked open a door.

Marco slowed at that, at the large suite of rooms they'd entered. "How do you know the way around here?" Something was very wrong.

"Time is short." Roman motioned to a thin door on the right. "Shower's there—real water. Clothes are on the bed there."

Shower? Clothes? He turned to the master hunter. "What is this? I don't understand."

Roman's mouth drew down. "I know. But you will." His shoulders sagged. "Go on."

He had been through much and would endure no more. "Nay, I would have answers."

"You will have them as you prepare. Go," Roman insisted.

Entering the bathing room felt like walking into an ambush. Mayhap he could sort what assailed his senses and mind. There was a glut of it. Beneath the water, he was glad to be rid of the swamp reek and the pain of that chair. Of that creature and her metallic-twangy voice that made his brain want to bleed.

"Do you recall your Reclaiming?"

Scrubbing his hair, Marco slowed at the question. Kynigos never spoke of the night they were raised from anonymity to embrace their *anaktesios* gifting.

"You heard my scout come in over the cliffs," Roman continued, sounding amused.

Marco lowered his hand, immersed in that moment. The echoes in the hall. The rattling of the leaded glass. His mother's cries. Suddenly, he felt small. "I'd forgotten."

"As you were trained to," Roman said soberly. "But now you must remember, Marco."

Scowling, he rinsed off, glad for real water and soap. "To think on those things only creates confusion and—"

"What is your name?"

Marco scoffed. "You just spoke—"

"The name bestowed by your parents."

He stilled. Cut the water. "Master—"

"The gift that the Ancient has given you is not best used as a Kynigos."

"What is this?" He jolted, snatched the towel, and stepped from the shower to look Roman in the face. "I am a hunter," he growled. "To the Decree. And the hunt. For honor!" He stabbed each phrase into the air. "I earned my place."

"Honor, yes." A thick startling scent roiled off his master. "But not to the hunt. Not any longer."

"Mas—"

"Dress, Marco." Roman was sad. Grieved. "You have little time." He nodded to the inner chamber, surprisingly extravagant, considering this was a house of priests.

The strange thrum through his brand forced him to eye it as he lifted the cream tunic, which seemed to have more fabric than necessary. Frilly.

Expensive. After stuffing it on, he stepped into slacks stitched with quality and gently weighted against his skin. The clothes were too expensive, too rich.

"Your mother and I argued when I arrived for your Reclaiming," Roman said. "Though notice had been sent that we would come, she had hidden that you were branded. I was furious."

Slowing, Marco threaded his hands through his hair, uncertain what to do with this story. Uncertain what it meant that Roman would even open the vault of the past.

"When your brand appeared, she had a vision that your heightened senses would be used against you. She came here to Iereania with you. Spoke with Kyros."

His mother had a vision? He recalled no such trip. But it both answered and created questions about Kyros. Donning the waistcoat and suddenly hungry for the puzzle to be assembled, Marco stared into the receiving room where Roman hovered at the large fireplace.

"They matched the brand to the Dragoumis heir—then but a babe. It was agreed that despite your mark, you must leave your mother's care and …" Roman roughed his palm over his chin. "Finish dressing."

"This is absurd," Marco balked, feeling every bit the petulant pup he'd been when Roman began training him. "You alarm me with these tales and ask me to dress as a clown. Speaking of my time before the Brethren is illicit, yet you are my master, so I would have the truth, the reason. How—"

"I will explain what I can. The rest …" Roman again indicated to the bed, his gaze on something. Something that twisted his features and scent.

Marco glanced down. Why the doublet had not registered before, why he had not even noticed it … Heart slowed, he stared. How …? He reached … Fingers touched the vibrant green brocade. The heavy embroidered lapels and stiff short collar. Gold buttons polished to a shine. The aetos stitched over the left breast.

Lifting him from the ground to the destrier.

"Vanko Kalonica, Father."

Beard twitched, rain dancing on it. "Vanko, Achilus."

Forever.

A piece of him tripped and fell down that memory from so long ago.

"Your father never wore the doublet after that night. He said you would return to them one day, and when you did, you would wear it."

Stunned—his adult mind chasing the steps of a small, frightened boy on a stormy night—Marco could not haul his gaze from the richly ornamented coat.

"The attack on Stratios Hall killed Medora Zarek and his sons." Roman was there, lifting the doublet. "Your brothers." He held it up. "*Your* father."

Marco angled away, shaking his head.

"As firstborn of Zarek and Athina," Roman said quietly, "*you* are heir to the throne of Kalonica … Achilus."

The name punched him in the chest. Taking another step back, he hit the bed. The mattress clipped the back of his knees. He dropped onto it. "No."

"I wish there had been a better time to tell you—"

"I am Kynigos." As if those words could change this.

"Aye, and one of our best. But Kalonica needs you. Now more than ever. What is happening, what is coming—they need a leader."

He rubbed his temple. "I am no leader."

"I would argue that, but time is not on our side." Roman held his gaze fast. "Bazyli and Ixion were informed of your identity after you fled the *Kleopatra*. They understand your obvious claim to the throne."

Marco jerked around. "You had no right—"

"Not only did I have the right, as a master of the Citadel I had a legal obligation to inform them." When they'd first met, Roman had always seemed impossibly tall and he appeared so once again. "While I understand your anger, remember what—who—you are and the training that has made you the man you are. That will be needed more than your anger and petulance."

It had been a long time since he'd received such a rebuke.

"Before you fall too deeply into that vat of self-pity," he continued with a smile, "come into the foyer when you are ready."

Swiping his hand over his face, Marco struggled to bring his thoughts into focus. To sort that petulance from legitimate frustration. He glanced down at the doublet again. Placed a palm on it, recalling doing the same when his father had filled out the fabric. A new ache bloomed there, sped along the seams with doubt and uncertainty. He had not been raised to rule a kingdom but to aid justice.

Are they not the same?

Voices drew him to the door. "You say you—" He stopped, staring at the dozen men standing in the foyer, especially one familiar face. "Mavridis." And beside him— "Bazyli." Inadequacy leeched from his pores. "I …" What was he supposed to say? How did he amend his totalitarian authority as a Kynigos hunting their relative?

"They know," Roman said, his voice resonating, "you had no knowledge of your lineage until now."

"Is it true," a man Marco did not recognize asked, "that you forgot who you were?"

"This is Elek of Trachys," Ixion put in.

The round-bellied man started. "Aye, yes. Sorry, my liege." He smiled. "So you forget?"

Cringing at the term, Marco eyed Roman, who had turned away. Leaving Marco to the hard task. "Kynigos are trained to set aside connections and memories to focus on the hunt. Until my master—"

"I am no more your master," Roman corrected.

Awkwardly, Marco hesitated. Glanced at the Kalonicans. He thought to tell them he never wanted this, but that would insult. "I know not what else to say or how to reassure you that, while deeply affected by this revelation, I never intended or imagined it." A weight settled on his shoulders. "What would you ask of me?"

Their scents were wary, guarded. Unsure.

After several long, strained moments of silence, Ixion stepped forward. "Say you will guard our laws and people as your own. That you will right what is wrong and fight for the innocent. That you will live with honor as medora just as you hunted as a Kynigos. That you will honor your father's name and memory."

Medora. King. Marco swallowed. "To say I would carry out my role differently because of where I laid my head would prove my honor is but hubris," he replied. "I have trained with the Kynigos not only in my gifting, but in my character."

Bazyli extended his hand. "That is why we can accept you."

"That and the Tyrannous blood in his veins," Elek said with a grin.

Tyrannous. The name threw grandiose images into his mind. "You are all agreed?" Marco said, surprised. "So easily?"

"We are but three of Five," Ixion clarified. "But we are agreed."

Marco realized he had hoped for rejection. He had come to Iereania expecting to deliver Kersei and be done with the chaos, only to find he'd entered a whirlpool of it.

"In time," Ixion said quietly, "you will stand before the elders and entolis to declare your claim to the throne. But since time is not on our side and technology is available, we have agreed that if your blood verifies you as Zarek's son, you will be set in as medora."

45

IEREANIA

For the first time, Kersei entered public with the brand uncovered. Cool air swirled around the edges of the wide silver sleeves, as if whispering her rebellion. But the matrons attending and dressing her had insisted. Though she could offer no complaints on the stunning silver crushed-velvet gown with dark gray brocade on the underside of the sleeves and overskirt, she ached for the bliaut and baggy omnir pants. For familiarity. Hair partially pulled up, she wore a thin silver circlet with crystal droplets and twining vines.

As they descended the stairs, she heard a titter of conversation passed among the matrons. Frustrated with the poke of crystals stitched into the bodice, Kersei looked around, wondering at their giggles.

One gasped. "There! The medora."

Medora? Kersei glanced down the staircase and across the abbey where a cluster of men in Kalonican dress strode forward. At the front, sweeping out of sight as he entered the chantry on the far side, was indeed the green doublet of the medora. She caught the black hair and broad shoulders. *Zarek?* He was alive? How could that be?

Hem lifted, she hurried down the steps, anxious to see what she knew to be impossible.

"Mistress, slow—"

Kersei aimed for the nearest door into the chantry, nearly running. If Zarek was alive, was her father? Ma'ma?

Two iereas swung into her path from their sentry posts, their blood-red robes blocking her.

She drew up. "I—"

They bowed at their waists, and when she backed away, they returned to their posts.

"Mistress." A woman pointed Kersei to gilt arches lining a path that led to a large round dome. Relentless light streaked through massive windows, making it blindingly bright. White. The stone was strange—like marble but not. Beneath that dome and carved of the same material as the intricate arches was a dais and podium of some sort. On her left, the men—Bazyli, Ixion, and other machitis who had traveled from Cenon with them. Sight of the Kalonican colors warmed her.

Her brand thrummed, and she tried to ignore it. Hated it uncovered so anyone could see it burning to life.

A gong reverberated through the chantry, and Kersei noticed the large dome overhead had clear hands that marked a clock or dial of some kind. With each movement of the hands, that deep, resonating sound trembled across the floor.

"Welcome!" intoned an iereas from the dais, his voice demanding silence and arousing curiosity. He wore a dark red cloak and white mantle.

They all drew closer, including Kersei, who itched to hurry across the stone.

"I am High Lord Kyros and with the assistance of Iereas Ypiretis and his apprentice, Duncan, we will commence the ceremony. Centuries ago, the revered Ladies of Basilikas handed down a prophecy known as the *Trópos tis Fotiás*, the Way of the Flame. Had I time, we would endure the full lecture on this ancient foretelling. Since we have experienced some … complications, and our enemy is nigh unto our doorstep, we will forgo it." He extended a hand to the left, where the men stood. "Hosts, would you announce yourself for all to hear?"

The Kalonicans parted and the medora—

Kersei gasped. It wasn't Zarek!

"I am Marco Dusan," he said, chin lifted, then glanced down, "only moments ago made aware of my true identity." He straightened. "I am … Tyrannous Achilus, firstborn of His Highness Medora Zarek and Her Grace Lady Athina."

Ears ringing with his pronouncement, Kersei could not breathe. Her mind refused to accept the words. Achilus. Marco was Achilus, the dead son? Zarek's son. She hauled in a breath—Darius's brother!

"Mistress?"

How … how could he not know? Why had she not seen the resemblance?

"Mistress!"

Kersei jerked to the iereas. "I beg your mercy," she said, her throat raw, sensing Marco's gaze but not meeting it. "I am Kersei Dragoumis, daughter of Xylander, one of the Five, elder of Stratios, and his bound, Lady Nicea."

Kyros motioned them both. "Bear you the mark?"

"I do." Kersei remembered the matron's instructions and extended her arm, the brand glowing bright blue. Heat writhed beneath the arcs.

"Indeed." Marco removed the doublet with the aid of Ixion and brandished his arm, which also glowed.

"Will the branded approach the dais," Kyros said.

Though at the door she stood a solid thirty paces from Marco, by the time they reached the dais, they were within touching distance. And he looked magnificent. Regal. Handsome. Yet somehow, it didn't fit him. But appreciation sparked in his eyes as he took in her gown and hair. Nodded.

"I thought you were Medora Zarek," she admitted.

He grunted, irritation pinching his mouth.

"That's a good thing."

"A strange thing."

"Agreed."

He smirked—ah, there was the Marco she knew.

Darkness fell over the chantry. Whispers and cries sailed up as they all looked skyward. A large ship blotted the sun.

"The light," Duncan shouted. "They're blocking the sun."

"They seek to interfere," Ypiretis said with a rueful smile. "As we knew they would."

Marco extended his hand to hers and she started to accept, but felt a tug on her arm.

"No skin touching," Ypiretis reminded.

Another gong.

"We must do away with ceremony and go for function," Kyros huffed. "To the stand. Hurry." He climbed the steps.

Above, a *whomp* sounded from the ship.

Crack! Creak!

Kersei gasped, glancing up. A large spiderweb crack splintered over the glass dome.

"Hurry, hurry!" Kyros barked. They rushed onto the dais and went to the stone stand, where they found a chest-high block of the unusual marble, divided into two troughs, which were separated by thin barrier down the middle. A long crossbar straddled the far end.

"Another hit," Ixion said from the side, "and that ceiling is coming down."

"Look! A corvette's fighting the battle cruiser!"

"Mistress!" Kyros indicated for her to face forward.

Drawn from the fright of the temple being attacked, Kersei lifted her arm, noticing how perfectly her sleeve fell apart. Kyros's hands were warm as he positioned it in the left trough.

Boom! Boom!

The ground shook. A great groan of supports warned of an impending collapse.

"Hand under the bar, then grip it so your brand faces up," he said hurriedly.

"The light is blocked," Marco muttered, mirroring the instructions given Kersei.

"The sun is not our source," Kyros said as he produced another bar and set it across their biceps. "The Ancient is."

When Kersei's fingers wrapped the cool iron, an acolyte approached and poured a thick, gelatinous substance into the troughs, encasing her and Marco's arms. Whatever the material in the trough, it hardened into a type of cast so they could not move. The vertical bar across her upper arm clamped into place, pinning her. A flicker of panic struck. Trapped.

Arms side-by-side and divided by that thin barrier, his forearm looked huge compared to hers. But it was the brand that captured her attention, seeing the two halves together, the completion of it. She thought of the last time they'd touched the branded arms. Knocked unconscious.

The ceiling rattled, spraying them with dust.

Marco hunched over her, still careful to avoid touching. She wished she could see his face, the truth of his identity a concept she could not yet wrestle into submission.

"If we survive," Marco said as a splintering crack ran through the glass, "I would be bound to you."

She gaped. "You must set petition."

"Then you say 'aye'?"

Crack. Thunk! Groaaann.

"It's coming down!" Ixion shouted. "To cover!"

Light bloomed through the chantry.

"It's getting brighter," Kersei said, looking up, amazed that it could be when war ships littered the sky.

"And hotter." Marco frowned at his arm.

Another gong.

"Marco, Kersei," Kyros nodded to them. "It is an honor to serve you both." And with that, he pressed a button and left the dais. Silence gaped through the ever-hotter chantry.

"Not comforting," Marco muttered.

"Are we supposed to do something?" Kersei asked, shifting

awkwardly—then sucked in a breath as the thin barrier separating their arms dropped out of sight and the cast pressed their arms together. The brand become one.

"I—"

"It is beginning," Kyros announced from behind the shielding.

Crack!

Whoosh!

Marco jerked her head to his chest, hovering over her as glass rained down. Brilliance shot through the room. Exploded. Consumed.

Scared the glass would slice them to pieces, Kersei ducked into Marco. Begged the Ancient and Ladies to protect them. Although her eyes were shut, light seared them. Fire raged in her brand. Violent. Furious. She cried out.

Glass. Where was the glass? Why hadn't it hit them? She felt the floor rattling. Felt the thud of columns collapsing.

Had a torch been held to her arm, the pain would not have been as great. She arched her spine, as if she could get away. As if she could break the hold of the trough. She understood the design—to keep her tethered even when her will broke. Her body broke. The attack on the temple fell away until her only focus was the raging fire in her veins.

Whimpering, she tried to be strong. Brave. "It hurts …"

"Put your mind elsewhere. Do not think on the pain," Marco breathed against her ear. "Remember, we will be bound. You will be my kyria."

A smile—

More light engulfed. Shrieked. Raged.

Another beam erupted. Shot more light at them.

The fire doubled.

Bending his mind around the attack, around the glass that never came yet fell, Marco's fingers tightened around the bar. Her body trembled against his, limbs shaking, wobbling. Marco shook from within. His bones rattled. It was … excruciating. He hunched. Growled. Aware but quickly forgetting how tightly he held Kersei. Seeking refuge in her signature. Desperate for relief. Terrified it would never come.

A blood-curdling scream pierced his heart.

Then silence.

Empty silence with a peculiar chill and signature. Marco unclenched his eyes, the vivid shock of white pulling at his corneas. Blinking rapidly, he tried to see their arms—were they still there? Burned to a crisp?

A flutter of movement snatched his attention. Different shades of white dancing.

"In the age of the Faa'Cris and the days of Vaqar and Basilia, peace was our honey and compassion our armor."

Gaping, Marco could not believe his eyes. Beauty without compare stood before him as a woman who had no remarkable feature, yet the sight of her put him in awe. White-blond hair hung in waves over delicate shoulders and framed unusually violet eyes. Wreathed in garments of white, she both possessed and reflected the light. *"We traveled the planets and dwelt among the people, gifted them, guided them until there came a time when we were driven out, hunted, murdered as mankind realized the gifts of the Faa'Cris could be harnessed for ill. The Faa'Cris were forced to take refuge deep in the heart to hide from the growing technology that would one day give rise to our annihilation. In an effort to preserve the sacred line, we buried two halves systems apart.*

"In severing the heart, we condemned ourselves to a lifetime of torment, suffering the effects of a gift stunted. Scattered among the stars are thousands of our children, though to them it is unknown. Long forgotten. Necessarily buried."

Her voice was hollow yet serene, and though Marco attempted to catch a signature, his receptors were flooded with a cool minty perfume that left room for nothing else.

"What you, Children of Basilikas, will face is a curse that will test your deepest convictions and character. Son of Athina, you are named Progenitor. At your right hand will walk chaos and at your left war. What is illuminated in your sight will be your burden and your measure. Daughter of Nicea, chosen wielder of light, you will awaken what lies dormant in the army that gathers. The days will be long, the heartaches endless, the battles cruel, and your enemies merciless, but remain strong. Understand that you stand between life and death. Between the Living and dead. As our defenders. Our Celeres."

And though she stood at least five meters away, in a blink she was directly in front of them. She placed one hand over Marco's eyes and the other on the branded arm. A white-hot beam that was perilously cold shot through him. Shocked him into darkness.

46

IEREANIA

Drums thundered in his head.

Marco groaned.

"He's coming around."

A few blinks delivered him into the same chamber he'd dressed in before the ... ceremony. Light punched his corneas. He cringed and closed his eyes, coming upright on the mattress. "The lights—kill the lights."

"My lord?" Ypiretis asked.

"The lights hurt. Douse them."

"There are no lights, sire."

Surprised at the iereas's words, Marco glanced around, blinking rapidly. Confused that the haze of white still filled his vision ... but slowly faded. How ...?

Ypiretis inched closer. "Are you well?"

"If being beaten to a pulp is well, then aye." He squinted and found Ixion and Bazyli in the room as well. "What happened?" He noticed the chamber. "The temple still stands."

Stalwart Ixion did not shift or hesitate like the others. "What do you recall from the chantry?"

"So much light it seemed the universe should now be eternally dark, and the ceiling blew, but we never got hit with glass," he muttered, glancing down at his arm. The brand still glowed.

"The chantry was destroyed—all save where you and the mistress stood at the trough," Ypiretis said. "It was a miracle that will be talked of for ages."

Marco didn't care about a destroyed temple. "Was anyone injured?"

"The *Macedon* fled, in the sky one second, gone the next," Ixion said.

"Wormhole," Marco growled as he swung his feet over the edge of the mattress. "The *Chryzanthe* is where they were developing it. At the cost of Brethren lives." He came to his feet, still shielding his eyes from the light radiating from the solar. "Oh, and the woman." Her voice—so melodious. Yet terribly fierce somehow.

"What woman?"

Marco hesitated, glancing around. Seeing the same concern, smelling the same anxiety on the three Kalonicans, as well as the iereas. "There was a woman. She spoke of … Celeres, of chaos and war." By their blank expressions and woodsy scents, he guessed, "You didn't see her."

Ixion started to shake his head but stopped. "The light around you and the mistress grew too blinding. We could not see even the two of you. Could not hear. It lingered for several long seconds. Then, like a band snapping, it vanished. We found you and Kersei limp and still secured to the stands, the ceiling gone, the supports in ruins. You were brought here and have been unconscious for the last three risings."

"Three risings?" Marco balked, his mind flinging to Kersei. "How is she?"

"She came to in the night, screaming, but she is well now. Resting."

Flinging wide his receptors, Marco searched for her signature. His nostrils were still cooled by the woman's scent in the chantry, but it actually enhanced his ability to draw in scents. Kersei's was there, calm with a hint of impatience. "I would see her."

"Jencir went for her when we saw you stirring," Bazyli said. "But we should speak of your role on Drosero."

Could he not have time to focus, to process? "Is there anything to drink here?"

Ypiretis nodded. "I've sent Duncan for a meal and drink. It will be here soon, but the machitis are right. You must be set in, informally, but officially."

He clapped Ypiretis's shoulder. "Thank y—" A waft of that mint struck him as he peered into the man's near-black eyes. Behind the pupil, a pale blue light stabbed the darkness. Disbelieving what he saw, Marco leaned in. *Pure,* he heard.

"Sire?" Ypiretis asked warily, leaning back.

Marco flinched. Turned away, roughed his hands over his face. He was losing his mind. Again, he glanced at the iereas, this time only seeing black eyes. What was that? He shook his head. He sighed and noticed the documents splayed on the table. The box carved with the Kalonican aetos. "What is this?"

"Since your blood has been proven, we three are enough to set you in," Ixion said, shoulders squaring. "Have you any objection to this?"

Aye. Many. He was not ready. He wasn't sure who he was—the hunter or the heir. He wanted Kersei. Instead, Marco shook his head, still feeling bullied. "Go ahead."

The three gathered around him, Bazyli with a scroll from which he read the rites of installment and had Marco recite the oath of medoraship. Fist over his heart, he vowed to uphold all the decrees and statutes—which he would have to learn quickly—as medora of Kalonica. The ceremony was a blur, his mind still drenched by the woman's voice.

Bazyli then lifted the twining circlet of the medora toward him.

At this, Marco objected. "There is little need for ornamentation now."

The elders glanced at one another, then agreed, and the crown was returned to the box. He shook hands with Ixion—and jolted again when that mint filled the air and he saw the shaft of light behind the pupil. What …?

Bazyli clapped his shoulder and gripped his forearm—and the same happened, menthol. "I am in your service." He knelt and inclined his head.

"Stand. No ceremony with me." Marco laughed awkwardly, wondering if there would also be light. The man glanced up and sure enough, it was there.

"Sire," Ixion said, shouldering in. "I would speak with you. I've been made aware of something … a great deceit that you must—"

Kersei's scent flew at him, pulled him to the doors seconds before they flung open. Fresh-faced and bright-eyed, she whirled into the solar. "You're awake!"

Three large strides had her in his arms. He buried his face in her neck, crushing her to himself. His anchor in this storm.

"Did you see her?" Kersei whispered in his ear, cupping the back of his head. "The woman?"

"Yes," he breathed. Kissed her cheek.

"I thought I was crazy." She held on as if he might dissolve. "Nobody else saw her, even though I felt her touch my heart and my brand."

"She touched my brand and eyes." He cupped her face, so relieved to see her well, loving the minty scent and the light permeating her irises. Loving her. Beautiful, fiery, Kersei. "You are well?"

"I am now," she said, her gaze darting over his face.

Bazyli cleared his throat. "I beg your mercy, my liege, but as you were a Kynigos for most of your life, I will take your … *handling* of the mistress as an innocent mistake."

Marco straightened, arm still around Kersei. "Mistake?"

Scent bristling, Kersei extracted herself. "He's right. It is"—she eyed the elder—"unseemly to hug one who is not your bound."

"Hugs are well enough," Bazyli allowed, "but that was much more than a hug. As she is not your bound, we demand to know your intentions and insist you offer recompense for your behavior."

Marco grinned at Bazyli. "Gladly. My intentions are honorable and clear. Your recompense as her nearest relative will be a bride's price"—he laughed—"paid by the crown."

"Then you intend to set petition for Kersei?" Bazyli challenged.

Noticing his brand still glowing, Marco smiled down at her. "Immediately."

"To that," intruded a new voice, "I most ardently object."

Alarm flailed through air. Kersei gasped and spun toward the door. She staggered. "Darius!"

Confusion choked Marco, making it difficult to think. Darius died in the attack. With the Stratios. Yet he stood there in a black-and-gold doublet, circlet on his head. Piercing blue eyes filled with warning and an efflux of fury.

"Sorry, *Brother*," Darius said, stepping in with two iereas. Scars carved his face and neck. "But as Kersei is bound to me, I insist you unhand her at once."

47

IEREANIA

"I daresay you didn't see this coming," Darius gloated, then focused his attention to her.

Rage had nothing on what Marco felt, at what he restrained. What vibrated through his being. Kersei's panic, her desperation smothered him. Pleaded. Her wide brown eyes were locked on him. She shook her head.

"Prince Darius," Bazyli growled, "how is it you are alive? You have much to answer for before any of us will see Kersei placed in your care."

"Why did you not make yourself known?" Kersei asked. "Why hide that you were alive?"

Darius shrugged. "Had I been stronger, I would have made my ... situation known sooner. As for Kersei"—he stepped forward and lightly caressed her cheek—"she is my bound." A sneer further marred his scarred face as she pulled back. He turned to Bazyli. "You have no say."

"The ceremony was never completed." Marco sensed his own desperation.

Darius laughed, but nerves rattled it. "You should know the laws that govern the land you're to rule, *Brother*." Anger. Fear.

Deliberately moving so he shielded Kersei a fraction, Marco glanced to Mavridis, hoping for a lifeline.

"I'm afraid," the Stalker said gravely as he drew closer, no doubt sensing the fury rumbling through Marco, "once Xylander accepted the prince's petition, the legality of their binding was complete. The rest is just ritual and ceremony."

I am medora! I can will it—order ... "There must be something," he growled to Ixion, struggling to breathe.

Gray eyes met his, forlorn as his scent. Then Ixion addressed the prince. "Darius, as elders of Kalonica and before your medora"—he let that sink in for a tick—"you are ordered to give an account of how you are still alive."

"Where have you been?" Bazyli demanded, teeth bared. "My father rots in the ground while you are here, in finery and health as if you'd danced through the explosion that leveled Stratios Hall."

"Why have you allowed the kingdom to struggle in ruin and despair," Marco added, "without declaring yourself a survivor?"

His brother shifted, his efflux saturated with myriad scents. But the anger gave way to uncertainty and … regret, then boiled again into a rage that made it to his face as he looked at Kersei, who had not gone to him—a fact that gave Marco a perverse pleasure.

When Darius reached for her, Marco lowered his head. "Touch her again before you answer these queries, and it will be the last thing you do."

Darius faltered. "You jest. She is mine!"

Marco's anger pounded war drums. "Are you so insensitive to the plight of the woman you claim as your bound?"

Drawing up, Darius lifted his jaw. "Insensitive? Only one who was not involved could ask such a cruel question! I have spent the last months trying to forget what I went through! Trying to forget the burns that leave me disfigured!"

His twisted words and deception boiled Marco over. He shoved forward. "Forget? How could you want to forget that our father was murdered? And Kersei's family slaughtered? Is this who you are, Prince of Kalonica? Are you only concerned for yourself?"

Darius went pale, his gaze skittering to Kersei. Then he panicked. Shoved him.

Lighting fast, Marco slammed into his brother. Pinned him to the wall. "Try that again. Lie to me again!"

"I was in that hall," Darius growled. "Following *our* father to find out why the iereas were there, why they said Kersei and I could not be bound, though we already were. They pulled ahead of me, and I took a wrong turn, down a sergii's passage. I heard the explosion." His face was a mask of stone, but his efflux was not. Carefully crafted, coiled tight, it reeked of deception. "Felt the walls rattle and the floor vibrate. I ran back. The explosion had leveled walls, and I saw our father crushed by that beam in an anteroom. I saw her sisters in the main hall. I tried to help but I was struck across the back of the head and shoulders by falling debris." His lips were trembling, spittle at the corners of his mouth. His grief—authentic. Rage, boiling.

"They were your memories," Kersei breathed, gliding forward. Her scent tumbled with anger and rage, then turned to black grief. "*You* saw them die. They used your memories to torment me!" She started. "You blinked."

Marco waited, his heart trampling that scent of hers that was wild with every emotion he could name.

"In the feed, I saw him blink, but I kept thinking it was my imagination."

"If it was his memories, how could you see the prince at all?" Bazyli asked.

"You said you were struck on the way back to the hall?"

Darius nodded.

She looked to Bazyli and Marco. "There was a gilt mirror there. Perhaps he saw his reflection and that's how I saw him."

Darius seemed dazed. "I have no idea what you're talking about."

Alarmed at what Kersei said, Marco considered the two. "Did you know they took Kersei?"

He frowned. "I woke up here in the temple wrapped in herbs and gauze for weeks, they said, before I could know my own name. How would I know Kersei was alive, let alone that someone had her?"

"*Here*?" balked Bazyli. "You were here? How did you get to Iereania?"

Darius huffed. "I was unconscious." His petulance far exceeded acceptability, and he knew it, for he huffed and continued. "The iereas told me they recovered me. When the shuttle that delivered them to Stratios Hall returned to retrieve their high lord and his acolytes, they found it smoldering. Found me alive and brought me here."

"Your story reeks." Yet it did not affect the binding with Kersei, and that is what Marco sought to undo. He pivoted and stalked to the window, palming the ledge. Heart roaring, he struggled to think. *There must be a way* … Strategy was always his strong suit, so why could he not find a way to extricate Kersei from that binding she never wanted?

He felt someone join him—Ixion by the signature. "Can I do nothing?" he murmured.

"Over the petition, no, my liege. I beg your mercy, but by all rights, she is his bound."

"If you are done interrogating me …" Darius's tone was every bit as petulant but now clouded with unease.

Marco pivoted. Glowered as he watched him take Kersei's hand.

"Nay," Ixion hissed, a hand to Marco's abdomen.

But when her large eyes sought him, her efflux drenched with grief, Marco flew at his brother, amid shouts and protests.

"Marco, no!" Kersei gasped.

Though Darius took a fighting stance, Marco slid in and grabbed his brother's collar. Hauled him up the two inches that separated their height. "On my oath—if you harm her …"

"I've loved her longer than you've known her," Darius snarled.

Marco pitched him backward. "You know not the meaning of love, or you would not have forced this on her."

Darius scowled, but then looked to Kersei. Held out his hand. "Princessa."

Tormented, her efflux slammed him. Her chest rose and fell unevenly as her gaze shifted from Marco to Darius and back. Her chin trembled. Defeat marred those beautiful features.

Marco balled his fists.

Darius led her toward the door.

"You forget yourself, Prince," Bazyli growled. "Do not show your back to your medora."

With a cocky nod, Darius shifted. Turned. Bowed. "Brother."

Kersei resisted, glancing at Marco, eyes molten with tears. His heart pounded with each step she took.

Grief hammered the now-stone walls of his heart. When a tear spilled over her cheek, Marco lurched forward, caught only by the lone remnant of honor he had left—and Ixion's strong hand. The man stood with his shoulder against Marco's, back to the departure.

Kersei was gone. Out of his chamber. Out of his sight. Out of his life.

The door shut with a bang. *Finality.* With each heaving breath, he felt his anger rising. The torrent of rage in him building.

"*The days will be long, the heartaches endless …*"

"She was right," he muttered miserably, trailing Kersei's scent that shifted from shock to grief. They shared that pain, just as they had the brand.

"Kersei was?" Ixion asked.

"The lady in the chantry." Marco returned to the window, ready to pitch himself down from the heights. He roughed both hands over his face. Then shifted and slumped against the window, staring at the marble floor.

"I beg your mercy," Ypiretis persisted. "But the lady? What did she look like?"

What did he care? He had lost the one woman he loved. But the men waited in expectation. "Beautiful yet ordinary," Marco groused. "She had an arm band with an interconnected emblem."

Ypiretis nodded to the wall. "Like that?"

Marco looked at the hanging with its rich oranges and golds. "Yes …"

Awe speared Ypiretis. "You've looked into our eyes, and each time, you startled."

Marco went to the forgotten food tray. "Hunger makes me twitch."

"I think it is more, Your Grace. I believe you saw a Lady—"

He lifted a cordi. "I've said that twice."

"No, I mean a *Lady*—a Lady of Basilikas," Ypiretis said, clucking his tongue when the machitis sniggered at him. "Otherwise known as a Faa'Cris. They have been gone so long they are relegated to lore."

Despite her departure and the distance Darius had no doubt put between her and this room, Kersei's signature reeked of panic and desperation.

Marco angled away, trying to hide from the rancid efflux. Was there nothing to be done? He should go, stop his brother. Stop this madness or Darius would take her. Make her his own.

It hurt to breathe. He had to stop it. Protect her. Curse the reek! The dream. In the dream, she carried another man's child. His legs grew leaden. *She was to be mine!*

Fury coursed and churned, demanded satiation. Driven frantic by the heady scent of her panic and Darius's determination, Marco tried to close his receptors. Shove it away. But it choked him. Taunted him. Scorned him. After all he had accomplished, this—*this* is how things ended?

"Leave me."

"My lord—"

"Leave. Me," he bit out, sensing the viper coiling in his chest. Tightening. He would injure them. Must hurt something. He palmed the cold table, clenching his teeth.

"Sire, I suggest—"

"*Leave. Me!*"

Their steps hurried out. Once the door closed, Marco upended the marble-top table. "Augh!" He pivoted, eyed the open balcony, and sprinted out into the evening. Toed the ledge and sprang into the gaping void.

There was no mercy in the heavens. He had returned physically exhausted in the middle of the night after climbing and scaling walls and rooftops. Tried to sleep. Waged a war against the scents pummeling his receptors— Kersei's grief and Darius's pleasure. Wrecked, he'd shut up the windows. Closed the curtains. Donned a cloth doused with herbs over his mouth and nose. All to no avail.

She was lost to him. Forever.

As dawn cracked the horizon, he poured warmed cordi—Ypiretis had learned quickly of the one vice for Marco—and gulped it down.

That blasted scent blindsided him again! He flung the goblet and palmed the large table with a growl. Breathing hard, he writhed against what he could not change.

A soft knock came and the door opened.

He caught Ixion's scent. Straightened.

Ixion said nothing. Wise.

Dragging another glass across the table, Marco hefted the pitcher, fermented cordi this time. Gulped it. "I am a Kynigos, Stalker." He glanced to the side. "In a hunt, we are trained to use our gift. Our instincts are honed to pinprick accuracy. Do you realize what that means in light of what I lost?"

"No, your majesty."

Marco shook his head and sighed. Poured more drink and tossed it back. "I can smell them," he sneered, again filling the glass. "Her grief is strong and … suffocating." He balled a fist. "It takes every measure of honor and self-control not to go for her." He huffed. "And his—" He growled. Banged a fist on the table. "I would kill him without a thought were I to see him."

Ixion's head lowered.

He swallowed the last and slammed down the goblet. "Why attach us to a prophecy, bleed brands into our arms, if we are not meant to be together? What manner of cruelty is that?" He stomped around the solar. "Kynigos pleasure themselves with chatelaine, but always—*always*—I refused because I wanted no woman, no distraction." He drew in a ragged breath. "Until Kersei."

He sighed, remembering her kiss. Her in his arms. "She saturated my receptors. I can pick her out leagues away. I went from one end of Zlares to the other and never lost her scent, though she remained unmoved." He rapped his knuckles on the mantle of the fireplace. "And this is the torment I am to now endure. Would that I had no honor, because I would—" He could not say it, would not. "I must leave."

Aye. The decision hardened quickly. He returned to his chambers, moving to his dressing closet.

"I agree." Ixion inclined his head. "It will only take a minute to pack, sire."

Marco pivoted. "No, Ixion. I go alone."

"Nay, sire," Ixion said. "As an elder, I cannot abide that. As a Stalker, I can protect you, help you learn the laws and the struggles of the people you will rule."

Marco appreciated the candor. "I guess that would make you my right hand."

The man twitched, surprised. "It would be an honor. I will pack at once and return."

Twenty minutes later, Marco secured a bag provided by the iereas and could not help but notice the pale blue glow beneath his tunic. Would the brand always burn now? A never-ending reminder of what he'd lost—being a hunter, loving Kersei.

He strode from the solar, determined to put this all behind him. He had been born to rule, so he would. He had been chosen by the Ancient ... Whatever that meant.

A flurry of movement grabbed his attention. Ypiretis and Duncan stood in the foyer. Satchel in hand, he strode toward them. "Thank you for your assistance, but here we part ways."

"Do not cast me aside—"

"Easy." Resting his hand on Ypiretis's shoulder, Marco quieted him, still marveling at the light he saw in the old man's eyes. "I do not cast aside my friends."

Ypiretis shot a startled expression to him. "What do you see when you look at me?"

Amused, he let himself smile. "Light, Ypiretis. Pure and minty."

"Minty?"

Marco shrugged. "They are paired in my receptors somehow." He squeezed the man's shoulder. "I ask that you go to Kardia. Be there for Kersei. She will need a friend. Would you do this for me?"

"Of course. It would be an honor—but where will you be?"

He did not know, but he was certain he could not endure living in the same residence with Kersei and Darius and that wretched efflux. "I will be there ... for a time." Stalking into the hall, Marco was met by the two remaining elders, as well as the two younger Xanthus.

Bazyli bowed curtly and the others quickly followed suit. "We have word you are leaving."

"Aye." Marco clapped arms with the Xanthus elder. "I look forward to seeing your lands for myself."

"It will be our honor, sire." Bazyli walked with him toward the front of the temple grounds. "I will send word of your coming to the others."

"Nay," Marco said, an idea taking shape. "I would see the lands in anonymity, if you please."

Surprise coursed through Bazyli's scent, followed closely by approval. "Of course, my liege."

Marco nodded, spotting Ixion by the main entrance. "Until then, Brothers." He strode toward him, but noted the man's furrowed brow. His scent … annoyed. Tense. "What vexes you?" It certainly vexed Marco how Kersei's signature persisted and with such strength.

Ixion's gaze wandered across the hall. The shadows seemed to swarm. Marco moved into the torch-lit passage, his eyes transfixed. Then it speared him like a javrod.

Kersei.

No. He could not face her, so he banked toward the courtyard, toward freedom.

Rustling material whooshed behind him. Marco quickened his pace. He could not do this. Could not.

No sooner had he reached the courtyard, than she caught his hand. "Marco, please." Darius's scent was all over her. It nauseated him.

He stopped and hung his head. "I cannot do this, Kersei."

"It's true then," she said. "You're leaving."

"I must." He trained his eyes on Ixion, who waited by the stairs that led down the mountain to the scout. Did not trust himself to look at her. "There is too much … I wish you and Darius every happiness—"

"Stop it! Why did you not speak for me?"

Anger erupted and he swiveled his gaze to hers. "And what?" he growled. "Dishonor myself with flimsy logic because I am in love with you? Defy the very laws I am sworn to uphold as medora? Fiery example that would set."

"I would never ask that of you—"

"Yet you do."

Grief strangled and she deflated. "I did not want this, Marco. Tell me you know this. That you can detect how much this tortures me."

He braved a glance and found fresh tears spilling over her cheeks. "Think you this is less a torment for me, detecting my brother's pleasure and his scent on you?"

Blinking, she drew back. "Then it pains you?"

His heart stopped for a beat. Then two. "No, it wrenches my gut. Sours my food. Fouls my drink. Skewers my head. Everything has become vile and cruel. I cannot stay and watch you with him or I will befoul my honor."

She sagged against him, her forehead pressed to his chest, sniffling. "That is why." She gripped his tunic in her fists. "I saw your rage in the solar." She shook her head, looking up at him. "I knew it was too much and feared …"

"That I would harm him."

She breathed a disbelieving smile. "That you would injure any and all who shattered our hope for love."

Her words were true, yet fell short of trusting him to be honorable.

Movement behind them reminded Marco they should not be seen together. He steered her to a corner, scanning the area and confirming their safety with Ixion. Then, gazing at Kersei, his heart clenched. Brilliant light, brighter than any he'd identified save Ypiretis's, burst from her pupils. But, also … a second light, tiny and blue, rose within it.

His heart sank. He legs threatened to fail.

"Marco, I need your strength. I love you!"

Mercy! He wanted to embrace her, kiss away this pain and torment. Instead, he allowed himself only to cup her face. "Remember the words of the Lady—stand strong." The words were so heavy, so raw.

Tears slipped silently down her cheeks as she stared up at him. Gave a faint nod.

"You are princessa now. The people will look to you—be of good courage. For them." His throat constricted and he pressed a kiss to her forehead. "And for my brother's son you now carry."

She gasped, her hands flying to her mouth, breaking away.

Her grief blasting his receptors and drenching his own courage, he strode from the Ierean temple, chased by Kersei's dolor. Escaping the gut-wrenching reality that had devoured his dreams, he hustled down the stairs with Ixion and into his scout. He pitched his satchel aside and stuffed himself into the pilot seat.

Ixion's signature wafted strong and insistent.

"Speak your piece, Ixion. You have nothing to fear of me, but I could do without a lecture, if you please."

"I do not know that your father could have handled that any better. I am proud to face whatever may come at your side."

Marco eased the thruster forward. "War and chaos, Ixion. The Lady said war and chaos."

EPILOGUE

On a cleft overlooking the Kalonican Sea, Marco crouched, his shoulder pressed into the wind that pushed hard against him. To the north, Kardia sat atop the hill in majesty and splendor. Despite the reports of the royal residence's disrepair since his father's death, the sun glinted off white stones and bled an eerie orange glow.

Four risings had passed since he'd kissed Kersei good-bye and journeyed to Drosero. Now, as he looked up the jagged face of the mountain where he had been born, he wondered if he could ever return here to dwell. Share the same halls with Darius and Kersei and their child.

He might as well cast himself down on the rocks, rid himself and the realm of such a man. For he could not live with this grief. He did not trust himself to be in the same home with her. It was too much … just too much.

I love my brother's bound. Forgive me, Ancient.

"Your majesty, the storm approaches," Ixion called from the scout door.

How was he to continue? What cruelty … Straightening, Marco struggled to push aside the heaviness. He glanced to the churning sea. Waves, blue-green and angry, rolled over one another. A clap of thunder thumped off his chest. Dark clouds spewed from the west with speed and turmoil as if racing for him, to spirit him away.

Come, you tempest, come.

Marco tugged the collar of his hide jacket up. Tendrils of light danced across the sky, illuminating the surrounding lands. Thunder roared again. Lightning splintered the dark sky and momentarily blinded him.

Something fumbled at his hand. He looked down. Delicate fingers wrapped his. Swathed in glittering white, the arm led to a face bursting with brilliance. A gold halo encircled hair barely visible beneath the glare. Marco shielded his eyes and squinted. In the vaguest of ways, he saw the face.

Kersei!

She smiled at him. "Our sons"—she nodded to the right—"have at last understood."

His heart raced. Sons? "What sons?"

"My lord?"

"What sons, Kersei?" Something tugged at his tunic. He pivoted to the left. A small boy of around five with a mop of curly black hair peered up at him. "Papa, will the baby be a girl this time?"

Marco whirled to face Kersei, seeing her swollen belly. "It's true then? Sons?"

"My lord?"

Gripping her shoulders, he begged her to tell him of the children. "Please, speak plainly."

"Your grace, I don't understand. The storm ravages. You must come out of the rain."

Storm? Marco blinked, and in that click, he once again stood in a horrendous downpour, hands planted on broad shoulders. "Ixion."

Concern touched the Stalker's brow. "Come in out of the storm."

Marco allowed his man to lead him into the scout. The vision weighed heavily against his heart and mind, as mercilessly as the rain that drenched him. Would there be a reprieve at the end of the storm?

Mayhap, just mayhap.

ACKNOWLEDGEMENTS

Special thanks to those who read this story in its raw infancy in 2005—Shannon McNear (you poor dear—you saw every variation of it and still loved it!), Robin Miller, Heather Tipton, Dineen Miller—and those who saw my first attempt at wrangling this story into submission years later—Narelle Mollet, Beth Goddard, Erynn Newman, Bethany Kaczmarek. Also to dear friends who recently gave feedback before this landed on my publisher's desk: Trissina Kear, Paul Regnier, John Otte, William Bauers, and Katie Donovan.

With humblest of hearts, I thank Kathy Tyers for forging the way for Christian space operas with her brilliant *Firebird* series (seriously, go read it if you haven't yet). And in 2012, taking a still-inexperienced writer's second attempt at a much-beloved story and offering feedback. You are a dear soul, and I'm so glad to know you!

Thanks to technical advisers: Steve Laube, John Otte, Paul Regnier, William Bauers, and E. Stephen Burnett for helping me get the "science" right—well, at least not catastrophically wrong. All mistakes are my own. Obviously.

Blessings and special dispensation should go to my inimitable editor, Reagen Reed, who knows how to drop encouragement and humor in her edits and emails. You are a genius at negotiating and solidifying storyworlds and a master at wrangling my contorted timelines into submission (so sorry … for the thousandth time). I'm very grateful for your care and friendship!

Mega thanks to Steve Laube for understanding my need and desire for this story to be published, who—like me—never gave up on *Brand* (though you did make me change names and I'm still in grief counseling for that …). Dreams do come true! Even if it takes fourteen years.

ABOUT THE AUTHOR

Ronie Kendig is an award-winning, bestselling author of over twenty-five titles. She grew up an Army brat, and now she and her Army-veteran husband live a short train ride from New York City with their children, V Volt N629 (retired military working dog), and Benning the Stealth Golden. Ronie's degree in psychology has helped her pen novels of intense, raw characters.

Ronie can be found at: www.roniekendig.com

Facebook: www.facebook.com/RapidFireFiction
Twitter: @RonieKendig
Goodreads: www.goodreads.com/RonieK
Instagram: @KendigRonie

THE ABIASSA'S FIRE TRILOGY

Available Now!

Embers

Accelerant

Fierian